# on second thought

# KRISTAN HIGGINS

## on second thought

CANARY STREET PRESS

## CANARY
## STREET
## PRESS™

Recycling programs
for this product may
not exist in your area.

ISBN-13: 978-0-373-78925-2 (trade)
ISBN-13: 978-0-373-80415-3 (Target edition)
ISBN-13: 978-0-373-80397-2 (hardcover)

On Second Thought

For questions and comments about the quality of this book, please contact us
at CustomerService@Harlequin.com.

Canary Street Press
22 Adelaide St. West, 41st Floor
Toronto, Ontario M5H 4E3, Canada
CanaryStPress.com

**Printed in U.S.A.**

This book is dedicated to Hannah Elizabeth Kristan,
who is one of the best people I know in all the wide world—
funny, kind, brave and brilliant. So proud to be your cousin, sweetheart!

# Chapter One

~⚬~

*Kate*

If I had known how things would play out on the evening of April 6, I would've brought my A-game that morning.

I would've set my alarm early so Nathan and I could make love. We'd been married for only four months, so that wasn't out of the realm of possibility. I would've brushed my teeth first *and* my hair. Afterward, I would've kissed him lingeringly, cupped his face in my hands and said, "I love you so much. I'm so lucky to be your wife." This would've probably caused him to give me the side-eye, because such gooey proclamations weren't my style, but the feelings were there just the same.

I also would've added, "Don't get me that second glass of wine tonight, by the way."

Instead, I did what I'd been doing almost every morning of our marriage; when Nathan's alarm went off—at 6:00 a.m., mind you, a cruel hour—I pulled the pillow over my head and muttered darkly. Nathan got up every day to spend forty-five minutes on the elliptical, which proved the old "opposites attract" theory, since I viewed walking down the block to get a coffee as my daily workout.

As I grumbled, Nathan laughed because my hatred of pre-dawn wake-ups had yet to grow old for him.

However, I did get up after he finished dressing, and I stumbled down to the kitchen in my plaid flannel pajama bottoms and NYU sweatshirt, the thrilling, awkward sense of newness at seeing my husband off to work still with me. I loved him like crazy, despite his addiction to exercise. At least he was healthy. (The Fates laughed merrily, the capricious bitches.)

He was already at the kitchen table.

"Morning," I said, tousling his still-damp hair. Hard to believe I'd married a ginger, which had never before been my type. And yet we'd had *fantastic* sex just last night. I leaned down and kissed his neck at the memory. See? I wasn't exactly in a coma, even if it was still too early to blink both eyes simultaneously.

"Hey," he said with a smile. "How'd you sleep, honey?"

"Great. How about you?" I took out a mug and poured some life-giving coffee, wondering if the fact that I still liked the smell meant I wasn't pregnant.

"I was very happily exhausted," he said with a smile. "Slept like the dead."

Nathan put his cup in the dishwasher, which he emptied every night before bed. He always used the same cup and put it in the same place on the top rack. He was an architect. He liked things neat and square, and his house was a showplace, after all. A literal showplace of his workmanship.

"We have Eric's party tonight, right?" he asked.

"What? Oh, yeah. His 'To Life' party." I took a long pull

of coffee and suppressed a grimace. Eric, my sister's eternal boyfriend, was celebrating his cancer-free status, and while I was obviously glad he'd recovered, the party seemed to smack of hubris. His health status wasn't exactly news, either—he'd kept us all up-to-date in searing detail on his blog, Facebook page, Twitter and LinkedIn accounts, Tumblr and the Pinterest board with photos of himself, his IV bag during chemo and, yes, his affected, er, area.

"He's a good guy. I'm so happy for him," Nathan said.

"I wonder if he'll run through a photo of himself, like they do on that weight-loss show," I said. Nathan laughed, his eyes crinkling with attractive crow's-feet, causing a warm tightening in my stomach.

Our togetherness still occasionally caused me a slight prickle of alarm. It was like waking up in a hotel room, that second when you don't know where you are before realizing you're on a wonderful vacation.

We looked at each other a minute, and the mood shifted slightly. *Don't ask if I'm pregnant,* I ordered telepathically. My gaze shifted to the window to dodge the unspoken question. Outside, a lion's head sculpture spit water onto a pile of rocks. I can't say I was comfortable living in a house that had "water features" just yet.

In a few weeks, we planned to survey my stuff, currently in storage, and see what we wanted to bring here. But for now, the house was Nathan's, not mine.

Nathan, too, did not yet feel like he was mine. After all, we'd known each other less than a year, and yet we'd vowed to love each other till death did us part.

So I did what I always did when I felt awkward—lifted my Nikon, which was always close at hand, and took his picture. I am a photographer, after all. Through the lens, I saw that he, too, felt a little shy, and tenderness wrapped my heart as I pressed the button.

"You'll break that thing, Kate," he said with a rather adorable blush.

Now, if I'd known what would happen later, I would've said, *Are you kidding? You're gorgeous*, even though his face was kind and interesting rather than gorgeous. Or even better, *I want lots of pictures of the man I love*. Even if it was smarmy, it was also true. Love had surprised me at the age of thirty-nine.

But in my ignorance, I said, "Nah. It's really strong," and smiled at him. He kissed me, twice, and I gave him a long hug, breathing in his good clean smell, then patted his ass, making him smile again as he left.

The minute he pulled his BMW out of the driveway, I bolted up the stairs and into one of the guest bathrooms, where I'd stashed the pregnancy tests. The lights there were motion sensor for some reason, and a little picky, so I jazz-handed and flapped until they went on.

Why the guest bathroom? Because Nathan was the type to sit on the edge of the tub and watch me go through the whole thing, stick in hand, trying not to pee on myself. I'd let him watch the first two times, but I really didn't want an audience.

Because no matter what the literature said, a negative pregnancy test still felt like my fault.

"Two lines, two lines, two lines," I chanted as I peed. After all, I'd be forty in a few months. No time to waste. We'd been trying since we got married.

I set the test on the edge of the sink, not looking at it, heart knocking. Three minutes, the instructions said. One hundred and eighty seconds. "Come on, two lines," I said, channeling my sister's cheerleader attitude toward life, minus the sugarcoating that she seemed to put on everything. "You can do it!"

A baby. Even now, the cells could be multiplying inside me. A mini-Nathan on the way. A boy. The image was so strong I could feel it in my heart, my rib cage already expanding with love—my *son*, my little guy, with blue eyes like his daddy's and brown hair like mine. I could see his little face, the soft blue newborn cap on his perfect head, a beautiful baby, warm in my arms. Mrs. Coburn—Eloise, that was—would look at me with newfound admiration (an heir!), and Nathan Senior would cluck with pride over Nathan IV (or perhaps a different name. I was partial to David).

One hundred and seventy-two. One hundred and seventy-three.

I decided to go for two hundred to give the pregnancy hormones a chance to really soak in. To give those two lines a chance to shout their news.

A *baby*. A husband was already pretty surreal after twenty years of singleness. Somehow, it felt greedy to be asking for a baby, too.

But I did want a baby, so much. For the past six or seven years, I'd been telling myself I was perfectly fine without one. I'd been lying.

One hundred and ninety-eight. On hundred and ninety-nine.

Two hundred.

I reached for the stick.

One line.

"Well, shit," I said.

The disappointment was surprising in its heft.

I wrapped the pregnancy test in some tissues and buried it in the trash.

*Not this month, little guy,* I told my nonbaby, swallowing. I wouldn't cry.

It was okay. It had been only four months. I could have wine tonight at Eric's party. And Nathan would be sweet when I told him. He'd say something like, "At least it's fun trying."

But if it took too much longer, it wouldn't be. I'd known friends who went through this, the grim tracking of the ovulation cycle, the way making love becomes insemination, as romantic as a turkey baster. One of my college friends, in fact, had said she *preferred* the turkey baster. "I don't have to pretend that way," she'd said.

I'd bought a six-pack of pregnancy tests. Hadn't really envisioned needing more. My periods had always been regular; a good sign, the doctor said. But now, there was just one lonely test left, since last month, because I hadn't believed the negative test, I had repeated it the next day.

The lights went off. I jazz-handed, and they came back on.

"Next month," I said, my voice bouncing off the tile of the bathroom. Then I looked at myself in the mirror and smiled until it felt real. I was lucky. Nathan was great. If we couldn't get pregnant, we'd adopt. We'd already talked about it.

I imagined my sister, Ainsley—my half sister, really— would get knocked up the first month she tried. She rarely had to work for anything. Happiness just fell in her lap.

Well. Sitting in the bathroom wasn't going to make me feel better. Coffee would, and now that I knew I wasn't pregnant, I could have another cup. I left the bathroom and made my way downstairs. It seemed like a five-minute walk.

Nathan's bread and butter came from designing high-end homes—faux Colonials and Victorians and Arts and Crafts "bungalows" that were 4,800 square feet on half an acre of landscaped perfection. Westchester County, just north of Manhattan, couldn't seem to get enough of them.

We lived in an older neighborhood of Cambry-on-Hudson, Nathan's hometown, the same town where my sister and parents lived. Nathan had torn down a house to build his masterpiece on this lot—a vast modern house with walls of glass and dark wood floors and minimalist furniture. He'd built it just after his divorce, thankfully; I didn't want to live in a house where another wife had made her mark.

But I needed a couch for flopping. The one drawback to living in this architectural jewel was the lack of a flopping couch. Yes. We could get rid of a couple of those angular chairs and replace them with my squishy pink-and-green couch from Brooklyn.

Not that pink and green matched the color palette of the house. Still, I could probably stick it in a bedroom somewhere. We had five, after all. Seven bathrooms (seven!), a huge eat-in kitchen, a dining room that could seat sixteen. Living room, family room, study, den—I still mixed them up sometimes. Laundry room, mudroom, butler's pantry, modest wine cellar (if any wine cellar could be considered modest), and even a media room in the basement with a huge wonking TV and six leather recliners. In the four months of our marriage, we'd managed to watch one movie down there. There was even a special bathroom off the garage to wash a dog. We didn't have a dog. Not yet.

I loved Nathan. I loved this house. I even loved (or really, really liked) his sister, Brooke, who lived three-quarters of a mile down the street, next door to Nathan's parents. This new life would just take some getting used to. Soon, I'd feel right at home. Soon, I'd even master the light switches. There were so many.

What I really wanted was for time to fast-forward to when

things felt more real, more solid. In three years, this house would feel like home. Our child's things would brighten up the place, a basket of toys, finger paintings hanging on the fridge and dozens of pictures of the three of us, laughing, smiling, snuggling. I would know how to turn on every light in the house.

I went into the study (or was it the den?) that served as both Nathan's and my home office. "Good morning, Hector, noble prince of Troy," I said to my orange betta fish. He was still alive, bucking the odds at the age of four. Nathan had bought him a gorgeous, handblown bowl when I moved in, replacing the one I got at Petco, and filled it with real plants to oxygenate the water. No wonder Hector was thriving. I watched my pretty fish for a minute, drinking my coffee, pushing against melancholy.

Tonight, when Nathan got home, I'd grab him the second he walked through the door, and we'd do it against the wall. Or on the floor. Or both. We'd be flushed and mellow at Eric's party. And tomorrow, I'd make crepes, one of my few culinary specialties. The forecast was for rain, so we could stay in and read and watch movies and make love all weekend long—just for us, not for the baby—and he'd smile at me every time he glanced my way.

My sister and Eric lived in this same town; in fact, they knew Nathan before I did. Ainsley had never mentioned Nathan to me back when I was dating; while I wasn't positive, I thought it was because she didn't want me on her turf. Our parents had moved to Cambry-on-Hudson a month after I started at NYU, when my brother, Sean, was a junior at Harvard, so only Ainsley spent her teenage years here. She viewed it as the epitome of perfection.

Me, I'd lived in Brooklyn since I was twenty, about a year before it became the capital of hipsters and microbreweries.

Yet here I was, in a town where the nannies had degrees from Harvard, where my mother-in-law invited me for lunch at her beloved country club each week, where my sister took hot yoga classes.

Speaking of my sister, there was a text. Can't wait to see you and Nathan tonight! ☺ <3 ☺

Her not-so-subtle way of reminding us to come. And the emojis… I sighed. All her life, Ainsley had been not-so-subtle. She was a people-pleaser and, I had to admit, it grated. I understood why, but I just wanted to take her aside and tell her to turn it down a few notches.

And then I'd remember how she used to crawl into my bed when she was four. I texted back. We can't wait either! Should be so much fun! Sure, it was a lie, but it was the good kind. I couldn't bring myself to emoji back, though. I was thirty-nine, after all.

There was a message on my phone from Eloise, left ten minutes before, when I was in the bathroom.

"Kate, it's Eloise Coburn. I'm wondering if we could schedule—" she said *shedule*, like a Brit "—a portrait of Nathan's father and myself for our anniversary. Please get back to me at your earliest convenience."

It always felt like my mother-in-law was about to catch me committing a petty crime. She was never rude; that would be to disobey the cardinal rule of Miss Porter's, of which she was an honor's grad and active alumna. But she was a long cry from warm and fuzzy.

Ainsley, who'd been with Eric since college, considered her own de facto mother-in-law as her best friend. She and Eric's mom went away for shopping weekends together and met for drinks at least once a month, laughing and giggling like…well, like sisters.

That would never be Eloise and me. I took a deep breath and hit Call Back. "Hi, Eloise, it's Kate."

"What can I do for you, deah?" She had an upper-crust Boston accent, rather sounding like Katharine Hepburn—that clenched jaw, the slight slur.

"You wanted to schedule a portrait?"

"Oh, yes, of course. Unfortunately, I'm terribly busy today. Would you mind ringing later? I'm afraid I must run."

"No, no, that's fine!" My voice was chirpy. Trying too hard. "Have a great day!"

"Well, I'm off to visit children in the burn unit at the hospital, so I probably won't, but thank you for your good wishes. Goodbye, deah." She hung up.

"Shit," I muttered.

I was determined that if Mrs. Coburn—Eloise—would never really warm up to me, I would never hate her. Nathan was close with his family—Brooke, his older sister, was married and had two sons, Miles and Atticus, who were in elementary school. Once a month or so, Nathan went out for a drink with Brooke's husband, Chase. (I know. The names came right out of the WASP directory.) Nathan played golf with his father and sent his mother flowers on the first of every month. I wasn't going to mess that up.

I thought of that pregnancy test, buried in the trash upstairs. Two lines would've made a lot of people happy. Two lines, and we could tell the elder Coburns that they'd have a Coburn grandchild. We could announce it just before their anniversary party, and by then, we might know if the baby was a boy or girl.

My parents, too, would be glad; Mom had thought Nathan and I were rushing (she had a point), and a baby would reassure her. My father adored kids in the "Let's see how high I can throw this little fella!" way. Ainsley would be a very fun aunt, I knew. My brother, Sean, had two teenagers, Esther and Matthias, and three years ago, he and his wife, Kiara, had a surprise pregnancy, resulting in the delicious and adorable Sadie.

A cousin, another baby in the family, would be very welcome.

Maybe next month.

But of course, Nathan would be dead by eight o'clock tonight.

I just didn't know it yet.

# Chapter Two

*Ainsley*

There, tucked beneath Eric's blue-and-red yacht flag boxer shorts, was a small turquoise box, the words *Tiffany & Co.* written across the top.

Thank the baby Christ child.

Not that I was looking, of course. No. I was *searching*. I was a bloodhound on the trail of a missing child who'd stuffed his pockets full of raw meat. I was Heathcliff looking for Cathy. I was Navy SEAL Team 6.

I'd been hoping to find this box for *years* now, and especially these past few months. But it was so like Eric to wait for tonight, for his "To Life" party, for a crowd. He'd definitely developed a flare for the dramatic since being diagnosed with cancer. And I had to hand it to him. Proposing to me tonight, celebrating not just his life, but *our* life, and our future…it would be perfect.

"Hon?" I yelled to ascertain that he was indeed downstairs,

rearranging the photo montage for the tenth time. Our dog, Ollie, the world's sweetest little dachshund mutt, was lying on the bed with the ratty blanket he dragged everywhere. He pricked up his ears, thinking I was talking to him.

"Yeah, babe?" Yep. Downstairs.

"Oh, never mind. I couldn't find my phone," I lied. "Got it right here."

Should I wait to see the ring? I should. Eric wanted to surprise me, and I should let him. "Should I wait?" I whispered to Ollie. He wagged his tail. "I don't think so, either."

After all, I'd opened other turquoise-blue boxes before, and they *hadn't* contained engagement rings. On our fourth Christmas together, upon seeing the small box, I burst into tears and threw myself into his arms.

Gold hoop earrings.

On my twenty-ninth birthday, an opal pendant.

Both lovely, mind you. Just not what a woman expects when presented with a box of a certain shape and color. So tonight, if there was anything other than an engagement ring in that box, I needed to know before a hundred people watched me open it.

Like a cat burglar, I slid the box out of the drawer and removed the turquoise lid. Inside was the black velvet box, just like those that had held the earrings and pendant.

I peeked, then inhaled sharply.

It *was* an engagement ring.

The diamond glittered at me, pulling me under its spell, the depth and sparkle of it, the mystery. It was perfect. A gorgeous solitaire, simple but so elegant, tiny diamonds on the band, the bigger stone dazzling. And *big*. A carat and a half. Maybe more. Oh, Tiffany! Well done!

"Check this out," I whispered to Ollie, showing him. He

licked his chops, and I idly petted his silky little brindle head, staring at the ring.

My eyes were wet as I closed the lid and replaced the velvet box into the blue one, then put the package back under the boxers.

Finally. *Finally.*

Then I pumped a fist into the air and did a little end zone victory dance around the room, happy little squeaks coming out of my throat. Ollie joined me, whining with joy, as he himself was an accomplished dancer.

At last! I was getting married! And the ring was flippin' gorgeous! And it was about time!

Eric was the love of my life. We'd been together since our senior year of college (eleven years ago, mind you). There'd never been anyone else. He'd been the third boy I kissed, the first boy I slept with and the only boy I'd ever loved.

And after the past year and a half, during the terror of his life-changing diagnosis, during the treatment and illness, I wanted to be married more than ever. No more *partner,* no more *boyfriend,* no more *significant other.* I wanted him to be my *husband.* The word was as solid and comforting as a bullmastiff.

In my heart, we already had a marriage-level commitment, but I wanted the whole package. You know how some people say, *Heck, we don't need a piece of paper to show our commitment!* They're lying. At least, *I* was lying and had been lying for, oh, ten years now.

The wait was over.

I glanced at my watch, then bolted into the bathroom. If I was going to be an engaged woman tonight, I was also going to get laid tonight, and I had to shave my legs. All the way up.

Two hours later, the party was in full swing. I wore a white dress (bridal, anyone?) and red heels, and I was nursing a glass of cabernet, feigning calm, though my palms were sweaty and my heart stuttered and sped. Ollie wandered around, greeting guests, sniffing shoes, wagging his tail, all shiny and sweet-smelling, since I'd given him a bath earlier that day.

This was Eric's big night, and soon it would be our big night.

The house looked fantastic. It wasn't as big or fabulous as my sister's new place, but it wasn't shabby, either. And unlike Kate's home, my house was lovely because of *my* work. Kate had walked into a fully furnished showplace designed by her architect husband, filled with custom-made furniture and tasteful modern art paintings.

Our place was my doing. Since my former career in television imploded, Eric funded 90 percent of our lifestyle, being the Wall Street wizard he was, but home was my domain. Every piece of furniture, every photo, every throw pillow, every paint color had been my decision, making this house our home.

Was our relationship a little retro? You bet. I liked it that way. And while Kate and Nathan's house was more impressive, I liked to think ours was a little more welcoming, warmer, more colorful. Kind of like Kate and me—her always a little reserved, me always trying too hard.

The caterers zipped around with trays of pretty food and bottles of wine (good wine, too; Eric had a man-crush on Nathan and asked for some recommendations, since Nathan had an actual wine cellar). There was a martini bar on the deck, and everyone was laughing and smiling with good reason. Eric had beaten cancer, and this party was his way of thanking everyone for their love and support since that awful day when he'd found the lump.

As if reading my thoughts, Eric glanced over at me and smiled, and my heart melted and pulled like warm taffy.

His dark hair was still short—it used to be longer, but after he shaved his head in anticipation of hair loss, he liked the cropped look. His black-framed glasses made him look attractively dorky, but the truth was, he was gorgeous, and since the diagnosis and his organic macrobiotic diet and exercise plan, his body was smokin'.

There was a velvet box-sized shape in his front pocket.

My fiancé. My *husband.*

The very first time I saw Eric Fisher, I thought, *That's the man I'm going to marry.* It had never been a question of if, just a question of when.

That question would be answered tonight.

"Ainsley, the house looks amazing!" said Beth, my across-the-street neighbor, who'd been wonderful about bringing food and leaving little bouquets of flowers from her garden when Eric was sick. "What a happy day!"

"Thank you, Beth! You've been so great. We can't thank you enough. Get a martini, quick!" She smiled and obeyed.

So many friends were here—Eric's fraternity brothers, his coworkers from Wall Street, Eric's parents and grandparents. My friends, too, from town and college and the magazine, though no one from my old job at NBC had even RSVP'd. My brother and his wife hadn't been able to make it, but their older two kids were here, not by choice. I had the impression Sean and Kiara left Sadie with a sitter, dropped the teens off here and sneaked out to dinner rather than come to the party.

Esther, who was thirteen, was slumped in a chair, the only sign of life her thumbs moving over her phone. Matthias, at fifteen, was similarly slumped, eyeing the young female servers when he thought no one was looking.

"You guys can go down to the cellar if you want and watch TV," I told them, stroking Esther's curly hair. They jolted back to life and practically trampled each other in the race to the cellar door, Esther shielding her eyes as she passed the photo montage. Poor kid. No teenage girl should have to see that.

"Hello, Ainsley."

I managed to catch my flinch at the sound of the voice. My boss was here—Captain Flatline, as we called him. Ollie trotted up to greet him, cheerfully sniffing his shoes, then putting his paws against Jonathan's knee. Jonathan ignored him.

"Hi, Jonathan!" I said brightly, though almost everyone else at the magazine called him *Mr. Kent*. I didn't. I had an Emmy, thank you very much (though I probably should've given that back after the debacle).

"Thank you for inviting me." He looked like he was at a funeral, still in a suit and tie from work, face as cheerful as the grave.

"I'm glad you could come," I lied. "Is that for us?" I nodded at the bottle of wine in his hand.

"Yes." He handed it to me. "I hope you enjoy it." Still no smile. "I'm sorry you couldn't make your employee review this afternoon."

I faked a frown. "Yeah. Me, too. That call with the pumpkin farmer went on longer than I thought."

He lifted an eyebrow. We both knew I was dodging the review. The thing was, the job wasn't that hard, and I did it well. Or pretty well, anyway. As the features editor, it was my job to assign articles to our vast army of freelancers, all of whom wanted to be the next host of *This American Life* and/or winner of the Pulitzer Prize.

*Hudson Lifestyle*, however, was glossy fluff. Lemonade stands and barn restorations, new restaurant openings and the history of Overlook Cemetery. Before I worked at the magazine, I'd been a producer on *The Day's News with Ryan Roberts*, the second most-watched news program in the country. I could handle Ten Ideas for Fall Porch Decorating.

That being said, yes, I had some difficulty in following every one of Jonathan's many rules to the letter. He liked us to roll in at exactly 8:30 every morning, which didn't take into account the fact that I might change outfits or get caught on the phone with my grandmother. He didn't allow food to be left in the employee fridge for more than four days in a row. No personal phone calls at work? Come on. No checking Facebook? What century was this?

These were the things Jonathan had discussed last year in my review, before I knew that dodging them was a friendly competition held among all *Hudson Lifestyle* employees. The current champion was Deshawn in Sales, who'd gone three years without one and was now flirting with Beth at the martini bar.

"Hello! Are you married?" Gram-Gram, my stepmother's cheerful and slightly senile mom, popped over and beamed up at Jonathan.

"Gram-Gram, this is my boss. Jonathan, my grandmother, Lettie Carson."

"Hello!" she said, taking his hand and kissing it.

He glanced at me, alarmed, then said, "Very nice to meet you."

"You, too! Ainsley, I was wondering if you could help me, honey. I'm on a dating website, but I can't seem to swipe. How do you swipe on your phone? My swipe is broken."

"Um…well, show me, and I'll help you." She handed me her phone.

Jonathan didn't seem compelled to move on. He watched us, expressionless.

"Tinder, Gram-Gram? It's kind of…trashy. And hey, that's

*my* picture! Not yours! You have to use a picture of yourself, you know."

Gram–Gram humphed. "I hate pictures of myself. Besides, you're so pretty."

"Well, you're misleading people."

She winked at Jonathan. "Maybe they'll date me if they think I look like her."

"Shame on you," I said. "Here. Smile!" Before she could protest, I'd snapped a shot, opened Tinder and changed her profile shot.

"Fine," she grumbled, scowling at it. "Thank you, I suppose. I'm getting more champagne! Nice to meet you, young man!"

"Go easy on the booze, Gram–Gram." She wandered away, patting people in her wake. I force-smiled at Jonathan. "She's quite a character."

"Yes."

I suppressed a sigh. Though my boss was somewhere around my age, he gave the impression of being a seventy-year-old minor British lord, an ivory-topped walking stick firmly impacted in his colon. In the two years I'd worked at his little magazine, I had yet to hear him laugh.

"Well, thank you for coming, Jonathan, and for the wine. That was very thoughtful. Here, come talk to my sister. I don't think you've met her. Kate! This is Jonathan Kent, my boss."

Yes. Let Kate have to deal with him. Like Nathan (and now Kate), Jonathan, too, was a platinum member at the Cambry-on-Hudson Lawn Club. From the corner, Rachelle, who answered phones at the magazine, made a sympathetic face. To be honest, I'd invited the boss only because he overheard me talking about the party this very morning. Jonathan was, to put it kindly, a downer.

But he *had* given Eric the online column—just a Word-Press spin-off that Eric posted himself, the magazine's website providing a link and a byline. Eric loved writing *The Cancer Chronicles*, so I guess we owed Jonathan for that, though it hadn't been easy convincing him to say yes.

"Nice to meet you," Kate said. "This is my husband, Nathan Coburn."

Being that it was Cambry-on-Hudson, Nathan and Jonathan had met sometime in the past. Ah, yes. *Hudson Lifestyle* had done a feature on Nathan's house a few years ago, before my time.

I wondered if I'd ask Kate to be my maid of honor, even though she'd eloped and hadn't even asked me to come as a witness. If I asked, would she somehow make me feel dumb? Then again, she *was* my sister...well, my half sister, but still. Nathan could be in the wedding party, too. He was a sweetheart, that guy. He caught me looking at him and gave me a wink. In some ways, he felt more like a brother than Sean, who was eleven when I was born, fourteen when I came to live with them.

Kate was lucky to have Nathan, though I never would've put them together. At least she seemed to know it. She and Nathan were holding hands, which was sweet.

"Hey,, Ains!" said Rob, one of Eric's fraternity brothers. "What kind of cancer was it again?"

I bit down on my irritation. If Rob had been a true friend, he'd have read *The Cancer Chronicles* (or the CCs, as Eric called them). Or maybe even called during the past year and a half. Like a lot of Eric's friends from college, he was something of a dolt.

I picked up Ollie and petted his fluffy little head. "It was testicular," I said, still wishing I didn't have to name boy parts. They all sounded so ugly. Penis. Scrotum. Sac. Girl parts, on the other hand, all sounded rather exotic and beautiful. When I was at NBC and we did a story on teenage pregnancy, there was a girl who wanted to name her daughter Labia. I could almost see it.

"Testicular? Shit!" Rob winced comically and turned to Eric. "Dude!" he bellowed. "Your nuts? Ouch, brother!"

"That's the good cancer, isn't it?" asked Rob's wife.

"There *is* no good cancer," I said sternly.

"I mean, the cure rate is really high. Like 98 percent?"

Her statistics were accurate. "Yes."

"So it wasn't like Lance Armstrong, then? The really dangerous kind?"

What was this? An interrogation? "It was the same type Lance had, but thank God, we caught it earlier. And *all* cancer is dangerous. I hope you never have to find that out."

Sure, sure, I sounded sanctimonious, but really, people could be such jerks. Eric had talked about this in his column, how people threw around terms like "good cancer" and "great odds" and just didn't understand.

No matter what, Eric had been afraid of dying.

There was part of him, I knew, that had wished his battle had been a little…well, a little more dramatic. He'd been prepped to be noble and uncomplaining. That was why he asked me to get him the column at *Hudson Lifestyle*. His journey, he said, would inspire people.

And it did. Well. *I* was inspired, of course. The blog didn't get a lot of traffic, and Jonathan was irritable about it, so I lied to Eric about the statistics. He'd been fighting *cancer*. He didn't need to know his views were in the dozens (sometimes not even that).

The truth was, the CCs were kind of…bland. Eric wrote about finding silver linings, living in the moment, being present, the transformation of the caterpillar to butterfly. There was a lot of detail about his treatment. Even a picture of the pre- and postoperative scrotum, which we had to take down as soon as Jonathan saw it, since it violated the magazine's pornography rules (*that* was an awkward meeting, let me tell you).

Eric liked to use quotes: Courage is not the absence of fear, but rather the realization that there is something more important than fear... Live to fight another day... You are braver than you know, stronger than you think... It's always darkest before dawn. (That one made even me wince.)

It wasn't exactly new territory, or great writing. Every Monday morning, Jonathan would fix me with a dead-eyed stare after he read the blog. I didn't care. It wasn't like *Hudson Lifestyle* was *Newsweek*. And besides, Eric was always very flattering when he referenced me. He called me Sunshine on the blog, rather than using my real name. To protect my privacy, he said, though I wouldn't have minded being outed.

"Why doesn't anyone comment?" Eric asked a few weeks after he started, and that was when I made up a bunch of fake usernames and started posting. Lucy1991, CancerSux9339, EdouardenParis, LivefromNewYork28, DaveMatthewsFan! and LovesToRead288 were actually all me.

There'd been this one woman who'd had chemo at the same place Eric went. Noreen. She'd been so, so sick, so thin it was a wonder her legs held her. No hair, no eyebrows, sores at her IV sites, yeast infections in her mouth, bleeding gums, yellow skin and slack, hollow eyes, a cough so hard I was surprised she didn't bring up her large intestine. It was her third time around with cancer. The odds were not in her favor.

But Noreen always smiled, asked after the nurses' kids by name, sometimes even crocheted little blankets for the preemies in the neonatal unit when she had the strength. Never lost her sense of humor, wore funny T-shirts that said My Oncologist Can Beat Up Your Oncologist and Does This Shirt

Make Me Look Bald? She was never anything but gracious, kind and happy. Every time I went in to sit with Eric, I was terrified Noreen wouldn't be there, that the cancer finally devoured her.

Against all odds, she made it. In fact, she ran a half marathon last month and raised more than twenty-five grand for cancer research. That was when Eric started training for one, too.

But Eric's cancer journey had been…well, it had been easy. Easy as cancer journeys go, that is. No hair loss (though he did shave his head). Only two days of puking and diarrhea that might've been caused by some iffy sushi. He lost fifteen pounds, but then again, he needed to, and it was more through our new macrobiotic diet than because of chemo. There was one week where he took a nap every day.

So what Rob's wife had said was true. If there was a cancer you had to have, testicular was the way to go. And Eric had sailed through it like a champ.

I knew he exaggerated on his blog, but I didn't bring it up. He had *cancer*, for the love of God.

And he won. Maybe his battle wasn't as tough as other people's, but he won.

My throat was tight with happy tears. I set Ollie back on the floor so he could win more hearts and minds, and took a breath, wanting to press our night into my memory forever. Three Wall Streeters were laughing in the corner. Lillie, my college roommate, was giggling with her fiancé. Everyone looked so happy.

Almost everyone, that was.

"You really went all out, didn't you?" My stepmother, Candy, appeared at my elbow. "I can't imagine what this cost."

"So worth it, though," I said, determined not to let her ruin my mood.

"If you say so." She gave me her patented, squinty look of disappointment—*I did my best, but look what I had to work with.*

A word about Candy.

She and Dad were each other's once and future spouses, as it were. The first time around, they met in college, got married, had Sean and Kate. Then, when Kate was seven, they got a divorce.

Not very long after the divorce—a few months, I was told—Dad married *my* mother, Michelle, who died when I was three. A pickup truck hit her one Sunday afternoon as she was riding her bike. Six months after that, Dad went back to Candy and married her again.

Candy wasn't an evil stepmother. She took care of me when I was sick and asked if I did my homework, but...well. She already had her children, and they were past the age when they needed help brushing their teeth. I was not encouraged to call her Mom. "Your mother is in heaven," she'd say calmly if the M-word slipped out, as it sometimes did. "You can call me Candy."

Dad, who had been a great baseball player in college but not quite good enough to play for a living, was an umpire for Major League Baseball. He traveled seven months of the year, so the bulk of my upbringing fell to Candy. And while she did take my father back, she never got over him dumping her for a younger, prettier woman. Every few years, she'd announce that she was divorcing Dad, though she never followed through.

Candy had a PhD in psychology and had authored several books on family dynamics, including *The Toxic Mommy* and *Stuck with You: Raising the Recalcitrant Stepchild.* Other cheerful titles included *Freeing Yourself from Your Family* and

*Parenting When You've Got Nothing Left*. She was a bit of a celebrity on the parenting circuit, and also the advice columnist for *Hudson Lifestyle*, which she wrote under the name Dr. Lovely.

She was great out in public and took her appearance very seriously—expensive blond hair, glaring white teeth, a perfect size four, five foot two, abs of steel. At book signings and whenever confronted with a fan, she'd morph into a smiley, warm, wonderful person who never minded taking photos.

With us—with me, I should say—she remained brittle. Which was okay. She had her reasons, and she'd never been cruel or angry toward me. Just resigned. She got her man back, but with the stiff price tag in the form of a toddler.

"Oh, honey, this is *gorgeous*," said Eric's mom, Judy, pouncing on me with a hug. "You're so wonderful, you know that? And look at you! So beautiful!"

"Thanks, Judy!"

"Candy, how are you? Isn't this a special day?"

"It is." My stepmother forced a smile, then backed away. Judy and I exchanged a look. We'd gossip about everything tomorrow. Tomorrow, when I'd be *engaged*.

"I love your dress. Perfect for tonight!" she said.

So she *knew*. Excellent. "Well," I said, feigning innocence, "white for a clean start."

She pressed her lips together so as not to blurt out the news. Her eyes filled with tears. "I don't know what he'd do without you, Ainsley," she said. "You're a treasure."

"Oh, Judy," I said, my voice husky. I gave her a hug, and my sister aimed her camera at us. Kate did take the best pictures.

"Where's my second-best girl?" Eric's dad asked, joining us. "You look beautiful, darling. Both of you do."

The Fishers were the best. "You're a daughter to us," his mother had been saying for the past decade. They had the kind of marriage I wanted—affectionate, open, happy and fun. My boyfriend had great role models, that was for sure. We went on vacation with them every year, and we always had a great time, a fact that befuddled my friends.

Judy and I would go crazy planning the wedding. It could be Jewish, since that would be important to them, and would win me even more points as best daughter-in-law ever. We'd have the canopy and the breaking of the glass and the fun dance with the chairs...

I looked over at my honey. He stood next to the huge montage of pictures of himself he'd put up. Eric before cancer, a little chubby. Going into the hospital for surgery. Lying in the recovery room afterward. Hooked up to an IV bag. (He asked me to take all these, for the record.) Just after he shaved his head. Wearing his Fuck You, Cancer T-shirt, sitting in his favorite chair, seven prescription bottles next to him.

He met my eyes and smiled, then clinked a fork on his champagne glass.

Oh, God, it was time. I looked around, my heart revved up and my toes clenched in the red shoes. Jonathan and Candy were talking in a corner. The frat boys were doing shots. Rachelle was taking a picture of Kate and Nathan, calling them Kate and Nate, and asking Kate about camera settings.

"Folks, if I could have your attention for a minute," Eric said. I swallowed hard. Everyone quieted and gathered around, ripples of laughter and conversation fluttering out. I hoped Kate would get a picture of the big moment. Oh, man, I was nervous! All these years waiting, and I was shaking!

"Folks," Eric said again, "I just want to thank you all for coming to this party. As of noon today, I am officially cancer free!"

A cheer went up, and glasses were raised, and I felt tears slipping down my cheeks.

"It's been a long, hard road," he said, "and I wouldn't be here without all of you. So this party is for you, all my friends and family who stood by me in this dark time. To life!"

"To life!" we all chorused back.

*"L'chaim!"* Aaron said. So *Fiddler on the Roof*! I loved that musical!

"And if you'll indulge me here," Eric continued, "there are a few people I need to thank specially. My parents, of course, the best people in the whole world. I love you, Mom and Dad. More than I could ever say."

Judy sobbed happily, and Aaron wiped his eyes. "Love you, too, son," he managed.

"My awesome team at St. Luke's, Dr. Benson, Dr. Ramal, Dr. Williams, and all the incredible nurses and staff at the infusion center." A round of applause followed, though none of the team had been able to make the party.

"My workmates, who were so great while I went through this ordeal."

The Wall Streeters gave themselves a rowdy cheer, and Blake shouted, "I'd give my left nut to be half the man you are!"

Eric pretended to smile; he hated that joke. He went on to thank his boss, his assistant, the receptionist.

*Come on, Eric.* If he went through the entire list (as he seemed intent on doing), he'd be here all night. Alas, he loved to give speeches. Next thanked: his cousin, who'd flown up from Boca to visit—for nine days, and let me tell you, that wasn't exactly a favor. Eric's golf buddy—Kate's husband, Nathan—for keeping his spirits up, though to the best of my knowledge, they'd played golf only once.

Next on the list: everyone who read and commented on *The Cancer Chronicles.* I sneaked a look at Jonathan, who remained stone-faced. Eric thanked Beth for her good cheer, the Hoffmans for plowing our driveway (once; I shoveled the other times). He thanked Ollie, "my little buddy when I was too weak to do anything other than nap."

*Come on, Eric.*

"And last on the list, but first in my heart, of course, is someone very special I need to thank."

He looked at me, his dark eyes wet, and my irritation vanished. My heart stopped, then surged forward, hot and full of love.

"Someone who stood by me every minute, who kept my spirits up when I stared down Death, when I was too weak to lift my head."

Granted, there really hadn't been a moment when he was too weak to lift his head, but yeah. I'd been great. Judy's quiet sobs resumed, and she gave me a watery smile. Aaron squeezed my shoulders.

"Babe, come over here," he said, and I went, my heart thudding, practically levitating from happiness and adrenaline. I was hyperaware of everything, like Peter Parker is in *Spider-Man*—the tag sticking up from Rachelle's neckline, the nice orange blossom smell of Beth's perfume, Ollie being fed an appetizer by Esther, Jonathan's constipated expression, my sister's sardonic smile.

Eric touched his pocket, where the box-shaped lump sat so promisingly, and I smiled through my happy tears.

It was about damn time.

# Chapter Three

◦⟡◦

*Kate*

I tried to remember a time when I loved parties. College, maybe?

This kind of party was the worst. I didn't know many people aside from my family members, and I'd talked to Esther and Matthias as long as they tolerated me, then trailed them down to the basement cellar, where they booted up *Mad Max: Fury Road*. When guilt forced me upstairs, I saw Nathan getting a plate of food for my grandmother.

An aching, lovely pressure squeezed my chest. He saw me looking and smiled.

"Kate, your husband is so wonderful!" Gram-Gram chirped. "I didn't know what I wanted, so he got me some of everything!" She popped a mozzarella ball into her mouth and chewed. "Delicious!"

"My pleasure, Lettie," Nathan said, sliding his arm around

me. "Is it me, or does all the food here look like testicles?" he whispered.

I choked on a laugh. Come to think of it, yes. Mozzarella balls, melon balls, grapes, cherry tomatoes, little round onion puffs, scallops…

Gram-Gram patted my cheek. "It's so good to see you happy, dear," she said. "Nathan, thank you for marrying this girl! We thought she'd be an old maid forever."

"Yes, thanks, Nathan," I said, nudging him with my elbow. "Community service and all that."

"It beat picking up trash on the side of the highway." He kissed my temple and dropped his voice so Gram-Gram wouldn't hear. "And thank *you* for the great shag earlier."

My cheeks warmed. "You're very welcome."

My grandmother ate another round thing. "You're in love! Oh, Kate, we'd given up on you!"

"That's enough, Gram-Gram." I smiled as I said it.

Eric started clinking his glass. "And here we go," I murmured, finishing my wine. Considered taking a photo of Eric, then opted against it. Clearly, he had too many as it was.

As he thanked the many people on his list, I felt myself getting drowsy. Nathan glanced at me and smiled. "No sleeping," he whispered. "If I can stay awake, so can you."

I smothered another laugh.

"…and my golf buddy, Nathan."

Nathan raised his glass and smiled. "We played once," he whispered as Eric kept naming names.

Uh-oh. I felt a case of the giggles coming on.

Nathan squeezed me a little closer. "Is my wife's glass empty? Uh-oh. I better fix that."

"Yes indeed," I said, handing him the glass. He went off to the back, where the makeshift bar was set up.

Eric paused and looked meaningfully at my sister. "And last

on the list, but first in my heart, of course, is someone very special I need to thank. Someone who stood by me every minute, who kept my spirits up when I stared down Death, when I was too weak to lift my head."

*Laying it on a little thick, Eric?* I chastised myself for the unkind thought.

He summoned Ainsley to his side.

It was about damn time Eric proposed. I mean, clearly, this *was* the proposal, finally. The fact that it was taking place in front of a collage of himself and himself alone bothered me, but it wasn't surprising. Ainsley had always been something of a groupie where Eric was concerned.

To each her own. Ainsley was glowing as she made her way to Eric, and that was what I should focus on. I adjusted my lens subtly, hoping to catch the moment.

"Everyone, raise your glass to Ainsley," Eric said.

Nathan was still waiting at the makeshift bar. He'd have to hurry so I could toast my sister. I'd sucked down that first glass fast to help me deal with that damn collage. There was a picture of his scrotum, pre- and post-op, with a little infomercial text underneath it. A quick wine buzz had been required. Even now, the scrotal sac photo seemed to beg me to look at it.

Behind me, I heard my mother sigh. She had a very distinct sigh, years of practice. Dad wasn't here; he was calling a game somewhere out West. A shame. Ainsley, product of the wife he truly loved, was his favorite.

Eric took my sister's hand. "Babe, I couldn't ask for a better woman in life. Ever since we met, I knew you were special, but my cancer journey has shown me that you're not just special…you're extraordinary."

Did the word *cancer* have to be in every other sentence? Still, Ainsley's chest was hitching; I could imagine how hard it was for her not to cry; she could cry at *Antiques Roadshow*. She bit her lip and smiled, her mouth wobbling a little. Sweet kid. Well, she was thirty-two. Sometimes I forgot, since she seemed so…naive.

Eric gazed out at the crowd. "Everyone, a toast to the woman who is not only kind and generous and strong and beautiful, but also…" He reached into his pocket, and I raised my camera. "But also the woman I want to spend the rest of—"

There was a little cry of surprise from behind me, and out of the corner of my eye, I caught a movement.

Nathan.

He tripped. *That* was embarrassing, right at the big moment.

It was just a flash of a second. Wine sloshed over the rim of the glass Nathan was carrying. A woman jerked as it splashed on her back. Nathan stumbled, and someone stepped neatly out of his way, and he fell.

There was a thunk, and I couldn't see my husband anymore.

A ripple of laughter rolled through the crowd. "Someone's cut off," a Wall Streeter said.

"Shame to waste good wine."

"Make sure he pays for that!"

My camera was still pointed at Ainsley. I looked at her, and she wasn't smiling anymore.

Her face was white.

Her boss, Jonathan, knelt down where Nathan had fallen.

I felt my heart roll. *Get up, Nathan. Get up.*

"Call 911," Jonathan barked, and then my camera hit my side as it fell from my fingers, the strap yanking against my neck.

Nathan was lying facedown.

Wait.

He'd only tripped. He wasn't a drama queen, not like Eric.

But he was just lying there.

A seizure?

Ollie the dog barked.

"Honey?" I said, but my voice was thin and weak. My wobbly legs carried me closer.

Jonathan rolled Nathan over, pressed his fingers against his throat.

Was he checking for a *pulse*? Why? Nathan just *tripped*, that was all. Big deal. Maybe his legs were a little weak because, yes, we'd done it against the wall not more than two hours ago, and it wasn't as easy as it looked on TV.

Jonathan started CPR.

Oh, *Jesus*. Jesus, Jesus, this couldn't be happening. This had to be a mistake. I'd never seen anyone do compressions before. It looked painful. Would Nathan's ribs be okay? Should Jonathan ease off a little? "Honey?" I said. I was on the floor all of a sudden, on my knees. *Please. Please. Please.*

Nathan's eyes were only open a slit. "Nathan?" I whispered.

"Help him," someone said. "Call 911." But that had already been said. 911 had already been called.

I could smell chardonnay.

"Help him!" my mother barked. "Somebody, breathe for him!" And somebody did, one of the frat brothers, the one who made the left nut joke.

Someone was saying "Nathan? Nathan?" in a high, hysterical keen, and I was pretty sure it was me. The dog was still barking. Then my sister's arms were around my shoulders, and she was telling people to step back, make room, get a blanket.

But a blanket wouldn't help him.

Nathan was dead.

# Chapter Four

*Ainsley*

I'd never seen anyone die before. Cross that off my bucket list. Not that it was ever on it, God!

I watched Nathan go from smiling to startled to dead. Just like that. My Spidey-senses had been going crazy, soaking in the happiest moment of my life.

There was the tag on Rachelle's dress. Jonathan's face of constipation. Nathan, carrying Kate's glass of wine.

Then he tripped on Rob's foot. It wasn't Rob's fault; it was crowded in here. The wine sloshed over the rim and sloshed down Beth's back, making her yelp, and Frank turned. If Frank hadn't turned, Nathan would've hit him, but he did turn, and Nathan fell forward, nothing to stop him.

His head hit the edge of the granite counter with a soft thunk, and his eyes widened, and just like that, he was dead.

I knew it before it was pronounced. I knew CPR wouldn't work.

Eric and I followed the ambulance, Candy and Kate in

Jonathan's car, since he was parked on the street and able to get out without ten other cars needing to move first.

As we drove, I knew the ER doctors would try and fail. I don't know how I knew, but I did.

"This is unbelievable," Eric said, his face grim as he took a turn too hard.

I realized I should call Sean. "The kids are okay," I said the second he answered, hearing laughter and silverware clinking in the background. So they *had* gone out to dinner instead of coming to the party. "But Nathan's in the ER, Sean. Hudson Hospital. It…it's pretty bad. Esther and Matthias are at our house with Eric's parents."

"Oh, my God. What happened?"

"We're not sure. He…he fell and hit his head. They gave him CPR."

"Oh, fuck," Sean said. He was a doctor, and his words didn't bode well. "I'm on my way. Jesus." He hung up.

"I can't believe this. I can't believe it," Eric said, careening into the hospital parking lot. "He has to make it. He has to pull through."

He wouldn't. Please God, let me be wrong about that.

We were put in a private waiting room while they worked on Nathan. I held my sister's hand, and she looked at me, her eyes open too wide, as if she didn't know who I was.

Sean and Kiara came, hugged and waited. The Coburns, thank God, someone had called the Coburns; Nathan's parents, sister and brother-in-law came in, white-faced, panic-stricken, and Candy opened her arms without a word and just held Mrs. Coburn, murmuring quietly.

Then the doctor came in and confirmed what I already knew.

I'll spare you the next hour.

In a weak voice, I offered to drive Kate home and stay

with her, but Candy said she'd take care of it. Sure. A person needed her mother at a time like this. That made sense. I called Dad's phone and left a message for him to call me, no matter how late, that it was important.

It occurred to me that Dad had gone through this, too, when my mother died. I remembered when the police came to tell us. One of them gave me a little toy, a cat whose head bobbled, how I had loved it and hadn't wanted to stop playing with it as my father tried to get my attention. He'd been crying and said Mommy had gone to heaven.

Was Nathan there yet? Did it happen that fast? Or was he lingering, here still, or with Kate?

I wiped my eyes and blew my nose.

"I'm gonna call my folks," Eric said. His eyes were red. He squeezed my shoulder and went outside.

My feet were throbbing. Right, I was still wearing those slutty red shoes. And the white dress.

I left our "quiet room"; it hadn't been quiet, not with the sound of poor Brooke wailing, and Mrs. Coburn's sobs, and Mr. Coburn breaking down, saying, "My boy, my boy." Oh, God, this was unbearably sad! The main waiting room of the ER was filled with the usual suspects—someone holding a bloody towel to her hand; a teenager slumped next to his mother, a little green around the gills; an older lady in a wheelchair with an aide, who was checking her phone.

And Jonathan. I'd almost forgotten about him. He stood up as I came over.

I swallowed, my throat aching. "He didn't make it," I whispered.

"No, I…I assumed. From all the… From their faces." He put his hands in his pockets.

"Thank you for trying." Tears sliced a hot path down my cheeks, and my face spasmed.

A normal person would've hugged me then. A family trag-edy had just occurred, for the love of God, and no one knew it better than the giver of the unsuccessful CPR.

But Jonathan was not normal. He looked like an alien's take on what a human should look like. Not enough emo-tion flowing through to really pass.

Instead of a hug, he looked at me, his pale blue eyes un-blinking, and offered his hand, as if we'd just been introduced.

I sighed and shook it.

Then he brought up his other hand and held mine in both of his. For a long minute, he just looked at my hand. *Human hand: warm, smooth. Interesting.*

"I'm very sorry," he said without looking up. He did have a nice voice.

"Thank you."

He let go. "See you Monday."

"Jonathan. My brother-in-law just died. I won't be in."

"Oh. Right." *Human wants time off. Fascinating.* "Call Rach-elle and let her know your schedule."

"I will," I said through gritted teeth.

He left—finally—and Eric came back in. His thick lashes were starred from crying, and my heart pulled hard. He was such a softy. "I just can't believe all this," he said, his voice rough.

"I know."

"I can't believe it." He hugged me for a long minute, and my tears dampened his shirt. "I love you," he said, his voice rough.

I started to cry in earnest.

My poor sister. Nathan was so nice! How could he be dead, just like that?

Eric's arms tightened around me. "I can't believe this hap-pened to me."

I jerked back and looked at him.

"To us, I mean," he corrected. "Tonight of all nights. You know?"

Right. The ring. The party. It seemed like a hundred years ago.

"Let's go home," I said, acutely aware of just how lucky I was to be able to say that, to have someone to go home with. Kate didn't have that anymore. Gone in an instant.

She was supposed to be a newlywed, not a widow. Nathan had *died* at Eric's "To Life" party. He was gone. Forever. How could that be?

One image kept coming back to me, over and over.

Jonathan, his hair flopping over his forehead as he did compressions, his face tight and grim.

He'd known, too—Nathan was dead. All the other stuff had just been for the living.

For my sister.

# Chapter Five

❧

*Kate*

It didn't surprise me to be widowed.

I mean, it surprised the *shit* out of me. Who the hell dies like that? What the *hell* had happened?

But what I meant was, Nathan always did seem a little too…serendipitous? Too good to be true? Just what the doctor ordered?

All of the above.

You have to understand. I was single for *twenty years*. Meeting the man of my dreams…well, come on. The phrase becomes ridiculous after you pass twenty-six or so.

I dated in high school and college, casual, mostly happy relationships that never ended horribly. After college, I dated nice men, though there was always a sense that maybe someone better would come along, someone I hadn't yet met, my soul mate. There was never that gobsmacked thunk, *oh, God, he's it,* as my sister had described when she met Eric at the age of twenty-one. My parents were hardly role models.

So if it happened, it happened.

It didn't happen.

In my two decades as an adult, I had three serious relationships. First was Keith, a fellow grad from NYU. He was terrifyingly handsome, the kind of guy who made people walk into lampposts. Beautiful smooth skin, green eyes, dreadlocks, six foot three, hypnotically perfect body. That relationship was tumultuous and spicy, lots of fights and making up and storming out (mostly on his part). I finally broke things off for good, unable to picture a future full of that kind of drama. He went on to become a model, and I got great pleasure out of pointing him out in magazines and telling friends that, no, seriously, I had seen him naked.

My next boyfriend, Jason, was the opposite. We started dating in our late twenties, which is still infantile by New York standards. He was a very nice guy. Things were steady and reliable…and bland. After a year and change, we just ran out of things to talk about and spent lots of time watching TV in a pleasant boredom until he finally euthanized the relationship by moving to Minnesota.

And last, there was Louis. We met at a gallery opening, just as cheesy as it sounds, when I was thirty-two. We enjoyed each other's company. Moved in together after a year, laughed a lot, felt comfortable enough that he knew that my eating popcorn drizzled with Nutella meant my period was nigh, and I knew that if he ate cabbage, he'd be in the bathroom six hours later. It felt real, and happy. Louis was smart, a psych nurse with a lot of compassion for his patients and great stories from work.

Then he got a tattoo. And another. And a third and fourth.

And then, just after he got a Chinese character depicting commitment, he dumped me for his tattoo artist.

Then came the online dating years. Sure, sure, we all know the happy couple who met online, who exchanged fun, flirty emails and then finally met, and voilà! They were in love. Oh, the fun stories of the losers they'd endured before they found each other! Daniel the Hot Firefighter and Calista, who lived on the same Park Slope street I did, had met online, though they divorced after a few years so Calista could devote more time to her yoga. But there were others who'd met online, married, and were still very happy together. I was game. I gave it a shot.

It was a fail. Same for my closest friend, Paige. Like me, Paige was abruptly and completely unable to find a guy. Like me, she was a successful professional—a lawyer—attractive and interesting. Like me, she'd had a slew of nice and not-bad dates, never to hear from the guy again. We both bought a few dating books and followed the rules assiduously. We both wasted our money.

Dating in your thirties becomes a second job. Some of the books remind you to *Have fun! If you're not having fun, what's the point?* The point was to find a mate. There was no fun involved, thank you very much. The fun would come after, when we could wear Birkenstocks and give up Spanx.

Honestly, it was more work than my actual career. I knew what I was doing with photography. This, though... The writing of profiles, the witty exchange of emails, the blocking of perverts. The careful mental list of what to reveal, how to make yourself sound interesting without sounding dysfunctional—should I mention my terror of earthworms? Do I admit that my parents have married each other twice? What about the fact that I binge-watched five seasons of

*Game of Thrones* in one weekend without showering or eating a single vegetable?

Sometimes, the men who seemed nice at first would reveal themselves to be not quite so balanced. After a really fun online exchange with Finn and a perfect first date that involved a tiny Colombian restaurant, much laughter and great chemistry, I got a text that was one giant paragraph without a single capital letter or punctuation mark.

kate you are really great i hate dating dont you we should definitely be exclusive because tonight showed me youre a good person i had a girlfriend who was such a slut she blew my brother in the gas station bathroom btw we were on the way to my grandmothers funeral then they wondered why i was mad seriously people can be such assholes but tonight your eyes told me you have compassion and are fun and wont judge me for things i maybe shouldnt have done

You get the idea. I printed it out for posterity. It was five pages long.

Even when I'd mastered the art of conversing politely yet genuinely and humorously yet seriously while making sure I listened carefully and attentively...well. All those adverbs were exhausting.

And even then, even if I liked a guy and the date went well, nothing came of it. In five years of online dating, I had two second dates. Zero third dates.

Paige and I would cheerfully obsess—*Why hadn't he called again? He said he would! We had a good time! We laughed! Hard! Two times!*—and complain—*His hair smelled like pot. A noodle got stuck in his beard, and then he got angry when I told him about it. He stormed out of the restaurant because they didn't have local sheep cheese*. We'd laugh and order another round, trying to protect ourselves from too much discouragement or hope.

The single guys we knew, like Daniel, the now-divorced and still-hot firefighter, dated twentysomethings—the False Alarms, Paige and I called them, since nothing serious ever developed after Daniel's divorce. The False Alarms were all pretty much the same—shockingly beautiful, thigh-gapped, vapid. There was a new one every month or two.

Occasionally, we'd run into Daniel, his cloud of phero-mones thick enough to make us choke. Paige called him Thor, God of Thunder, and yeah, he had that kind of effect. Once, Paige and I were sitting in at Porto's Bar & Restau-rant, and Daniel walked in at the very moment the jukebox started playing "Hot Stuff" by Donna Summer. Even the machinery knew.

He was friendly, sure, slinging an arm around my shoul-ders. "Hey, Kate!" he'd say, his eyes flickering from their usual good cheer. After all, I'd known him as half of a cou-ple, back when he and Calista were newlyweds. I'd seen him sitting on their front steps, waiting for her to come home, unsure of where she was. I knew that he'd been heartbroken, and she had not. Calista moved to Sedona after the divorce, taught meditational movement and spiritual cleanses. I still got a *Namaste* card for winter solstice each year.

But Daniel and his ilk—the cheerful man-children of Brooklyn—didn't give women like Paige and me a second glance. Marriage? Tried that, didn't work. Those guys just kept buying lemon drop martinis for their just-graduated girlfriends, women a decade (or more!) younger than I was, who considered Britney Spears songs classics. They didn't care about things like fatherhood potential, didn't care about depth of character. They were simply smitten by the FDNY insignia on Daniel's T-shirt and the bulging muscles that were showcased by it. (To be fair, I'd once seen Daniel shirtless, and I stopped caring, too.)

The other single men I knew…well, the truth was, I knew only a few. Most of them were ex-cons, as I volunteered at the Re-Enter Center of Brooklyn, a place where parolees could take classes to help them adapt to life on the outside. I taught small business management with a little photography thrown in for fun. And while I was all for forgiveness, chances were quite small that I'd marry a guy with a teardrop tattooed under his eye.

Paige and I would assure each other that being single was *great*. Our lives were *full* and *fun* and we *loved* our careers. Look at other women! Just because they were in relationships didn't make their lives meaningful! Paige had two sisters and seven nieces and nephews, and both sisters were wretched and exhausted. One was contemplating a mommy makeover to lift her boobs and shed her fat and get her husband to sleep with her again; the other, Paige was pretty sure, was about to come out of the closet.

My own sister…well, okay, Ainsley was happy, but kind of…how to put this? Naive. Retro in her worship of all things Eric, always putting herself second, despite the fact that she'd had a very impressive job. She took care of Eric in a way he never took care of her; he was the star in the couple, and she had a supporting role. It bugged me.

I was different. Paige, too. We were self-fulfilled. And what about that fabulous trip we'd taken last year to London, huh? We should plan another! Vienna this time? Or Provence?

Then a couple would walk by, a baby strapped to one parent, an adorable toddler wearing an ironic T-shirt holding hands with the other, and we'd falter. "Screw it," Paige would say. "If only there were mail-order husbands."

If only I had a gay male friend who'd pony up and co-parent with me! Not only would we have a wonderful child, we could write a great screenplay about it. Alas, no—my gay friends, Jake and Josh, already had Jamison, so that was out.

I told myself it was okay. After all, I didn't *need* a baby. The world was overpopulated, there were teenagers I could adopt, etc.

But then I'd visit my brother and watch him and Kiara with their kids. The rush of love and gratitude I'd always felt over the years when my niece or nephew would run to see me, or more recently, at least come out of their rooms to see me. Sadie still snuggled, at least. Granted, I wasn't like my sister, who had to sniff the head of every baby we saw and chat up the mother for details on the birth, but I loved kids.

Brooklyn was full of babies. I wanted someone to cuddle, someone I could carry and stare at during naptimes—not in a creepy way, but in a loving, maternal glow. Someone who would call me Mommy and reach for my hand without thinking, the way Esther still did with Kiara, the way Sadie reached out for my brother. I found myself eyeing pregnant teenagers, wondering what they'd say if I casually asked if they'd consider giving me their unborn child.

It was always there, the primal call to procreate and protect. The maternal instinct is the strongest force in nature, they say. But I wanted the whole package, too. I wanted there to be a daddy. Aside from the maternal thing, there was that secret desire to be…well…adored.

It was not something that was cool to admit. With each passing year, the idea of being smitten with someone, having someone smitten with me, became more and more distant, even a little absurd, as if I still expected Santa to come on Christmas Eve.

Birthdays became a bit of a shock. Thirty-five, thirty-six… they were fine. They were great, even. I knew who I was, my reputation was growing, I was making a nice income, teaching classes, traveling.

But thirty-seven…and then thirty-eight…the very digits had a tint of desperation to them. *Late thirties* sounded so much older than *midthirties*. Checking the box "never married" made me feel as isolated as an Ebola patient. I found myself getting more and more obsessed, looking at every passing male as my potential mate—the guy at the dry cleaners, the guy who delivered my pizza, the guy who bumped into me in front of Whole Foods.

And then came thirty-nine, and something great happened. I just…stopped.

My friends and siblings took me out for a surprise dinner—Paige; Ainsley and Eric; Jake and Josh; my occasional assistant, Max, and his wife; Sean and Kiara. They toasted me and gave me insulting cards. Paige gave me a box of Depends diapers, which was a little mean, I thought. She was only two months younger than I was. Jake and Josh gave me a full cadre of crazy-expensive skin care products specifically designed for aging skin. From Sean and Kiara, a day at a spa for a *rejuvenation package*. From Ainsley and Eric, same spa, same treatment.

"No embalming fluid?" I asked, getting a laugh.

"This is from the gentleman at the bar," our server said, setting a fresh martini in front of me. I turned; there was Daniel the Hot Firefighter, who winked at me and resumed fondling the ass of his latest False Alarm. Sure. He'd buy me a drink. He'd never sleep with me. I'd aged out fifteen years ago.

I waved my thanks, looked back at my friends and family, smiled and simply gave up.

No more dating. I took down my online profiles, stopped scanning Prospect Park's softball teams and forbid myself to watch anything on the Hallmark Channel.

I was surprised by what a relief it was.

Suddenly, I was happier than I'd been in years. I'd lived in the same gorgeous apartment since college, bought with a hefty loan from my parents just before Brooklyn prices boomed. If I ever needed the money, I could sell it for nearly five times what I paid for it. My classes at the Re-Enter Center were always full. I had a small but tight circle of friends and a slightly dysfunctional but pretty good family.

I had a well-established career I loved, clients who were generally overjoyed with my work. There was nothing like showing a couple their wedding photos—proof of their love— or seeing a mom tear up over the photo of her laughing child, that one moment in time that tells her everything she hopes. I loved how my camera could capture a fleeting moment and all the emotions it held, how a good photo could stop time forever.

At night, I'd come home to the third floor of my brownstone, make myself some dinner or eat leftovers, sit on the steps in the nice weather, talking to the neighbors—the Kultarr family who lived on the first floor, Mrs. Wick from down the street and her poodle, Ishmael. In the winter, I'd plunk myself down in my gray velvet chair, open a book and drink a glass of not-bad wine. Movies, the occasional concert, walks in Prospect Park, drinks with friends.

For children, I had my nieces and nephew. Ainsley and Eric had been together for a thousand years, and I imagined they'd have kids pretty soon. I often babysat for Jake and Josh and got my baby fix from the adorable Jamison, who loved me because I never tired of giving him horsey rides, extra dessert, and would read story after story until he was sound asleep.

If this was all there was, it was plenty. Constantly scanning for more—the baby or the guy—had chipped away at my soul. Life was good. Single, Solitary Me was enough. Call me a Buddhist, but it worked.

Shortly after that birthday, I shot a wedding of a woman who reminded me of my earlier self. She was thirty-seven, quick to tell me she and her fiancé had been together for twelve years, lest I think she was *alone* until now. (I always wondered about those couples, my sister and Eric included. A decade is a long time to wonder if you should marry someone.)

The bride was grim in her victory. Huge fluffy dress, six bridesmaids, four flower girls, high Anglican mass at St. Thomas on Fifth Avenue. Her tiny, elderly parents walked her down the aisle to Wagner's *Bridal Chorus*. The sense of *I've earned this, goddamn it* was as thick as fog in London.

As was often the case, I could see through the camera what wasn't visible to my naked eye; the groom was itchy, his goofy antics masking his resentment. I guessed she'd given him an ultimatum about marriage; I imagined they'd fought bitterly about it until he caved.

The bride's smile was tight at the corners, her eyes flat, her forehead Botoxed. Even the kiss at the altar had been quick and hard. Some of the guests rolled their eyes, and rather than the lightness that so often radiates from weddings, regardless of the age of the bride and groom, this one was dull and heavy.

Every wedding tradition was honored—the engraved program announcing the readings, the lifting of the veil, Handel's *Trumpet Voluntary* blaring at the end. At the reception, which was held at the Peninsula Hotel, the bride and groom were introduced as Mr. and Mrs. Whitfield, the three hundred guests dutifully applauding, the bride snarling at her sister for not securing the train properly. There was the first dance, the father-daughter dance, mother-son dance, the cutting of the cake, the tossing of the bouquet.

As I held up the camera to photograph the bride getting ready to chuck her flowers, I could see through the viewer that, yep, she was rubbing it in, calling some of her reluctant friends by name to get on out there. *I am no longer one of you, hags! And the world shall know that you are still single!*

Those older (my age) friends muttered resentfully as they stood on the dance floor, third martinis in hand, not even pretending to try when the bouquet was tossed. The bride's college-age niece caught it, still young enough to think it was fun.

Then the call went out for the single guys to catch the garter—another baffling tradition: *Would you like to have my wife's pointless underwear accessory as a memento? Maybe keep it under your pillow and sniff it from time to time?* The men were the usual suspects—the teenage boys, the already drunken groomsmen, an elderly uncle, the guys whose dates were pretending not to watch but were shrewdly assessing how hard the men would try to make the catch.

Someone caught it; I didn't see who, as he was in the middle of the pack. But then came the obligatory dance for him and the bouquet-catcher, so I dutifully took a few pictures, congratulating them both on their dexterity. The niece was quite beautiful, the guy good-looking without being too handsome, his reddish hair and blue eyes giving him the boy-next-door appeal. My money was on him taking the niece home.

Imagine my shock, then, when the garter-catcher left the niece at the end of the song and came right over to me. Asked about my camera. Listened as I described it, then admitted he took pictures only with his phone. Further admitted he was talking about cameras only to see if I was single and might want to have a drink with him.

"If that's code for 'I have a room here, want to hook up?'" I said, "then sadly, the answer is no."

"There's a code?" he asked, grinning.

"There is."

"Well, what's code for 'Will you have a drink with me after the wedding? Or sometime this week?'"

*It's Hi, I'm an alien*, I thought.

Because good-looking, age-appropriate men didn't date thirty-nine-year-olds. (Daniel the Hot Firefighter, anyone?) Even if, unlike Daniel, a guy my age wanted to settle down, they focused their sights on women in their twenties or early thirties, still secure in their fertility. Not women who'd been single for the entire two decades of their adult lives.

Up until this moment, I had never been approached by a stranger and asked out. Not once. It just wasn't how it happened anymore.

I gave him my business card and smiled, hopefully hiding my befuddlement, then went off to photograph the hissing bride and pissy groom twining arms to sip champagne. I would've bet my left ovary that I would never hear from the garter-catcher again.

He called me the next day and asked me out for a drink on the Lower East Side. Not knowing how to handle such a bizarre turn of events, I accepted.

The restaurant was agonizingly trendy; I'd Googled it earlier in the day and saw it marked as one of New York's hippest bars with egotistical cocktails and flattering lighting.

"Nice place," I said, though it wasn't really my style.

"I picked it because it was a straight shot across the East River for you," he said.

"That was very thoughtful," I said, sliding into the booth. "I'm guessing you're either gay, a serial killer, a gay serial killer or a bigamist, charming his way across America, occasionally calling his children by the wrong names, his wives thinking he's just distracted because he works so very hard."

He laughed, and I felt a purr of attraction low in my

stomach. "No," he said. "Just one ex-wife. Sorry to let you down."

His name was Nathan Vance Coburn III, an architect and fourth-generation son of Cambry-on-Hudson. I told him my folks lived there, that my sister and her boyfriend had recently bought a house there, as well. We played Six Degrees of Kevin Bacon, figuring out who we knew in common. He read my mother's column and had met Eric at a fund-raiser.

I didn't bother trying to impress him or monitor myself; those days were done, those long mental lists of what to say and ask, which topics to avoid. His average looks were appealing, and he wore a suit but no tie. Long blond eyelashes gave him a sweet, almost shy look, though he seemed relaxed and funny.

Men like this just weren't single.

It seemed contradictory, because I personally knew at least five really great women in their late thirties and early forties who were looking for love. Statistics would say there'd be at least five similarly great single men in the same age group, but statistics would be wrong. I didn't know one man my age I'd want to date, and believe me, my criteria had been low. Forget about living with his mother or having a job. We were talking "no recent murders" by the time I called it quits.

So Nathan Vance Coburn III... I was obviously suspicious.

I shook his hand at the end of the date and said it had been very nice talking with him. He called me two days after that. We met for dinner, and he insisted on paying. I let him kiss me good-night, and he did it just right; no tongue, long enough to convince me, short enough to avoid embarrassment.

I smiled all the way home, the only person on the subway to do so.

We started dating, and by dating I meant just meeting and talking and some kissing. We held hands sometimes.

No sex, because I was having fun the way things were. My newly acquired Zen kept me chill about the whole thing—if it worked, yay. If not, no biggie.

Nathan seemed freakishly great. I quizzed him on the social issues that mattered to me, showing him pictures of my brother's biracial kids. Nathan's only comment: "Gorgeous," with a sweet, almost wistful smile. I mentioned my gay friends. My voting history. My feeling that people who stole handicapped parking spaces should be hobbled. I told him about my fear of earthworms. He sympathized and admitted his fear of potato eyes.

Nathan didn't mind the old-fashioned courtship. Sometimes, he'd bring me a bouquet of flowers. Once, a small cardboard box tied in twine, containing a perfect red velvet cupcake. I'd send him photos from our dates, since I was never without my camera—the old woman on the bench, the sun glinting off One World Trade Center. I took him to the best Polish restaurant in Brooklyn and introduced him to the wonders of homemade pierogi. We went for a walk in the Brooklyn Botanic Garden, the golden aspen leaves drifting down around us, and went to the top of the Empire State Building, something he'd never done, which I found incomprehensible. He was an architect, after all.

"We ever gonna sleep together?" he asked amiably as we surveyed the miracle of New York's skyline.

"Someday, maybe," I said, running a finger along his wrist, feeling the heavy thud of his pulse. "If you're very lucky. Keep up with the cupcakes."

The next day, two dozen cupcakes were delivered to my studio.

The truth was, I was almost afraid to sleep with him. What if I found out that he liked to use a riding crop on his lovers, or could get it up only if I called him Caesar?

Nope. When the day came, after seven and a half weeks and nineteen dates, he asked me to take the train up to his place in Cambry-on-Hudson. Asked me to pack an overnight bag. Gave me a tour of his massive, beautiful house and, when he showed me the master bedroom, said, "Please note the California king-size bed comfortably accommodates two."

He made me dinner. We had a bottle of wine. And we did sleep together.

It was lovely. *He* was lovely.

Finally, I asked the question that had been bugging me from the first day we'd met. "Nathan, why did you ask me out?"

"It was an impulse," he said, and I gave him points for not delivering a schmaltzy answer. "You just seemed...together. And happy."

I liked that a lot.

One night, after a long kiss good-night that made my stomach gather in a giddy, delicious squeeze, he whispered, "I love you, you know," and my whole chest ached with heat.

"I love you, too," I breathed without thinking.

My next thought was *Too early. Too easy. Too soon.*

Six weeks later, he proposed.

It was fast. But we weren't kids. He'd been married already. And children, which seemed like an elusive dream akin to spending the summer horseback riding through Montana with Derek Jeter, were now a possibility. One way or another, biological or adoptive, we both wanted to be parents. He loved his two nephews like crazy. Always wanted to be a father. Madeleine, his ex-wife, had changed her mind on that; it was the issue that ended their marriage.

And, I thought, life was uncertain. Look at Eric, hit with cancer at thirty-two years old (though thankfully, he caught it early, and it was a cancer with a high cure rate). My sister could've lost him. Live life to the fullest. Seize the day. Et cetera.

His parents weren't thrilled; well, his father seemed fine, kissing me on the cheek and forgetting my name almost immediately in a benign, scotchy way. His mother looked elegantly perplexed but was classy enough to say, "I'm sure we'll become quite close." His sister, Brooke, was warm, and her husband was quite nice, as well. Their little boys were beautiful; cousins for my future children. The thought caused a palpable tremor of joy.

My own family was mixed. Dad, who was enduring the off-season by rewatching every game he hadn't personally called, tore his eyes off the TV and said, "Good for you, Poodle! About time! You've been with him what, ten years?"

"No, that's Ainsley," I said. "This is kind of a whirlwind thing."

"Those are the best. Like me and Michelle," he reminisced fondly, naming Ainsley's mother. My own mother's lips disappeared. "Well, good for you!" Dad continued. "Will I have to pay for the wedding?"

I patted his arm. "I think we're gonna keep it small. Elope, maybe. I'm forty, after all. Almost."

"You are? Good Lord! Well, elopement is a good idea. Very romantic. Bring him by sometime. Does he like baseball?"

I winced. "He's a Mets fan." We were pin-striped, of course. Dad was an American League umpire.

"Pity. Well, I'm sure he's nice."

"Why would you want to be *married*, Kate?" my mother asked over lunch with Ainsley and me. "Just live together. It's less messy when you break up."

"Thanks for the vote of confidence," I said. "And aren't you pro-marriage? I'm sure you mention it in one of your books."

"You've been on *my* case to get married for years," Ainsley said.

"Well, you're wasting your life with Eric, honey. If he liked it, as the song goes, he would've put a ring on it."

"Should you be quoting Beyoncé when you have a PhD from Yale?" my sister asked. "Also, Eric's recovering from cancer, if you remember. Weddings are kind of low on our priorities list."

"How's he doing? Still clear?" I asked, hoping she wouldn't launch into too many medical details.

"Yeah," she said, "but he's waiting for the eighteen-month mark. That's when he's officially better."

"Fingers crossed," I said.

"Kate," Mom said, turning to me, "you can hardly expect me to be wholehearted about this. You've known him what? Six months?"

"Five."

"Five. Do you know the statistics for people who marry knowing each other less than two years?"

"Nope. But I'm almost forty. Old enough to make my own decisions, Mom."

Ainsley chattered cheerfully about flowers and dresses, but she gave off an air of confusion. After all, as Mom pointed out via Beyoncé, Ainsley was the one with the decade-long relationship. She already lived with Eric in Cambry-on-Hudson. She clearly was supposed to be first down the aisle.

"Well, Eric thinks the world of Nathan," she said gamely. "He's a total catch!" The words made me wince. So 1950s, as if we women had to trick men into marriage.

But he did meet every criterion a single woman could have—kind, steady, interesting, intelligent, attractive, financially secure. Even his divorce spoke well of him; he hadn't been hanging around, not committing (as I had been). He had no pit in his cellar, no devices for torturing women, no collection of Nazi uniforms. I looked, believe me, making him laugh and laugh as I poked around his enormous home.

There was absolutely no reason not to marry him.

Except...

There's always that, isn't there?

Marriage, as nice as it might be, would throw my life into upheaval—Nathan wanted me to move to Cambry-on-Hudson, relocate my studio, sell my apartment. Of course he did. COH was his hometown, and though I hadn't grown up there, it was where I went on holidays. It made sense. He had a gorgeous house perfectly suited to children and entertaining, with plenty of space for us both.

But still. All the adjustments, all the moving, most of the changes would be mine. Ideally, I'd take more time to ease into this. I knew I wasn't used to being part of a couple, of joint decision-making.

Not to mention that five months wasn't enough time to truly know each other. This would be a leap of faith that everything I believed to be true about Nathan would hold fast. If I was wrong—or if he was—we'd look like idiots.

The changes would be worth it, I believed. But it would be upheaval nonetheless, and twenty years on my own...well, it was hard to walk away from. I couldn't bring myself to sell my apartment. Instead, I rented it and put my things in storage. It was December. Who wanted to schlep furniture?

If I'd been even a few years younger, I would've waited. There was a small, annoying voice—my mother's—telling me that a reason *not* to marry him didn't mean a good reason *to* marry him. That you can't really love someone you've known for five months.

I confessed my concern to Paige. We were at Porto's, our favorite bar, one of the few places in Brooklyn that predated the influx of cool people and was therefore übercool, the *not* locally farmed, *not* organic, *not* microbrewed, *not* free-range food and drink deemed delightfully retro by the hipsters.

We were drinking vodka tonics at a table, idly watching Daniel the Hot Firefighter flirt with what seemed like identical blonde women who couldn't be more than twenty-two. "Maybe I should wait," I said. "Just see how things go."

"I think you're a fucking idiot," Paige said, taking a slurp of her drink.

"No, no, tell me what you really mean," I said. "Don't mince words."

"Seriously, Kate. He's great. Marry him. Move to the 'burbs and have twins. I'm so jealous I could stab you in the throat."

"Will you be a bridesmaid?" I asked, grinning.

"Piss off."

She wasn't smiling. My own smile died a quick death. "Paige," I began.

"I don't want to talk about it, okay? You were the last single friend I had. I'd *kill* for a guy like Nathan, and you sit there wondering if you should marry him. Who do you think you are?"

"Um…a person? With feelings and thoughts? Come on, Paige. I thought I could talk to you—"

"Yeah, well, don't. Okay? You have a two-carat ring on your finger. Wear white. Register for new china and, hey, how about a destination wedding to make your single friends use vacation time and spend their own money to cheer you on?"

With that, she threw down her napkin and left.

"Did you and Paige break up?" Daniel asked, appearing at my side. "Was it over me?"

I laughed reluctantly. "No. I'm getting married. Paige is…" My voice trailed off.

"A bitch?"

"No. Just feeling a little left out, maybe. I'm moving to Westchester."

He shuddered. "Well, mazel tov, Kate. Nice knowing you."

"I'm not dying."

"You're moving out of the city. Same thing. See you never." He smiled and went back to his fan club.

I forgave Paige the bitchiness, but I knew she wouldn't forgive me. I was getting what we both always wanted, and she was not. I understood. The little voice in my head, that tremor of warning, was snuffed out.

On New Year's Day, Nathan and I went for dinner at a restaurant with a view of the Brooklyn Bridge. It was snowing, and we had a window table. I wore a glittery white cocktail dress and slutty black shoes, and Nathan gave me a red rose. The justice of the peace came in, and in front of a room full of strangers, with New York shimmering through the windows, I became Nathan's wife.

Ninety-six days later, I became his widow.

# Chapter Six

❧

*Kate*

Taking a pregnancy test moments before leaving for my husband's wake…the sense of the ridiculous was not lost on me.

I locked the guest bathroom door and tried to take a deep breath. Since the moment Nathan went down four days ago, I'd been in a dream-state of panic and disbelief, the edge of hysterical laughter never far from my lips, as if at any minute, Nathan was going to jump out of the broom closet and say "Surprise!"

I hadn't cried yet. Not exactly. There'd been some…well… noises. A sense of strangulation if I dozed off. No tears, not yet. I did, however, seem to be hyperventilating rather a lot.

Ainsley used to have panic attacks when she was little. Mom dutifully taught her to breathe slowly—in for a count of three, hold for a count of three, exhale for three, hold for three. *In for three, hold for three, out for three, hold for three.* I used to chant it during thunderstorms when she was tiny and would climb into my bed, shaking with fear.

I tried it now. It wasn't working. All the air wanted to do was rush in-out-in-out-in-out.

*Two lines, goddamn it*, I mentally ordered. *Two lines. You owe me.*

I wrestled my Spanx panty hose back into place (because one must look smooth and sleek at the wake of one's husband), pulled down my black dress and waited.

*Come on, Universe. Throw me a bone here.*

The seconds ticked past. No rush. Wasn't like I was going anywhere fun. My chest bucked with an aborted sob. Someone had told me I was in shock. Kiara, that was it. She was a doctor, she knew these things. Also, there was no normal reaction to a sudden death. Nothing I felt was wrong.

Except *everything* I felt was wrong.

I *so* did not want to do this widow thing. For a flash of a second, it seemed possible that I could say, "Yeah...no. I'll pass." Then I'd revive Nathan and go back to being married.

Eloise and Nathan Senior were waiting downstairs with Brooke, Chase and the heartbroken boys. The thought of their sweet, bereft faces made my throat feel like a nail had been driven through it. A spike, actually, a big rusty railroad spike. Their uncle. Their *only* uncle.

Four days ago, I was *married*. That had been enough of a trip. Now I was a *widow*. I ask you—how weird was that? (My brain seemed to be generating only italicized words, like an overdramatic narrator.)

Brooke lost her beloved younger brother. The Coburns no longer had a son.

Nathan was *dead*.

I mean, really. What the *fuck*?

Maybe I could stay here all night. It sure beat what lay

ahead. I could simply wait for everyone to leave, creep out of the bathroom and watch *Orange Is the New Black*. I could make popcorn. Better yet, I could buy some of that popcorn with the salted caramel and chocolate in it. Get a bottle from Nathan's wine cellar, climb in bed with our big TV on. Nathan wouldn't be able to resist that. He'd *definitely* come back from the dead for that.

Funny—horrible—how fast I'd gotten used to sleeping with another person. For twenty years, I'd had my own bed almost without interruption. Two weeks into our marriage, and Nathan and I had already figured out how to sleep together, how we fit together, when to cuddle close, when to pull away.

Now the bed was like the vast Arctic Ocean, freezing cold and lifeless.

The panic was back, little squeaks coming out of my throat, my lips clamped tight.

*Please don't make me do this, Nathan. Please.*

There was a gentle knock on the door, and I jumped. "Kate? Are you okay?" It was Brooke.

"Coming," I said too loudly. My watch told me I'd been in here for seven minutes.

In a movie, there'd be two lines. After all, we *did* shag before the party. I would have a baby in my grief, and the baby would be a memorial to Nathan and our tragic love, and such a comfort to the Coburns. He *absolutely* would be Nathan the Fourth. I'd be really noble and quite beautiful, probably played by that chick who cried so well… What was her name? Rachel McSomething. Yes. Nate IV and I would make a new life together, and he would have his father's blue eyes.

I looked at the test.

One line.

Insult to injury. "Fuck you, test," I whispered. "You're wrong."

★ ★ ★

The carpet at the funeral home was so plush and soft that I wobbled every time someone hugged me. And *everyone* hugged me. I definitely should not have worn heels. Why didn't anyone tell me this? Also, the Spanx panty hose kept threatening to roll down. Every few hugs, I'd have to reach behind and hitch it up a little. I had to pee, which would give me the chance to pull the panty hose back where it belonged. Was I allowed to leave the line? Probably not.

"I'm so sorry for your loss."

"Thank you," I said to the tie in front of me. If I looked only at the necktie, it was easier not to lose my shit and start with the *hehn-hehn-hehn* sounds of hyperventilating. It was so *fucking* embarrassing. I sounded like a dying duck.

My language had seriously deteriorated since my husband died.

"Bernard, how good of you to come. Thank you for being so kind," said Eloise next to me. She wore a black knit St. John dress and pearls. Her eyes were dry, her heart broken, and she made Jackie Kennedy look like a strung-out wreck. "This is our daughter-in-law, Kate. Kate, our very dear friend Bernard Helms."

"Great to meet you," I said, then covered my mouth with my hand. "Oh, shit, I didn't mean that. Obviously, I wish we'd met under different circumstances. But you know, thanks for coming." My left heel wobbled. I felt drunk with fatigue and grief. Now I *looked* drunk, too, wobbling around, constantly off balance. Eloise's heels were higher than mine, but she was not the wobbling type. Brooke wore flats. Smart of her. "Did you know Nathan well?"

Bernard's eyes filled. "I've known him since he was a baby. Such a good boy. I remember this terrible snowstorm, oh, maybe ten years ago. My wife had cancer, and we lost power, and I look out the window, and there's Nathan, coming up our driveway. His place had an automatic generator, and damned if he didn't take the both of us to his house and treat us like royalty the whole four days. Cooked us dinner, played Scrabble." Bernard was now openly weeping. "I'm so sorry for you, my dear. Such a tremendous loss."

I seemed to be gulping and sort of barking with a little choking thrown in for good measure. Pressing my hand against my mouth, I glanced at Eloise helplessly. Pain was carved so deeply on her face that it hurt to look, but she smiled sadly and patted Bernard's arm, murmured something.

I felt like a junkie next to her.

My sister slipped up with a box of tissues. I didn't need them, though. I was just barking, like a dog, or a fox, or a…a…stegosaurus. Did they bark? What was the question? Oh, tissues. The really good ones, with lotion. Ainsley was still waiting, so I took one, blew and wobbled. Ainsley steadied me, and I hated that she was being so nice. I didn't *want* her to be nice. I wanted to be home with Nathan. "Hang in there," she whispered, then went back to her seat.

"I'm so, so sorry," said another one of Eloise's friends, her eyes red and wet. "You just got married! How can you stand it?"

*I have no fucking idea, lady.* "I… It was a terrible shock." Eloise had been saying that, so I borrowed her line.

"Awful! Did he…" She lowered her voice. "Did he make any noise?"

*Jesus.* "I… No. It was very fast."

"This is why Indian women throw themselves on the pyre, isn't it? You must want to do the same thing." She looked at the casket. "He almost looks alive, doesn't he?"

Yeah. We had an open casket. I wasn't sure who said yes to that. It might have been me.

Most of the people here were strangers to me—friends I hadn't met, friends of the elder Coburns, friends of Brooke. The boys' classmates came, which was just brutal, seeing Miles and Atticus trying not to cry, and failing. The Little League team Nathan and Chase coached together came in as well, the little sweaty boy hands shaking mine, the kids unable to look me in the eye.

As wife, I came first in the reception line. Then Eloise, her finishing school posture ramrod straight, and Nathan Senior, who was medicated, I was pretty sure, the lucky dog. God. No, he wasn't lucky. The rusty spike twisted.

Then came Brooke, who was being so brave and kind, though how, I could not imagine. Chase was solemn, nodding, speaking in a low voice, moving the line along, putting his arm around Brooke. At the end were Atticus and Miles in their little navy suits, which just ruined me.

My sister and Eric sat in the front row with Matthias and Esther, Esther crying quietly, Matt giving me a sad smile when our eyes met. And Mom, who wore a *you should've listened to me* look on her face. What was she? A fucking gypsy? Sean and Kiara were murmuring in the back, shaking hands, listening sympathetically. They'd left Sadie with a sitter, but they'd brought a drawing she made for me, smears of pink and green paint.

"Oh, *Kate*! I'm just so sorry!" Hugging me now was one of Nathan's workmates, a fellow architect whose name I couldn't summon. Her body shook with sobs. "I am so, so, *so* sorry."

Three *so*s. He deserved them.

"He was so happy with you," she whispered, pulling back to look at me.

"Oh. Yes. Thank you." My throat was so tight, the words croaked out. "He was—" *was?* Shit, all this past tense! "—so fond of you." *Whoever you are.*

The coworker's mouth trembled, her eyes red. "Anything you need, just call me," she whispered, moving on to Eloise.

"Susannah," my mother-in-law said, never one to forget a name. Her Boston accent made the name sound like *Susahn-ner*. "You're so kind to be here. I know Kate appreciates it very much, as do we."

Nathan and I would never make fun of his mother again. Oh, he'd loved her, all right, but he could do a killer imitation of that upper-crust accent, her soft *R*s and long vowels. "Is this hahf-and-hahf?" he'd say. "Hahven't you any skim, my deah?"

I'd never hear him do that again. How was that *possible*?

"Hello. Thank you for coming," I said to the next tie, my voice wobbling.

"Kate, these are the Parkersons," Eloise said, her voice trembling slightly. "Our next-door neighbors when Nathan was a boy."

"We can't believe it," Mrs. Parkerson said, tears pouring down her face. "We just can't believe it. He was such a good person!"

"I'm Kate," I said. "Thank you so much for coming."

"We flew in from Arizona. Terrible storms in Chicago."

"Well. We appreciate it."

"He used to rake our leaves," the husband said. "We'd pay him a dollar, remember, Eloise? Imagine that. Kids today can't drop their iBoxes to do a damn thing, but Nathan did our whole yard for one dollar."

*So you were cheap and took advantage of a kid. Got it.*

"At least you don't have children," the woman said. It felt like a punch in the throat. Before I could answer—and what do you say to that?—they moved on to Brooke and fell on her like vampires.

Poor Eloise. I had no idea how she could hold it together

like this. On impulse, I reached out to squeeze her hand, but she turned away to say something to the neighbors before I could, and my hand was left floating, awkward and alone.

Impressions of people swarmed me like bats after dark. There was what's-his-name, the guy whose office was next to Nathan's, covering his face with his hand, crying. They'd worked together for a long time, I thought. Just inching through the doorway now was one of the shop owners from downtown—Jenny, who owned the wedding dress shop, and her boyfriend. Lenny? No. Something cooler. Leo. So nice of them to come. We were going to have dinner, Jenny and Leo, Nathan and I. Not now. No more foursomes. Not unless I found another husband, quick.

The thought made me sputter with a laugh, the edge of hysteria that much closer. I turned it into a cough. I wasn't sure anyone was fooled.

I met Nathan's Boy Scout troop leader; the woman at the post office; the mayor of Cambry-on-Hudson, who used to babysit him. His cross-country coach from middle school, his cross-country coach from high school, his teammates, his classmates, his college mates, his graduate school mates, his workmates. Everyone knew Nathan. Everyone had a story.

Another person from downtown Cambry-on-Hudson stood in line. Kim from Cottage Confections, who'd made us a tiny, beautiful wedding cake when she heard we'd eloped. She and Jenny the wedding dress designer and I had drinks when I moved into my new studio, all of us linked by the wedding industry. Kim had gone to school with Nathan. She'd told me a funny story about him at an eighth-grade social, when he danced right into a pole and got a bloody nose.

She saw me looking now and gave a little wave, tears in her eyes.

I wasn't sure how I could keep breathing. The spike seemed

to be cutting everything off. Maybe I'd faint. Fainting would be good. I wouldn't have to be here if I was unconscious.

Ainsley had sent a mass email to my friends, letting them know about Nathan. But Cambry-on-Hudson was far to come for a wake, I guessed. Brooklynites were notoriously reluctant to travel past Manhattan. Out of the entire City of New York? Please. There'd been a lot of emails I hadn't yet read, and many flower arrangements, some fruit baskets and donations to charities. Cards had been pouring in.

The only representative from my Brooklyn life was Max, my soft-voiced assistant, standing in the back with his wife, eyeing the crowd like a member of the Secret Service. He didn't like most people, which was ironic, since we were always photographing them. So the fact that he was here…

Ainsley hopped back up like a well-trained service dog and gave me a few more tissues, assuming I was crying. Nope, still no tears. Panic, yes. My skin crawled like fire ants had attacked. Adrenaline, shock, whatever. I took the tissues and balled them in my hand.

Behind me was Nathan's body, post-autopsy.

"You doing okay?" Ainsley asked.

"Nope. Really shitty," I whispered. The carpet sucked at my heels again, and I staggered a little.

My father appeared before me. "Hey, sweetie. I'm so sorry." Then his face crumpled a little.

Sometimes I forgot that Dad had lost a spouse, too.

He composed himself, his face changing back to that jovial *how 'bout them Yankees* expression he usually wore. Hugged me hard, the kind of hug that I hadn't had from him in twenty years or so.

"Thanks, Dad," I whispered. My father had liked Nathan, despite the Mets. Swore he'd win him over to the dark side by taking him to a Yankees game.

So that would never happen, either.

Dad let go of me rather abruptly and moved down the line to Eloise. He hated funerals and wakes. Most people did. I *definitely* did. I wondered if I could say, "I hate these things. Who wants to grab a burger instead?"

Had Nathan been scared? Did he know? *Please, please, don't let him have been scared*, I begged the higher power that I've been clinging to these past four days. Heaven, which I never really believed in, had become awfully important this week.

Nathan deserved heaven.

Maybe if I could cry, this horrible spike in my throat would disintegrate. But the tears didn't come.

Another man stood in front of me. No tie. Kind of refreshing, really. Just an unbuttoned gray polo shirt revealing an attractive male throat, a hint of chest hair. I waited for the *I'm so sorry for your loss*. It didn't come. I raised my eyes.

The face was gorgeous. And familiar, but I couldn't place it for a second. Green eyes. Dimples. Mischievous eyebrows.

"Hey, beautiful," he said in a low voice, and he gave me a hug, and then I knew who he was, and I was suddenly so unexpectedly *happy* that it took me by surprise. Someone from my old life was here, someone I would never have expected to see. His neck was solid and warm.

"God, you smell good," he murmured. "Sorry. Inappropriate?"

"Very," I said, hugging him back. "What the *hell* are you doing here, Daniel the Hot Firefighter?"

The room went quiet.

Oh, shit. I mean, that *was* what we called him, but still.

"It's the grief talking," he said to Eloise, releasing me. "Hi, I'm Daniel Breton, a friend from Brooklyn. I'm so sorry." He looked back at me. "So. Shitty luck, huh?"

"Yep."

We just looked at each other a second. "How are you?" I asked, not wanting him to go.

"Better than you." He cocked an eyebrow.

"True enough." It was so strange to see him in my new life, in Westchester County. Aside from a few parties in the apartment he once shared with Calista, the only time I'd ever seen Daniel the Hot Firefighter was in bars or riding past in a fire truck.

We'd never been friends, exactly. Calista had been my friend before she got so spiritual and limber. Daniel was just her man-child ex, fun eye candy. At most, Paige and I had let him sit with us for a drink while he was waiting for a False Alarm to wander past.

But here he was. And it probably took him two hours to get here.

"Were you happy together?" Daniel asked.

The question brought the spike flying back. "Yes," I whispered.

"Good. That's good."

The line was stopped, the endless mourners waiting. "Thanks for coming, Daniel."

"You bet. See you around." He moved on, shaking hands with the Coburns.

For a second, I pictured four of us—Daniel and one of his False Alarms, Nathan and me, back at Porto's Bar, laughing. We should've done that. Why hadn't we ever done that? They would've liked each other, maybe.

Unfortunately, Nathan still seemed to be dead.

So no beers with Daniel the Hot Firefighter.

I glanced at the casket, which I'd been trying so hard not to do.

Nathan wore a blue suit and a tie I'd given him for Christmas. Or had I? He had lots of ties. This one was purple with red polka dots. From now on, I'd be obliged to hate red polka dots.

This was just not funny. Seriously. I was not amused. For a second, I felt like kicking his casket and saying, *Wake up, you selfish shit. Look at your poor mother! Look at Miles and Atticus! How is your sister supposed to go through life without you? And what about me, huh? What about our baby? Remember that little project? Huh? Huh? You can't just run out on all this, you know!*

"I'm very sorry for your loss."

Another tie. This one was navy blue with silver. "Thanks." I raised my eyes. It was Jonathan, Ainsley's boss.

He'd been great that night. When I started, ah, screaming and stuff—Nathan's slits of blue eyes, those unseeing blue eyes, and please, Higher Power, take that image away from me—Jonathan had been busy. Chest compressions until the paramedics arrived. He drove me to the hospital, I think. It gets blurry around that point. No. He did.

"He seemed like a very nice person," Jonathan said, and the simple words caused another agonizing swallow.

"Thank you," I whispered, and he inclined his head in a courtly nod and moved on to shake Eloise's hand.

"Kate," said a quiet voice next to me. Brooke. "Can I have a word?" She guided me a few steps closer to the...the...the casket and lowered her already quiet voice to nearly inaudible. "Kate, Madeleine is here and wants to pay her respects. Is that all right with you?"

"Madeleine? Nathan's ex?"

"Yes. She...she was devastated when Mom called her." Brooke's eyes filled with tears.

"Oh. Um...well, sure. I mean, is it okay with you guys? The family?"

"It's up to you."

Well, I couldn't exactly bar the door, could I? "Sure. Of course."

Brooke nodded, then walked from the room, and I went back to the hated line.

Nathan never told me much about Madeleine; it was one of the few subjects he was touchy about. It hadn't been easy, I knew. They'd been married for six years. She'd had a difficult upbringing and was, in his words, brilliant. She worked in…in something cool. I couldn't remember. Otherwise, I knew nothing.

"Thank you for coming," I said to the next tie.

"I'm very sorry," said the man, and I was so tired, I didn't bother asking how he knew Nathan.

"Thank you," I said.

"At least you didn't have children," his wife said, patting my arm, and I felt like stabbing her.

And then in came Madeleine with Brooke.

My husband's ex-wife was *stunning*. He hadn't mentioned that part. *So you were married to Jessica Chastain, huh?* I thought. *Why isn't she your widow? Doesn't seem fair that she had you for six years, but I'm the sap who has to stand here. Also, my feet are killing me.*

Madeleine was slim in that "*Diet?* What do you mean by this foreign word?" way. She was a vegan, Nathan had told me; he'd been watching me lay waste to a bacon cheeseburger and seemed quite content with my meat-eating habits. Vegans were difficult, he'd said.

But they did tend to have great figures. Her dress was navy blue, simple but fascinating, too. Chic, smooth haircut, expensive-looking gold earrings that twisted and swung.

She saw the casket and froze, her face turning white as chalk.

Then she let loose a wail that made my blood run cold.

The place fell silent.

She collapsed right there, folding (gracefully) to her knees, and put both fists up to her face. "No!" she sobbed. "Oh, Nathan, no!"

I hadn't wailed, or collapsed. Was this a point in my column, or a demerit?

A demerit, it seemed. Eloise rushed to her side, helped her up and put her arms around her. "My deah Madeleine," she said. "Oh, my deah." They hugged, and finally, it seemed, Eloise cracked. Her face spasmed.

Just for a moment, though. She led Madeleine to the casket, where Madeleine put her hand on my husband's chest— my *dead* husband's chest—and shook with sobs.

Six years, the lucky bitch. Eloise murmured to her, and Brooke came in for a group hug.

Them, the popular girls in high school. Me, my panty hose rolling down.

"Where's the bathroom?" my grandmother asked loudly. "I shouldn't have had all that Pepsi at lunch."

"Come with me, Gram-Gram," Ainsley said.

"Kate." The ex-wife was in front of me, trembling, pressing her lips together. Should I try to out-grieve her? Should I also wail and collapse?

Then I looked in her eyes, and all my bitchery evaporated. She had really loved him.

"Hi. I'm…I'm so sorry," I said, and my mouth wobbled, because I *was* so sorry, so sorry I hadn't taken better care of Nathan. She'd kept him alive for six years. I lost him in our first.

"Forgive me for…that," she whispered, tears spilling out of her beautiful eyes.

"No, no. It was an honest moment." Sheesh. Listen to me. "I'm sure he loved you very much."

"Right back at you."

Eloise gave me an odd look.

How did he ever get over her? She was flippin' beautiful. *I* would marry her, she was so stunning. And why didn't she want his babies? It would make things a *lot* better for the Co-burns if there was a little Nathan running around this place, let me tell you. Madeleine was probably a selfish whore.

Eloise put her arm around her and ushered her away. I wondered if I said that *selfish whore* bit aloud.

"Thank you for coming," I said belatedly, my voice sound-ing cheerful, as if I were waving fondly as best friends left after dinner.

*Cause of death: blunt trauma to the head.*

If my sister had gone for wood counters, or soapstone, would Nathan still be alive?

Apparently, he had a tiny little oddity in one of the blood vessels in his brain. Not a problem, unless one's wife needed a second glass of wine.

*Cause of death: wife wanted to have buzz on during irritating speech by sister's boyfriend.*

Couldn't Eric just have asked Ainsley to marry him in private, like a normal person, I don't know, like maybe five years ago? Instead, he had to make a big production in front of everyone, in front of his *Wellness Montage* (it had been la-beled, and really, who the *hell* photographs the removal of a testicle?). No, we all had to drink a toast to my little sister, and boom, I'm a fucking widow.

I looked at the line, which went out the door, out into the foyer and down the street. When we pulled up to the fu-neral home, the line of mourners was four people thick and wrapped around the block. So much black it looked like the Night's Watch from *Game of Thrones* had descended. That was two hours ago, and the line showed no sign of thinning.

Everyone loved him.

Nine months ago, I hadn't. Nine months ago, I hadn't *known* him. I'd finally gotten to that happy Zen place, and life had been really, really good.

If he had tripped nine months ago, I wouldn't have even known about it. Seven months ago, I would've lost a very sweet guy I'd been seeing. I would've been melancholy for a while. Would've made a black joke about how the universe was telling me not to date. Five months ago, I would've mourned him, would've wondered if we had truly been in love or if it was just infatuation. I would've gone to his wake and introduced myself to his mother as a friend, smiled sadly when I thought of him.

Four months ago, I would've lost my fiancé, but I still wouldn't have known the reality of living with him day after day.

Ninety-six days of marriage.

I drifted over to the casket and, for the first time this endless evening, took a long look at my husband's body.

That woman had been wrong. He looked *absolutely* dead. His face was hard and stiff, like one of those plastic surgery addicts, pumped up on filler. I wondered if the funeral home used the same stuff. Juvaderm. Botox.

*Oh, Nathan.*

At least his hair felt the same. My fingers stroked it, gently, trying not to make contact with his scalp. Just his hair, soft, silky hair that curled a little when he was sweaty. Roman emperor hair, I said once. We were in bed at the time. His smile…

"Hey."

It was Eric. *Cause of death: extremely long-winded speech.*

"Hey," I bit out.

"You doing okay?"

"Not really."

He put his arm around me, and I felt a pang of regret. Eric had always been a decent guy, if self-absorbed. "I was telling Sean about how weird this was, given my cancer. Like there's some meaning here."

The irritation came swooping back like a vengeful eagle. "There's not, so please. None of your platitudes, Eric."

He blinked. "I...I just meant life is short. You have to live life large."

"Not *now*, Eric."

"It's almost a message from the universe. You know I loved him, too. And I thought *I'd* be the one who died. You know? From my cancer?"

"I vaguely remember, yes."

"It's just so random. When I was getting chemo, there were days when I thought this was the end, and I said to myself—"

"Here, Kate." My sister pressed a glass of water into my hand. "Mrs. Coburn wants you to meet someone. Nathan's friend from Columbia."

Saved by the mourners. My sister steered Eric away, and I took another long look at my husband.

*I love you*, I thought desperately, and at almost the exact same time, another thought came, hard and defiantly ugly.

*I wish we'd never met.*

# Chapter Seven

*Ainsley*

"Just when I'd accepted the divorce," Candy liked to tell people on book tour, "Phil showed up with his child."

I remembered thinking at age three and a half that it would be fun to live with a lady named Candy, that her house would be sparkly and we'd eat mostly pink foods. There'd be a lot of singing, I imagined.

There wasn't. Candy sighed a lot. She had a daily headache.

Hence, my childhood of guilt. Candy would buckle me briskly into a car seat, then wince as she stood up, hands on her back. She was in her forties when I came to live with her, and she'd tell her friends that she'd forgotten just how hard little kids were. She was dutiful, showing up at parent-teacher conferences because Dad was off with the boys of summer. She made sure I ate nutritious—and tasteless—dinners, but it was pretty clear. I was not her daughter. She already had one of those.

When I came along, Candy had been working on her PhD. It took her four more years to finish her dissertation, which became her most famous book—*Stuck with You: Raising the Recalcitrant Stepchild*. It took me decades to figure out it was about me.

Unlike Sean and Kate, I was a day-care kid. From their stories, it seemed they were raised in a magical kingdom of sibling friendship and parental delight. Candy baked back then, coconut cookies and angel food cake. Kate and Sean had stories of the time their mother made a tepee in the living room over winter break, or read *The Wind in the Willows* out loud, doing all the voices to perfection. Sean and Kate even shared a room until he turned seven.

There were dozens of pictures of them before I came along, laughing together, arms slung around each other, Sean steadying Kate on her bike, the two of them eating Popsicles on a summer day, or standing in front of the house on the first day of school, Kate's hair in neat ponytails, Sean's freshly cut.

Day care was fine. To the best of my knowledge, I was never dropped on my head or burned with cigarettes or put in toddler fight club. When I started kindergarten at the age of four and a half, I went to after-school programs, envious of the kids who got to ride the bus home.

As I got older, Candy signed me up for pretty much anything that kept me out of the house. I was a Daisy/Brownie/Girl Scout, played soccer from the age of five, was forced into volunteering at Adopt-a-Grandparent, spending many a high school afternoon talking to elderly people who kept asking me to take them home.

My father liked me quite a bit, though he wasn't around too much, always flying off somewhere to do his umpire thing. But when he *was* home, life was a lot happier. "I'm taking the Ainsburger on some errands," he'd call to Family 1.0, and once or twice a month he would take me off, my little hand so happy in his. We'd visit one of his friends, and I'd get to have ice cream *and* watch TV, maybe play computer games, something Candy forbid. Dad and his friend would go into the bedroom to "have a little talk in private," and hey, I didn't care. Dad often took me to the toy store for a new stuffed animal after the visit. For years, I thought *errands* meant visiting ladies.

Kate and Sean were fine. They didn't hate me, beat me, tease me. They just kind of…ignored me. Not in a mean way, but in a slightly confused way. I remember knocking on Sean's door, asking him if he'd play with me. He looked utterly baffled as he groped around in his desk for something I could do with him. (He showed me how to shoot an elastic band, then told me he had to study.) Kate wasn't the type to brush my hair or play dolls with me, though she would, if I asked.

I just got a little tired of asking.

So instead, I made up friends. Lolly and Mr. Brewster, the tiny humans who lived in the mountains of my blankets, would ski and slide down the hills made by my knees and have terrible crashes and vivid arguments about whose fault it was. There was Igor, a tiny elephant who lived in shoe boxes I decorated with scraps of fabric and paint.

I sound tragic, don't I? I wasn't, I'm pretty sure. By the time I was eight or nine, I had friends, and it was such a *relief*, having people who really seemed to like talking to me. In middle school, I joined everything, did the grunt-work jobs (always secretary, never president, equipment manager rather than star player). High school was the same; I was always Switzerland, staying friends with everyone, never taking sides.

I didn't have a boyfriend. But I was great at giving advice to my friends who *did* have boyfriends, and I got a vicarious thrill every once in a while, approaching Seth to tell him that Lucy really liked him, and did he like her?

When Kate went off to NYU, my parents and I moved to Cambry-on-Hudson, and I made the most out of being the new girl. I'd learned long ago that being a superfriend was the way to make people like me back. Adore, and ye shall be adored.

Sean went from Harvard to Columbia Medical School, because he was a show-off. After NYU, Kate got an MFA in photography from Savannah College of Art and Design and immediately started working as a professional photographer. She was dazzling to me, so sophisticated and urbane, living in Brooklyn (I barely knew where that was back then, but it sounded so cool).

I went to a pretty nice college in New York City—well, it was Wagner College on Staten Island, in the shadow of the mighty skyline but technically still in New York City.

Unlike my siblings, I wasn't driven to achieve or study anything in particular. College was wonderful, and I loved being away from home. My siblings were off leading their fabulous, very adult lives; Sean married Kiara, also a surgeon, specialized in some kind of brain surgery and did the occasional TED Talk. Kate lived in her brownstone, a world away, it seemed, though she had me over for dinner once in a while, always nice but a little unsure where I was concerned.

Then, junior year, I met Eric.

Wagner was a small school, but somehow, we didn't know each other. He was an accounting major; I was studying philosophy, because doesn't the world need more philosophers?

I saw Eric as we were moving back in on the first day of the new school year. His parents were saying goodbye, hugging him, and his mom was laughing and wiping tears. He kissed her on the cheek, hugged his dad, not the awkward *thanks, gotta run* hug of most boys our age, but a real hug, a loving hug.

And Eric was handsome. Dark hair, dark eyes, attractively dorky glasses, lanky build.

He looked up, saw me watching and smiled, and that was it. I fell in love.

It took two weeks for me to speak to him, which was getting awkward, since we lived in the same dorm that year. But one happy night, my key card wasn't working, and I was patiently reinserting it for the fifteenth time when Eric came up behind me and said, "Want me to try, girl who doesn't talk to me?"

I blushed.

He smiled. "Maybe we could grab a coffee," he suggested, and my heart ricocheted around my chest.

We grabbed a coffee.

By the weekend, we were a couple. It took him all of two weeks to get me into bed; basically, the amount of time it took for the Pill to kick in. I couldn't believe love had finally found me in the form of affable, well-liked, dorktastic Eric Fisher...my boyfriend!

And even more remarkable...he felt the same way about me.

We could talk all night. It was more important to talk than sleep. He was funny, and he was so *nice* that it took my breath away. I hadn't met any boys like that. Boys who held the door and bought you cold medicine when you were sick and snagged a blueberry muffin from the dining hall just because you loved them.

With Eric, I finally belonged. Finally, I was special.

That summer, we both got internships in Manhattan, me with a tiny publishing house, him with a bank. His parents let us stay in their apartment on 102nd Street—the building was named The Broadmoor, which I thought was so sophisticated. I'd never lived in a building with a name before. The apartment had belonged to Eric's maternal grandmother, and it was a tiny, unglamorous place with a bedroom so small it could fit only a double bed. The living room was also the kitchen, and our table could fit only two people, and even then, our knees had to touch.

Mr. and Mrs. Fisher approved of me, which in itself was dazzling. "Are you religious, sweetheart?" his mom had asked on our third dinner together.

"Not really, Mrs. Fisher. Don't let the name O'Leary fool you," I said. "I can't remember the last time we went to church. Maybe when my cousin got married a few years ago?"

She beamed. "Call me Judy, honey."

"Sorry about my mom," Eric said, smiling at his mother. "She wants to make sure the kids will be raised Jewish."

Kids! Raised! My knees thrilled with adrenaline and love.

After graduation, we stayed together. It was always *we*. "We should go to San Francisco," Eric said late in our senior year, "though it would kill my mother. By the way, she wants to take you to *Phantom* again. I'm sorry."

I *adored* him. He was smart, kind and thoughtful. He told great stories, making his happy, normal childhood seem utterly hilarious without ever mocking his parents. His devotion to me didn't even flicker. That was another thing I loved about him. His constancy.

The difference between being someone's friend, sister (or half sister, as the case was), daughter (or stepdaughter)...and being someone's *love* was breathtaking. I felt like the most wonderful creature in the world.

Upon graduation, Eric and I got jobs in the city, making Judy just about cartwheel with joy (they lived in nearby Greenwich, Connecticut). My B+ average and philosophy major qualified me to be nothing, but I got a job as a receptionist at NBC. Eric got a position at the bank where he'd interned, and we moved back into The Broadmoor, much to the jealousy of our friends, who had to endure complicated commutes from Queens or Yonkers.

It was perfect. The thrill of our first real jobs, riding on the subway, getting pad Thai for dinner and watching TV, fooling around in our tiny bedroom…it was everything I imagined adult life should be.

I loved working at Rockefeller Center, liked seeing the celebrities going in and out. I liked dressing up for work in my retro-cute dresses or sweater sets and A-line skirts. I was outgoing, I was cheerful, I said hello but didn't ask for a selfie with the talent or try to kiss up to the producers and writers (though I did text Eric every time I saw Tina Fey). The job wasn't rocket science, but I did it well.

Eric had a higher-paying job, and I encouraged him to look into MBA programs, because he had a really good brain for numbers. After just two months at the bank, he was already restless and irritable about his entry-level position. He wanted something with status, with an office and a personal assistant.

Personally, I felt there was a lot of peace in doing a not-hard job. Besides, my real adult life lay ahead of me, in some happy, vague fantasy that involved me wearing a lot of Armani, but still being a stay-at-home mom to our kids. Surely Eric and I would be getting married soon; we talked about it without reservation, not the specifics, but just *when we're married* or *that would be a nice place to settle down* or *when we have a baby*. There was no rush. We were just out of college, after all.

NBC was fine. I never minded delivering lunch to the newsroom or standing in the rain to grab a taxi for someone who'd forgotten to book the car service. Then one day, a reporter from *The Day's News* asked me to run out and buy him a new shirt and tie; he had to go on air unexpectedly and had sweated through his original shirt running back from lunch. "I hate to ask you," he said. "But I'm in a jam, and my assistant isn't in today."

"Oh, I don't mind!" I said. "No problem at all."

He gave me four hundred dollars. "Buy yourself something for your trouble," he said, "and thank you. Really, Ainsley. I appreciate it."

How nice that he knew my name! Well, I wore a name badge, but most people just called me "Hey," as in "Hey, I need a cab/lunch/reservation…"

I went to Brooks Brothers, got him a blue shirt that would bring out his nice eyes and a cool blue-and-purple tie with a pattern that wouldn't strobe on TV. I brought the stuff up to the office and left the receipt and change in an envelope on his desk.

Two days later, there was a beautifully wrapped box on my desk. *I told you to buy yourself something nice*, the note said. *Thank you again. —Ryan Roberts.* Inside was a stunning pink-and-red silk scarf, so fine it practically floated. As Candy had drilled into me, I handwrote him a thank-you note.

Three weeks later, Ryan asked if I wanted to work on *The Day's News* as a production assistant. There was an opening, and he'd thought of me. Eric just about fainted when I told him. "That's great! Honey, I'm so proud of you!"

So even though I had only a vague idea of what a production assistant did, I said yes.

And here's a secret. If you didn't mind doing anything anyone asked, you were an *amazing* production assistant. Make coffee, get lunch, proofread this copy, get the art department to change this graphic, cut this story down to three minutes, call this restaurant and make a reservation for this anchor… it was easy. Other production assistants ran around sweating and panicked, trying to outsweat and outpanic each other to show how very important they were. I didn't. I knew I wasn't.

That was the thing that really stood out at NBC—my complete lack of ambition. I didn't want to be a journalist or an on-air reporter. I didn't want to go to Beirut (are you even kidding me?). Let other people go to dangerous places filled with bombs and rubble and gunfire. Me, I liked running water and flirting with the seventy-five-year-old doorman at The Broadmoor. I liked sleeping with Eric, because even though we both worked long days, we still fell asleep cuddled together every night.

I didn't want a corner office. I never asked for a raise or a promotion.

This somehow got me a raise and a promotion every six months. For some reason, Ryan thought I was invaluable.

I know what you're thinking. That he put the moves on me. Nope. He took Eric and me out to dinner with his wife. He showed me pictures of his kids, whom he truly adored. He thanked me for remembering his mom's birthday when he forgot.

I went from production assistant to assistant producer, making my colleagues grind their teeth. Six months later, Ryan was tapped for more airtime, and I got another promotion so I could go along with him (associate producer). A year and a half after that, he was made lead anchor of *The Day's News*, and at the age of twenty-six, I was made senior producer of the country's second-largest news show.

Eric was so proud. He took both the O'Leary and Fisher families out to celebrate at a superfancy restaurant, and everyone came, even Dad, who happened to be in town for a Yankees-Orioles series. Judy and Aaron continually toasted and praised me, and Kate asked for celebrity gossip. Even Sean was impressed. Candy wondered how I was qualified, and Eric said, "Because she's wonderful at everything she does."

Ryan's popularity soared; he was young enough to still have boy-next-door good looks, old enough for a sense of gravitas. He had a great sense of humor (hosted *Saturday Night Live*, in fact; I got Judy and Aaron tickets) and was adored by everyone at NBC. He treated me like an equal, listened to my suggestions and took them.

When he interviewed the President, I told Ryan to ask about the day his kids were born, and sure enough, the leader of the free world teared up, and ratings and social media went wild. Ryan knuckle-bumped me after the interview and introduced me to the President. Of the United States.

Meanwhile, Eric graduated from Rutgers with his MBA, got a job on Wall Street, and we were living the Big Apple dream. We traded in The Broadmoor for a two-bedroom in Chelsea (no name for the building, alas).

Despite my shiny title and brushes with the rich and famous, I made only a fraction of what Eric did at his job. Unlike me, he was very ambitious. But he was also fretful about work. On Wall Street, in a job with three hundred other bright, ambitious people, it was hard to stand out.

So I jumped in, his secret weapon. I had him invite his boss over for dinner, where I cooked and charmed with work stories and befriended the boss's wife. I urged Eric to join the company softball team and volunteer for the American Lung Association stair climb in his building. When the CEO had twins, I had Eric make a donation to Save the Children in honor of the newborn boys. (She came down from the top floor to personally thank Eric, by the way.)

Ryan liked to say I had my finger on the pulse of humanity—yeah, yeah, a little over the top—but I did read people well. Eric…not as much. He was a little too used to being the worshipped only child to see what other people needed. I was the opposite. Unworshipped and clear-eyed.

Every so often when we passed a jewelry store window, Eric would look at me and grin. I'd feign innocence, and he'd say, "Just trying to see what you're looking at." So there were assurances and hints and references to us getting engaged… but still no ring.

One night, when we were having a rare dinner together in our beautiful apartment, and were both happy and full of good wine, I heard myself ask, "Hon? When do you think we'll get married?"

He put down his fork; he'd cooked shrimp risotto, my favorite. Nodded, and gazed at me with his kind eyes. "I want that, too. You know I do. I love you so much, Ains. But the last thing I want to do is start our married life at a time when I'm so busy that I can't spend time with my wife. Another year and a half, maybe two, and I'll be over the hump. Can you hang in there that long?"

And not wanting to sound like a dependent, weak female, I said, "Of course! I'm busy, too, definitely. No, it was just a… I just wondered."

"Obviously, we're gonna get married, babe. You're the love of my life." He smiled, poured me more wine, and we had a lovely night. With great sex, I might add.

And then…well…then the shit hit the Peacock, as it were.

In addition to being the country's most trusted source for news, Ryan Roberts also seemed to be a bit of a magnet for the action.

There was the time a bullet whizzed past his head during a hostage situation, and Ryan had the cameraman shoot him giving the update live, pointing to the hole in the building behind him. How about the time his car was lifted right off the ground in Tornado Alley? The fire in Queens, the terrorist threat in California. Exciting, terrifying stuff, right? I'd write the lead-in: *This evening on* The Day's News—*Ryan Roberts on the DC hostage situation, too close for comfort. Tune in at five!*

At first, I didn't know anything was amiss. I thought he just wasn't that good at remembering the details when he called in. *I was just down the street from the gunfire*, he told me on the phone, but in our news meeting, it was a lot more dramatic—*bullets streaking past my head*. The big explosion that rattled the windows in the building down the street became a hair-singeing brush with a fireball.

Details can come back to people. It happens all the time. Besides, I trusted Ryan. He was the best boss in the world.

But it became a pattern. His SUV was fired on in Afghanistan. In Botswana, he held a dying AIDS patient in his arms. The news story—and ratings—were so much better, so much juicier when Ryan was part of the news, not just reporting it. And he *was* on the scene, after all. It was his job.

It didn't happen all the time. Maybe every few months, but enough that my antenna started to twitch. I finally asked him about it over a late dinner in his office one night. It was hours after a hurricane had socked Brooklyn, and Ryan had been on the scene. "There I was, just trying to get a feel for the area," he said, "and this woman called out from the subway. She was drowning, Ains! I ran down the stairs, into the water, which was completely filthy, by the way, and dragged her out. She was barely conscious."

The antenna quivered. Why would he wait all day to tell me this? "Where'd you take her?" I asked.

"Huh? Oh, someone helped her to the hospital. She was fine."

The antenna twitched.

"Did you get her name? It would make a fantastic piece."

"I should've asked, right? Guess I was just too caught up in the moment." Except he was a newsman. Getting the story was his life.

The antenna began voguing, Madonna-style.

I took a bite of my sesame noodles. "It's funny. Sometimes it seems like you only remember the best details after you've had a couple hours." I didn't look at him as I spoke, and I kept my tone careful.

This was my *boss*. He made sixteen million dollars a year. He'd given me an incredible career, and I wasn't exactly awash in life skills.

Ryan didn't answer. Just looked at me and took another bite of his Reuben.

"I just want to be sure the story is…clean," I said.

"Of course it is, Ainsley," he said with that crooked grin America loved. "Sometimes it takes a little while for everything to filter through. The adrenaline, you know? Well." There was a significant pause. "Maybe you don't. Since you don't go on scene."

In other words, *don't push it.*

Every news show probably did the same thing, right? I mean, it didn't simply rain anymore—we had rain events. Fog warnings. Anchors were sent to stand in front of empty buildings in the middle of the night to create a sense of drama. "Earlier today, a shocking story…"

Really, what did I know? I wasn't there. My antenna knew nothing.

Then came the point of no return.

It shouldn't have been such a big deal. Really, of all of Ryan's exaggerations to cause a frenzy, this one was the most harmless. But the frenzy happened just the same.

Ryan was doing a story on the cuts Congress had just made to veteran benefits. He was interviewing a vet who'd lost both her legs and part of her face to an IED. They all sat in the humble living room, the husband's voice gruff as he spoke about his wife's courage and determination, the American flag in its triangle box on a shelf behind them.

Ryan looked so gentle and concerned that I myself teared up. He asked about what the benefit cuts would mean to the family, how much her physical therapy (no longer covered) had helped, and what her prosthetics and additional plastic surgery would cost.

Then the kicker. The couple's three-year-old wandered into the shot and climbed right on Ryan's lap. "Hello, there, sweetheart," he said, and he carried on the interview just like that. She fell asleep with her head on his shoulder.

You could feel America sigh with love.

I mean, talk about good TV! The noble warrior, her hard-working husband, their adorable toddler and America's most trusted face. You couldn't script that stuff.

Except apparently, you could.

Two weeks later, the *New York Post* ran the headline: Ryan Roberts Bribes Military Family for America's Tears. An email had been leaked—the veteran's husband wrote to thank Ryan for doing the story and apologized that it took so long for Callie to warm up to you. Hope your ears don't still hurt from her crying!

Crying? There'd been no crying!

The email went on. The extra money sure will help. We really appreciate it.

Ryan could not be reached for comment.

Turned out, he'd offered the couple a thousand dollars to have their kid come sit on his lap, coached into the shot by the grandmother. It had taken quite a few tries before little Callie trusted Ryan.

Bill, the retirement-age cameraman, had leaked it. Though he'd been in on Ryan's exaggerations all along (for a few extra thousand each time), this story was the straw that broke his back. He was a veteran himself. The couple admitted they simply needed the money for better prosthetics, due to the Congressional funding cuts.

Long story short, Congress got off their asses as if they were on fire.

A GoFundMe page was set up for the family, and more than $1.4 million was raised in the first day.

Ryan's other stories came to light. The tornado. The bullets. The drowning woman in the subway. He was fired, and after a six-month period of head-hanging and sheepish apologies, he was rehired at another network for a paltry half of his sixteen-million-dollar salary.

I was fired, too. I was *not* rehired. It was my job to make sure the news was clean, to know if Ryan was stretching the truth, to *keep an eye on these things, goddamn it!* as the head of NBC screeched.

So I joined the ranks of the unemployed, as appealing to other networks as an Ebola-riddled leper holding an open jar of typhus.

After my one hundred and fiftieth job rejection in four weeks (Starbucks wouldn't have me), I lay on the couch, ten pounds heavier than I'd been a month ago. It was okay, I told myself between bouts of sobbing and Ben & Jerry's. I never wanted to be a producer in the first place. At least I had Eric. And Ben. And Jerry.

Eric sighed as he came in; I was in the "pajama" phase of grief. "Babe, come on. You were gonna leave anyway once we had kids."

"It's just... I didn't do anything wrong. Technically."

"I know. We've been over this."

Oh, God. If *Eric* didn't want to talk about it—Eric my rock, my love, my best friend—I was really, *really* pathetic.

Then he threw me the best bone ever. "Listen, with my salary, you don't need to work. Take your time, find something you really love, something that will work in the next phase of our lives. Besides…" He paused and stroked my unclean hair. "Don't you think it's time we bought a house?"

Hell's to the *yes*! It was exactly what I needed. I'd figure out what the next phase was (marriage and children, thank you very much). First step, a home for all of us.

We found a house in Cambry-on-Hudson, where I'd spent my teenage years, where Candy and Dad still lived, forty-five minutes from Judy and Aaron in Greenwich. An easy commute for Eric via the train, close enough to the city that we could still pop in for a show or to see friends, far enough away that it felt like the country. The posh little town was filled with interesting shops, some great restaurants, a couple of little galleries and a bakery that could be compared only with paradise. A marina jutted out into the Hudson, and high on a hill sat a huge white country club that we nicknamed Downton Abbey (which would be perfect for our wedding).

"Wait till we have kids," Eric warned me when we found the house. "Don't be surprised if my parents buy the house next door." That would be great with me.

Our house was a little soulless from the outside, but fabulous on the inside. Huge bedrooms, a sunken living room, a kitchen with granite countertops and a nice front porch. It was in a development, which I hadn't wanted, but the yard was landscaped and pretty.

We went to the animal shelter and picked out Ollie, then a skinny little bag of bones who'd been found tied to a phone pole. Still, when we reached out to pet him, he wagged so hard he fell down.

"Our family has begun," Eric said, kissing the dog on the head.

When it came time to sign the papers, I had a little shock.

"Um…my name isn't on here," I told the real estate agent.

"Oh, no! Did I make a mistake?" he asked. "I can draw up new papers. I just… I'm sorry, it must've been a misunder-standing."

"No, let's do this," Eric said. "We can fix it later, babe." He signed with a flourish, grinning at me, and when the Real-tor left, we made love in the empty living room. His parents came over that night, and even though we drank champagne and laughed, I kept thinking about that. Eric Fisher. Not Eric Fisher and Ainsley O'Leary.

"I wonder if we'll ever have grandchildren, Aaron," Judy said, subtle as a charging lion. She held Ollie, stroking him as he crooned with joy. "Grand-dogs are lovely, too, but…"

"Mom," Eric said. "Why do you think there are four bedrooms?"

He kissed me, and Judy sighed, and Aaron chuckled, and I put my worries aside and waited for a marriage proposal. Kept waiting. Waited some more. Started volunteering at the local senior housing complex where Gram-Gram lived, bringing Ollie in for pet therapy. Planted tulip bulbs. Painted rooms, refurbished a table, bought furniture.

Two months after we moved, Eric got another promo-tion. He apologized, saying he really, *really* wanted to tie the knot and spend more time at home but this job would put us over the top. I tried not to feel glum. His career was on fire; I was an anomaly in Cambry-on-Hudson—a stay-at-home person. Like a shut-in, Kate mused, or a kept woman. She smiled when she said it, but I knew she meant it.

I missed my old job more than I ever would've guessed.

That was when Candy got me an interview for features edi-tor at *Hudson Lifestyle*. "Don't mess this up," she said over the phone as I stood in front of the fridge, eating Ben & Jerry's Chunky Monkey, Eric in Dallas yet again.

"Thanks for your faith in me, Candy," I said. "I'll try not to blow it."

"It's just that I have a professional reputation there. I recommended you for this job. If you don't make a good impression, it will reflect badly on me, and let me tell you, I worked very hard to get where I am. It wasn't easy, especially having a toddler thrust on me when I was forty years old."

Lest we forget. "Got it, Candy. And really, thank you." I hung up and polished off the entire pint of ice cream like any good American.

The offices of *Hudson Lifestyle* were in a brick building in the old part of downtown. There were six people on the staff, most in cubicles, most dealing with advertising and bookkeeping.

A secret about print journalism—the writers are often the least valued people on the job. Advertisers keep any paper afloat, and the graphics people have to set the thing up, and someone makes those irritating calls to see if you want to subscribe, and someone has to empty the trash and clean the bathrooms, but writers? Pah. A dime a dozen. There's always some college intern who can do what you do. Besides, everyone reads only the *Huffington Post* and *BuzzFeed*.

I waited in the reception area, which was small but nicely furnished. The glossy magazine was spread out on the coffee table—a picture of a farmhouse on one cover; a head of lettuce on another; a sailboat on another. Headlines such as Best Plastic Surgeons in Westchester! and Farm to Table Dining and Area's Top Garden Centers! told me all I needed to know about the magazine, which I'd never read before. The receptionist told me to have a seat, then disappeared (probably to clean the bathrooms and empty the trash).

I missed my old job. I missed Rockefeller Center. I missed Ryan. I missed being important.

Tears filled my eyes, and my nose prickled. Did I have a tissue? No, I did not. It's just that this job…after my other job…it was such a step down. It was humiliating. I'd produced news stories on rebels in Afghanistan. I'd met the leader of the free world. Now I'd have to write about lettuce. I wiped my eyes on my sleeve, leaving a smear of eyeliner and mascara. Great.

A man came out to greet me, already seeming pissed off, as if he could read my mind. "Ashley?" he said.

"Ainsley. Ainsley O'Leary. A pleasure." I stood up and stuck out my hand, which he looked at and didn't shake.

"Are you crying?"

"Oh… I just… I'm a little, uh, premenstrual." Shit.

He gave me a long, unblinking look. Strange, pale blue eyes, like an alien. "Will that be a problem during this interview?" he asked.

"Let's hope not. But those first two days can be murder." I smiled. He did not. I felt my uterus shriveling, as if his disapproving gaze was bringing on menopause.

Finally, he blinked. "I'm Jonathan Kent. This way." I followed him into a big, sunny room divided into cubicles. One of the men gave me a half smile and, unless I was wrong, an eye roll.

"You have an appointment at eleven, Mr. Kent," the receptionist said.

*Mr. Kent*, huh? He couldn't be past forty, but he sure didn't give off that easygoing Mark Zuckerberg vibe.

There was only one office on the floor—his. It was scary-neat, a clean desk (sign of a sick mind), one photo facing him. On the wall, a painting of, you guessed it, the Hudson River. A bookcase that contained books only, no statues, no photos, nothing personal at all.

"Remind me why you're here," he said, sitting behind the desk. "You want an internship, your mother says?"

"No, and she's my stepmother. Not my mother. Candy, that is. Um, you're looking for a features editor?"

Another long, pained, uterus-shriveling glance. "How old are you?"

"I believe it's against the law to ask that question." He stared. "Thirty," I added.

"You look younger." It wasn't a compliment.

He stared at my résumé, glanced up at me. I smiled, or continued to smile, as the case was. He didn't smile back. Looked at the papers again. My smile felt stiff. The left corner of my mouth was twitching.

People usually liked me right away.

Jonathan Kent wore a suit, and his tie was not loosened. He was clean-shaven, which was kind of rare these days. Dark hair combed back severely. Cheekbones like dorsal fins, and those pale eyes. He was neither attractive nor ugly. *Generic Caucasian male with potential to be a serial killer, please.* Back when I was the receptionist at NBC, I'd made calls for the casting director.

"Do you really want to work here?" he asked, looking up at me.

"Yes! I'm here for an interview, after all."

He blinked. Finally. "Why?"

*Because I'm bored* didn't seem like a great answer, though it would be honest. "Well, I really, uh, respect what you do and think I could positively contribute to the content of the magazine." Ta-da! The perfect answer.

"What do we do?" he asked.

"Excuse me?"

"What is it you think we do?"

"Is that a trick question?" No answer. "You publish a regional magazine."

"And why would we do that?"

*Because it's a cash cow.* "To showcase the beauty and vibrancy of life in the Hudson River Valley," I said with my best Girl Scout smile.

"Your résumé says you graduated from Wagner College. I assume you have a degree in journalism?"

"Uh, no."

"English?"

"Nope."

"Do I have to keep guessing, Ms. O'Leary?"

I winced, then smiled to cover. "Philosophy." Another stare. "It's one of those degrees that can be used for anything," I said, echoing the duplicitous guidance counselor at Wagner.

"Is it?" Mr. Kent said. I couldn't argue that point. "You worked for Ryan Roberts." He waited, expressionless.

"Yes."

"Who was fired for an egregious breach of professional ethics."

"And rehired by another network. But yes. That's correct."

"Putting aside your possible complicity in his journalistic deception, do you have any actual skills or education to recommend you?"

I felt a sudden rush of anger. What a *rude* man. Ryan had not been my fault. (Okay, fine, a little bit my fault, but mostly not.)

"Wow, Jonathan," I said. "Those are a lot of big words. I'm not sure I follow you." Clearly, I wasn't going to get the job, so why not go for broke? "But after seven years with NBC, I think I can write about the great lettuces of Westchester County and who does the best boob jobs."

His expression didn't change.

"Have a lovely day," I said, standing up and reaching for the door.

"You're hired," he said. "You'll have a three-month probationary period. Be here tomorrow. We open at 8:30. Don't be late, Ms. O'Leary."

And so I went from writing news that tens of millions of people would hear to editing fluff pieces—the historic Groundhog Day parade in Smithville and the artisan potter who'd had a piece bought by the White House. Where the prettiest wedding venues were (okay, that piece I enjoyed), and how shipping lanes had changed on the Hudson.

It was fine. It was pleasant. I made friends fast, as I always did, though Jonathan failed to succumb to my charms and didn't eat the cookies I occasionally brought in. I was just killing time, waiting for Eric to propose so we could get married and have kids.

Instead, he got cancer.

# Chapter Eight

*Kate*

My brother and his family stayed with me for three days after Nathan died, and thank God for it. Dad was helpless and overly jocular because of it. And Mom...though she didn't say the words, there was definitely a grim sense of *I told you not to get married so fast.*

It was good to have the kids there, the two teenagers making heroic efforts to talk about movies or books or school. Kiara was lovely and kind, telling me nondeath stories about the hospital. I was invited to stay with them in the city. Esther said she'd give up her bed for me. Matthias told me he'd take me out for sushi.

Sean didn't say much. There wasn't much to say, of course. But part of me wanted him to come up with something for me to grab on to; he was my older brother, after all, always with that slight air of superiority granted to him by being the firstborn and only son.

He had nothing other than an occasional shoulder squeeze.

Ainsley, on the other hand, had been strangely practical, dividing up the food people brought into single-serving blocks, wrapping them in foil and labeling them, leaving a few in the fridge, most in the freezer. She and Eric had come for dinner last night, along with our parents, and I saw her and Eric dragging the trash cans down to the curb. Yesterday, when Sean and I went to the lawyer's and Kiara was out with the kids, Ainsley came in and cleaned up the kitchen from our breakfast mess. She left a sweet note and a mason jar full of tulips on the kitchen table.

Sadie, the three-year-old, was the one I really wanted to be around. She didn't really know or remember Nathan, only that "Auntie was sad" and thus appointed herself to be my keeper. Every morning they were here, my little niece climbed into my bed and ordered me to make animal sounds. Happy to oblige, I nuzzled her soft, fuzzy curls, pulling her close against me. "Kitty!" she demanded.

"Mew! Mew!"

"Gog!"

"Woof, woof!"

"Effalent!"

I took that to mean elephant and trumpeted obligingly.

"Wacoon!"

"Purr, purr."

Her laughter sounded like water over rocks, and for a second, I'd thought that if she stayed, I could totally handle widowhood. Surely Sean and Kiara would give her to me. They had two other kids, the selfish things.

Alas, they were rather attached.

When they left on Wednesday, Kiara and Sean hugged me, and the kids tried to smile, and I tried not to cling too hard as my brother took Sadie out of my arms.

Then they pulled out of the stone driveway, leaving me alone in Nathan's house.

A storm of panic started flinging debris in my head. What would I do? Could this really be my new life? Was it possible to rewind and skip Eric's party? Or maybe…rewind and just say no when Nathan called for that first date? How could Nathan be *dead*? What was I supposed to do? Actually *do* in the next few hours?

I didn't know.

I had no idea how to be a widow. I *wanted* to be brave. To make Nathan proud of me. To be elegant and kind. I could see myself in Paris, wearing a black Audrey Hepburn–style turtleneck, a glass of red wine in my hand as I stared out at the street, melancholy but noble. Perhaps I would take up smoking, just one a day, for effect. Men would look at me, intrigued, but that slight air of sorrow would keep them at arm's length. I'd walk back to my garret, where I would continue to work on my…uh…my poetry, let's say, and not the more realistic scenario of ripping open a bag of Cheetos and watching HBO.

I shivered. It was cooler than normal, and rainy.

I guess I had to go inside, into that enormous, empty house.

Okay. First step. A shower, probably. And then groceries. People had been bringing food over, lots and lots of food, but I hadn't left the house since the cemetery. I needed half-and-half, which Matthias had mistaken for milk this morning and finished off. I couldn't face the morning without coffee back when I was happy, let alone now. Ainsley would be happy to get it for me, I was sure, but I had to leave the house sometime and do something normal.

Nathan's bathrobe was still on the hook on the back of the bathroom door. I didn't touch it, afraid that something inside me would break. His toothbrush was still in the shower. I hated that he brushed his teeth in there, for some reason. It struck me as wrong, spitting at your own feet. So far, I hadn't said anything.

I caught myself. *So far.* I wouldn't have the chance to say anything, ever. Nathan's legacy of spitting in the shower would last forevermore.

"No, no, that's good," I told myself. "He wasn't perfect." Yes! Remember his flaws. He spit in the shower! I'd never have to put up with *that* anymore! Score one for widowhood!

My chest hurt so much it was hard to take a full breath. I almost wished it was a heart attack. Then I could go to the hospital and get taken care of. Maybe they'd put me in a medically induced coma, and when I woke up, everything would be okay again. Maybe Nathan would be by my bedside. Or maybe I'd die and see him in heaven, the heaven I couldn't quite picture.

I showered fast, threw on some yoga pants and a sweatshirt. Dared not look in Nathan's closet, where all his beautiful clothes were. He had a thing for cashmere sweaters. Probably had twenty of them, and if I saw one now, I'd crumple.

I went downstairs, couldn't find my phone and went into the den (or study). There it was, right in front of Hector's bowl. "I'm leaving," I said to my fish, who mouthed obligingly. "Need anything? Tampons? Got it."

Speaking of tampons, I still didn't have my period. Probably, I was pregnant. Screw those tests that said I wasn't. It was just too soon to show up, that's all.

I got in the car—a battered Volkswagen Golf that was good for holding all my photography gear. It had more than a hundred thousand miles on it, and Nathan and I had discussed getting another car, one with four-wheel drive, big enough for car seats and diaper bags. He'd blushed, and that awkwardness wriggled again—kids with a guy I hadn't known for even a year.

That conversation had taken place just a few weeks ago.

I realized I was gripping the steering wheel, my knuckles white.

"Turn on the radio, Kate," I said aloud. I hadn't slept much lately, and my brain was fuzzy. I started the car, backed carefully out of the driveway, still worried that I'd take down the mailbox, then headed out. On the radio, a man-child scatted and falsettoed about being dumped. "Maybe if your testicles dropped, she would've stayed," I said, then laughed. Hey, look at me! Laughing! See? All was not lost.

I rolled down the windows, the smell of rain and soil hitting me. Spring was here, wedding season. I was booked almost every Saturday from May through August. Maybe going to weddings wasn't a smart idea. Would I cry? Would I run out, sobbing? Or would I just do what I'd been doing for the past fifteen years?

Oh, goody, a song I liked! "Lose Yourself" by Eminem. Good, good. Very inspirational, seize the moment, step into your power, all that Oprah-speak, but with cussing.

At a stoplight, I found that I was singing the bass line—"Whump whump whump whump bump bump bump bump. You better lose yourself—" And that was where I didn't know the lyrics but kept singing anyway. You go, Eminem, foul-mouthed genius from the bad side of town! Yeah! "You only get one shot something something something yo!"

My eye caught the car next to me. The driver gave me a nod. I smiled and kept singing. Maybe she liked Eminem, too. She didn't smile back.

Ah, shit. It was Madeleine, Nathan's first wife.

Here I was, pretending to be a skinny white rapper, and she looked like...well, like someone had died.

The horn behind me blared, and I floored it, then braked hard as I turned into Whole Foods.

For a second there, I'd forgotten that Nathan was dead.

Inside the grocery store, it was as cold as a morgue. Poor choice of words.

I couldn't remember what I'd come for. Vegetables? Why not? Whole Foods did have the prettiest produce in the entire world, even if it did cost a million trillion dollars. I tossed a cucumber into my cart. Too bad I didn't have my camera; the eggplant was downright seductive, all that smooth, dark color gleam. I grabbed one of those, too. I loved eggplant parmesan, not that I'd ever made it before. But I had lots of time on my hands now, didn't I?

Yes. I'd become a great cook. I'd channel Ainsley and tie on an apron and cook really nice dinners. Salads and everything. Candles on the table, because Nathan had the coolest candle-holders. He actually bought those Jo Malone candles that cost the earth and smelled like heaven. Did straight men buy Jo Malone candles? Did they? I guess it didn't matter anymore.

Nathan had plenty of china, too, and glasses for every beverage under the sun—water, wine (red, white, champagne), whiskey tumblers, martini glasses, all matching, which I still found thrilling. Not to mention his enchanting silverware, designed by a Hungarian woman whose work was featured in the Cooper Hewitt. I knew this because Nathan told me. He was very proud of those forks and spoons.

He'd never eat off those plates again. Never sit at his own table again. Never use one of his perfectly balanced, adorable spoons for ice cream.

Then again, I could paint the dining room. Honestly, every room in the house was white. I was dying to slap some red on a wall somewhere.

That rusty spike seemed to slam through my throat again in an actual, physical pain, as if someone with very strong hands was intent on killing me.

"Kate, isn't it?"

I looked up. An older woman was addressing me. "Yes. Hello."

"I'm Corinne Lenster. Eloise's friend? I was at the funeral, but of course, so was the entire town."

"Oh, sure," I said, though I didn't recognize her. "How are you?"

She smiled sadly. "I'm so sad for you, dear. Nathan was such a wonderful young man. He and my son were friends in high school. He and Robbie—my son—went skiing in Utah their senior year, and they got stuck on the lift, and Robbie..."

Her voice droned on, but the words started blurring together.

Nathan had never mentioned this story. I didn't know he'd gone skiing in Utah. Did I even know he liked skiing? Yes, yes, I did. We actually went skiing in Vermont over Thanksgiving weekend. Right, right.

But this story? This Robbie-stuck-on-a-lift person? I didn't know him. Why hadn't Nathan ever told this story? What else didn't I know? How was it that there was a great (maybe) story from his youth, and I didn't know it? Hmm? Huh?

What's-her-name kept talking. She was extremely well dressed for the grocery store, I noted. I was wearing my If Daryl Dies, We Riot T-shirt. Must avoid *Walking Dead* references when one is a new widow. Must also remember to wear a bra.

God. She was *still* talking. Was this normal, people ambushing widows in the grocery store to tell them things they didn't know about their husbands? I nodded as if I was following the story, and the spike in my throat turned harder.

In the background, I suddenly heard the piped-in music. "I Will Always Love You" by Whitney Houston (who was also dead).

"You gotta be fucking kidding me," I said.

"Excuse me?" the woman said.

"It's the grief talking." Someone else had said that. It was a good line. I planned on using it often. Horribly, laughter rolled through my stomach. I clamped my lips together hard. *Nathan, do you see this?*

The lady nodded. "Dear...you're not wearing shoes."

I looked down. "Huh. Look at that! I wondered why the floor was so cold." My toenails were still bloodred. Nathan had painted them for me as I lay on the couch one night a couple of weeks ago.

"Perhaps you should go home," she said.

"I need half-and-half," I said. Aha! That was what I was here for! "Bye. Nice talking to you." With that, I pushed my cart down the aisle, my eggplant and cucumber trembling with the cart's faulty wheel action. Over the PA, Whitney changed keys, bringing it home. "And I-aye-aye...will always...love you-ooh-ooh-ooh..."

Maybe I should sing along. *This one's for you, Nathan Coburn!* I could grab that cucumber and pretend it was a mic and let loose.

Puffs and squeaks of laughter leaked out—poor dead Whitney was killing me.

Oh, what was this? Organic pumpkin pie ice cream sandwiches in April? Hooray! Someone up there must like me, and three guesses as to who it was! The hysterical laughter wriggled and leaped inside my chest, making me snort some more.

Probably, I looked insane. No shoes, no bra, Daryl Dixon on my chest, eggplant, cucumber, pumpkin pie ice cream bars in my cart.

The floor was really freezing. My feet would be filthy. The polish needed changing. But if I changed the polish, it would be gone forever, The Polish That Nathan Applied. Nathan would not return from the dead to give me a pedicure.

The laughter stopped.

I'd leave that bloodred polish on until it chipped off.

*Cause of death: cerebral hemorrhage.*

Please, Higher Power. Please that it was painless. Please that he wasn't scared.

He hadn't looked scared. He'd only looked...dead.

In front of the dairy case was an old, old woman, creeping, creeping, inching along. She stopped right in front of the half-and-half and opened her purse. Shuffled through it. She had several thousand coupons to consider. I considered reaching around her, then decided it would be rude. Waited. Waited some more.

I had the sudden urge to ram her with my cart.

Why was *she* still alive? She looked to be a hundred and forty-three years old, and she was *still* alive! Why wasn't she the one who'd died, huh? Riddle me *that*, Batman. Why was my thirty-eight-year-old husband *dead* and this *crone* still allowed to be here, trying to save a dime on nondairy creamer?

"Would you help me, dear?" she asked. "I can't see if this coupon's expired." She held out a piece of paper in her age-spotted, gnarled hands.

I took it. "It's good till next week."

"Thank you so much, sweetheart."

"You're very welcome. My pleasure." I waited till she got her tiny carton, then grabbed a half gallon and walked to the self-checkout as fast as I could.

Driving home, I passed the movie theater where Nathan and I had gone last week. Last *week*! Last week, he'd been alive. It was the night before Eric's party, in fact, and the thrill of going to the movies with my *husband* had engulfed me like a hug. He'd held my hand. He'd eaten popcorn like a ravaging Hun. The movie had been terrible, but that was okay, because we were together.

Last week.

What had we seen? Sci-fi? No. Horror? No. Frat-boy stupidity? No.

It was suddenly incredibly important that I remembered. I pulled over abruptly and fished my phone from my purse. Clicked the calendar and scrolled back a few days.

April 6, Friday. *Eric's party. Bring wine.*

I wondered if the wine we brought was the one Nathan had poured for my refill.

April 6. His last day. His last night.

I paused. Should I write that down? *Nathan dies.* Should I black out the date? Maybe I could take it out of the calendar altogether.

Here it was. April 5, Thursday.

Nothing. I had nothing in there.

Right, because the movie had been a spur-of-the-moment kind of thing. Neither of us felt like cooking or eating out, so we decided to have popcorn for dinner because we could. But what was the movie? I didn't remember. What a shitty wife I was. Widow. I was a shitty widow. I bet Madeleine would remember, she of the collapsing and wailing.

When I got home, I'd check. I could find it. Then I'd write it down and remember every single thing about our almost nine months together. Nine months, like a pregnancy. And if I wasn't pregnant right now, someone was going to pay, yes sir. The universe and my higher power owed me big-time.

All of a sudden, I couldn't even remember his face.

All I could see was the face in the casket, the strange, artificial face. Madeleine breaking down, Eloise comforting her.

My hands started tingling.

My breath sawed in and out of me, and I couldn't grab it, couldn't hold it. I was hyperventilating. *Hehn-hehn-hehn-hehn*.

Maybe I'd faint. Maybe I was dying. In for *hehn* three, hold *hehn* for three *hehn*, out for *hehn-hehn* three, hold for hehn-*hehn*-hehn.

It took fifteen minutes to get under control, and by the end, I was sweaty and limp, my arms so weak I could barely grip the steering wheel.

*This is your life now.*

The thought almost felled me.

# Chapter Nine

*Ainsley*

A couple of weeks after Nathan died, Eric called me at work and told me he was taking me out for dinner. A *special* dinner, he said. He'd leave work and meet me at Le Monde, Cambry-on-Hudson's newest restaurant overlooking the Hudson River.

I sensed the proposal was nigh. He'd been edgy all week.

I knew it sounded selfish, picturing that diamond on my finger. But there'd been so much sadness these past few weeks. My heart broke for my sister, and I found myself missing Nathan, even though I hadn't known him very well, waking up with tears in my eyes before I even knew why I was crying, Ollie licking my face, offering me his ratty blanket.

Eric had been taking it hard, too. It would be awfully nice to have something happy to look forward to, something happy and hopeful.

I hesitated a minute, then picked up the phone and called

Kate. I wasn't sure I was being helpful, but it was better to try than not. I thought so, anyway.

"Hello?" she said, sounding groggy.

"Hi! Did I wake you?"

"Um...yeah. That's okay. I have to get up anyway."

There was a pause. In the past three weeks, my sister and I had seen each other more than we had in the past three years. We'd never been on the outs, but we'd never been exactly close, either. After all, I stole her father. It was only because my mom had died that she got him back, and while she never outwardly blamed me for that, I'd been feeling it all my life.

"How's it going today?" I asked, my voice too bright.

"I'm fine," she lied.

"Did you call that group yet?" Unable to not do *something* to help her, I'd Googled some info for her. There was a bereavement group for spouses right here in Cambry-on-Hudson.

"Which group?"

"The, um...the grief group? It might be nice—I mean, good—to talk to other people who...you know." I always said the wrong thing where Kate was concerned.

"Right. I'll take another look."

A quick knock on my cubicle frame. "Ainsley, have you finished that piece on— Oh."

Jonathan, wearing his resting bitch face. *My sister,* I mouthed. He hated personal calls at work, but for God's sake, he himself had tried to resuscitate Nathan. Even Captain Flatline had to let me talk to Kate.

He sighed and went off to bother someone else.

"You should get back to work," my sister said. "Thanks for checking in, though."

"Can I do anything for you? Maybe stop by tomorrow?"

"That's okay. I think I'm going over to Brooke's."

Jealousy flashed through me, followed by its twin, shame. *I wanted to help.* Sean and Perfect Kiara had stayed with her for a few days after Nathan died; Kate and Sean had always been closer, since I was the half sister, and significantly younger. And now there was Brooke, who was suffering, too, of course.

But I wanted desperately to be helpful. I wanted to cook for her, except she said she had too much food. To let her cry on my shoulder…not that I'd seen her crying. I wished I had. Instead, she looked like a little kid left on the side of the highway, terrified and alone.

"So what's new with you?" she asked. "How's Ollie?" She had a soft spot for my dog.

"He's good. If you want to borrow him for a night, just say the word."

"I might just do that."

There was another silence. "Hey, I think Eric might propose tonight," I blurted, then winced. "I'm sorry. I shouldn't have said anything."

"No, no, that's great. That'll be really nice. I'm happy for you."

"Thanks," I mumbled.

"Is he taking you out somewhere?"

"Le Monde."

"Oh, very nice. Nathan and I…" Her voice trailed off.

"Did you eat there?" I asked, my voice husky. *It's okay,* I wanted to say. *You can talk about him.* The words stuck in my throat.

"We always meant to. Never got around to it. Oh, shoot, Eloise is calling. I better go. Let me know how it goes tonight, okay? Congratulations. I'm sure he'll do a lovely job."

She clicked off.

Kate had always been like her name: brisk, efficient, classy. It's not that she was a bad sister; she was a dutiful sister. We never shared giggles over boys, but she showed me how a tampon worked. She let me believe in Santa as long as I wanted to (an embarrassingly long time). She gamely took me to the mall with my friends, where she'd sit with her camera in the courtyard while we tweens tried every makeup sample known to womankind.

I just never felt that she really *liked* me. I was the daughter of the woman who stole her father, after all. Sometimes I'd see her looking at me, judgment in her eyes, and I'd wonder what I was doing wrong. She was never mean, but she was never truly there.

The dynamic didn't change when we became adults. Kate lived in Brooklyn. She was cool, and I was not. She was thin and elegant, and I was round and cute. She was a successful photographer (and a great one, really, her pictures were stunning); I was excellent at unjamming the printer. She'd never relied on a man for anything, and I'd been living with my boyfriend since I was twenty-one.

Sensing that my phone call was over, Jonathan reappeared at my desk. "Are you finished with your personal calls?"

"Yes, Jonathan, I am. Kate sends her best."

"And are your cramps sufficiently muted?"

Right. I'd pulled the period card when I got back late from my lunch hour. "I'm feeling much better. Thank you. That's very sweet of you to remember."

"Believe me, I'd love to forget. Are there any other personal problems interfering with your ability to work? A lost kitten, perhaps? A sick goldfish?"

I pretended to ponder. "I don't think so."

"Then please finish editing your mother's column." His pale blue eyes were a little eerie. Plus, he didn't blink. I was almost positive he was an alien.

"Stepmother. She's my stepmother. Um, I'm almost done. I'll have it to you any minute."

"It was due at noon."

"This is a difficult time for my family, Jonathan." I raised an eyebrow.

"And yet your mother has her work in on time."

*Stepmother.* I closed my eyes briefly. "Well. Candy loves her job." Then, realizing how that sounded, I added, "Like all the O'Leary women. I'll get right on it. Sorry for the delay."

He gave me a pointed look and went off to stare down someone else.

I opened Candy's emailed file and started reading.

Dear Dr. Lovely,
My daughter lost her husband suddenly, and I don't know what to do for her. She's in a fog. The thing is, I'm not sure she really loved him, so it's more shock than heartbreak. Some days I want to slap her, and others, I want to hug her. She—

I picked up the phone and dialed. "Candy. You can't write about Kate."

"What are you talking about?" she said in that faux inno-cent voice. For a shrink, the woman was a terrible liar.

"*You* wrote the letter to Dr. Lovely!"

"No, Ainsley, I *am* Dr. Lovely."

"Oh, please. You can't fool me." There had been one about two years ago involving a laid-off daughter who was *content to clean up after her live-in boyfriend and make door wreaths.* "Don't make me tell Jonathan."

"Tell Jonathan what?"

I dropped my voice to a whisper. "That you write some of these letters."

"Prove it."

"Candy. Your professional reputation is at stake."

She sighed. "The coincidence factor is high, I'll grant you that. But I picked it because it did remind me of Kate, and she needs to get out of her funk."

"It's been three weeks, Mom." Whoops. The M-word slipped out sometimes.

"I know how long it's been," Candy said after a pause. "And maybe it would do her good to read that other people are going through similar things."

"I actually recommended a group for widows and widowers," I said.

"Did you! Good. She needs help. I hope it's led by a professional grief therapist and not some quack with a piece of paper she got over the internet."

"Me, too. So what should I do with this letter?" I asked.

"Just cut it, I suppose," she said. "There are two more after it."

"Got it. Have a good day, Candy."

"You, as well." She hung up without saying goodbye.

Just then, Rachelle came into my cubicle and leaned against the frame, dunking a tea bag into a cup. "So there I was last night at the park by the river, okay? Guess who I ran into?" She had a gift of spotting celebrities and would often post pictures of them from behind on Facebook. *Robert Downey Jr.'s butt in Southampton!* or *You're goddamn right that's Jennifer Hudson!*

"Was it Chris Hemsworth?" I asked, brightening.

"No."

"Derek Jeter?"

"No. Jonathan."

I made a face. "I was hoping for more."

"*And* his ex-wife."

"Oh! Do tell." It must've taken a strong (or masochistic) woman to be married to our boss. I sympathized with her already.

"She looked like she was being stabbed in the liver, you know?"

"Don't we all when we're around him? What else? Is she pretty?"

Jonathan's door opened. "Oh, Mr. Kent," Rachelle said. "How are you? I love your tie."

He glanced at the two of us. "Did you need something from Ainsley?"

"I did. And I got it. Thanks, Ainsley, hon!"

"Are you done with your mother's column?" he asked me. "It's only six hundred words."

"Yep! Sending it now," I said, smiling. He walked down the hall, and I scanned Dr. Lovely's work, fixed a comma and emailed it to Tanya, who did the layout.

To be fair, Jonathan wasn't a horrible boss. He was just incredibly stuck-up and rigid and irritating. And private. He never mentioned his children (the one photo in his office showed two little blonde girls, and I assumed they were his). He never came to happy hour with us or lingered in the staff kitchen asking about our weekends. Then again, we were his employees, and apparently we weren't supposed to know he had a beating heart. He wasn't called Captain Flatline for nothing.

I concentrated on work as best I could for the rest of the day, but my thoughts kept skimming to tonight. To the ring, that gorgeous, glittering diamond. Eric and I had talked in the past about what kind of wedding we'd have someday— fun and breezy with a great band, the kind of wedding where people ate and drank and danced and hated to leave.

And then, the bliss of being married. I'd make sure we

were the kind of couple who hired a nice babysitter and still did fun things together. I wanted at least two kids. Maybe we'd name a son Nathan, even. Or use it as a middle name. Kate could be godmother, if Jewish babies had godmothers. I glanced at Jonathan's door (closed) and Googled it. Yes, they could have godparents. Perfect. Kate would be little Nathan's godmother.

My eyes filled up with tears on that one, and I grabbed a tissue and blotted them just as Jonathan opened his door, doing another office scan for slackers. He looked pained at the sight of me but didn't speak.

At last, five o'clock came. We all left like little soldiers, except for Jonathan. He owned the joint, after all.

"Good night, Mr. Kent," said Rachelle, shooting me a wry look.

"Have a good weekend, Mr. Kent," said Deshawn, holding the door for us ladies.

"Bye, Mr. Kent," said Francesca, the bookkeeper.

"See you Monday, Mr. Kent," said Tanya.

"Good night, Jonathan," I said.

"Good night," he said, deigning to look up at us for the briefest instant before returning to his work.

Whatever. I had a dog to feed and hair to curl. The black velvet fit-and-flare dress? Too wintry. The white dress with red polka dots? Too Betty Boop. The green and gold? Too Christmassy.

I might just have to buy something new.

Le Monde was gorgeous, flickering with candlelight, the floor-to-ceiling windows overlooking the Hudson. I wore a new navy dress with a wide, pretty neckline and navy lace overlay and a pair of very high nude heels. Creamy satin clutch (also new) and a gold bracelet on my right hand. Didn't want the diamond to have to compete with anything.

"Your party is already here," the maître d' said, smiling at me. "Please, come this way."

As I wove my way through the tables, a familiar face caught my eye.

Jonathan, talking with an attractive woman. Dear God! A date? A sister? His ex? A prostitute? A robot-companion? I'd text Rachelle the first chance I got.

I paused at their table. "Hello," I said, smiling.

He looked up, nodded and went back to cutting his fish.

Nice. "I'm Ainsley. I work with Jonathan," I told his companion.

"Adele. Nice to meet you," she said pleasantly.

"I don't mean to interrupt."

"And yet you did," he said, tilting his head. *Human contradicts her words through actions. Strange.*

"Jonathan," the woman chided fondly. "Be nice."

"Enjoy your dinners," I said. Maybe he had Asperger's. Then again, he was generally rude only to me.

Didn't matter. There was my beloved, dressed in a gray suit, white shirt and the red tie I'd bought him for Valentine's Day. Tonight, we'd be engaged. I paused for a second, taking it all in. Taking in Eric.

Sometimes, the image of him when we first met didn't match this handsome adult in front of me. We'd been kids, after all. Then, his black hair was longer and curly. Now it was cut short, and the black had a few silver strands shot through it, though it was as thick as ever. He'd broadened in the shoulders this past year, thanks to his cancer journey and CrossFit regimen. But his eyes were the same, dark and thoughtful and kind.

My guy. He stood as I approached.

"Hey, babe," I said, a happy lump in my throat.

"Hi," he said. He kissed me on the cheek. Didn't say anything about how I looked, which was a little unusual. He almost always noticed a new dress, and this one was killer—demure yet sexy, exactly the way you'd want your wife to look.

"Thank you for thinking of this," I said, spreading the napkin on my lap. "It's good to get out after all the sadness."

"I still can't believe he's gone," Eric said. "Life will never be the same."

I suppressed a flash of irritation. While a true friendship between Nathan and Eric might've developed, they were really just casual acquaintances. We'd seen Kate and Nathan only twice during their marriage—dinner at our house, dinner at theirs. (Theirs was better. On top of everything else, Nathan could cook.)

"I talked to my sister today," I said, hoping to remind him whose life would really never be the same.

"How is she?"

"She's hanging in there. She's always been strong."

"Good, good. I've had to call on my own strength, too."

"Eric. I think Kate is probably suffering a little more than you are." I raised an eyebrow.

He blinked. "Well, I think no one is suffering more than anyone else. There's no measure. We're all in pain."

"No, *Kate* is suffering more. Mr. and Mrs. Coburn and Brooke and her sons…they've lost their husband, son, brother, uncle. Let's not make everything about you, hon."

"I'm just trying to say that I feel this deeply. Is that so wrong? And since when has everything been about me?"

I took a deep breath, remembering that tonight we were probably getting engaged. "I'm sorry. Let's talk about something else, okay?"

"Fine," he grumbled.

I knew Eric was self-centered, the classic only child, son and heir of adoring parents. It left a mark (or a crown). But he was also generous and smart. He loved the life we'd built, loved our home, loved that at company dinners, his bosses would chuckle and say, "That's a great girl you've got there, Eric," because I knew how to work the crowd. He was faithful, funny and kind.

Also, he was really good in bed. Did I mention that? Not that I had anything to compare it with, but yeah. He was.

The cancer...well, I was tired of thinking about it, but cancer had scared him to death, despite all his positive affirmations. No one got through an experience like that unscathed.

"Candy's column was pretty hilarious today," I said, and he brightened and listened as I told about her advice to a woman with a horrible mother-in-law (a problem I would never have). We ordered wine and appetizers, and I made a point of being my best self, chatty and flirty, to put him in the mood. From time to time, I'd glance over at my boss, but he never glanced back.

It was in the middle of dinner that Eric finally got things rolling.

He cleared his throat and put down his steak knife—he always ordered filet mignon. Every time. I was eating the lobster, which wasn't the best choice, since my hands were a little buttery. Then again, the ring would slide right on. It was also the best lobster I'd ever had, succulent and tender, and the butter, my God, I wanted to drink it.

Using great self-control, I took one more bite of the lobster, then subtly wiped my hands thoroughly on the napkin. Took a sip of water to cleanse my palate for when Eric would kiss me, his fiancée.

"There's something I've been meaning to ask you," he said.

Oh, goody! My heart squeezed hard, then seemed to expand to fill my entire chest. Love, baby! Love.

"Really?" I asked, keeping my voice casual. He liked to surprise me, though he rarely pulled it off.

"Yes. But…well, I'm not sure how you'll react."

"Hmm. Give it a shot and see," I said, smiling. In about thirty seconds, our fellow diners would see Eric on bended knee, would hear me say yes, and maybe even Jonathan would be happy for us. Maybe he'd even smile, though his face would probably crack.

"Okay," Eric said, taking a deep breath.

Then…nothing. He just sat there, not smiling, not frowning, just looking at me.

*Reach into your pocket*, I mentally urged him, smiling a little harder. Still nothing. "What is it, babe?" I asked. My smile was feeling a little forced. Was he trying to remember a speech? He did love a speech.

"Um…okay." He sat up a little straighter. My left ring finger raised itself in anticipation. He looked me in the eye, face serious, and said, "I'd like you to move out."

Though my ears heard the words, it took a little longer for my brain to process them.

*Was there a proposal in there somewhere?* my brain asked.

*No, I don't think there was*, I answered.

*What was the question again?*

*I'm not completely sure.*

"Excuse me?" I asked. I was still smiling. My ring finger was still waiting.

"This is hard for me," he said. "But it's time. I'll always cherish our years together."

"What?"

"It's just that Nathan's death…it was so profound, you know? It was a message."

"Wait, wait, wait. Hang on one second." My thoughts were just a gray blur. "Um...Nathan's death? What has that got to do with us? I mean, besides the obvious."

"It was a message. To me. A very profound moment."

"No, it wasn't! He tripped and hit his head and died. That is *not* profound. That's an accident, Eric. The opposite of profound."

What the heck were we even talking about? Had he said something about me moving out? It looked like he had surprised me after all. But I— We— My brain was stuttering in shock. Jonathan was looking at me. I took a bite of lobster and chewed, smiling at my boss. *Nothing to see. We're all good.*

Eric cleared his throat. "Babe. Look. I've been thinking. There's a reason we haven't gotten married, right? That says something."

I swallowed the wad of lobster meat, nearly choking on it. "Yes, there's a reason, and no, it doesn't! The reason is, you've never proposed! Not officially, anyway." My voice was shrill, and people were starting to look. Let them.

"I know," Eric said. "We talked about it, but we never did follow through." He gave me a steady look. "That tells the whole story, don't you think?"

"No! I absolutely do not!" *Where's the ring?* my brain asked. *We would really like to see that ring.* "We live together. We bought a house together. We take vacations with your parents!"

"We did. That's true."

We *did*? What was this past tense thing? "Eric...you can't be breaking up with me..." My voice cracked in disbelief.

He gave a sort of crooked nod/shrug, like he regretted that, yes, he was.

"What about the ring?" I asked. "You bought me an engagement ring."

He twitched. "How did you know?"

"Because I know *everything*." Yes. Pull the Angry Mother. Eric was a nice Jewish boy. Angry Mother Voice scared him. "Eric David Fisher, you bought me a one-and-a-half-carat engagement ring from Tiffany's because you want to *marry* me! Not break up with me!" People were now openly enjoying our drama (minus Jonathan, who was eating again), but I didn't care.

"Ains, look. You're right. I *did* want to marry you. There I was at the party, about to propose, you're right. And then the universe *literally* stops me by killing a guy."

"Oh, for God's sake, Eric! He tripped! It was completely random!"

"Well, *I* think it was more than random. It was the universe saying life is short, life is uncertain, live life large."

"I am going to stab you with this fork if you don't knock it off."

"Ainsley. Honey. I'm so grateful for everything. I really am. It's been an amazing run. But I'm putting the house on the market. I quit my job today, and I'm going to Alaska."

"*Alaska!* Are you drunk? You're not moving to Alaska!"

"I am."

"Does your mother know?" Judy would lie prostrate in front of his car if he tried to move to New Jersey, let alone Alaska.

"Not yet. But you need to move out."

"I am *not* moving out! Are you kidding? Is this a joke?"

"I'm so sorry. I really, truly regret hurting you." He looked at me steadily, kindly.

There was...something...in his expression. In his voice, too. *Sincerity*, my brain said.

*Shut up*, I told it. "You can't break up with me," I ground out. "I nursed you through cancer, Eric." I raised my voice so the onlookers could hear. "I nursed you. Through *cancer*. Remember?"

"I do. And I will always be grateful."

My hands were shaking, wanting to throttle him. I took a deep breath. Glanced around at my fellow diners, who were rapt, save for Jonathan. *Thank you for not caring about anything, Captain Flatline.* For once, it was in the plus column.

I chugged my wine and refilled the glass.

"How is dinner tonight?" the waiter asked, smiling.

"It's great! Fantastic. Best I ever had," I said. I took another defiant bite of lobster "My boyfriend is just about to propose."

"No, I'm not," Eric said. "We're breaking up."

"Oh! Uh...I'll let you decide, then." The server backed away.

Eric pushed back from the table as if to leave.

"No, no, no," I said, wiping my mouth. "We're still talking. You stay right here." He closed his eyes briefly but obeyed.

Okay. Eric always shut down when I was mad, so I wouldn't be mad. I'd be logical.

"Eric," I said in a calmer voice, "honey, I know you really liked Nathan. And I know—believe me, I know—how terrifying this past year and a half has been. It's natural to reexamine your life."

"Thank you for understanding," he said.

"No, no, not yet," I said. "Look. I understand you want to, uh, live life large. But you don't dump the person who's been with you, by your side, for eleven *years*, who adores you and wants to have your children, who helped fight your battle with cancer—" yes, yes, bring up his favorite subject "—who cleaned up your puke and gave you sponge baths."

Let my fellow diners suck on *that* little tidbit. Granted, the sponge bath was one time, and it was more like a practice run (at Eric's suggestion) in case he got so weak that I'd have to do it for real. We ended up playing Naughty Nurse. He could also chew on that for a minute.

"You were wonderful," he admitted.

"Thank you, honey. In sickness and in health, right? In my mind, we're as married as can be. You said the same thing. The paper is just a formality, you said."

"Oh, sweetheart, my old boyfriend used that same line on me," murmured a blonde woman to my left. "Right until he left me for his third cousin."

I ignored her. Clearly, she and I had nothing in common. "Eric, I think you're just…reacting. Nathan's death has hit us all hard. But breaking up…no."

It just would not be allowed. *I* would not allow it.

He nodded slowly. "Yeah. I…I knew you'd say that. I'm sorry, Ains. I really didn't mean to hurt you, and I acknowledge that I have. That I am. I own that. But I need to start over. I need to go to Alaska."

"Why? So you can be a crab fisherman?"

"I'm going to take three months and camp in Denali."

"This from the man who can't go outside after dark because of the mosquitoes. What about grizzly bears and wolves? You'll be eaten within an hour."

He smiled. "I need to change. I need to live life to the fullest. I was given a second chance. Nathan wasn't. I can't ignore that, Ainsley."

"Well, you can't break up with me, either." I smiled firmly. "What about Ollie, huh? You can't leave us."

He smiled back sadly. His eyes, those brown eyes that I loved, were a little shiny.

*I hate to break it to you*, my brain said, *but he looks like a man resolved.*

My own eyes started to fill. "Eric," I whispered. "I love you. I've loved you my entire adult life. If you need to go to

Alaska, that's fine! That's great! I'll go with you. Or not. Go and come back. But we…we love each other."

He reached across the table, his hand so familiar on mine. "That was true."

"It still is!"

"For you, maybe. But I have to do this. I know you think this is a knee-jerk reaction, but I've thought about this constantly since Nathan died, and the truth is, I haven't been happy for a long time."

*That* one stabbed me in the heart. Like a child telling his mother he doesn't love her, even if she knows it's not true. The words still sliced right through.

"I don't believe you," I whispered.

"It's true. Our life is not the one I want."

No, because who would want unconditional love and fun and friendship and happiness and security and great sex… and…and… My chest was hitching. "Then you're an idiot," I managed.

"You haven't been happy, either. That job of yours doesn't fulfill you. It's a huge step-down from NBC. You complain about it all the time."

I glanced at Jonathan. Sure, *now* he was listening. "But our *life* fulfills me," I said to Eric. "I'm very happy. My job," I added, lowering my voice, "will be fine until something better comes along."

"But that's the lesson of Nathan's life! You might not *get* something better coming along!" He leaned forward, eyes intent on me. "Don't you see, Ains?"

"No, I don't see a damn thing! I repeat. You're not thinking clearly. We should get married. It's time. Don't be ridiculous."

"I'm sorry to hurt you. I really am."

"You did not invite me to this gorgeous dinner to dump my ass, Eric."

"I thought, wrongly, that you wouldn't make a scene here."

"You want a scene? I'll give you a scene! How can you do this to me? How can you be so selfish?"

"I guess you're well rid of me, aren't you?"

*He's not serious. He'll rethink this.* "I'm going to leave now," I said. My throat felt like it was jammed with broken glass. "I'll see you at home."

"I'll be at my parents' house tonight."

"Fine! By all means, go home to Mommy. Maybe she can talk some sense into you."

"Again, Ainsley, I'm so sorry, and I'll always be grateful you were my partner during my cancer journey."

"Oh, shut up."

I rose from the table and glanced at my lobster. Considered taking it with me. Decided it wouldn't be a dignified exit if I had a crustacean clutched to my breast.

This wasn't really happening. He couldn't break up with me. We were special.

I spent a restless night, alternating between fury, confusion and the urge to drive to Greenwich and slap him silly. I also stomped through the house, with Ollie bouncing after me with his blanket, trying to find my engagement ring.

I didn't find it. But I did open the box that contained every single card Eric had ever given me, every note, every funny little drawing.

The notes made my eyes spill over with tears. He *loved* me. I knew that. It was right there in black and white.

In the garage, I found a huge box from Eastern Mountain Sports, containing a tent, cooking gear, hiking boots, hiking socks, hiking shirts, hiking shorts, hiking hat. Eric was nothing if not a man addicted to gear, after all. There was a subzero sleeping bag, backpack and trekking poles (to ensure he'd look like a total ass if he did manage to get on a trail). There was even bear repellent.

So he was Cheryl Strayed now? Taking a hike to find himself? That was so last year!

I resisted the urge to burn everything camping-related, went inside and turned on our giant TV. Watched *Game of Thrones*, ate Wheat Thins dipped in Nutella (I should've taken that lobster, damn it) and tried to distract myself by lusting after Jon Snow, Ollie in my lap.

It didn't work.

Tears leaked out of my eyes. This was the worst fight we'd ever had. Ever.

I was scared. In eleven years together, we'd never once talked about breaking up.

This had to be a blip on the screen of our life together. This wouldn't last. He loved me. He loved our dog. He loved our life together. How many times had he told me that? A hundred? More?

But my heart seemed to be shivering.

I didn't get much sleep that night.

Eric's mother called me in the morning. "He's here," she said. "I don't know what's gotten into him. He's being an idiot."

There was a rattle in the background. "Are you making him pancakes?" I asked. Judy's pancakes were the stuff of legend, and she made them every time we came for breakfast.

"He's hungry. Here, Eric," she said, her voice growing distant as she breasted the phone. Yes, I knew her that well. "There's bacon. I'm on the phone with *Ainsley*, you know, Ainsley—" her voice came back louder "—the woman who loves you? Remember her? Ainsley, sweetheart, I want you to know that Aaron and I are completely ashamed at how our son has treated you."

"I appreciate that."

"It's like he's forgetting the most important person in his life," she boomed. "Here's the butter, honey. Quitting his job? A job that pays him that salary plus a Cadillac health-care program, plus that office and his nice secretary? And the *gym*, Ainsley! Right there in the building? The gym!" Judy had always been dazzled by Eric's Wall Street office. "Not so much syrup, baby, it's just sugar, you know. Anyway, we *told* him he was being a fool. Alaska! Who lives in Alaska? He'll die in Alaska."

"People die in Alaska all the time," Aaron echoed.

"Exactly," I said.

"He'll come around, sweetheart. He's not *that* dumb." There was a pause, in which I imagined her glaring at her son, then putting another pancake on his plate. "Are we still on for shopping on Thursday? I have nothing to wear for my cruise."

See? Things were fine if she still wanted to go shopping with me. I assured her I was, then hung up.

I was supposed to have lunch with Rachelle. Good, that would be good. I'd get my mind off things, and who knew? By the time I got back, Eric might well be sitting on the front porch, waiting for me with a bouquet of roses in his hand and regret in his heart.

I wouldn't tell anyone about this. It would only make things awkward when Eric and I got back together.

I showered and dressed with care, trying to empty my mind. Put on a cute checked dress, long silver earrings and strappy sandals. There. I looked like myself again, slightly plump (curvy, Eric liked to say), cute as a bug's ear.

Except I could see the shadow of anxiety in my eyes.

We'd never parted on angry terms. We'd never gone to bed mad. We were that special couple, two halves of a whole.

Rachelle and I were meeting at the Blessed Bean, a sweet café in the historic downtown section of Cambry-on-Hudson, not far from work. I rode my bike into town, past Kate's still-new studio, photos of brides, grooms, babies and animals in the window. She liked to say that photography showed the truth of people, and over the years, she'd taken a few pictures of Eric and me. We looked happy in every damn one. There was no *I haven't been happy for some time* anywhere.

Or maybe there was. Maybe I should check.

As I passed Bliss, the bridal gown boutique, I tried not to look in the window. The dresses were works of art (especially the short lace one I saw out of the corner of my eye). But I couldn't be thinking about weddings right now. No. Eric had some crawling to do.

There was Rachelle, checking her phone in front of the restaurant. "Hey!" I called, plastering on a smile.

"Don't you look cute!" she said. Like me, she loved clothes. Shopping was one of the ways we'd become friends. "Did you check out the lace dress in Bliss? Oh, my God, I have to get married just so I can wear that!"

"It would look great on you. I'm starving," I said. "Let's go in."

We were seated by a window and she flirted with the waiter. Rachelle was single and on the prowl, and he was pretty cute.

"So guess what?" she said after we'd ordered. "I have office gossip."

"Oh, goody! Do tell."

"Captain Flatline went on a date last night. Can you believe it?"

"Really?" I drank some water to cover. Of course, I'd seen Jonathan last night—not that I'd realized it was a date. It had looked about as romantic as a bunionectomy. But I didn't want to tell Rachelle. After all, Jonathan had seen me in my moment of humiliation. He'd ignored me as I left the restaurant, and I was grateful. I knew he'd never talk about it with anyone.

Rachelle chattered and speculated away, and I nodded and smiled but didn't comment. We then moved on to where she could meet a nice guy—her last date had tried to convince her to become a Druid—and I promised to give her the number of one of the Wall Street crew she'd met at Eric's party.

"I could use a rich boyfriend," she said. "I had to cancel my cable and I'm in deep mourning. And what's-his-name was pretty cute."

God, if only we could do that party over. I'd make sure Kate's glass was full. Nathan would still be alive, and I'd be engaged.

When the bill came, I grabbed it, handed over my Visa and subtly checked my phone.

Nothing from Eric. Maybe he was home by now.

"What are you guys doing tonight? Anything fun?" she asked.

"Oh, no plans yet." I forced another smile.

The cute waiter came back with the bill. "I'm so sorry," he said, "but your card's been declined."

My mouth fell open, and humiliation burned its way up my chest and throat, into my cheeks. "Oh…uh, right! I…I forgot, our card number was hacked. I'm so sorry. I was supposed to throw that one out. Here."

Our credit card had not been hacked.

I dug in my wallet and handed him two twenties. "Sorry. Keep the change."

Eric had canceled the card. I knew it in my bones.

Holy guacamole. Fear pricked my knees. "Listen, I should

check in on my sister, so I'm gonna cut this short," I told Rachelle.

"Of course," she said. "Give her my best, okay?"

"Will do. See you Monday!" My heart thumped erratically. *I'd like you to move out.*

I raced home, burst through the front door and went straight to my laptop—the latest Mac, a Hanukkah gift from Eric—and logged into our bank account, the one I used to pay the household bills.

My password was accepted, thank God. The dread didn't lift. Ollie whined, and I petted him automatically, waiting for my bank account to appear. Our bank account.

There.

Checking Account Ending in 7839: Balance: $35.17.

A cold sweat broke out on my forehead and back.

Last week, there'd been more than twenty grand in there.

Savings Account Ending in 3261: Balance: $102.18

Last week, fifty grand and change. My breathing was fast and shallow.

All our—his—other money was held in a conservative stock portfolio. He kept some aside to play with; it was what he did for a living, after all. He liked to take some chances on new companies, always on the lookout for the next Google.

I sat back and tried to take a calming breath.

Back when Eric started making more than I did, I insisted on paying for half of our expenses (except rent, because there was no way I could've afforded our second apartment). But I paid for half the gas, half the electric, half the building fees. I didn't want to seem like a kept woman, even if his job on Wall Street had boosted us into another tax bracket. And now, please. I didn't earn enough at *Hudson Lifestyle* to live in the area the magazine covered. The irony was not lost on me.

When we bought the house, Eric told me to save my share

of the down payment "for when we have a baby." Logistically, I couldn't manage a tenth of it, let alone half. I'd worried— a little, anyway—at the time, wanting a more modest house, but Eric had smiled, kissed me and said, "Honey, we can easily afford this."

By which he'd meant *I can easily afford this.*

Otherwise, I never thought much about money. Stupid, stupid, stupid. The name on the deed...only his. We'd never changed that, had we? Had that been deliberate? My God, had he done that on purpose?

I never once questioned that it was our money, our house, our families.

Once or twice a year, I'd wrestle Eric for the check and say, "This one's on me," and we'd laugh, and he'd let me pay.

I realized I was sweating.

I did have my own savings account, which I checked now. The balance was the same as last week: $12,289.43. Not a lot to show for a decade of work.

My heart should probably be broken, or I should be furious, but right now all I felt was numb.

He didn't mean this. A day or week from now, he'd be on his knees, begging me to forgive him. He loved me. He had *always* loved me.

But there was a voice in my head that sounded a lot like Candy's, and it was saying Eric was doing exactly what he wanted to do.

# Chapter Ten

*Kate*

On the twenty-second day of My Exciting Adventures as a Widow, I found myself in a gas station bathroom, peeing on a stick.

Why? Because I was *fun*, that's why.

Still no period.

So I *had* to be knocked up, right? Right?

I recognized my own desperation. Eleven pregnancy tests had told me I wasn't pregnant. I opted not to believe them. Fuck 'em! So what if the Mayo Clinic, WebMD and the National Health Service of Great Britain said they were 99 percent accurate? If that was true, I'd have my period, so clearly, I was pregnant.

"I am going to have your baby, Nathan," I said aloud, setting the test on the sink to do its thing. My voice bounced off the tiles on the bathroom walls. "You and I are going to be parents, honey!"

Keep on the sunny side, right? That was me! Widowed but not broken.

Why the gas station? Well, let's just say I was tired of irrationally hiding my used pregnancy tests at home. Having to do jazz hands to keep the lights on took away from what should be a special moment. Also, what if Brooke stopped over, unannounced, as she was prone to doing these days, and rifled through my trash (which she hadn't done, but still, it was possible) and found a pregnancy test, and her hopes got so high, and then I had to dash them?

What if my mother-in-law (was Eloise still my mother-in-law, since I was technically no longer married?)...anyway, what if Eloise brought her little dogs over, and they ran into the bathroom and grabbed one out of the trash and ran out and dropped it at her feet, the same way my childhood dog had barfed up a tampon in front of my first boyfriend?

I'd run out of pregnancy tests two days ago, so I had to go to the CVS three towns north (in case I ran into someone who knew Nathan, and their name was legion). The CVS was conveniently located next to a gas station.

And really, the two lines were much more likely to show up here. Right? Wouldn't this make a great scene in a movie? It was all so...grimy. If I was a teenager, I'd definitely be pregnant.

I *had* to be pregnant. I had never once missed my period, which had been such a faithful pain in the ass since it had first debuted when I was twelve during my great-aunt Marguerite's one hundredth birthday party. "I see your Cousin Tilly from St. Louis has come to visit," Marguerite whispered in my ear.

I thought she was having a stroke. Turned out I had a big splotch of blood on the ass of my white (of course) sundress. Ainsley thought I was dying and had been inconsolable.

And since then, every friggin' twenty-eight days.

So where was my period, huh? Making a placenta, that was where.

"Placenta," I said out loud, just to make sure I wasn't in some weird dream. The difference was very hard to tell. I was drunk with exhaustion.

Since Nathan's death, I'd slept only in twenty-minute spurts, jerking awake in a panic. Was it true? Was he really gone? Or had I dreamed his whole death thing? Or maybe our whole *life* was the dream, those nine bizarrely idyllic months just an incredibly vivid product of my imagination.

Already, our marriage felt like it was dissolving. I could picture Nathan only in shimmery waves, as if I was looking at him across a hot parking lot in August. I could picture a photo of him, but not him in real life.

"Please come back," I whispered. "Please, Nathan."

There was no answer.

I glanced at my watch. In twenty minutes, I was meeting Eloise at the Cambry-on-Hudson Lawn Club for lunch. We were now shackled together in grief, she and I. This would be my first public outing aside from that trip to the supermarket, three late-night drives and today's fun-fun-fun outing to CVS.

Twenty minutes. Plenty of time for my hormones to create the appropriate lines on the pregnancy test. I wouldn't tell Eloise that I'm pregnant until I was well out of the first trimester, when the pregnancy was more assured. And then, oh, what happy news it would be!

I picked up the test.

One line.

"Well, fuck you, shit-bird," I said and threw it in the trash as hard as I could.

★ ★ ★

"Kate, my deah," Eloise said as I came into the club. "Thank you for joining me."

"Thank you for inviting me." I went to kiss her just as she hugged me instead, so the end result was that I kissed my mother-in-law on the neck, like a teenage boy going in for a hickey. She kindly ignored it but did step back a little. I couldn't blame her. Looking down, I saw that my shoes didn't match. Classy. I tried to hide this fact by standing with one foot behind the other, like a tightrope walker.

Looking Eloise in the eye was just too hard. Though I wasn't a mother (thanks for nothing, pregnancy test), it seemed to me that suicide might feel like a very reasonable option if your child died. Then again, Eloise had Brooke and Brooke's sons. And Nathan Senior.

"Right this way, Mrs. Coburn, Mrs. Coburn," the maître d' said.

Technically, I wasn't Mrs. Coburn. Four months ago, changing my name had felt awkward and pretentious, as if I'd be flaunting my married status. Now I wished I had.

I followed Les or Stu or Cal—I knew his name had three letters in it—to a table by the window.

"Please let me say how very sorry I was to hear about young Mr. Coburn," he said.

"Thank you, Bob," Eloise said. Bob. That was it. "You're very kind."

"Yes. Thank you," I added.

"I remember his sixteenth birthday party here, when he—" Bob's voice broke off.

I swallowed. Everyone knew him. Better than I did, in many cases. Everyone had more memories. And rather than comfort me, these stories made me jealous and confused. *What do you mean, you played poker with him? He never played poker!*

*Not in the whole nine months I knew him!* I wanted to bark. Or, *Who gives a rat's ass that he got you through algebra? He was my husband, and he's dead!*

"That was a happy day," Eloise said, graciously covering for poor Bob, who was struggling to maintain control. He gruffly assured us that our waiter would be right over and left the table.

Unable to avoid it any longer, Eloise and I looked at each other.

"So how are you?" I asked, my words squeaking, crushed by the vise in my throat.

"I'm doing as well as can be expected."

She looked good, that was for sure. Tall and slender, her thick blond-gray hair cut in a bob, Eloise was the type of woman who didn't own jeans or Keds. She wore a beige dress with a matching jacket and low heels. Very stylish, very flattering.

What was I wearing? I didn't remember, so I glanced down. Linen pants (points for that), a white shirt with a faint stain of spaghetti sauce. That's right. The meatball stain from a night at Porto's. A stain that predated Nathan.

"And how are *you*, Kate?" Eloise asked.

My stomach chose this moment to growl. Loud and long, too, thunder rolling across the plains. "Hungry, I guess." I laughed.

Whoops. No laughing allowed. My husband was dead. Her son. The laughter stopped.

Eloise's face didn't change. She gave a small nod.

"Sorry," I whispered. I looked away.

"Have you gotten back to work yet?" she asked, folding her hands.

"Not yet," I said. "I had a wedding this past weekend, but my assistant covered it. Max. You met him, I think."

"Yes. A nice man."

"Yes." Another stomach growl. We both ignored it this time.

The waiter came over. "I'll have a martini, three olives, very dry," I said, even though it was only 1:12 in the afternoon. But wait! I might be pregnant. "Actually, just water. And a Caesar salad, and the filet mignon." Because the baby would need iron and stuff. Until Cousin Tilly from St. Louis came to visit, I was pregnant, goddamn it.

"House salad for me, thank you," Eloise said. "Dressing on the side, please."

Our waiter nodded and left.

From where we sat, we could see the golf course, acres and acres of unnatural, perfect green. Nathan had sponsored a charity golf event. I wasn't sure how golf charities worked, but he had one, and it was supposed to have been in August. Who would take over? Who cared?

"How's Na—Mr. Coburn?" I asked.

"He's…he's struggling," Eloise said. There was a pause. "And how are you holding up?"

I took a shaky breath. "It's hard," I said.

"We have to be strong."

I nodded, pressing my lips together.

How could she do this? How could she even be upright? "Eloise," I said, reaching across the table to hold her hands, "I'm so sorry you have to—"

She squeezed my hands hard, then pulled back. "Please, Kate. Not here, my deah."

My hands stayed across the table for a moment, like dead fish. "Of course. You're right."

Everyone grieves differently, the saying went. And I knew Eloise was devastated inside. Her *boy*. Her baby. He was everything a person could want in a son. He'd never disappointed her…well, not that I knew of. Except, perhaps, in marrying me.

"Have you seen any of your friends, deah? Or your sister or brother?"

I took a deep breath. "My sister calls every day. Otherwise, no. Not yet."

I'd had a thousand texts and emails, cards and phone messages, though. *I don't know what to say* was a popular theme. Also, *Call me if you need anything.*

Nothing from Paige. That really stung. We'd been friends for so long.

Daniel the Hot Firefighter had emailed. Just a Thought you might like this and a link to a *BuzzFeed* article about why men shouldn't own cats. #4 had been *because they'll try to see if the cat's head will fit into their mouths* with a GIF of someone doing just that, and I'd laughed out loud, startling myself, startling Hector into a rapid swim across his bowl.

Otherwise, it had been mighty quiet in Nathan's house. Mighty quiet. I was considering getting a dog.

My stomach roared again.

"You're not eating well, are you?" Eloise asked.

I shook my head, swallowing, forcing my throat muscles past the rusty spike that seemed to be wedged there.

"Well. We cahn't have that. You'll have a good lunch."

But when lunch finally came, I could barely get down a mouthful.

I did it. For the baby's sake, no matter what those ignorant tests said. Chewed and chewed and chewed. Swallowing was an act of will.

This was my life now.

"Mr. Coburn and I have decided to go ahead with our anniversary party," Eloise said. She ate the European way, fork in the left hand, knife in the right. "And of course we'd love for you to do the photos."

"Sure. Of course."

"We cahn't just abandon the charity."

"That's very…good of you."

I'd be going to the party without Nathan. His parents got fifty years; we didn't get one.

Until April 6, I'd had a civilized relationship with my in-laws. Nathan Senior often called me Karen, and finding things Eloise and I had in common had been nearly impossible. We didn't read the same books; she didn't watch TV or go to the movies. Once we'd exhausted the topic of how perfect Atticus and Miles were, we were pretty much done.

Brooke had said all the right things when Nathan and I were dating, and she urged her kids to call me Aunt Kate after we got married. She'd invited me to one of those parties where guests buy jewelry made by African schoolgirls, and I sat there, trying to be open and positive and interested in everyone, buying lots of jewelry I wouldn't wear.

Before April 6, my still-shaky place in the family had been natural, normal. All I had to do was be pleasant and hang in there, and eventually, I'd belong.

Now I'd forever be a reminder of their lost son and brother, forever included in family events that would be steeped in grief for the rest of our lives.

How did people survive this?

*I can't believe you abandoned us like this, Nathan. Pretty selfish, don't you think?*

He didn't respond.

"Let's do this again next week, shall we?" Eloise said when the interminable lunch was finally over, and I couldn't help flinching.

"Sure!" I said. "That would be great!"

The food sat heavily in my stomach as I drove home. Eloise followed behind me the entire way, which made my driving jerky and uncertain. Their house was less than a mile from Nathan's place. Our place, I meant. Mine, actually.

I pulled into the driveway. Someone was standing on my doorstep, surrounded by suitcases. Someone holding a little dog.

"Ainsley?"

"Eric and I broke up," she said, and my mouth fell open. "Dumped me, cleaned out our account and told me to move. Can I stay with you for a few days?"

"Yes! Of course, come on in."

The joy that flooded through me was shameful. But thank God, I wouldn't have to be alone in this house another day.

# Chapter Eleven

❧❦❧

*Ainsley*

As Kate helped me lug in my three suitcases, as Ollie charged through the exciting new space, a corner of his blanket clutched in his mouth, I seemed to be stricken with verbal diarrhea, hoping desperately that she didn't mind me showing up here. For a flash of a second as I drove over, I'd forgotten that Nathan was dead, and in that flash, I felt such relief… Nice Nathan, who really seemed to like me, would *definitely* be on my side.

But he was dead. And his death was why Eric decided to move to *Alaska* (the state's name now imbued with dripping sarcasm).

"Yeah, so he dumped me Friday. I thought he was going to propose, but no, and the thing is, the lobster was so *good*, and all night long, I kept thinking about it. And the ring, Kate! The ring was so sparkly! I found it in his underwear drawer the night of—um, a few weeks ago. Anyway, no proposal. He dumped me, so I figured I'd do exactly what he said, right? He wants me out, I'm out."

"Good for you, Ainsley." Rather than the typical expression of slight concern whenever she saw me (and a little condescension), she looked genuinely pleased.

I lifted the heavier suitcase so as not to scratch the floors. "I think if I just leave him alone for a few weeks—um, or days—" *she doesn't want you here for weeks, dummy!* "—he'll come to his senses. Wow, this place is beautiful! Eric always had a woody for it. I swear to God, he wanted to be Nathan."

*Who died on your stupid granite countertop. Shut up, Ainsley.*

Kate just looked at me. "Well, come on upstairs and pick your bedroom, okay?"

We went up the stairs and down the long, white hallway, which Ollie was using as a racetrack, filled with glee. I looked in the first bedroom. "This will be fine," I said.

"No, no, take your time. Look around. The corner room has a great tub. But this one has a skylight. And I love those red pillows." She paused, pushing her hair back. Her shoes didn't match, I noticed, and my heart twisted.

"They're all beautiful. I really appreciate this."

"Nathan has—had—great taste."

"Absolutely! That's for sure. I still can't believe you actually live here. You're so lucky."

Ah, yes. Just what to say to the grief-stricken widow. Maybe I should write for Hallmark Cards. *Your husband may be dead, but think of the extra closet space you'll have!* "I...I meant I love this house."

"I know. Don't worry. You don't have to walk on eggshells." She gave me a rueful smile, and I felt a twinge of little-sister hope. Then again, I'd felt that twinge once a year for my entire life.

"Thanks. We'll have a great time." And there I went again,

saying the exact wrong thing. "I should shut up now. Sorry again."

She laughed a little. "It's okay. You're a breath of fresh air."

"Are you hungry?" I asked.

"Um…yeah. I think so. I just had lunch with Eloise, but I didn't eat much."

"I'll cook us dinner! Okay?"

"There's lots of food in the freezer. Well, you know that already. Thank you, by the way. For coming by and organizing stuff." She swallowed with difficulty, it seemed. "Anyway, get settled in, and I'll pour you some wine and you can tell me everything. It'll be nice not to think about…my own stuff."

"Kate." I hesitated, then gave her a hug. "He was the nicest guy in the world."

"You know what's funny?" she said, her voice husky. "You knew him longer than I did." She gave me a brisk pat on the back, then pulled away. "Check out all the rooms and pick your favorite."

She went down the hall to her own bedroom, and I caught a glimpse of her giant bed. My heart wobbled with grief. Thirty-nine years old, and a widow.

And here Eric was having a midlife crisis. If anything, Nathan's death should've taught him to cherish the people around him, the ass-hat.

This Jack London phase wasn't going to last. Really. Eric shuddered at those shows about the Alaskan mountain men on the Discovery Channel. If he made it out of New York, I'd be stunned. But right now, I was furious. I deserved to be married. I wanted that ring, that piece of paper, that Mrs. title in front of my name, and I'd earned it.

I loved Eric, had always loved him, had always been his biggest fan.

What an idiot. Me, I meant. I wiped my eyes with angry hands.

Okay, well, I had to unpack. I opened the door to the corner room and sucked in a breath. It was impressive, all right, and so different from my bedroom at home. One entire wall was brick, and a black, modern four-poster sat in front of it, made up entirely in white. Fluffy white pillows, white on white duvet cover, a fluffy white throw. There was a vast black bureau topped with three modern long-necked bird sculptures. A furry, blissfully soft white rug on top of the cherry-stained floors. Ollie ran to it and flopped down, rolling in delight. Against one of the white walls was an asymmetrical couch, a fainting couch, I think it was called, upholstered in gray velvet with a small red pillow. The wide windows overlooked the courtyard or patio or whatever they called it. A Japanese cherry tree was in bloom, its elegant branches swaying slightly in the breeze.

I couldn't help the juvenile pang of envy I felt. Let's face it—Kate walked into this life without any effort on her part. A wonderful husband (I would've dated him if I'd been single), the prestige of marrying into the Coburn family, this incredible house.

Everything I had, I worked for. Yearned for. Spent years planning.

My own house—*Eric's* house—was filled with color and comfort. Sure, we had nice things, too, but not like this. This was the kind of room an Oscar winner would sleep in.

But it was mine for now. I would read on the couch, I thought, and sip tea, and look out at the cherry blossoms while Eric rued the day.

The bathroom…whoa. I walked in and the lights turned on automatically, dimly at first, then to full power. Wow! A little room for the toilet, a separate shower and a huge wonking bathtub with eight (count 'em) jets. Long quartz countertop, strange, beautiful sink, four little succulent plants in a row.

I went back into the bedroom and pulled out my Winnie the Pooh, who'd been with me since birth. For the past eleven years, Pooh had been relegated to a shelf or chair in the guest room, as it didn't feel right to have my beloved cuddle friend watching as Eric and I had sexy time. Now I wanted him with me again.

"I love you more than Eric," I told Pooh and kissed his worn little nose. He wasn't the classic Pooh; he was Disney's version—red shirt and denim overalls. After thirty-two years of love, he was missing both eyes, just a black thread trailing down from one socket like a worm, and his red shirt had more patches than original fabric. Kate used to sew him up for me.

I set him on the bed between the pillows, a splash of comforting tackiness in all this sophistication.

Then I took out the picture of my mother and me, and put it on the night table. It was the only picture I had of the two of us.

My mother had been a beauty, that was for sure. She'd had black hair like mine. Hers was wavy in the way of a 1950s pinup girl, as if she'd slept in rollers all night. To the best of my knowledge, it was natural. Talking about her had never been encouraged.

Once, when I was about seven, I'd asked Candy if she knew my mother. "Only in the sense that your father and she were having an adulterous affair," she said, aborting the conversation with surgical efficacy. Dad tended to say things like, "Oh, Michelle was…well. She was terrific, your mom." And not much else.

In the picture, she was holding me on her hip, smiling right into the camera. Pooh was clutched to my chest, both eyes then intact, his fur a yellow not found in nature. My mother's hair was blowing in the breeze, and I had on a rather adorable pout.

I'd tried a thousand times to remember that moment. Tried, and failed.

I liked to think she and I would've been friends. That we'd be close still, like Judy and I were, except even better. That she'd have visited me at NBC and would've loved Eric, would've helped me paint the rooms in our house and gone shopping with me for all the little things that made our place so cozy and fun.

I used to think she'd have been proud of me.

Today, though, a rejected, underemployed woman who wanted nothing more than to get back together with the man who'd dumped her...today, I wasn't so sure.


By Monday morning, I still hadn't heard from Eric.

That scared me, but I was trying not to think about it. After all, it had been only two days. And Kate seemed quietly glad for my company. On Saturday night, we'd watched the last half of the Yankees game to catch a glimpse of our father behind home plate, not that you could see much with all his gear.

While staring at the TV, stroking Ollie's belly as he lay in the chair next to her, Kate told me she hadn't had her period since Nathan died, but didn't seem to be pregnant, either.

"I always thought you'd make a great mom," I'd said, once again sticking my foot in it. Her face rippled with sorrow, and she didn't look at me. When our father called the batter out, Kate said good-night. Ollie, good doggy that he was, trotted up after her.

And yet, yesterday afternoon, we'd played Trivial Pursuit, the first time we'd played a board game since Candy Land. Sean called, and I talked to him a little bit—a rarity, as he never deliberately called me, though Kiara did once in a while. Sean was under the impression I was staying here out of the goodness of my heart, rather than because I was currently homeless.

It would be good to go to work. Get my mind off things and on to such burning issues as the latest trends in local goat cheese. I poured myself some of Kate's great coffee—an Ethiopian blend Eric would covet if he knew Nathan had once loved it.

Kate wandered into the kitchen, her hair a little matted. "How'd you sleep?" she asked.

"Like the dead," I answered. "Oh, shit. I'm *sorry*. Like a rock. Very well. I slept well." I closed my eyes for a second. "How about you?"

"Not bad," she lied. The shadows under her eyes told the true story.

"I have to get to work. Jonathan's really anal about us showing up on time."

"Okay. Have a good day," she said.

"Can I do anything for you while I'm out?"

"No, no, I'm fine." She rubbed her eyes. "I have to go to the studio and return some phone calls and stuff."

"Good, good," I said. "Tell Max I said hi." Once upon a time, I had a huge crush on Max and his whisper-scary voice.

"Will do. And, Ainsley...you know, stay here as long as you want. Even if Eric comes crawling back—as he should—you're welcome to have a little breathing room here. But I don't need you to stay, either. I mean, just do what you want. You're welcome here." Grief and exhaustion had softened her a little; she was usually a lot more brisk where I was concerned.

"Thanks, Kate. And hey," I added, "remember that, uh, that grief group I found? It meets tonight. Maybe, if you don't want to go alone, I could go with you the first time. Or something. If you want."

She nodded. "Yeah, that might be…good." Her mind was already wandering. I wanted to hug her, but I always felt a bit like an ass, hugging my ultracool sister (*half* sister, I could hear Candy saying).

I went out to my car, breathing in the sweet springtime smells from the gorgeous flowers and trees of the landscaping. The exterior of the house was just as sleek and fabulous as the inside. A sweep of grape hyacinth grew along the steps and four flowering pear trees marked the curve of the driveway.

I wasn't sure I was doing Kate any good by being there.

Then again, I wasn't sure where else to go. Candy and Dad's—no. Candy would let me stay, of course, but I couldn't bear to be another nail in her crucifixion. Plus, I didn't want her and Dad to think badly of Eric, because once we got back together, it would be awkward.

Same with a friend's place. So it was Kate's, or Gram-Gram's. Despite not being my biological grandmother, Gram-Gram adored me. And speaking of the sweet old lady, I hit her name on my phone. "Hi, Gram-Gram!"

"Is this Ainsley? Hello? The name says Ainsley on the phone. Is that you, honey?"

"It is! Hi, Gram-Gram!"

"How are you, sweetheart? Are you married yet?"

"Nope, not married. Just calling to say hi."

"Oh, dear. Was it your husband who died?"

"That was Kate, I'm afraid. Remember? Nathan was her husband."

She sighed. "That's so sad. Do you think she wants to be fixed up? I know a nice young man."

"It might be a little soon."

"How about you? Would you like to meet someone?"

"No, not right now. I'm on my way to work, Gram-Gram. I just wanted to say hi, and I love you."

"Aren't you sweet! Thank you, darling! You made an old woman's day! Oh, I wanted to tell you something! Last night, I heard a noise! And you know I live here by myself, of course."

Not exactly. She'd recently moved to a swanky senior housing development, the same one where I brought Ollie once a week. She had her own apartment, but it was in a giant building with about three hundred other residents.

"Anyway, I went outside, and I took a butcher knife with me! Just in case!"

"Oh, Gram-Gram. That's not a good idea."

"Well, guess what it was?"

I glanced at my watch. It was 8:28, and Jonathan hated when we were late. "What was it?" I pulled into the lot behind the *Hudson Lifestyle* offices. Of course, there were no free spaces, so I had to back out on the street and try to parallel park.

"It was a skunk! Can you believe it? A little black-and-white skunk! Oh, it was adorable! I left it some cat food."

I turned off the engine and grabbed my purse and phone. "You probably shouldn't feed it, Gram-Gram."

"Well, I did. I'm an independent woman. I can do what I want."

I laughed. "I guess that's true. I have to go now. Love you!"

"I love you, too, honey. Come visit me! We can go to Walgreens together."

It was her favorite place. "That sounds like fun." I did love the As Seen On TV aisle.

"Or a wake. Someone's bound to die soon. All these old people. An ambulance comes here every day! And you never know. Wakes are great places to meet someone."

I snorted. "Bye, Gram-Gram." Granted, I didn't really want to go to a wake with my grandmother, but her friends *were* dropping like flies, and she liked to show me off at wakes and funerals. She always called me her granddaughter. Never once used the word *step*.

I ran up the stairs to the office. Everyone looked up and went quiet. Lateness was on par with beheading puppies as far as our boss was concerned. His door, at least, was closed. "Hi, everyone," I said in a low voice, hoping to slip into my cubicle like Bob Cratchit avoiding Scrooge.

His door opened. "You're late," he said. "Please come in for a moment."

"Hi, Jonathan." I stood up, my face flaring with heat. Was he going to bring up Friday night? Or the fact that Eric announced that I complained about my job? More likely, he was going to deliver another lecture about punctuality and godliness. He did have that Calvinist preacher vibe.

Jonathan closed the door behind me and sat down, regarding me with his unblinking, pale blue eyes. His office was not a place where happy conversations occurred. Not with me, anyway.

"I'm sorry I'm a tiny bit late. I was talking to my grandmother, and she has dementia, a little anyway, and it was hard to get her off the phone. But she's very sweet. A widow for a long time. How was your weekend?"

"Please sit down," he said. His voice was very deep, almost a growl, like the dragon Smaug from The Hobbit movies. Rachelle was convinced it was the one sexy thing about him, but everything he said to me always sounded very...disdainful.

"Have you seen *The Cancer Chronicles* this morning?" he asked.

"Uh, no." The CCs were supposed to be done, though Eric had run a maudlin piece about Nathan just after he died.

"Jonathan, speaking of Eric, I'd like to keep our, um, little scene from the other night to ourselves, okay? We're...well, we're getting back together."

"Are you?" An eyebrow lifted.

"Yes. Probably. I mean, definitely. It's just a blip."

He sighed, then turned his monitor around so I could see.

It was Eric's blog, running as usual under the banner of *Hudson Lifestyle Online*.

*The Cancer Chronicles* by Eric Fisher, it said, and then the headline:

Cutting Free from the Corpse of My Old Life.

On Friday night, it began, I made a difficult, exciting decision. To live life large. In order to do this, I had to assess what had been holding me back. Now that my Cancer Journey has drawn to a close, and because the Universe has shown me how fragile life is, I had to make some changes.

The first step was big. I had to separate myself from a person close to me, even knowing it would cause her pain. But sometimes pain makes you stronger. It did in my case. The pain of cancer was the fire that burnished my soul. (Sigh. There really hadn't been much pain.)

On Friday night, I used my strength to cut free from the person who represented the old, sick me: Sunshine.

The corpse of his old life was me.

My lips started to tremble, and the words jumped around on the screen.

He *had* to break up with me, the blog said, despite my tender loving care during his "life-and-death battle" because I was "the weight around his ankle," dragging him under.

My lack of support, my love of the status quo, my failure to understand that life "demanded more" now that he had "stared Death in the eye."

He described my anger on Friday. How I kept eating lobster (I regretted that now). My insistence that we should get married.

Rather than focus on the heart of the matter, she repeatedly asked me about the Tiffany engagement ring I bought her. And I had bought her one, but that was before I understood my life's new meaning.

And while he regretted having to hurt me, he was nonetheless "ready to take on the challenge of living life in the moment."

Jonathan was silent. Outside his office, the rest of the staff was silent. So they already knew.

"Please," I whispered. "Take...take it down."

"Look at the comments."

I tried. I was blinking rapidly, as if the computer were about to slap me, which, metaphorically, it already had.

There were 977 comments.

The blog posted at 6:00 a.m. every Monday.

977 comments in two and a half hours. No, 979. Nope, 985. 993. 1001. 1019.

Oh, my Jesus.

This guy is a total dick, the first comment read. She's better off without him.

Bruh, good for you! said the second. Women always think it's about them.

As a leukemia survivor, I also had to scrape some people off my shoe…

This column makes me sick. He used her, plain and simple. Live life large, my ass. He should be...

Outside Jonathan's office, the phone started to ring. Another line. Another. I could see the lights on Jonathan's phone.
The magazine had five dedicated lines. All were lit up.

"Take it *down*, Jonathan," I said, my voice shrill.

"I'm not going to do that. I'm sorry."

"You have to! You hate this column anyway."

1034. 1041. 1075. God, it was going crazy! I put my hand
over my mouth, unable to process what I was seeing.

Jonathan turned the screen back and clicked a few keys.
"Our Facebook page has seven hundred new likes since yesterday. The story has been shared on social media more than
a thousand times."

Oh, shit. Shit! The blog automatically linked to our Facebook, Tumblr and Twitter accounts...all of which I'd set up
when I started work here.

"Take it down!"

"Ainsley, I can't. It's gone viral. I'm sorry." He almost
sounded sincere.

"So? That's my life there! That's me being humiliated!
Please take it down." Tears were spurting out of my eyes.

Jonathan folded his hands together. "You're the one who
fought for this column. I'm sorry it's your personal life, but
that was exactly what you and Eric wanted. And clearly, we
can't turn away this kind of exposure."

"Do you have a beating heart, Jonathan? Come on! Please."

His door opened, and Rachelle stuck her head in and looked
at me apologetically. "Mr. Kent, *Good Morning America* is on
the line."

"I have to take this," he said. "Excuse me."

# Chapter Twelve

❧

*Kate*

My mother called seconds after Ainsley left. "How are you?" she asked. I could hear the clatter of something in the background. My mom was a multitasker; unless you hired her, she would never just sit in a chair and talk. "Things good?"

"Yeah, they're, uh, fine. Fine." As fine as things could be, considering my husband was dead. I didn't mention that Ainsley was staying here. Mom would not approve.

Today was May 1. Our five-month anniversary. No one had mentioned that so far. I was probably the only person who knew. Nathan would've known. He would've bought flowers.

"It's important when dealing with grief to continue self-care and your normal routine." That was probably a line from one of her books.

"Yes. Well, I'm going to the studio today."

"Good! Work is balm for the soul at a time like this."

"Yes."

"We'll talk soon. I'm here if you need me."

"Okay. Thanks for—" Nope, she'd already hung up.

My mother had never been warm and fuzzy.

I had a vague memory of Dad's second wife, Michelle. She smiled a lot. Baked cookies on the weekends Sean and I came over. When Ainsley was born, Michelle let me give her a bottle, even though I was only seven at the time. But Sean and I didn't go over a lot. Our father's job as an umpire meant that he traveled from April through October, home infrequently for short visits. And Mom didn't like us going to see Michelle if Dad wasn't there.

And then, of course, Michelle died.

The divorce and Ainsley were never discussed at home; Sean and I were little, after all. Or little-ish. Mom had suffered the all-too-common indignity of being dumped for a younger, shinier woman, who'd been pregnant before the marriage, before Dad left. After the divorce, Mom had to work more hours, and dinnertimes were tense affairs with dry chicken and vegetables from a can.

It was before Mom's books were published, before she'd invested in a face-lift and started coloring her hair white blond and taking karate. Back then, she was just used up, like an old paper bag.

And then Michelle was gone, and Dad came knocking, and Mom took him back. Him, and the progeny of the other woman.

I knew my mother loved Ainsley...in her way. It was just that her way wasn't the most demonstrative, not even with her biological children. The fact that Ainsley looked so much like Michelle didn't help.

I was glad Ainsley was here, even if she kept putting her foot in her mouth. She gave off a lot of energy, and while that often irritated me a little, I welcomed it now. Without her, the house was very quiet.

I fed Hector, who ate his flakes with gusto. Funny, that this fish pre- and postdated Nathan. A fish with a life span of what?—three years?—bore witness to the beginning, middle and end of my time with Nathan.

"That doesn't seem right to me," I told Hector. Considered flushing him down the toilet to balance the (fish) scales of justice. "I'm just kidding, buddy."

On the shelf above Hector's bowl was my everyday Nikon, the same one I'd been using the night Nathan died.

I hadn't looked at the pictures yet, terrified of what I'd see. Once Nathan fell, my memory of that horrible night was sketchy. I hadn't taken a picture of Nathan going down, had I? I mean, I did have professional instincts. What if there was a picture on there of my husband dying or…dead?

The clock ticked.

I actually had an appointment today. Jenny Tate, who owned the wedding dress boutique around the corner from me, needed some pictures for her website. I didn't realize just what a big deal she was in the wedding dress world until I'd gone to her site. She'd made a dress for a member of the Liechtenstein royal family, and one for an Emmy-award-winning actress, and she'd been featured in all the big bridal magazines.

Time to start getting back to the land of the living.

I showered, not looking at Nathan's toothbrush, and got dressed in jeans and a T-shirt, Converse sneakers and a peach-colored cardigan.

Outside, it was shockingly lovely. I'd almost forgotten it was spring; the past few days had been gray and rainy. But today, the air was soft and clean, and crab apple and pear trees were fluffy with blossoms. I got my bike out of the garage—what was I going to do with Nathan's car?—and got on.

I rode past the tasteful homes and tidy lawns. Nice porch on that house. Pretty pansies there. Maybe I should do something like that. Then again, pansies wouldn't look right at Nathan's place. Something more stark and bold. A cactus, maybe. A statement tree, a phrase he'd used without irony when he first showed me the courtyard.

It seemed like such a long time ago.

*Are you there?* I asked. *Are you watching me? Are you okay, Nathan?*

There was no answer, no sign. I didn't really expect there to be.

But I was out, and it was beautiful, and I had to keep going, keep moving, or be caught by the heavy, dark fog of grief.

I coasted up to the Blessed Bean with its green-and-white-striped awning and wonderful smells. It was past the morning rush, so I didn't have to wait in line, just ordered a large coffee and a larger muffin. Seriously, the thing was the size of a human brain. I was suddenly starving.

Without Nathan at my side—or his mother or Brooke— I was still a stranger in Cambry-on-Hudson. Right now, I was grateful for that. I was just nobody buying a muffin, not a mother with diamond studs in her ears, not a Mercedes-driving businessperson. Just someone passing through, maybe. Someone nobody knew.

"You're Nathan Coburn's widow, aren't you?" the barista asked, handing over my change.

There went my mood. "Yep," I said. "Have a good day."

"His sister babysat me," she said. "Sometimes Nathan would come over and help me with my math homework, and he was always so—"

"Okay, bye," I said, walking out. Kept walking right down the street to my studio, passing Bliss and Cottage Confections.

It was pretty neat, three women who owned wedding-oriented businesses on the same street. Kim and I did events other than weddings, but it made up the bulk of our work. Nathan had been so pleased the one time we three women had gone out for a glass of wine.

"See? I *told* you you'd make friends," he'd said when I got back, and it irritated me, since I'd never said I wouldn't. It also seemed as if he'd been implying that… I don't know. That my move from Brooklyn hadn't been as difficult as it had been.

Because yes, I missed the most beautiful borough. Sometimes I'd mention that, how I missed the smell of garlic at Porto's or Ronny, the homeless guy we all bought food for, and Nathan would look a tiny bit peeved, as if he was disappointed that I didn't say, "Gosh, Cambry-on-Hudson is the best place ever! I hate Brooklyn!"

Now I was stuck here in Cambry-on-Hudson, husbandless in my husband's town, where everyone knew him better and longer than I did.

I missed being alone by choice, not by a freak accident and a tiny venous malformation and granite countertops.

There was the rusty spike again.

"Hello," said an older man walking his little mutt.

"Hi." I gave him a fake smile and unlocked the door of my studio. Mercifully, he didn't pull me aside for a tearful memory of my husband. If he tried, I might've punched him.

And then I was inside, and safe. *Kate O'Leary: Award-Winning Photography*, the sign proclaimed in tasteful letters. The space still felt new to me. New, but clean and bright. Creaky old oak floors and a little courtyard in the back, where Max and I ate lunch the day Nathan died.

My office was its usual mess. I'd come back here for something after Nathan died. Couldn't remember what now. Papers or something. There was a picture of us on the shelf above my desk. I turned it facedown.

Why was I here again? Oh, right, a shoot in about ten minutes. Max wouldn't be in for that; he helped only on outdoor shoots, when the lighting was trickier, or at big events. I had plenty of time to eat breakfast. Had to keep up my strength and all that. I took a big bite of muffin. Cranberry-orange, and damn, it tasted so good. The coffee, too. Crumbs rained down on my sweater, and I brushed them blithely into my keyboard. I was glad it was as big as my head. I might have another one later. Two head-sized muffins in one day.

My thoughts sounded a little crazy even to me.

Maybe tonight I'd go to that grief group Ainsley mentioned.

Three and a half weeks since he died. Almost a quarter of our married life. Almost a month. I wondered if this would be how time was measured now. The days and weeks, the minutes since.

I think I knew the answer.

Oh, and by the way, still no period. I was throwing caution to the wind. *See this huge wonking coffee? Damn right, I'm gonna drink it! Take that, Two Lines! I'll be as surprised as anyone when you show up!*

Yes. The group might be good.

I went into the other room, where the indoor portraits were done, and started setting up, placing the kicker lights to cast shadows and light on Jenny's face. Checked my portrait camera, made sure I had the mirror angled so she could see herself.

The bell in the front jangled. "Kate? It's Jenny!" In she came, a big black bag over one shoulder, her dark hair shiny.

"Hey, girl!" I said, my cheery voice sounding odd. She wore a soft black leather jacket that I wanted to marry. Oops. No jokes about marriage. I was a widow now. She also had a bag of fabric; I'd asked her to bring some different material to use in the background.

"This is such a great space!" she said, looking around like an eager sparrow. "Oh, here, I brought coffee." She handed me a big cup. "One of those mochaccino caramel things."

"Thanks." I probably shouldn't have more caffeine. You know. Just in case. My uterus snickered.

"You bet. And hey...about Nathan." Her dark eyes were painfully kind. "I'm so sorry." She squeezed my shoulders. "I'm going to email you every week and invite you out for dinner, and you can turn me down as much as you want, but when you're ready, we'll go somewhere fabulous with huge drinks, my treat. And you can tell me about him, or we can talk about bridezillas or gossip or go to a movie. We can talk now if you want, or we can just get down to work."

I should type up what Jenny just said and send it to everyone who said *I just don't know what to say*. This. This is what you say.

"Let's work," I said, my voice a little husky. "And thank you. I'll take you up on that."

"You better." She paused. "You know, Leo's a widower. My boyfriend."

Oh, God. "No, I didn't know that." He seemed so...normal the only time I met him.

"Yeah. It's an ongoing thing, you know? He goes to this grief group once in a while. Have you looked into anything like that?"

"Actually, my sister found one. It meets at the Lutheran church."

"That's the one he goes to. He says it helps." She smiled a little, such a nice person. I tried to answer, but the spike wouldn't let me.

"Okay," she said. "Let's do this. I watched *America's Next Top Model* last night to prepare. I'm ready to smize." She grinned, and I found that I could speak once again.

"That show has ruined high school girls for years now."

"I know, but I can't help it. It's like crack."

"That and *Project Runway*," I said. "I watched a marathon last summer." Before I knew Nathan. Before I was a wife, before I was a widow.

"I know Tim Gunn!" she said, pulling me back from the black fog, and we chatted about New York and celebrity sightings.

I kept her talking while I shot. She had a great smile, and her nose was a little big, which saved her from being forgettably pretty and made her beautiful instead.

So her guy was a widower, and he was in the land of the living. Maybe the grief group had something going for it.

Half an hour later, I took the picture I knew would work best. "We can stop now. This is the one," I said. I downloaded it to my computer and pulled it up in black and white.

Perfect. Jenny sitting on the floor in the middle of a mountain of white tulle, her legs crossed, black leather jacket gleaming. She was looking just a bit off camera, and her face was open and friendly with a smile that was the slightest bit mischievous. Happiness shimmered off her in waves.

"Oh, wow," she said. "This is perfect, Kate! I love it!"

I smiled. "Great. I'll email it to you."

"Super. Would you make up a few prints, too? I'll give one to my sister, and one for Leo if the big dope wants it."

"You bet."

She gathered her fabric up and stuffed it back in the bag. "Hey, doesn't your mom work at *Hudson Lifestyle*?"

"She does a column there. My sister is their features editor. Why?"

"Oh, then you probably already know."

"Know what?"

She put her phone in her purse and slung it over her shoulder. "The cancer guy? Now that he's all better, he dumped his girlfriend. And *blogged* about it. It's everywhere now. Do you know him?"

My skin prickled with dread. "A little," I said.

"Sounds like a dick. Well, I have to run. See you around the neighborhood. And thanks, Kate. This was really fun."

"Yeah. Definitely. See you soon."

The second she was out, I opened my computer. Googled *Cancer Chronicles, Eric Fisher.*

0.0042 seconds later, I had my answer.

That bastard.

The little *worm*. When I was done with the article, I read it again. Maybe I should go to his house and beat the living crap out of him. After all, I was a new widow. I'd be forgiven.

I scrolled through the comments.

There were four *thousand* of them.

From what I could see, they seemed to be split fairly evenly; people saying Eric had the right to do what he wanted, the other half saying he'd done Ainsley terribly wrong. "You think?" I asked the empty studio.

At least he'd never named Ainsley in the blog. Nope, he called her Sunshine all this time.

I called her. It went right to voice mail. "Hey," I said. "I just read the blog. I'm so sorry. I'll see you at home, okay? Call me if you want. I'm free all afternoon."

The rest of the day, I was consumed with thoughts of my sister, and guiltily grateful because of it. It beat wondering if I was pregnant, thinking about Nathan and trying not to think about Nathan.

Sean called me around five. "Did you see Eric's blog?" he asked.

"Yeah."

"I never liked him."

"Me neither." We were quiet for a minute, bonding over our irritation with our sister's boyfriend. Sean had written him off long ago as a bit of a tool.

Eric had his attributes. He was always very nice to me, friendly and upbeat. But he took Ainsley for granted; she was always Gayle, and he was always Oprah.

"Was he really that close with, uh, with Nathan?" Sean didn't like talking about unpleasant subjects.

"No. They were on some charity committee together last year. Nathan's golf thing."

My brother grunted. "How are you doing, by the way?"

"Good, I guess. I had a shoot today. How are the kids?"

"They're great. Maybe you can Skype us some night this week. Not tonight. Matthias has karate."

"Okay. Sounds good."

"Tell Ainsley I'm…well, whatever. Tell her I called."

"Will do. Thanks, Sean."

I grabbed my knapsack and headed home on my bike. Ainsley was there when I went in. She was dressed, as always, in a cute outfit, the kind I never could pull off—an ivory skirt printed with black bicycles, a red shirt with a boatneck collar, little black ankle boots. All part of her 1950s housewife vibe.

Her eyes weren't red. That was a good sign, I guessed.

"So," I said.

"Yep," she said, pouring herself a big glass of wine.

"Can I do anything?"

"Nope."

"You gonna kill him?"

"I think his mother will take care of that."

I smiled. Eric did have nice parents. "So…are you guys…?"

"I think he's having a nervous breakdown."

He'd sounded pretty calm on the blog to me. Sanctimonious, hell yes, but calm. First, he broke up with her. Now he put it out there for the universe to read about. And knowing Eric, he was loving the attention.

"You seem pretty chill," I said, accepting the glass of wine she handed me.

"Well, I've had all day to read comments. That dickhead boss of mine wouldn't take it down."

"Too much free publicity?"

"Exactly. I can't decide which man I hate more, Eric or Jonathan. I think it's Eric. Yes. Definitely Eric."

"We can burn him in effigy if you want. That Japanese maple is perfect for it."

She snorted. "I appreciate that." But her eyes flickered and welled. Like a normal person, she cried when the situation demanded it. Me, I was still dry. I handed her a tissue and she blew her nose, then took a swallow of wine.

"Are we going to that grief group tonight?" she asked.

"Oh, we don't have to," I said. "You've had a rough day."

"No, let's," she said. "It'll be fun."

I waited.

"Not fun. Shit. It'll be helpful. It'll be helpful and cathartic. Or horrible, and if it is, we can ditch it and go bowling. Let's order a pizza, okay? I need dairy and gluten."

"Coming up," I said.

At 7:00, my sister and I drove to St. Andrew's Church, where the grief group met. We got out, a fine mist blanketing my hair almost immediately. No one told me how much it rained in Cambry-on-Hudson. Almost a completely different weather pattern than in Brooklyn.

"You really don't have to come in, Ains," I said. "I can walk home or get a ride."

"No, it's fine. I'm here for you." She looked at me, as if really seeing me for the first time today, and gave a little smile. "No one should have to do this alone. Not the first time, anyway."

She was so damn nice. "Okay. Thanks."

Time to open a vein.

# Chapter Thirteen

❧

*Ainsley*

Apparently, St. Andrew's was the happening place when you had a problem. There was an AA meeting going on in one room, an NA meeting in another, a divorced people's group and ours—I mean, Kate's. *One Step Forward: Support Group for Widows & Widowers*, the sign said.

Kate's shoulders were clenched around her ears. "Maybe this isn't a good idea," she said.

"Why don't we give it a try?" I countered. "You might be surprised."

"You'll stay, right? God, I sound pathetic."

My heart pulled. "Of course I'll stay." Finally, I was needed. It felt good after the battering my ego had taken today. God, was it only today? I felt a million years old.

My phone buzzed with a text from Eric.

Guess what? GMA wants to have me on the show!!! Jimmy

Kimmel, too!!! Seems like the CCs have really struck a chord. Did you see today's post??? Went totally viral!

My eye twitched. If Eric was here right now, my phone would be shoved into his frontal lobe. Or up his ass.

I'd received three hundred and seventeen emails today. Eleven of those were from Judy, panicking about what her son wrote about me with just a hint of pride thrown in, as well. *And now* Men's Health *wants him to write a column about his fitness regime! He does look good these days, don't you think?* Then, seconds later, another email, *But don't worry. He'll come to his senses. He loves you.*

The urge to go back to Kate's fabulous house right this minute and guzzle piña coladas was strong within me.

Then Kate reached out and grabbed my hand. My sister needed me. Whatever I was going through, Kate had it worse. In the thirty-two years I'd known her, I'd never seen her lost before.

The group was held in what was clearly a nursery school classroom by day. There were little tables and tiny chairs, and cotton-ball lambs decorated the wall along with the alphabet and numbers. A bookcase and carpeted area were on one side of the room, and the place smelled comfortingly of paint. In the middle of the room was a circle of gray metal chairs, looking out of place in the cheerful, diminutive decor.

There were six or seven people here. Two men, one *extremely* attractive… Too soon to fix Kate up? Yes, of course it was. Jeesh. I sounded like Gram-Gram. The rest were women, one about Kate's age, one older, one younger.

"Hello, I'm Lileth," said one of women in a smooth voice. "I'm a licensed clinical social worker, and I run this group. You're welcome here, and I'm so glad you came. Here are the rules." She smiled sadly, a professional mourner's smile, and handed us a ream of papers.

"Wow. Lots of, uh, information. I'm Ainsley, and this is my sister, Kate," I said. Kate said nothing, so I felt obliged to fill the gap. "Her husband died a few weeks ago."

Kate cleared her throat. "Yes. April 6."

"Nathan Coburn?" one of the women asked.

"Yes."

"I know his sister." She smiled.

"Hey, Kate," the hot guy said. "Sorry you belong to this shitty club. Jenny told me you might show up." He smiled.

"Hi, Leo," she said.

Right, right. He'd come to the wake with the wedding dress designer.

Who wouldn't be making my dress, as I wasn't engaged.

But it was Kate's turn to be miserable. "Is it okay if I stay? Since it's Kate's first time?" I asked Lileth.

"We prefer that you don't," she said.

Leo sighed dramatically. "It's fine with me," he said.

"Me, too," said one of the women.

"Me, too," said another.

"I don't mind," said a little old man.

"It's just that you don't *share* the *experience*," Lileth said. "And the group might not be *comfortable* with someone who's not a widow."

"So she's not a widow," a woman said. "Good for her. It's not like we're going to stone her."

"That's a relief," I said.

"The *rules*—which exist for good *reason*—say only widows and widowers." Lileth cocked her head, fake-smiled and waited for me to leave.

"Are *you* widowed?" I asked, raising an eyebrow.

"No. But I'm a licensed clinical *social* worker."

I felt myself bristling. Kate was still clutching my hand, and I liked the sense of being needed. "Think of me as a therapy dog," I said.

"Oh, let her stay, Lileth, for God's sake," one of the women said. She had a glorious Bronx accent, the orangey skin of a tanning addict and crispy dyed black hair. "We're all bored with ourselves and our whining, anyway." She patted Kate's shoulder. "So sit already, tell us your story."

Lileth didn't look happy. I hated her already.

We sat on the cold, hard folding chairs. "A few *ground* rules," Lileth said. "Which are covered in the information packet I just gave you. One. Our group, One Step Forward—"

"Two steps back," Leo interjected. Lileth ignored him.

"—is a *safe place*, and everything we share is meant for this group *only*. Two. *Confidentiality* is expected." She glared at me, as if I was live Tweeting already. "And this *one* time, I suppose it's all right if—I'm sorry, what's your name?"

"Ainsley."

"—if Ainsley stays. Unless anyone has a *problem* with that? This is *your* group, and if anyone has even the slightest bit of—"

"Let her stay," said the man who was not Leo. "She's pretty."

He was about eighty and gave me a smile. I smiled back. *Take that, Lileth.*

"Three. We take *turns*. Each person may *choose* how much to share, but everyone—"

"It's not rocket science, Lileth," Leo interrupted. "Kate, if you feel like talking, talk. You already know me a little, so I'll go first. Here's the sad story in a nutshell. My pregnant wife—Amanda—died in a car accident. I was driving. They both died, our unborn son and her." His face seemed to change without actually moving, and suddenly his tragedy, easily spoken of, filled his eyes. Filled the whole room. I teared up, trying not to picture what that day, and all the days after, must've been like.

Leo cleared his throat. "That was three years ago. And now I'm with Jenny, and she's really fantastic, but I have my moments of deep dark despair. She thought this group might help. And it has." He smiled, the sorrow shifting, if not leaving, and I found myself liking him.

I looked at my sister. Still had that deer-in-the-headlights look.

"I'm LuAnn," the orangey woman said, her Bronx accent so thick you could practically taste the Yankee Stadium hot dogs. "Cop's wife. Widow. God, I hate that word! Anyways, last year, Frank, my husband, he goes on a DV, right? Domestic violence for you civilians. Worse kind of call. Knocks on the door, the husband answers, shoots him point-blank, dead. We got four kids."

"Oh, God, I'm so sorry," Kate said, her voice tight and strained.

LuAnn shook her head. "Here's the thing, Kate, hon. I am so mad at Frank, okay? Seriously. How the hell could he do this to me? If he was alive, I would kill him. I would kill him in cold blood."

"Of course you don't *mean* that," Lileth said, "though it's *natural* to indulge in—"

"Oh, give me a break here, Lileth! I'm in the anger phase today, because our son? Frankie Junior? He comes home with an F—an F!—on his math test, and I'm like, 'If your father knew how you were screwing around, he would smack some sense into you and don't you roll your eyes at me!'"

Lileth made a sympathetic sound. "Hmm. Mmm. Children can—"

"—And Frankie Junior, he says, 'Ma, who even cares?

Dad's dead, you can't use the guilt card on me forever.' So that's what *I'm* dealing with. A no-good son. Who even knows with the girls? They'll probably be pregnant before long. My twelve-year-old, Marissa? She tells me she has a boyfriend, and I'm like, 'Not while I draw breath, you don't,' and then it's tears and drama, and shit, I could use a vacation already!"

I *loved* her. I grinned at Kate, but she just sat there, a little frozen.

"I'm George," the older guy said. "My wife and I were married for forty-three years, and she just slipped away in her sleep. Bad heart. That was last year." He paused. "It doesn't seem possible that I've made it this long without her. Every day is so long. But I can't complain. We were lucky, Annie and me. We had a lot of good times."

My sister gave a small squeak, and I squeezed her clammy hand.

The other women went. Janette's husband died of pancreatic cancer on their fifteenth anniversary. "His last words to me were 'I'm sorry to be dying on our special day,' and I said, 'Well, you've always been a selfish bastard,' and he laughed, and then he just…sank a little into the pillow. He died at that exact moment. And I panicked, you know? Like, seriously? *Those* were my last words to him? So I grabbed him and shook him and said, 'Hey! I love you, idiot!'" She laughed through her tears.

My sister's forehead was shiny with sweat.

"You okay?" I whispered.

She nodded.

Bree's husband died after a sheet of ice flew off the truck in front of him on Interstate 87 last winter. "It's hardest when I try to talk about him with the kids," she said to Kate. "Camden is four, Fiona's eighteen months. I don't know how to keep his memory alive. The other day, I asked Cam if he remembered the time he went fishing with Daddy, and he didn't. He's forgotten. And Fiona thinks *Daddy* is the word for picture. We went to Target the other day, and in the frame section, she kept pointing at the shelves and saying 'Daddy? Daddy? Daddy?'"

Someone was panting.

It was Kate.

At first, I thought she was crying, but no, she was hyper-ventilating. Drenched in sweat, too. "Uh-oh," I said. "Okay, slow down. In for three, hold for three, out for three, hold for three." There was the rare occasion when Candy's profession came in handy. Panic attacks had dotted my early childhood, and she'd taught me how to breathe through them.

Kate sounded like an overheated dog in the middle of sum-mer. "In for three, hold for three, out for three— Okay, she's gonna faint. Lean over, Kate."

Leo helped me maneuver her head between her legs. "I'm s-s-so-sorry," she managed. She gripped my hand hard enough that bones crunched. "I think I'm having a heart attack."

"Nah. Just hyperventilating," I said. "Remember me and the thunderstorms?" She nodded. "Does anyone have a paper bag?"

George (I was already crushing on him) found one, and Kate held it against her mouth, her eyes wide, face white. "In for three, hold for three, out for three, hold for three," I said, rubbing her back.

"We all lose it at one point or another," LuAnn said. "Me, the first time after Frank died, I was watching *Real House-wives*. We watched it together, right? So it's two weeks, maybe three, after he died, and I sit down and I say, 'Frank! *House-wives* is on!' and then he doesn't come, and I actually call him again. And then it hits me. He's dead. No more TV watching together. I freak out, just like you."

"Our bodies sometimes *acknowledge* what our brains can't," Lileth said. I wondered what fortune cookie she got that from.

"Doing better?" I asked Kate. She nodded but kept puffing into the bag.

"So let's get it out of the way, hon," LuAnn said. "How did your husband die?"

Kate was in no shape to form words. "Want me to tell them?" I asked.

She nodded.

I kept rubbing her back. "He, uh…tripped and hit his head. Freak accident, really."

"He was getting me wine," Kate said into the bag, which expanded and contracted with each breath. "I needed more wine. Because Ainsley's boyfriend was making a speech, and he wanted us to toast her, and I hate parties, so I drank my first glass really fast, and I needed more, so Nathan got me more, and now he's dead and it's my fault." The bag inflated and deflated faster now.

There was a pregnant silence, just the sound of the paper bag. I could've sworn Leo was trying not to laugh.

"It's really Eric's fault, though, isn't it?" I said, still rubbing her back. Soon, I would burn a friction hole in her shirt. "He's the one who said to raise your glass. Plus, he's an asshole."

Leo did laugh then. So did LuAnn. Kate may have smiled, but it was hard to tell with the bag over her mouth.

"Speaking of assholes," Bree said, "did anyone read about that guy who ditched his girlfriend once he got over cancer?"

For a second, I didn't remember it was me she was talking about. But no, *I* was the lucky girl, wasn't I? "That was my boyfriend," I said. "I'm Sunshine of *The Cancer Chronicles*."

Bree's mouth dropped open.

"That dickwad is your boyfriend?" LuAnn asked. "Holy crap. Want us to kill him for you?"

Turned out most of them had all read or heard about *Cutting Free from the Corpse of My Old Life*, not including Lileth, who was probably above social media and read self-help books instead.

I was famous.

Since they were abuzz with questions, I relayed the story of my lobster dinner, the ring, the denied credit card. The eviction.

Janette threw up her hands. "He kicked you out? I can't believe it."

"Thank you."

"And here's the other thing," LuAnn said, leaning forward. She looked a bit like Steven Van Zandt when he was in *The Sopranos*. "So many assholes out there agree with him! What's that even about, am I right?"

"He's going on *Good Morning America* this week," I said.

"Are you kidding?" Kate asked, sitting up. The color had returned to her face a little.

"I forgot to tell you," I said. "And listen to this. My boss wants me to get him to sign an exclusive contract with our magazine. Put him on the payroll and everything."

I sat back and enjoyed the group's moral outrage. Kate even patted my knee.

"Sounds like you dodged a bullet," Leo said.

"You know whachoo need?" LuAnn said. "A rebound fling. Pronto. I have brothers, I can help."

"I'm good," I said. "But thank you. I...well, I actually think we'll get back together. This is just a...meltdown or something. A lapse."

"No, it's not," Leo said. "Sorry, kid. There's a pound in Tarrytown. Time to get a cat."

I shook my head. "No, really. I know he sounds like an idiot, but he's been an amazing boyfriend for a long time. Eleven years. He just freaked out when Nathan died. Before that, he was almost perfect. Right, Kate?"

"There's a group for *divorced* people down the hall," Lileth said, smiling her fake smile. "I'm sure they'd be more than *supportive* with your, ah, *unfolding* drama. But we have our *own* issues—"

"I'm sick of our issues," Janette said.

"Me, too," said George. "Kate, was he really perfect?"

Kate blinked. "Um…well, no one's perfect."

"So what you're saying is, he was a self-centered bastard," Leo said.

Kate winced. "No, not…well, not a bastard. He was—is—self-centered, though. I mean, don't you think so, Ainsley?"

I shifted in the hard chair. "Yeah, well, he's also smart and funny and nice."

"He called you a corpse," Leo said.

"Metaphorically." My face was hot. Defending Eric wasn't easy, but we had eleven good years. Great years. "It was the cancer, then Nathan dying. He just panicked. He'll come around."

"Before or after his Alaskan adventure?" George asked.

"The Discovery Channel makes it look so great, doesn't it?" Bree said. "I wonder if I should pack up the kids and go up there."

"There *are* a lot of single men," I said. "You know. For when you're ready."

"Keep us in the loop," Janette said.

"Will do."

It seemed as if my public humiliation had greatly cheered the mourners, and for that, I was genuinely glad. Our hour was up; Lileth pointed out the cookies and coffee and her availability for one-on-one discussion and reminded Kate to read the tome of rules before next week, then smiled that mournful, practiced rictus.

I snagged a couple of cookies and walked with my sister down the hall.

"How do you feel?" I asked as we went outside. The earlier mist had stopped, and the air smelled like wet soil and copper. Kate stepped around an earthworm—funny, I'd forgotten that she was afraid of them.

"I'm okay," she said. "A little embarrassed."

"You're entitled, Kate. And everyone in the group has been through it, and here they are," I said. "Doing okay. Still alive."

"True."

"I really liked Leo. And LuAnn. My God, that eye shadow is fantastic! And I think I might fix Gram-Gram up with George when he's ready."

Kate smiled a little. "Yeah, everyone was very...kind."

"Think you'll go again?" Since this had been my suggestion, I really wanted it to work in my endless need to win Kate's (or anyone's) approval. For a second, I pictured her calling Sean to complain about me. *Ainsley forced me to go to this horrible group, then all she talked about was Eric.*

"Maybe. Yeah. It was a good idea, Ainsley. Thanks for coming with me."

"Of course! Anytime."

The church basement door opened, and there was Jonathan Kent, still dressed in his suit, a trench coat draped over his arm. He lurched unsubtly to a stop at the sight of me.

AA? NA? It gave his personality a little color, if also a crippling addiction.

"Hi," I said, since he obviously wasn't going to.

"Ainsley." His strange blue eyes shifted to Kate. "Hello," he said.

"Hi, Jonathan. How are you?"

"I'm fine, thank you. It's good to see you."

"Thanks. You, too." She sounded sincere.

For a second, I pictured them as a couple, then rudely shoved that image away. No. Jonathan Kent was not her type.

Even if he was.

Which he wasn't.

"Can I have a moment of your time, Ainsley?" he said.

"Of course, Mr. Kent." I batted my eyelashes at him, strangely and suddenly irritable. "I'll just be a second, Kate."

"Take your time," she said, getting into the car and checking her phone.

Jonathan came around to my side of the car and looked at the pavement, a lock of hair flopping over his forehead as if he were a Regency duke.

His hair had flopped the night Nathan died, too.

"You need a haircut," I snapped.

He looked up, startled.

"Sorry," I said. "What is it, Jonathan?"

He lowered his gaze to my chin. Probably I had a pimple there. My fingers twitched, wanting to find out. "I would appreciate it if you didn't mention my presence here tonight."

"At Alcoholics Anonymous?" I suggested.

He didn't blink.

"NA, then?"

Still nothing.

"I won't say anything. I assume it's the divorce group."

His face didn't change. Then again, it never did. "Have you spoken to Eric yet?" he asked. "I would very much like a commitment from him."

*I would very much like?* People didn't talk like that in real life. "No, I haven't. He's on my shit list at the moment."

"I thought so. I sent him a message this afternoon after your early departure. We're meeting him in the city next Friday for drinks. Eric, you and I."

"What? No, we're not!"

He looked to the left, his jaw tightening. "Ainsley, you petitioned very hard to get *The Cancer Chronicles* linked to *Hudson Lifestyle*. Now—finally—people are reading that ridiculous blog. Traffic on the entire site today was up 9,000 percent. If you'd like to keep your job—indeed, if you'd like to *do* your job, which would be refreshing—I strongly suggest you make yourself available. I'll see you tomorrow."

I was busy sputtering and therefore unable to answer. It was probably best... I didn't want to cuss my boss out—but how dare he? I didn't want to see Eric!

Except I did. I wanted to see the old Eric, the one who loved me and didn't think I was a corpse.

Jonathan had already walked away. I got in my car and slammed the door.

"You okay?" Kate asked.

"Peachy," I said, started the car and headed for Kate's. A bath in that soaking tub was definitely on the agenda. And a nice violent television show. *Game of Thrones.*

I was in the mood for beheadings.

# Chapter Fourteen

*Kate*

I woke up the day after the grief group with a glorious revelation.

I didn't have to be sad anymore! I'd been *so* sad these past few weeks, shaking in my sleep, for God's sake, scared and stunned, feeling like a cannonball had gone through my chest and taken out everything.

But I could be done with that. My duty was fulfilled. Already, the grief group had worked wonders.

Symbolically, I was lying in the middle of our huge bed. *My* huge bed. No more sleeping on the left side. Also, the sun was streaming through the windows, and I could see the Japanese cherry tree, laden with impossibly pretty blossoms, gently swaying in the wind.

The mourning period was over.

Those others in the group last night—Leo losing his pregnant wife, poor Bree with the little ones, Janette watching her husband waste away, George after forty-three years—*they* had it rough. *They* had processing and stages and stuff.

Me, let's face it. I'd known Nathan only nine months. It was deeply sad, but it didn't have to be crippling. I'd be noble and, um, clean, that would be great. I'd get back to showering every day, and I'd go back to enjoying single life again.

I'd be so good, so kind, such a role model. My ex-cons (who'd sent a joint card, by the way) would love me all the more, and teenage girls would look up to me as an example of a life well lived, a person worth knowing. I'd be dignified yet also the life of the party (not that I'd ever been that, but it could happen). People would hear that I'd been widowed and be amazed. *Kate? But she's so happy! She's so giving and wonderful and fun!*

I lay there a minute, picturing this, feeling better for the first time since Nathan died.

Then I felt the familiar warm rush and accompanying cramps in my upper legs, flung off the covers and ran into the bathroom. Jazz hands didn't work. I flapped, jumped, the lights finally went on and I yanked down my sock monkey pajama bottoms.

My period. And not just any period, either, the Biblical period, the *is this a period or did I accidentally sever my femoral artery* period, the pajama-destroyer, the burn-the-mattress, and God! It was so unfair!

I wasn't pregnant. I wasn't pregnant. I *really* wasn't pregnant, and the throat-squeaking began. *I'm sorry. I'm sorry. Oh, little nonbaby, I'm so sorry!* My breath slammed in and out of me, *hehn-hehn-hehn-hehn*. My arms and legs buzzed with tingling so intense it hurt.

I was probably dying. My heart raced and zipped, and my vision started to gray, and I knew, I just knew, my life was ending, and anxiety and fear engulfed me in a cold wave. What about my nieces and nephew? Sadie wouldn't remember me! Would I see Nathan in heaven?

I bent double on the toilet. *Don't let me die here*, I begged my vague higher power. *Please don't let the paramedics find me like this. I don't mind dying, just not in a pool of menstrual blood with my sock monkey pajamas around my ankles.*

In for three, can't hold anything, can't think, jeez, listen to me, *hehn-hehn-hehn-hehn.* In for three, hold for three, out, *oh, Nathan, I'm so sorry I can't even have your baby and I wanted one so bad and I miss you, I miss you so, so much, I want you to be here, blinking those long blond lashes at me, saying something sweet, please come back, please, I just can't do this, please help me.* My hands fisted in my hair as I struggled not to list to one side.

Some distant part of my brain gave a wry smile. I guess the whole *not being sad* thing was off the table, then.

In for three, hold for three, out for three, hold for three.

In for three, hold for three, out for three, hold for three.

"Kate? You okay?"

I pressed my hands against my hot eyes. "I'm fine," I said, my voice wobbling and strange. "I got my period."

"You want me to come in?"

"No. No. I'm…"

"I'm right here. I won't go anywhere."

Thank God. I wasn't alone.

The lights went out; I flapped and they came back on. "Thanks, Ains," I said. I sounded more normal now.

Could I stand? Would my legs work? The answer was yes. I washed up, dug out the box of tampons, did what I had to do and pulled on Nathan's bathrobe.

It still smelled like him.

*Oh, Nathan, please help me. Give me a sign.*

There was no answer.

"Hi," I said, opening the door.

Ainsley had already stripped the bed. She hugged me. "I'm sorry," she said.

The spike was back in my throat. "I knew I wasn't. I took fourteen tests."

She laughed a little. "I was hoping anyway."

"Me, too." Never too comfortable with physical contact (except for when I was a wife), I stepped back. "You headed for work?"

"Yep. Guess what? Eric's blog has more than fifty thousand shares. Nice, huh?" She rolled her eyes. As always, she looked like Betty Boop in that 1950s, adorable style she had. Circle skirt printed with little umbrellas, white blouse with a Peter Pan collar, bright red lipstick. The only thing modern about her was her adorable cropped haircut.

I'd heard her crying last night, but she was smiling now, probably because I needed her to.

Eric was *such* an ass to leave her.

"What do you have going on today?" she asked.

"I actually have a shoot," I said. "A teenager who wants to be a model."

"Oh, fun! And it's gorgeous out, too. Where are you going?"

"Prospect Park. Brooklyn."

"That sounds great! More fun than my night. I'm going to Gram-Gram's for dinner. She needs help with her dating profile."

I felt a pang that Gram-Gram hadn't asked me, followed by relief. "You're a saint."

"Tell me about it." She smiled again, her sweet apple cheeks plumping. "You okay now? Sounded like maybe another panic attack in there."

I nodded. "I'm good."

"Okay. I have to go. Jonathan pops another hemorrhoid every time someone's late."

"Have a good day, Ainsburger."

She laughed at the nickname Dad always used and left the room, her nice orangey smell going with her.

I was so glad to have her here, and not at all sure I deserved her.

I'd always tried to be nice to my little sister, but it was hard sometimes. For one, Sean and I didn't remember a time without each other; Ainsley was thrust upon us. There was always the schism: if I loved Ainsley too much, I'd be too sad at the end of our weekends with Dad. If I found myself missing her, it meant I didn't love Mom enough.

When Ainsley came to live with us, it was even worse, because she was so little, so cute…and yet Dad wouldn't have left us without Michelle getting knocked up. For three years, I'd watched Mom's heart petrify, and then he was back, and with a cherubic toddler, too. Any time I spent with Ainsley, I felt like I was betraying my mother.

I should've done more. She was just a little girl. I shouldn't have been torn at all.

Just another item for the guilt pile.

Well. I had a shoot, and I had to get to Brooklyn by ten, and traffic would be hell because it was New York. Max was meeting me there. I threw some tampons in my purse and swallowed some Motrin.

The model in question was Elizabeth Breton, younger sister of Daniel the Hot Firefighter. She'd emailed me last week and said that her brother said he knew a professional photographer, and did I do head shots for modeling? She had a day off from school and she'd saved a hundred dollars of her babysitting money, less than a tenth of my fee.

She sounded so sweet and earnest that I said yes, that would cover it. Fashion shots weren't my specialty, but I'd done enough to be competent.

And it was awfully nice of Daniel to recommend me.

I still couldn't get over the fact that he'd come to the wake, all the way from Park Slope.

And that Paige hadn't. I did get a sympathy card with a white dove on it and the generic card message: *Sending you caring thoughts.* She'd written only her name.

Whatever. I had bigger sorrows than a shitty friend.

After I'd showered and dressed in jeans and a flannel shirt (no need to look pretty; that was the model's job), I went downstairs to make sure I had everything.

There was my Nikon on the shelf in the study. Or den. I'd never know for sure which room it was, since Nathan was dead.

Usually, I'd take that camera and my Canon; I liked to use a couple of cameras for their different qualities. But the last photos of Nathan were on my Nikon. Once I saw them…

My hands tingled, and the spike in my throat seemed to materialize like dark magic. I looked at my fish, swimming laconically in his pretty tank.

"Hi," I said. He mouthed back. *Hang in there*, I imagined him saying. *You still have me.*

When I arrived at the park, lugging my bag of lenses and filters, my camera slung over my shoulder, babies were out in full force. Beautiful, lovely babies in every color and age, running, yelling, crying, laughing, nursing and, in one case, being ignored as a mom complained loudly on the phone. For a second, I considered just pushing the stroller away and stealing the kid, but no, she gave me the side-eye.

I guess I'd been staring.

I hadn't *really* thought I was pregnant.

When I was about ten, my second cousin invited me to go on a trip. Our mothers had been close as children, and Mimi and I were about the same age and played together at Christmas. She was an only child, and when her parents booked a trip to Hawaii, they invited me to come along. We would helicopter over a live volcano and swim and take a surfing lesson.

It was, by far, the most exciting invitation of my young life. For weeks, Mimi and I talked on the phone—we would tame a dolphin, ride horses through the rain forest, and eat pineapples and coconut ice cream. It was incredible to think that I'd be going anywhere so exotic and different, that I'd have actual adventures.

The day before the trip, Mimi came down with appendicitis, and the trip had to be canceled. I was crushed, but as I cried into my pillow so my mother wouldn't hear, I also acknowledged I never really expected the trip to actually take place. It was too good to really happen.

That was how it was with Nathan and me and children. Unimaginably wonderful, so close…and then no.

"Kate. How are you?" Max appeared, unshaven, his white skin, dark eyes and black stubble making him look like a somewhat sickly vampire. Still, he had a thing going on. Balding, midfifties, that scary assassin voice… Women loved him.

"Max." We hugged briefly; he wasn't touchy-feely, and neither was I.

"You good to go?" he asked.

"Yep. We're meeting over by the Boathouse."

We walked under the Cleft Ridge Arch, where a toddler was testing the echo, and down Prospect Park's winding paths. The grass had been cut recently, such a happy smell. Overhead, the branches of the towering trees interlocked like a couple holding hands.

A beautiful, gazelle-like young woman wearing jeans and a T-shirt stood by one of the iron lampposts. Next to her was a suitcase, for wardrobe changes, I assumed. "Elizabeth?" I said.

"Hi! You're Kate?"

"Yes. This is my friend Max," I said. "Great to meet you. You're gorgeous!"

She beamed. "Thanks. I'm so glad you could do this. I looked at the rates for a fashion photographer and I almost had a heart attack, and that's when Daniel said to call you."

"I'm glad you did. Do you have a makeup artist?"

"No. I'm doing it myself."

"Got it. Max can help if you need to."

"I used to work for Bobbi Brown," he said.

"Really? I love their lip gloss."

"Hey. Sorry I'm late," came a voice, and there was Daniel the Hot Firefighter, clad in faded jeans and the requisite FDNY T-shirt, a denim jacket slung over his shoulder. Cue Donna Summer. *I need some hot stuff, baby, this evening…*

"I told you not to come," Elizabeth said, scowling.

"Sorry, Lizzie. It's my job to make sure you don't look like a slut. Mom's orders." Daniel winked at me, oozing testosterone as one did when one was FDNY. "Daniel Breton," he said to Max.

"Max Boreo." They shook hands.

"So Lizzie here thinks she's pretty enough to model," Daniel said.

"More than pretty enough," I agreed, though models had to be more than just pretty. Lizzie had dark brown hair and green eyes, perfect skin and a full, smiling mouth.

She and I talked about the looks she wanted for the portfolio—couture, which would involve the usual strange, heron-like poses; girl-next-door, which I was fairly sure she'd rock; drama, which would entail some crazy makeup and a close-up of her face. "Daniel says we can use his place for the indoor shots," she said.

"Where do you live, Daniel?" I asked.

"St. John's Place. Not too far."

I suddenly remembered a night at his and Calista's apartment nine or ten years ago, when we'd lived on 4th Street between 5th and 6th Avenues—how happy Daniel had been, pouring us wine, looking at Calista like she was the sun and stars. That was one of the things that made him so likable— he'd been an adoring husband.

I wondered if a person got over a love like that. Based on Daniel's dating history with the False Alarms, it seemed the answer was no.

Daniel caught me looking at him, and I turned my attention to my camera, adjusting the lens.

While Lizzie changed in the Boathouse, Max and I set up. Daniel texted and leaned against a tree. Max got out the reflector to make sure we'd have enough light on Lizzie's face. I checked the light meter and did a few test shots of the building.

Then Lizzie came out wearing a formfitting gold gown, her hair in a sleek twist, shimmering gold eye shadow and dramatic blush. "Holy shit," Daniel said. "How old are you again?"

"Almost seventeen."

"I thought you were twenty-four."

"That's Sarah, dumb-ass. I'm still in high school. If I was twenty-four, I'd be totally too old to start modeling."

He groaned. Max murmured something to Lizzie, and she opened her makeup case and handed him a tube of gloss and let him touch up her lips.

"We good to go?" I asked, and she nodded. "Okay, Elizabeth, show me what you've got."

She struck a pose, and all of a sudden, she went from cheeky girl arguing with her brother to a gorgeous woman, looking disdainfully at the camera while she raised one arm over her head. I crouched and snapped, circling around her, and she worked with me, following the camera with her eyes, angling her body. Then she shifted, hand on hip, one leg behind the other. Now an over-the-shoulder look. She arched her back and put her hand on her collarbone. Profile. Three-quarters. Her long neck arched gracefully, and she knew how to make her lines long and interesting.

"She's good," murmured Max, which was high praise, coming from him.

Some people gathered around to watch as Lizzie fluffed her gown, lifted its hem, leaned forward and smiled, then pouted, then glared. I gave her some instructions—*relax your hand, lower your chin, look down, close your mouth, use your neck.* Max moved the reflector and fixed her hair from time to time, and Daniel just watched.

"Come and take a look," I said after about half an hour, and she hiked up her dress and ran over. I clicked through the pictures, pointing out the ones I thought were best.

"When you're putting together the portfolio, use two or three for each outfit," I suggested. "Less is more, you know? And go with the wow shot. This one," I said, stopping at a shot of her standing in some impossible way where her long, slim body curved for miles from head to toe. "And this one." The shot of her glaring at me, eyes murderous.

She grinned, looking like what she was all of a sudden—a girl playing dress-up.

"Let me see." Daniel came over and stood behind me. "Shit," he murmured, his chin somewhere around my ear, his body pressed against my back. "She's beautiful." His breath tickled my hair, and my sad empty uterus tugged with attraction. Of course it did. He was Daniel the Hot Fire-fighter. Every uterus in the entire borough felt the same way.

I clicked to the next photo. "This one's nice," he said, and my entire left side shivered. Click. "But this one's slutty." Click. "Slutty. Slutty. Slutty. Beautiful." There went my left side again, buzzing with lust.

"Daniel, you don't get a say," Lizzie said. "Ignore him, Kate."

*Yes, yes, good advice.* After all, I was a widow who shouldn't be lusting after Brooklyn's Bravest, which was like saying "See that Border collie puppy? Do *not* think it's adorable."

Lizzie went to change again, and Max went with her, taking her makeup case for her girl-next-door look. When she came out, her hair smooth and parted on the side, a cropped top under a cute tweed jacket, skinny jeans and adorable high-heeled ankle boots, she looked like someone else entirely.

We walked to a different area to change up the setting.

"Let's have her lie down on that bench and let her hair stream down," Max suggested.

"Nope. Slutty," Daniel said.

Max sighed.

"Let's just go with sweet and happy," I said. "Think Maybelline or Dove soap, that kind of thing. Imagine you're waiting for a guy you like, and this is your first date."

Daniel scowled. "How about if she imagines she's about to go into the convent and can't wait to turn her life over to God?"

"You're such a loser," Lizzie said. "Okay. Waiting for boyfriend, check."

But when I held the camera up to my eye, I paused.

There it was, the little hint of what I couldn't see without the camera. While Lizzie was smiling, her eyes were different.

She glanced to her left and fixed her smile more firmly. A corner of her mouth twitched almost imperceptibly.

She was worried. Nervous.

I clicked the shutter button. Looked up at her and smiled. "Sweetness and light," I said, hoping to put her at ease. "You two will get ice-cream cones. He has a surprise for you, and it's a kitten! Aw! A kitten, how cute!"

She tried to look excited, but whereas she'd totally brought it earlier, her face was weird, shoulders tense.

"Does she have a boyfriend?" I murmured to Daniel, who was standing at my side.

"She better not."

"Does she, though?"

"Lizzie!" he barked. "You got a boyfriend?"

I sighed. There was a reason I'd asked him, not her.

"No," she said. "Not that it's any of your business." But she started to pick at her fingernail, then stopped. Tried to readjust, but her neck muscles were stiff. She glanced to the left again.

I put the camera down and went to sit next to her. "Does he come to the park a lot?"

She looked at me for a second, then her eyes filled with tears. "I broke up with him, and he's…he's not taking it well. I think he's…stalking me."

Daniel was at her side in a flash, kneeling at her feet. "Who? Who's the guy? Where does he live? What do you mean, not taking it well? Did he threaten you? Want me to talk to him? Let's go right now."

"No! Daniel, you'll just make thing worse." She looked at me. "I'm sorry."

"Don't be stupid," Daniel growled.

"He's probably not going to do anything." Tears spilled over and ran down her perfect cheeks.

"I'm less than reassured," Daniel said. "Come on. Tell me. Right now."

Lizzie looked at me, rather than her brother. "It's just…like, I was walking home the other day, and I heard him laughing, but when I turned around, I didn't see anyone. And then… I don't know. My phone rings at two in the morning, and it's 'Unknown Caller.' He never liked the idea of me trying to be a model. Yesterday, there was a note in my locker that said I was ugly."

Daniel started to say something, but I put my hand on his arm to stop him.

"You know," I told Lizzie gently, "if I had a pesky ex and a big strong firefighter brother, I'd probably work that angle."

"Listen to her. She's smart," Daniel said.

"I just want him to leave me alone. I don't think he'd…*do* anything. You know. Hurt me."

Daniel's arm turned from old-fashioned hard to iron under my hand. I squeezed his biceps to keep him calm (and for the thrill of it). "Right," I said. "But even if he's harmless and just being a jerk, it can't hurt for him to know you have this guy, you know what I mean?"

She picked her cuticle again. "Yeah. I guess."

"So maybe your brother should have a word with him."

"She's right," Daniel said, standing up. "Let's go."

"Daniel! Not this second! I'm getting my pictures done!"

"What's more important, you idiot?" he snapped. "Pictures, or your safety?"

"God! I knew I shouldn't have said anything!"

"Okay, how about this?" I asked. "Does this boy live fairly close?"

"Yes. Over on 8th Avenue."

"Let's finish this part of the shoot. Then you and Daniel

can go talk to the guy, Max and I will get a coffee, and we'll meet you at Daniel's after."

"Perfect," Daniel said, crossing his Thor-like arms.

"No. Please come with us," Lizzie said. "Daniel will beat Ewan up, and then the police will come and Daniel will get fired and Mom will have a fit and tell me how she'd only planned to have four kids, not five."

"Ewan?" Daniel said. "You dated a guy named *Ewan*? You didn't sleep with him, did you? Because that would break Ma's heart, and then I *have* to kill him, and you *will* go to the convent."

"Daniel, shush," I said. "You're not in a position to criticize names. Didn't you date a girl named Waterfall once?"

He glared at me. "I don't remember."

"Of course you don't, you slut," Lizzie said.

Max sighed, which silenced the rest of us. "Let me fix your makeup, honey. Then your brother can go scare the shit out of this boy, and we'll all be in the mood for drama shots."

"Like there's not enough drama with her already," Daniel muttered.

But Lizzie perked up, and within fifteen minutes, I had some gorgeous shots of her, her shiny hair and lovely smile.

"You just glow in this one," I said, showing her the shot. "And your eyes here are gorgeous."

Daniel was pacing, his arms crossed, which made for some first-rate arm porn. "Can we get going here? Someone threatened my little sister. I'd like to take care of it."

The little sister sighed. "Chill, Daniel." Now that the problem had a solution, she seemed back to normal.

Max glanced at his watch. "As much as I'd love to come and stand in the background like the angel of death," he whisper-said, which was exactly what I'd pictured, "I have to pick up the boys from soccer."

"Okay. I can handle the rest without you. Thanks, Max."

"Talk to you tomorrow." He walked off. A nearby toddler looked at him and ran wailing to her mommy, making me smile. Good old Max.

I put my camera in the bag. "You sure you guys want me to come?"

"Yes!" Lizzie said. "Please. If you don't mind."

"No, no, it's fine. It's kind of…" *Fun*, I was going to say. But it was, sort of. So much better than being back home.

Daniel grabbed my bag and the light reflector. He already had Lizzie's suitcase. "Want me to carry something?" I offered.

"Please. I'm a New York City firefighter. I could carry all this, you, her and a German shepherd."

"Be careful. My ovaries are melting," I said, getting a snort from Lizzie. "And *are* you a firefighter? I somehow forgot that."

"Right?" she said. "I don't think he owns a shirt that doesn't have FDNY on it."

"Hush up and lead the way, Lizzie," he ordered.

Despite the fact that we were on our way to deliver a verbal and hopefully not physical ass-whupping (or because of it… there was something very appealing about the outraged Brooklyn male protecting one of his own), I felt unexpectedly… happy. I snapped a few candids of Lizzie, who was bouncing around like a puppy now, swinging around a lamppost, hopping up on a rock, even doing a cartwheel on the grass.

We came out of the park into my old 'hood. Oh, the *buildings*.

There must be a term for us real estate junkies, who cooed over every building, every door, every planter. I took a few pictures of them, too, the gentle brownstones. A boy of about seven or eight skateboarded past me wearing a David Bowie T-shirt and pink-printed jeans. Ah, the hipster spawn.

When was the last time I'd been back in Park Slope? Two months? More? Nathan and I had come out for the biannual dinner to benefit the Re-Enter Center in February, and he'd grumbled about the traffic on the West Side Highway. It was one of his rare bad moods; the weather wasn't great, and parking, of course, was nonexistent, and the dinner was not the type of gala he usually went to; it was a spaghetti supper in the cafeteria filled with parolees.

Daniel hadn't been there; he'd been working, and I remember wishing he'd been there to meet Nathan and see that I was happily married. And maybe—maybe—to show Nathan that I had an extremely good-looking friend. You know how we women are.

Speaking of the man, the legend, the hot firefighter, Daniel was half a block ahead of me, his long legs and fury making him a lot faster. I ran to catch up. Lizzie pointed to the door and then cringed as Daniel ran up the stairs and pounded on the front door.

A young man opened the door. "Is this him?" Daniel asked his sister.

"Yes," Lizzie said.

Daniel grabbed him by the shirt, earning a yelp, and hauled him onto the stoop. Closed the door behind him so no parents would interfere (I assumed). The boy was cute, already manly but like a blade of grass compared to Daniel.

Daniel gave him a shake. "Did you threaten my little sister?" he growled. "This angel? This beautiful girl who means the world to me? Did you scare her somehow? Did you in any way make her life less wonderful for even one minute?"

The boy's eyes were wide, and he wisely opted not to struggle. "I...uh— Hey, Elizabeth, um, I... No? I mean, if I did, I didn't mean to?"

"What did he say to you again, Lizzie?"

"He said he'd make me sorry for breaking up with him."

Daniel gave Ewan a disappointed look. "Well, I'd say that sounds like making her life less wonderful, Ewan. What did you mean by that?"

"Um…I don't know. Nothing?"

"So you didn't mean you'd hurt her or scare her or follow her or bully her or spread rumors about her or make her life less wonderful in any way."

"No," squeaked Ewan. "I…I wouldn't do any of those things."

"So you were just hurt because she's moved on."

"Yeah."

"And she's perfectly safe in every conceivable way a person can be safe, is that right?"

"Yes."

"Did you know that in addition to me, she has forty-nine other firefighters in Park Slope who care very deeply about her personal happiness and safety? And not just that, Ewan. Did you know that we firefighters consider each other brothers and sisters? We do. So in a way, Lizzie here has more than ten thousand firefighters here in the greatest city in the world who are her brothers and sisters. Isn't that great?"

"Um…wow, yeah, that's great."

"It *is* great, Ewan," Daniel said. "It's so great. Lizzie is probably the most loved and protected girl in all of New York, don't you agree?"

"Yes."

"Is there something you'd like to say to my precious, angelic, perfect baby sister, Ewan?"

"Sorry?"

"Now, Ewan. You can do better than that."

I had to admit, this was *really* fun.

Ewan looked at Lizzie and swallowed. "I'm sorry if I scared you. I'd never do anything, not really. I was just…" He looked down. "Sad."

"And in the future, you'll just let yourself be sad, Ewan. Feel the feelings and leave my sister alone. Got it, son?"

"Yes."

"Yes what?"

"Yes, sir."

"If *anything* happens to her," Daniel said, "if a dog bites her, if a bridge falls on her head, if she's attacked by a shark, I'm holding you responsible." He looked at his little sister. "We good here?"

She nodded, smiling.

"Okay, you can go, Ewan," Daniel said, and the kid scrambled back inside the door.

Daniel and Lizzie came down the steps. "So much testosterone," I said to Lizzie, getting a smile from Daniel. "Where does he keep it all?"

"In barrels behind the garage," she said. "Can we still do the drama shots?"

"My place is way on the other side of the park," Daniel said, hefting her suitcase.

"So?" she said. "I thought you were Superman. Just fly us there."

"You know what? I'll call my tenants and see if they're in," I said. "My old place is three blocks from here. Maybe we can use it if they don't mind."

I texted my tenants, both doctors, who were at work. I'd given them a nice price on the rent, since they were both residents in pediatric oncology, and they always included a nice note with their rent payment about how much they loved the place. Take as long as you need, the husband texted.

So Daniel, Lizzie and I headed over to 4th Street. I glanced at him as we passed the house he used to live in with Calista, but he didn't look at it. If Lizzie was aware that he used to live there—she would've been a little kid back when he was married—she didn't say anything.

Funny, how simultaneously familiar and odd it felt to be back in my old building. The walnut railing felt as smooth and cool as ever, but I hadn't set foot in here since December. As we reached the third floor, it smelled different—a hint of curry and cardamom, and just the smell of someone else's house. I opened the door.

Home, yet not.

Different furniture, bright tapestry wall-hangings, a row of potted herbs on the kitchen windowsill. In place of my pink-and-green couch, there was a futon, and the TV sat on the floor amid a nest of wires and an Xbox. Still, the view across the street, through the branches of the locust tree, grabbed my heart and squeezed.

I missed it here.

"Okay," I said, clearing my throat, "why don't you change, Lizzie? The bathroom's down the hall."

An hour later, we had some great photos of the chameleon-like Lizzie, who'd opted for some very well-done Kabuki-style makeup; white skin, white lashes, black eye shadow and red, red lips. Daniel sighed wearily, muttered something about how she was playing with dolls not that long ago and stared out the window.

"Thank you so much for doing this," she said when she was back in her street clothes. "Here's your check. Totally worth it."

Daniel reached over, ripped up the check and said, "I got this."

"Really? Daniel! Just when I thought I hated you, I totally love you." She punched him in the stomach. Fondly.

He rolled his eyes. "I'm putting you in a cab."

"Mom thinks you're coming for dinner."

"I'm not. I'm taking her out." He jerked his head at me.

"You are?" I asked.

"Yeah. You free?"

"That was beautiful, Daniel," Lizzie said. "You've got game, big bro."

"Shut up. Her husband just died."

"Oh, my God! I'm so sorry!" Lizzie said, covering her mouth with her hand.

I shrugged, a little sad that the specter of my widowhood had been brought in. "Thanks."

Daniel looked at me. "Can I buy you dinner? Since you put up with me and my sister all day long? If you don't have plans, that is."

I hesitated. It sounded a little...date-ish. Then again, it was just Daniel the Hot Firefighter, and I'd aged out of False Alarm status fifteen years ago. "That would be nice," I said.

He smiled, and a lovely warmth filled my chest.

I wasn't sure that was allowed for a grieving widow, but it sure felt good.

We put Lizzie and her suitcase in a cab, and I assured her I'd get her the photos as soon as possible. I waved as she drove off. "Great girl," I said.

"Ah, she's not horrible, anyway."

"Didn't you use the words *perfect* and *angelic*?"

He laughed. "Maybe. You think she can be a model?"

"I don't know. I mean, in my opinion, sure. She has a lot of looks, understands angles, and she's definitely beautiful."

"She's watched that dumb modeling show since the beginning of time."

"I also watch that show. That's quality television."

He looked down at me and grinned. "Wanna go to Porto's? I'm starving."

The old hangout where Paige and I had spent so many evenings. "Sure."

A soft spring night, walking through my old neighborhood with Daniel the Hot Firefighter, who was not just hot but insisted on carrying my stuff, really good Italian food ahead... it was a field trip from my life. I could feel the sadness waiting for me once I crossed the Harlem River and headed back to Cambry-on-Hudson, but for now...for now, I was okay.

Porto's was exactly the same, thank God. It was still pretty early, before six, so we got a table. "Good to see you," Al said, the eponymous owner. "You want wine?"

"Um...sure."

"I'll get the wine list." He squeezed my shoulder—maybe someone had told him about Nathan—and walked away.

This would be my first alcohol since Nathan had died. Four weeks. Now that it was really, really proven that I wasn't pregnant, I could have a glass of wine.

Strange, to miss something that never was. To miss even the remotest possibility that I was pregnant with my dead husband's baby.

"So how you doing?" Daniel asked.

"Okay," I said, snapping out of my fog. "I mean... I don't really know. Today was a good day. Other days are...not good. How's that for eloquent?"

He nodded, looking right at me. That was something that was uncommon lately; people couldn't bear to look me in the eye.

Over the years when I'd run into Daniel, he'd be flirting, smiling, flexing and generally looking hot in a way that I appreciated but didn't really feel. His green eyes slanted down a little, and he had a killer smile (and knew it). His hair was cut very short, almost a crew cut, possibly because of work. Like all the other man-children in Brooklyn, he didn't shave daily. He was tall and had those ridiculously beautiful, strong arms; I'd once seen him flex his biceps for a False Alarm and actually tear his T-shirt. So yeah. I knew all that.

But today, he'd acted like any good big brother would, and now...well, he looked very... He looked *kind*.

"It's nice to be back here," I said, my voice a little husky.

"Good. How much do I owe you, by the way?"

"A hundred bucks."

"I'm guessing you charge more than that."

"Not today."

"How about three hundred? Would that cover it?"

"Daniel, you did me a favor. Plus, I plan to eat a lot tonight. A hundred is all I'll take."

He smiled. "Then make sure you order a bottle of expensive wine."

We ordered, and I picked out a not-too-expensive bottle of wine. "How are things at the Re-Enter Center?" I asked.

"Not bad. I got a good group this year."

"Carpentry, right?"

"That's right."

I had a sudden idea. "Hey, do you ever make furniture?"

"Sure."

"Do you think you could make a porch swing?" It would be the perfect present for my in-laws on their fiftieth. A beautiful, one-of-a-kind swing where they could sit and remember their dead son.

I swallowed. The spike was back.

"Sure, I could," Daniel said. "I made one for my sister a couple years ago. Is it for you?"

"My in-laws."

"Got it. Sure, I'll send you some pictures and you can see what you like." His phone chimed, and he glanced at it. "It's my lieutenant. I have to call in, but I'll be right back, okay?"

"Is it really work? Or is it a False Alarm?"

He looked confused. Right. He didn't know our name for his bimbos. "I'll just be a second."

"Yes. Go protect and serve."

"God, Kate," he said, tousling my hair. "Get it right. The cops protect and serve. We're New York's Bravest."

"Go. Be brave. Make that call." I smiled at him.

Al brought over a bottle of fumé blanc and poured me a glass. I took a sip. *Hello, wine, my old friend.*

The last time I drank wine was the night my husband died.

The wine soured in my mouth, and I had to force myself to swallow. If wine was ruined, Nathan's death would *really* be a tragedy. Right? Get that? Gallows humor. Ha. I forced myself to take another sip to ease the spike in my throat.

I'd brought Nathan to this restaurant a couple times. We'd sat in that booth over by the window. Once, we'd come with Paige, before we were engaged, before Paige had such a bug up her ass. Something got us women so silly we couldn't talk, and Nathan just sat there, smiling, and I remember just *loving* him so much, feeling my whole insides warm and—

Porto's door opened, and there was Paige as if I'd conjured her. She did a double take when she saw me, then came over.

As ever, she wore an awesome suit; she was the real deal of a corporate attorney. Heels, too. She looked fantastic.

I felt a stir of oily black anger.

"Kate?"

"Hey."

"What are you doing here?"

"Work."

"Oh." She set down her gorgeous leather bag. "Um, can I sit for a minute?"

I didn't want her to, but I shrugged. She sat.

"So. How are you?"

*Well, my husband died, and I seem to be having heart attacks every other day or so, and thank God my sister got dumped and moved in with me, because I'm so sad my bones hurt, Paige. They actually hurt.* "I'm fine."

What *was* it about female friendships? Why was it so crushing when they failed?

"Look," she said, and her tone was a little impatient. "I've been wanting to call you, but I really didn't know what to say. But you're good?"

"Fine."

I guess she could read something in my face. "Well, you're here, having dinner with a friend, I guess. That's a step in the right direction. It's good. You *should* get out, see people."

"I appreciate your input."

She took the veiled insult.

I'd talked to Nathan quite a bit about Paige after she dumped me. His take was that I was better off without her. Men never could understand women and their friends.

But I was a little obsessed. Who dumps a friend because that friend is happy? Though I did it on the sly, I checked her Facebook page, her Twitter, looked at her Pinterest board. She had one for wedding dresses, for God's sake, and it was public and under her real name. If there was a better way to scare off a potential boyfriend, I didn't know what it was.

She'd been my closest friend, and I didn't make friends easily. My *very* best friend, and all she could manage was to write her name at the bottom of a shitty card from Duane Reade.

"So you're just going to sit there and judge me?" she said.

"Pretty much, yes."

"Hey, Paige." Daniel returned, shoving his phone into his jeans pocket.

Her mouth fell open and her eyes widened. "Really? *Daniel?*"

"Yeah," he said. "Hi. How are you?" He sat down. "You joining us?"

"No," she said. "Wow, Kate. You're doing *much* better. Better than I would've thought."

That oily black anger bubbled, hot and sticky.

"Paige, don't be such a bitch," Daniel said easily. "She took some pictures of my sister as a favor. It's dinnertime. We're eating, not getting married, and how about a little compassion for your friend? Her husband died, in case you forgot."

Damn. That was perfect.

"Who can forget?" She stood up. "You two have a nice *dinner.*"

She left. My cheeks were hot with all the things I didn't say. The wine went down faster now.

"You okay?" Daniel asked.

"Yep. Fine."

"Why would you say fine? She's a pill. It's okay to admit it."

"We were friends for years."

"I know." There were those kind eyes again.

"So what's going on with you these days, Daniel? Got a girlfriend?"

"Nah. Not really. You know me." I smiled. "Family's good. Well, not really. My sister Jane, you know her?"

"No." I'd never met any of Daniel's family until today.

"Well, her husband left her. And she's seven months pregnant."

"Good God."

"Yeah. So I've been helping her out. She's got three other kids. My other sister has six."

"Nice. I have two nieces and a nephew myself. The baby's only three."

"Great age." He smiled.

We ordered, eggplant parm for me. He got steak (such a cliché) and a side of pasta, and a Caesar salad, too, and ate four pieces of garlic bread. Hungry lad.

He told me about work, brushing off the danger, sadness and fear that his job must entail, as was the way of every firefighter I'd ever met. I told him about Ainsley coming to stay with me, though not why, as well as some of the lesser challenges I faced as a widow: not understanding the complexities of Nathan's light switches, and having to jazz-hand in the bathroom, and eating under what seemed like an interrogation light because I couldn't figure out the dimmer switch in the kitchen.

We'd never really talked before, other than a few *hey, how's it going* conversations. Once in a while, we'd run into each other while teaching the ex-cons. Otherwise, no.

This was nice. Daniel laughed in the right places, kindly. There was that word again.

He paid for dinner, and I realized with a little shock that it was past eight.

"I'll walk you to your car," he said.

"No, it's fine. This is my old turf."

"I'll walk you, Kate."

"Okay. Thank you, Daniel the Hot Firefighter. And thank you for dinner."

We headed down the street, Daniel carrying my camera bag and reflector over one shoulder. The lights from the town houses glowed warm and little bits of music threaded through the air, but it was quiet, as Park Slope tended to be. Prospect Park was quiet, too. You'd never know you were in the city.

It was getting cold, and I shivered a little. Without a word, Daniel put his arm around me.

I wasn't sure how to feel about that. On the one hand, he was just Daniel the Hot Firefighter. On the other, he was Daniel the Hot Firefighter. He smelled good, a combination of soap and a little sweat and garlic.

I wasn't cold anymore. There was that, too.

When we got to my car, I stashed my bags in the trunk. "Thank you," I said. "This was an unexpectedly nice day."

"Well, thank you for doing this for Lizzie. She's already texted me six times about how great you are."

I smiled.

"Kate…" He shifted his weight and crossed his arms. "My sister Jane? The one who's pregnant?"

"Yeah?"

"Well, she lives in Tarrytown." It was the town south of Cambry-on-Hudson. "Maybe when I go up there, we could grab a beer sometime."

I hesitated.

"As friends," he added.

"That would be really nice," I said, a wave of relief washing over me. I liked Daniel. I always had. Just not that way. And obviously, I didn't want to date anyone.

"Good. I have your number. From your website. I'll call you sometime."

"Have a good night, Daniel. Be safe."

He winked at me, back to Daniel the Hot Firefighter, Conqueror of Vaginas, and headed off.

I took the long way home, opting to cross the East River via the Brooklyn Bridge and go up the West Side Highway, since it was more beautiful that way. I'd driven this route many times, back when Nathan and I were dating.

For a cruel, beautiful instant, I forgot he was dead. I

imagined telling him about Lizzie and Daniel and seeing Paige, imagined him waiting for me, his sweet, shy smile, his good clean smell.

The image was so powerful that I didn't realize the light had changed, and horns were blaring behind me.

# Chapter Fifteen

$\sim\!\!\!\gg\!\!\bullet\!\!\ll\!\!\sim$

*Ainsley*

In the past week, Eric was on TV four times.

It seemed that dumping your girlfriend after "surviving a horrific battle with cancer" played well in Peoria. *Good Morning America*, *The Doctors*, *Live with Kelly* (and I loved her, damn it!) and *Jimmy Kimmel Live!*. I DVR'ed them all. Of course I did, and watched it in Kate's media room one night when she was asleep, furiously eating popcorn, weeping, yelling at the TV and nearly choking at least twice.

He looked fantastic, the bastard, not like me, with red-rimmed eyes and popcorn in my cleavage. He said all sorts of sanctimonious things about the death of *this great friend of mine* ("One game of golf and your man-crush doesn't make him your great friend, you dick!") and about how *Sunshine was one of those people who had a pretty strict agenda of her own* ("To raise your children? That agenda? The reason we bought a house with four bedrooms?").

Wine was chugged from the bottle, I'll admit it.

To my relief, the hosts all gave him a hard time. He answered their questions with ease. "I do regret hurting her, believe me. But you can't live your life according to what you once wanted when something as radical as a near-death experience completely changes your priorities."

He used the words *live life large* eleven times in the four interviews. He'd gotten two tattoos since posting the Corpse blog. One said—surprise!—*Live life large!* The other was *NVC*... Nathan's initials.

I hoped the Coburns weren't watching my ex-boyfriend use their son for his fifteen minutes of fame.

Eric wasn't the only one who'd been approached by the media. Oh, yeah. I'd been called, too. Thanks, but no thanks. I let them all go to voice mail.

The Friday meeting with Eric that Jonathan had set up loomed like a tornado on the horizon. Eric had even sent me an email to confirm. And another to Jonathan, cc'ing me, saying how much he was looking forward to our "pitch" and seeing how it compared with the others he'd been fielding.

Jonathan had sent me a memo with bullet points on the pitch. It was color-coded.

At least I had Kate to look after. Though I felt guilty about it, I was glad to have a purpose. I baked her a chocolate cake to temper her cramps and found some sci-fi movies for us to watch. Brooke and her sons had come over the other night, and the second she walked in the house, Brooke started to cry. I took the boys into the media room and played astronaut with them, tipping them back in the chairs and doing a countdown with all sorts of drama and blastoff noises. At least I'd been able to make them smile.

Kate was quiet and appreciative. She'd always been on the reserved side, always seemed so together, always a little removed from the complicated, messy, intense feelings the rest of us dealt with. Maybe it was the camera, always by her side, always documenting life rather than making her live it, in a way.

Even so, I still felt fairly useless. I wasn't able to think too far into the future. My job wouldn't cover rent on a decent place in town, and I loved Cambry-on-Hudson. I scanned the internet for jobs that might pay more than the magazine, but there wasn't much out there. Nothing for philosophers, nothing for disgraced news producers.

Interior decorating might be fun, but I quickly learned that was a field glutted by housewives who thought they had good taste (like me); any real career came only after a degree and an apprenticeship.

Dog-washing? Dog-sitting? Ollie told me with his beautiful brown eyes that I was the world's greatest person. At least I had him.

On Monday night, Kate told me she was going back to the grief group, and I perked up. "That's great!" I said. "Hey, do you mind giving me a ride? Not to your group this time, but, well...maybe the divorce group."

And so it was that I walked into the basement of St. Andrew's, waved to the adorable Leo and the even more adorable George, then went into the next room. Alas, it was AA, where they were chanting the Serenity Prayer. I finished with them—"And the wisdom to know the difference" could be applied to so many situations, after all—then went into the correct room, according to the sign. *DWI: Divorce With Integrity.*

"Catchy name," I muttered.

And there was Jonathan, who did a double take at the sight of me. Super. Still, I smiled. It was not returned.

There was no Lileth for this group, just four people, two middle-aged women: one wearing yoga pants and a tired

T-shirt, no makeup; the other decked out in skintight leather pants, stacked heels and cropped top more suitable for an eighteen-year-old French prostitute than a fifty-year-old soccer mom. Tiny frame, double D boobs, tight eyes. Her teeth were so white they hurt my eyes. Seemed like she'd coped with divorce by becoming a plastic surgery junkie. She reminded me a bit of Candy.

For men, we had Jonathan and another guy, about forty.

"Hi," I said. "I'm Ainsley. I work with Jonathan, and my boyfriend of eleven years dumped me on his blog. Do I qualify for this group? The widows and widowers kicked me out."

They swarmed me (minus Jonathan). Marley and Carly were the women, each divorced in the past year, both with kids. Henry was the other guy—midforties, good-looking, well dressed and possibly in the closet. If not, I might introduce him to Kate. When the time was right, of course.

The metal chairs were in a circle, same as the grief group.

"Sit, sit," Carly (or Marley) suggested. "We'd love to hear your story. You're Sunshine, right? Sorry, I read the blog. Who hasn't?"

"Yep. Feeling more like a little black rain cloud these days." I looked at the chairs. "Can I make a suggestion? Is there any reason why we can't go out for a drink instead of staying here?"

"We always meet here," Jonathan said.

"You have a point," Marley (or Carly) said to me. "I could go for a strawberry daiquiri. Why *do* we meet here, anyway?"

"To avoid becoming bitter alcoholics?" Jonathan suggested.

"Who's bitter?" Henry said. "A piña colada would taste great right now. And if things go south, we know where to find AA."

Twenty minutes later, we were sitting in Cambry Burgers & Beer. I'd suggested Hudson's, which was closer, but

Jonathan grimly insisted on this place, which was lively and fun (surprising, because Jonathan had picked it.)

We ordered drinks and appetizers and exchanged the usual getting-to-know-you chitchat. Except Jonathan, who already knew me, of course.

"So I went on my fifteenth first date this weekend," Marley said (I'd ridden with them and figured out who was who on the ride over). She had an inch of gray roots showing and cracked her knuckles as she spoke. "He won't call. I'm surprised he even made it through the entire drink."

"What did you wear?" I asked.

"Does it matter?" Jonathan said.

I turned to him. "Yes. It's all about first impressions, Mr. Kent." I looked back at Marley. "I would love to give you a makeover."

"I've been asking her to let me do the same thing for a year," Carly said.

"So I can get a pair of these, Barbie? No, thanks," she said, jabbing Carly fondly.

"Maybe we could do mutual makeovers," I suggested. "All us women style each other."

"Except you, Ainsley, you're adorable. I wouldn't change a hair," Marley said. She chugged half her margarita. "You really think you could help me? I'm old, honey. I'm fifty-four."

"That's not old, and sure!" I said. "I love clothes. And makeup. And shoes."

"That would be fun," said Henry. "I'm a hairdresser. I'd love to have at you both. Not you, darling, you're perfect," he added, adjusting a strand of my hair. "Though a streak of gray would be very on fleek."

"I've thought about it," I said, smiling at him. "So on this first date, Marley, did you talk about your divorce?"

"Of course. He has to know what I've been through."

"Ah, that's a no-no. My mom is Dr. Lovely, the advice columnist. She just wrote about this."

"Really? I love her! I read her online every day! No wonder you know so much."

I smiled, oddly proud of Candy.

Jonathan stared fixedly at a point past my head. Carly detailed a wretched first date she'd had with a ninety-one-year-old man who'd lied about his age by three decades, and Henry told us he wasn't quite ready to put himself out there just yet.

I did wonder about Jonathan. I'd seen him on that date the night Eric dumped me. And I was dying to know what my stick-up-the-colon boss did in his spare time. Taxidermy seemed about right.

"Okay," Marley said after we'd put a dent in the appetizers. "We actually do talk about divorce stuff, Ainsley, so let's get down to business. Everything's confidential, okay? That's one of our rules."

"Nothing is confidential, since we're in a public place. Anyone could overhear us," Jonathan said.

"Who wants to go first?" Carly asked. "How about you, Ainsley? Since you're new?"

I had just taken a bite of a very delicious slab of quesadilla, but I nodded and chewed, held up my finger and chewed some more. "Well," I said finally, "my boyfriend seems to have had some kind of nervous breakdown or something. The man I love is not the man who's doing all this. But all this *is* being done just the same, you know? So how do you reconcile that? I mean, I want to get back together with him. How long do I put up with this? And how do I forgive him? And when do you think he'll snap out of it? He really was the best boyfriend ever."

Three sad, sympathetic faces looked back at me. Jonathan rolled his eyes. "Oh, save your contempt, Jonathan," I said.

"You didn't know him before cancer. He was *great* before cancer."

"He was your only boyfriend, isn't that right?" Jonathan asked.

"Yeah. So?" I was a little surprised Jonathan knew this.

"So you have no point of comparison."

"I didn't need one," I said.

"I told myself the same thing," Henry said. "That Kathy was going through a midlife crisis, that she wasn't herself and that we could get back to the way things were. Hasn't happened, and the truth is, I'm starting to feel...happy. Like I'm free from all the expectations of our life together and can start to be the real me."

Hairdresser, piña colada, free to be the real me. Yep. Henry would be marching in the gay pride parade next spring. Maybe Deshawn and he could hook up. The old opposites attract thing.

Carly talked about how her ex never spent any time with their kids, just kept sending checks, and how the kids' resentment was aimed at her. Henry commiserated, saying how much he missed being in the same house with his sons every night. Marley was going to be an empty nester this fall and was dreading it. "It feels like the world is going to end, and I have to sit there and pretend to be happy about it," she said. Henry handed her a napkin so she could blot her eyes.

I wondered if I knew someone for Marley. She seemed awfully nice. I'd visit Gram-Gram and check out the younger residents. She might like being a trophy wife.

"What about you, Jonathan?" Carly asked, leaning forward to flash a few inches of cleavage. "Last week, you said... How did you put it? There was someone you thought you had feelings for, remember? But it was difficult?"

*Thought he had feelings for.* The man was Mr. Spock. *What are these emotions I'm experiencing? Let me do a brain scan and analyze the results.* I bet it was the woman he'd been with on that date. She'd seemed nice. Nicer than he was.

"I'd rather not discuss it," he said. "Ainsley is my employee, and I'm not comfortable sharing details of my personal life with her."

"But she's so *nice*," Marley said. Aw. "Maybe she could help you. And Dr. Lovely is her mother."

"Well, stepmother," I said. "Jonathan knows her, too. She writes for his magazine."

"Of course, of course."

I shifted to see my boss better. "I am pretty good with that kind of thing. Maybe I could help you."

"You couldn't."

"I bet I could."

"While I admire your confidence, no, thank you."

"I see. You're chicken."

He sighed. "No, Ainsley, it's not that. It's that I have two children to consider."

"I use that excuse, too," Henry said.

"And second, I don't think you're in a position to offer relationship advice. Forgive me if that sounded rude."

"It *is* rude. Just own it," I said. "Was it that woman from Le Monde? Points to you for taking her somewhere nice."

"So you've already been on a date with her?" Marley said. "What about a second date? Is that when people typically have sex?"

He closed his eyes. "As I said, I'm not comfortable discuss—"

"Send flowers," Carly suggested. "Every woman loves flowers."

"Nah," I said. "That's for later in the relationship. First he has to show her he has what she wants. What all women want."

"A lot of money?" Carly suggested.

"No, no. Though it never hurts."

"And what do all women want, in your vast experience?" Jonathan said.

"Honesty." I sat back, proud of the answer.

"Oh, good one," Carly said. "My ex had an entire apartment in Manhattan I didn't even know about. But since we're a fifty-fifty state, he had to buy me out, so I got the girls done—" she pointed proudly to her bosom, which was big enough to hold a generous plate of pasta "—had a little *refreshing* done and took my sisters to France for a month. Oh, that made him mad!" She smiled fondly.

"Sense of humor is another one," I said. Poor Jonathan. I might as well have said *grow sparkly wings*. "Being open to new things." Pause for laughter. "And kindness, that's the most important."

Trying to save Nathan's life...that had been kind. Or a reflex. But he'd stayed at the hospital. That had been very decent of him.

"It's the little things," I went on. "Holding doors and such. Let her talk and pretend to pay attention."

"Pretend? That's your advice? How fascinating."

"See?" I said. "You're doing it already."

"I still say you can't go wrong with flowers," Carly said. "Or just whisk her off to the city for dinner. Shock and awe, razzle and dazzle."

The others continued with their suggestions. Buy her a puppy, send her secret notes, flirt with her (like he could pull that off).

"I appreciate your suggestions," he said. "Perhaps we can move on."

"Did anyone ever tell you you talk like you're on *Downton Abbey*?" I asked, smiling at him.

"Not until just now."

"You do. You have a very formal way of talking."

He blinked at me, clearly pained.

"I love it," Marley said. "If you were ten years older, Jon."

He smiled at her.

Huh. I couldn't say I'd ever seen him smile before. It was an unexpectedly sweet smile, just a curve of the lips and a slight crinkle to his eyes.

And he was still wearing the suit he wore to work, except his tie was a tiny bit loosened, and...well...he was suddenly... attractive.

"I'd better head off," he said.

"Would you give me a ride home?" I heard myself ask.

The smile was gone. "Of course."

"It was great meeting you," I said, putting down my share of the tab as well as a healthy tip. "Hope to see you again." They answered in a chorus of goodbyes.

We walked out to Jonathan's car, a very sleek Jaguar. Maybe the magazine industry wasn't so bad after all.

He held the door for me. I got the sense that his nanny would beat him with a cane if he didn't. "So why did you get a divorce, Jonathan?" I asked as he got in.

He didn't answer for a minute, just pulled carefully onto the street. "I'd rather not discuss it," he said.

"Okay. Sorry."

"It's all right."

"I really could coach you on dating, you know," I said.

"I appreciate the offer, but no, thank you."

"How old are your children?" Apparently, I was not the *sit in comfortable silence* type.

That smile, though. That had been a very nice smile.

"Emily is eight, and Lydia is six."

"Do you get to see them a lot?"

"Yes. My ex-wife and I share custody. A week with me, a week with her." He turned, knowing where Kate's house was, I presumed, because he knew everything about this area. It *was* a famous house in our fair city.

"Does your ex live in Cambry-on-Hudson?"

He glanced at me. "Yes. We didn't want the girls to have to experience any more change than was necessary."

"Right. Of course."

We were quiet for a minute, and I looked out the window at all the pretty houses. If we took a right at the stop sign, and then a left, and another right, we'd be on the street where I used to live.

Used to.

"I won't say anything," I said, still looking out the window. "About your divorce or anything. You don't have to worry about that."

"I'm not."

That was all he said. I wasn't sure if it was a compliment or a threat.

A minute later, he pulled into Kate's driveway. The house was lit up, glowing from the exterior lights that my sister couldn't manage to turn off. Several trees and a modern statue were lit from the base.

"How is your sister these days?"

"Quiet. Sad."

He nodded. "Please give her my best."

For once, his formal language didn't put me off. He looked at me for a long minute, not blinking.

If I'd been with anyone else, I would've thought he wanted to say something.

I wasn't used to just looking at him; in fact, I rather specialized in avoiding exactly that, since he was usually frowning in disapproval at me. But in the glow from the car light, it seemed that one of his eyes had a flake of gold in it. Yes. It did. The other one did not.

"Your eyes don't match," I said. My voice was a little strange.

He blinked. "Sectoral heterochromia," he said, glancing at his hands, then back at me. "A color abnormality in one part of a person's eye."

"Oh." It was rather hypnotic, that mysterious bit of gold in the pale green…or blue. His eyes weren't the lifeless alien pale color I'd always thought. No, on closer inspection, they were made up of pieces and shards of blue and green, and that one little patch of pure gold sitting at eight o'clock in his left iris.

I was staring.

Jonathan's mouth moved. It wasn't exactly a smile as much as…well… I didn't know what.

"Good night, Ainsley. Try to be on time tomorrow."

I cleared my throat. "Will do. Thank you for the ride."

Then I got out, the spring air cool on my surprisingly hot face.

The next morning, I made it to work at 8:31. I would've been in at 8:30 if not for a school bus driver who decided he had to have a chat with a kindergartner's dad. I slid into my desk, but not before Jonathan looked up, irritation quirking his mouth downward. Because I was sixty seconds late.

If there had been a moment in the car last night, it was probably only in my imagination. In fact, thinking about it, I was sure it was.

Ten minutes after I sat down, Rachelle's voice came over the intercom. "Ainsley, there's someone here to see you." Her usually mellow voice was tense.

Oh, God. Eric. Was it Eric? Finally! My knees and elbows

tingled, and my heart seemed to lurch into my throat. "I'll be right out."

Everything was going to be all right. Everything would go back to normal. He'd have the ring. He'd apologize. Once I saw him and how sorry he was, all the love would come flooding back and I'd forgive him. We'd never gone so long without seeing each other, and just the thought of being close to him again made my whole body thrum. I hadn't let myself miss him yet, too consumed with anger and embarrassment. But God, I'd missed him.

I checked my reflection in my computer screen, fluffed my hair a little and pinched my cheeks, like Scarlett O'Hara. Eric! I was about to see Eric at last. My knees tingled as I walked into the reception area.

It wasn't Eric.

It was his mother. My heart fell into my shoes.

"Honey," she said, rising, tears filling her eyes. "Can we talk?"

"Is Eric okay?" I asked.

"See, I knew you'd ask. I know you still care, I do, honey. Yes, he's fine. Well, if you can call this grizzly bear fixation *fine*. Can we go somewhere private? He's losing his mind!"

I ushered Judy into the conference room. Jonathan came in almost immediately, as I knew he would. It was his magazine, after all, and he had to monitor all activity, especially anything personal.

"Good morning," he said, leaning in the doorway. "I'm Jonathan Kent."

"Judy, this is my boss, Jonathan Kent. Jonathan, this is Judy Fisher. Eric's mother. Did you meet at Eric's…um…" My voice trailed off.

"You were so wonderful to try to help poor Nathan," she

said, holding his hand with both of hers. "And of course, Eric loved having his blog here. Oh, dear, this is such a mess."

"Would you like some coffee?" he asked.

"No, no, I'll just be a moment. Thank you."

He glanced at me, and I could see the irritation in his special hetero-something eyes. "So. Ainsley, you'll have that piece on Labor Day events for me soon?" The reminder that we were at work, in case I forgot.

"You bet." I would have to *start* it soon, actually. He left, closing the door behind him.

"Did you see Eric on TV?" Judy asked. "Our hearts are broken! He looked so handsome, though, didn't he? I don't know what to do, Ainsley! Please don't give up on him yet."

"Judy, believe me, I—"

"You *know* how he is with stress. He wet the bed when he went to camp the first time! When he was eleven and had his first erection, he was afraid it was cancer. Oh, God. How's that for irony? Maybe we should've taken him to the doctor back then. Maybe we would've caught it early."

"He did catch it early."

She gripped my hands. "Listen. He's not going to backpack through Alaska. What if he falls and gets hurt? Who will take care of him?"

"I don't know. I don't care at this point." If only that was true.

"Oh, honey! Don't say that! He's had a meltdown. You can't stop loving him! You're the best thing that ever happened to him. You do still love him, don't you?"

I pulled my hands free and rubbed the back of my neck. "I don't know, Judy. I mean, of course I do. But this new guy... the one who calls me a corpse and goes on *GMA* and *Jimmy Kimmel*...he's completely different."

"I know. It's shock. He loved Nathan like a brother."

"No, Judy, he barely *knew* Nathan. Nathan was *my* brother-in-law, and *I* barely knew Nathan."

She looked at me, her face drawn in concern. "Ainsley, honey. You have eleven years with our son. That's a third of your life. Don't forget that!"

"I know. But..." My throat closed, my eyes filled. "He's the one who forgot, Judy. It's like I'm a stranger he doesn't care about at all anymore." I swallowed a sob. "He hasn't even been over to see Ollie."

We'd had Ollie for two years. How could a person just ditch his dog like that?

Or his woman?

"He does love you," Judy said. "You just wait, and you'll see. Please. This cancer scared him so badly. You know that better than anyone. I think it's post-traumatic stress, that's what I think."

I took a breath and swiped under my eyes with my fingertips. "You could be right."

"I am. I know it. I'm his mother, and I know." She kissed my cheek with vigor and looked into my eyes. "Aaron and I love you, sweetheart. We want you to be the mother of our grandchildren. You're like a daughter to us, you know that. Please, just keep an open mind."

"Okay." I hugged her. "I have to get back to work. Talk to you soon."

"I love you."

That caused more tears to flood my eyes. "Love you, too," I whispered.

Judy and Aaron were more like my parents than Candy and Dad. If I lost Eric, I lost them, too. No more annual Broadway shows, no more mani/pedis with Judy where we gossiped and laughed. No more beautiful Hanukkah nights, lighting the candles, Judy exclaiming over the gifts I chose so carefully. No more vacations where the guys played golf and Judy and I had a fruity cocktail on the beach.

No more unconditional love.

I went to the bathroom to make sure my mascara hadn't smudged. It had, of course. I ran a tissue under my eyes, blew my nose and washed my hands.

When I got back to the desk, there was an email from my boss.

Please refer to page 29 of the employee handbook about personal matters being handled during work hours.
Jonathan Kent, Publisher
*Hudson Lifestyle*

I typed back, my fingers hammering the keys.

Please refer to the fact that the publisher of *Hudson Lifestyle* is making me meet with our problematic blogger, so maybe getting some insight from his mother about his current mental state isn't the worst idea in the world.
Ainsley O'Leary, Features Editor
*Hudson Lifestyle*

A second later, my computer dinged.

You may have a point. Please try to refrain from crying in the bathroom, however. It's bad for morale.
Jonathan Kent, Publisher
*Hudson Lifestyle*

I typed my response, then deleted all the F-bombs, then realized the F-bombs made up the whole email.

Whatever. I had an article on pumpkins to write.

# Chapter Sixteen

❧

*Kate*

When I got home that night, the house smelled fantastic. Ainsley was in full 1950s housewife mode, still wearing blocky little heels, an apron over her cute little flowered dress.

"Wine?" she asked with a smile. "I'm making a roast with mashed potatoes, braised carrots, a little wilted spinach on the side. And there's coconut pie for dessert."

"You're amazing, Ainsley." I raised my camera—the Canon, not the Nikon—and took her picture.

Ah. There it was, the real deal. She was confused and angry and sad. What Eric was doing was a joke—another idiot being controversial whose fifteen minutes would soon be up.

"How was your day?" she asked, pouring me some vino.

I put down my camera and sat at the soapstone counter. "It was okay," I lied. "I had lunch with my mother-in-law at the club." There'd been a line of people—a *line*—who wanted to talk and pay their respects. My cheek had been kissed so many times I had a headache from all the Estée Lauder perfume that seemed to be a requirement of female club members over sixty. "Eloise is…" My voice choked off.

"I can't imagine how she's coping."

I shook my head. "She always says the right thing, she's nice to everyone." I hesitated. "But she doesn't want to talk about Nathan. At least, not with me."

"How's Mr. Coburn?"

"Medicated. Drinking a lot. So we talked about nothing. The only safe topic is Miles and Atticus."

"They're so cute."

Atticus resembled Nathan an awful lot. It was hard to look at him. I cleared my throat. "I went back to the house, and Mr. Coburn asked if we could blow up a picture of Nathan for their anniversary party. As a cutout, you know? He'd been drinking, and…"

Those little strangled noises were coming out of my throat. Not crying, no, that would be too normal. Just vocal chord spasms as the air tried to escape from my locked throat.

"Oh, honey." My sister came around the counter and hugged me. Her dog whimpered, dragging his little baby blanket to me. Sweet puppy.

Last night, I'd had a dream about Nathan. We were hosting a party. I didn't know anyone there, but it was our house, and as I went to find Nathan, I saw him heading for the cellar door. I knew in a flash that if he went through that door, he wouldn't come back, that he'd cross to the other side. I called to him, and he turned and smiled, that sweet, sweet smile…and went in anyway. I tried to follow, but the door had disappeared, and everyone was telling me what a great party it was while I groped along the wall, trying to find a spring or latch so I could find Nathan and bring him back.

Ainsley was back on her side of the counter, checking the roast.

"I'm so glad you're here," I said, and her face lit up.

"Really? I feel like an idiot half the time."

"You're not. You've been fantastic, Ains." Ollie, aware that someone other than himself was getting praise, put his paws against my legs. "And so have you, Ollie-Dollie," I said, picking him up. He had the silkiest ears in the universe. I could well understand the value of therapy dogs.

"So what's new with you?" I asked, dipping my finger in the wine and letting Ollie sniff it. Not his vintage, apparently, because he jumped down and trotted back to his blanket.

"Oh, let's see. Judy came to see me at work today," Ainsley said. "To beg me not to give up on Eric just yet. She thinks he's got PTSD."

I thought he had asshole-itis, personally. I'd seen a snippet of him on *Good Morning America* and hit Off so fast I nearly broke the remote. "What if he does come crawling back, Ainsley? Would you give it a shot?"

She didn't answer right away, putting the spinach in the frying pan. "I never pictured a life without him," she said, not looking at me. "I know we had a...retro kind of relationship, but it really was all I ever wanted. So I guess I'd try to forgive him, sure. He'd deserve that after eleven years, right? I mean, what else would I do? It's not like I love my job. I was never the career people you and Sean are."

"You were so good at NBC," I said.

"You mean covering for America's most lying newsman?"

"You can't take the blame on that. You didn't know."

She was quiet for a minute. "Eric exaggerated on his blog, too."

"Yeah, no kidding."

"You knew?"

I snorted. "Of course I did."

"Do all men lie, do you think?" she asked.

"All people lie at one point or another." I paused. "Dad lied to Mom for years."

"Right." She nudged the potatoes. "Did Nathan?"

I paused. "No. I don't think so."

"He was so nice."

For a second, I imagined Nathan coming in here, wearing one of his beautiful suits, tossing his keys into the tasteful wooden bowl he had for the sole purpose of holding keys, and saying, *Was? What do you mean, was?* He'd kiss me and then go hug Ainsley and say something nice to her...and...and...

His face was growing blurry to me.

That horrible spike was back in my throat. I took another healthy sip of wine.

"What's it like?" Ainsley asked, her pretty face kind. She still looked twelve to me.

I didn't answer for a moment. *It feels like someone peeled off my skin. Everything hurts or stings or bleeds. I don't even feel like a person anymore, just a raw piece of meat that has to get out of bed.*

Some things you just didn't want to put into words. "It's like being in a dream. Like I'll wake up in my old apartment and think, 'Wow, that felt so real!'"

"Does the group help?"

I'd gone twice now. "Yeah, it does, actually. Just knowing they're alive. Leo's really happy these days. Even LuAnn—you know, the one with the makeup and the Bronx accent? She's heartbroken, but she's still laughing. So. Maybe I'll get there."

"You will."

The wine was giving me a nice buzz. "That photo shoot I did in Brooklyn the other day? That was a good day. I saw an old friend. It was fun."

"You deserve some fun."

"It was nice while I was there, like yeah, I lost my husband, but I could handle it. And then I got back home here, and I ended up sleeping on the couch, because our bed is just so big."

I wasn't used to this…heart-to-hearts with my sister, who'd always seemed so different from me, so much younger. Yet here she was, pretty much saving my life by living here, even if it wasn't her choice. "I felt like I was cheating on him," I went on. "Because I'd had a nice day. Had dinner with a friend, who's a good-looking guy."

"So no nice days for the widow. And you have to ditch all your good-looking friends. Got it." She cocked an eyebrow at me. "You think Nathan would want you to be miserable? Don't you think he feels guilty enough, dying and leaving you alone? Get real, Kate. If you have a good day, grab on to it. Now sit. Dinner's ready."

She chattered about work, about a coworker named Rachelle who'd gone out with a guy who owned seventeen ferrets he regarded as his children, but because he had a job and paid for dinner, Rachelle agreed to a second date. About how the magazine would be sponsoring a Thanksgiving pie contest, and all the ingredients had to be from within a fifty-mile radius.

She was gifted at charm. I never valued that in her before, but I felt like kissing her hand now. I should write to Eric and thank him for being a self-centered idiot.

I ate enough to get me to the next meal; food had lost its taste, though Ainsley was a great cook. Then I shooed her off to do her thing and cleaned up the kitchen. I still didn't know where everything went, but cleaning was satisfying, making everything perfect again, the way Nathan had liked it. I oiled the soapstone and scrubbed the sink and looked for the switch that would turn on the undercounter lighting, because that was how my husband had liked it.

"Nathan?" I whispered. "Are you okay?"

There was no answer.

Maybe I'd call a medium, someone who'd know where Nathan was. She could tell me he felt no pain and that he loved me and I should live a happy life.

Except I already knew those things, mostly. The coroner said he died instantly.

I gave up on the light switch and went into the den (or study), found the switch on the first try and sat down. This was where Nathan had worked from home.

The room still smelled like him.

He'd been making a plan for his parents—a home expansion so they could live on the first floor. Their house was huge, but formal, and he'd had this idea of knocking out the back, redoing the kitchen and putting on a big bedroom with a huge, wheelchair-accessible bathroom, should that day ever come. It was going to be a surprise, these plans. Their gift for their fiftieth anniversary.

I had a sudden flash of inspiration. I'd have someone at Nathan's firm finish the plans—Phoebe, was that the name of the nice woman? I could give the plans to the Coburns, and they'd have part of him, his beautiful work, in their home for the rest of their lives.

I clicked on his mighty Mac and waited. The desktop background was our wedding picture.

There he was. The little mole on his cheek, his reddish blond hair, the slash marks (not dimples) that showed when he smiled. Pathetically, I touched the screen, wanting to remember what his cheek felt like.

At the bottom of the screen, the little red number on his email icon went from three to seventy-four.

Shit. I should've checked this before. I'd have to close his account.

I clicked the icon and started scrolling through the new messages.

Three were from coworkers on April 6, before he…fell. The other seventy-one were junk mail about exciting investment opportunities and seminars and a few for cheap Viagra.

"He didn't need it," I said to the computer.

His email folders were neatly labeled: Wildwood, Jacob's Field, Oak Park—all developments his firm was building. I wondered if I should forward these folders to the firm. I'd call Phoebe, if that was her name.

There was another folder called Travel, which contained details on a few upcoming business trips he wouldn't go on. Another called Computer Info, which had warranty information and the like.

And there was a folder called Kate. Unable to resist, I clicked on it.

All the emails I'd ever sent him.

From the first one, sent not even a year ago, to the last—the day he died, I'd asked him to pick up (you guessed it) wine. I'd signed it *Love you, you big dork.* I can't remember why I'd called him that. I mean, he *was* a big dork, but… And he'd saved even that note. Something as mundane and ordinary as that, but he'd taken the time to file it away.

I felt the tears coming, felt my eyes moistening, and thank *God.* All this time, I hadn't cried a single drop. Surely, this would make me feel better, more normal, would start the healing process. If I could have a good cry, maybe that spike in my throat would start to disappear.

Out of the corner of my eye, I saw another folder.

MRT.

The tears paused. *No, no, keep coming,* I told them, but even then, my hand was on the mouse, clicking the folder after only a second's pause.

All these emails were from Madeleine Rose Trentham, the former Mrs. Nathan Coburn III.

There were quite a few of them. Twenty, twenty-five. All read, some with the little purple arrow indicating a reply.

The first one was dated September 28, four or five weeks after we'd started dating.

The last one was dated April 5.

The day before he died, ninety-five days after we got married, he'd been talking to his ex-wife.

# Chapter Seventeen

*Ainsley*

On Friday at 5:01, Jonathan and I got into his stupid Jaguar and headed into the city.

"Are you prepared for this?" Jonathan asked.

"No!" I snapped. "I told you this is a terrible idea."

He sighed and put on his signal to turn onto Route 9. "Ainsley, I realize this is painful for you on a personal level. But professionally, you have to acknowledge that *you* were the one who forced the issue with *The Cancer Chronicles*. The fact that Eric finally managed to write something interesting, while shocking, *was* the original point of the column. Eric's notoriety will increase readership. Controversy sells."

"I *know*, Jonathan," I snapped. "But this isn't exactly *Time* magazine featuring a mother nursing her fourth-grader! This is Eric being a dick. How does that fit into a lifestyle magazine? Our last cover was about the lost art of blacksmithing!"

"I remember," he said drily. "You did a nice job with that, by the way."

"Was that a compliment?"

"It was."

I stared straight ahead. "Well, it doesn't make up for this."

"While we're discussing work, perhaps we could schedule your employee review."

"I think I'm suffering enough, Jonathan, don't you?"

"You can't avoid it forever."

"Can't I? I'm going to try."

"Now that you're here, and I'm here—"

"Jonathan. Please. Not now. I'm doing this pitch for you, okay? We'll do the review next week." Or not, if I could help it.

"You were late again this morning. That makes seventeen days in a row."

Jesus. "I'm sure you have more statistics back in a file in your office, just waiting to humiliate me. Let's wait so we can milk it for all it's worth, shall we?"

He sighed.

"You can always fire me, you know," I suggested.

"I was thinking that if you landed Eric as a columnist, I'd have to give you a raise."

I hadn't had a raise since I'd started.

And now that I was trying to support myself, a raise would be really helpful.

Jonathan glanced at me.

Funny. His eyes, which I could've sworn were blue this morning, looked very green now. And I wanted to see that little flake of gold again. I'd Googled the term he used—*heterochromia*. Very cool, making my own run-of-the-mill brown eyes feel very dull by comparison.

I adjusted my skirt. Oh, I'd gotten dressed very carefully

this morning, let me tell you. I wanted to look chic, sophisticated, calm and so frickin' beautiful Eric would feel like his legs were shot out from underneath him. I'd squeezed myself into some horrible thigh-to-neck undergarment to make me look smooth and curvy, if not exactly svelte, and chosen a sleeveless black turtleneck dress, wide red leather belt, oversize mustard bag and leopard-print shoes with red soles (fake Christian Louboutins, very affordable). It had taken twenty minutes of blow-drying, ten minutes with the hair iron and three hair care products to get my cute little elfin cut to look completely natural and unself-conscious. Of *course* I'd been late for work.

"Having Eric with us would be very good publicity for the magazine," Jonathan said.

"I *know*." It irritated me that he had such a beautiful speaking voice.

"I think the pitch would be more effective coming from you."

"I know."

"And I appreciate you doing it. Thank you for not quitting." He slowed down for the Henry Hudson Bridge tollbooth.

So Jonathan was being nice, which made me even more off balance.

The thing was, I hadn't seen Eric since he dumped me.

I missed him so, so much. I missed feeling special. I missed his laugh, his beautiful thick hair, the way he got down on the floor and played with Ollie, barking at him till our dog ran in circles of joy so fast he was just a little brindled blur. I missed sex. I missed feeling like I was home.

"So where are we meeting?" I asked.

"The Blue Bar at the Algonquin."

Of course. If you were an aspiring writer, as Eric now

seemed to be, you'd pick the most pretentious (and expensive) bar in New York City.

I let out a huffy breath.

By the time we'd inched through Times Square traffic, I was seething inside. I loved Eric. I hated Eric. This was not going to go well.

We parked in one of those underground garages that charges a kidney and both retinas for two hours, and walked up to the Algonquin. I might have to break it to Eric that Ernest Hemingway was dead, and they weren't about to be best friends.

Jonathan held the door for me, and I took a deep breath, sucked in my stomach (why couldn't I be more like Kate and lose weight in times of stress?) and went in.

There he was, already at the bar, martini glass in hand.

Everything inside me squeezed. Love, betrayal, anger, loneliness, everything, wadded into a tight ball of emotion.

"Hi," I said, and to my irritation, my voice was husky.

"Ainsley." He got up and kissed me on both cheeks. He smelled different, but the same. A new cologne, but still my Eric.

I had to press my lips together to avoid crying.

"You look beautiful," he said, smiling. I didn't answer. Round one went to Eric—I was more shaken by seeing him than he was at seeing me. "Jonathan. Good to see you. How are subscriptions?"

"Very healthy, thank you. We've seen a bump since your column."

Eric smirked. How gratifying for him that Jonathan, who'd clearly thought his blog was idiotic, was now wining and dining him.

"Shall we get a table?" Jonathan suggested, and we did,

the blue light making us all look like aliens. The waiter came right over.

"What would you like to drink, Ains?" Eric asked. "I'm having The Hemingway, and it's delicious."

I glanced at the menu. Name aside, it was a girlie drink with fruit juice and a sugar rim. To be true to Hemingway, it should've been a shot of whiskey mixed with bull semen. "I'll have a Ketel One martini, extremely dry, two olives, please," I said. *I* could drink a real martini, thank you very much.

"Bowmore single malt," Jonathan said.

"On the rocks?"

"Good God, no." So round two went to Jonathan.

"I'll have another Hemingway, Jake," Eric said. Ah. He was friends with the server. How cute.

My chest hurt.

Eric wore a dress shirt unbuttoned a few, a gray suit jacket and jeans. His hair had grown in the weeks since I'd seen him, and he'd gelled it to stick up in front.

He looked hot, in other words.

"Ollie says hello," I said.

His eyes flickered. "How's he doing?"

"Great. Sweet as ever. Perhaps a little confused."

Eric looked down for a second. "Maybe I'll come see him before I leave."

"Still planning to go to Alaska, then?" Jonathan asked.

"Of course." He looked meaningfully across the table. "I made a commitment to Nathan's memory. I'm doing this for him, on some level."

"What about your commitment to me?" I couldn't help saying.

"We didn't have one." He gave me a sad smile. A sad, fake smile. My fists clenched in my lap.

"A trip that big must take a lot of preparation," Jonathan

said, and Eric lit up and started talking about walking sticks and ice picks and the best kind of tent.

Our drinks came. Mine went down fast.

"I don't know if I told you, Ainsley," Eric said, "but I may have a book deal in the works! Isn't that great?"

"So great."

"It's about my cancer journey and, of course, the trip to Denali. My agent is fielding offers."

He had an *agent* now?

"Congratulations," Jonathan said. "And it brings up the reason we'd like you to stay with *Hudson Lifestyle*. Obviously, your column struck a nerve."

*A nerve right in my heart, you asshole.* I narrowed my eyes at Eric, who just smiled back.

Jonathan looked at me. "Ainsley? Why don't you tell Eric what we have in mind?"

"Before you start, Ains," Eric said, "I just want you to know that my agent is in talks with *Outdoor Magazine*, *GQ* and *Maxim*." He smiled. "So *Hudson* is feeling a little...provincial."

"That's incredible," I said. "I mean, they were never interested when the blog was just about you and your testicle. It was only when you crapped all over our relationship that things heated up. How will you sustain interest? Just keep dumping women after they've given you everything?"

"I understand your anger," he said. "Thank you for sharing it with me."

"And thank *you*, Eric, for so generously understanding."

Jonathan took a sip of his scotch and said nothing.

It didn't take a shrink to figure out why I was really here. I wanted to see him, to see if he was really sticking to his *corpse* guns.

God. What if he did come back to *Hudson Lifestyle*?

On one hand, it would be nice to be able to edit Eric's

column each month, which would consist of me putting a big red X through it and saying *you can't write for shit* in a helpful, constructive way.

"A very big raise." Jonathan's voice was extremely quiet.

Eric frowned. "Excuse me?" he said.

"Nothing," Jonathan answered.

My ex-boyfriend looked pissy at that. "Tell me why I should stay with your magazine," he said, sitting back with his girlie grapefruit drink. He smiled, fully prepared to enjoy our sucking up.

I fake-smiled right back. "Well, Eric, as you no doubt recall, *Hudson Lifestyle* gave you a column when no one else would. You might remember that you did indeed pitch many magazines and blog sites to carry *The Cancer Chronicles*, and no one so much as returned an email."

His smile slipped for a second, then returned. "Times have changed. *Fox News* said I was the voice of the modern male."

"Actually, it was a reader comment on the *Fox News* website—in Sioux City, Iowa, that is—who said you were the voice of the modern male," I corrected. "Other commenters had more colorful names for you, which I'd be happy to list. Or maybe I'll start my own blog about men who exaggerate when they're sick."

A nudge from my boss.

"Anyway, Eric," I muttered, "we hope you'll do the honor of staying with us."

Eric cocked his head. "But why would I?"

"Gosh. I don't know," I said. "Maybe you owe me. I was the one who wiped your fevered brow, remember?" He'd had one fever. One. "I cleaned up your puke after the bad sushi… I mean, after your chemo. I wrote on your scrotum so the doctor would be sure to take out the correct testicle."

Jonathan choked.

"You were very good to me, Sunshine," Eric said, and I wanted to break my martini glass and stab a shard into his neck. He never called me Sunshine in real life. Never. "But I don't operate in a world of debt anymore. I have to do what's right for me. I know you don't want to take advice from me, Ainsley, but I think you have to try harder to—" he paused for dramatic effect "—live life large."

"Good God," muttered Jonathan.

"And you should release those toxic feelings, babe. They'll eat you alive."

The rage that had been building in me rose like a fireball. I slammed both hands on the table, rattling the glasses. "You know what, Eric? You're unrecognizable to me. To *me*, who's loved you for eleven years. I'd give anything to see that terrified, weepy, shaking guy who cried for three days straight after his diagnosis instead of the ridiculous, self-centered, smug asshole I see before me."

"I'm sorry you're feeling so victimized," he said. "I choose not to move through life that way. Getting cancer was the worst thing that ever happened to me, and yet it taught me so much. There's only the now, only answering the inner voice."

"Let's go," Jonathan said. "Thank you for your time, Eric."

I stood up, shaking with rage. "Getting cancer wasn't the worst thing that ever happened to you, Eric. Getting *over* cancer was. Admit it. You *loved* having cancer. It gave you permission to worship yourself, and you haven't stopped yet. You're breaking your parents' hearts, and you broke mine. I don't even know how you look at yourself in the mirror."

Eric took his phone out, clicked a button and spoke into it. "Getting over cancer was the worst thing that ever happened to you. Worshipping yourself. Breaking parents' hearts." He clicked again, then looked up at me. "Thanks for my next blog."

I lunged.

Luckily, Jonathan grabbed me around the waist, stopping me before I made contact. "We're leaving," he said, dragging me back a few paces.

"Then she attacked me," Eric said into his phone.

"*Attempted* to attack you," I said. "Lucky for you, someone stepped in, because God knows, I could take you."

"And threatened me, even though I'm still in the recovery phase."

"No, you're not!" I yelled, in case there weren't enough people looking at me. "You recovered six months ago, and it's driving you crazy!"

Jonathan towed me away. "Let's go before we're thrown out, shall we?" he murmured.

"Did you *hear* him?"

"Inside voice, and yes. Come on."

The air was cool and rich with the smell of New York— that strangely sweet tang of subway, food and exhaust. "Let's walk," Jonathan suggested, and I stomped down the street, my thoughts just an angry, pulsating red smear. Turned on Fifth Avenue and headed uptown, plowing through the crowd.

Powered by fury, my legs ate up the blocks, arms swinging, bag hitting my hip, my leopard-print shoes biting my heels, cramping my toes.

I *hated* him. Who the hell *was* that? What had happened to the gentle, funny, loyal man who hugged his parents and told me on more than one occasion that he'd be nothing without me? Where was *he*?

Who was that other guy, that pretentious ass who dictated my words into a phone so he could *blog* about me?

How the hell were we going to get over this?

I got to the edge of Central Park and jerked to a stop, unsure of where to go now.

"Here."

Jonathan. I'd almost forgotten about him. He held out a handkerchief.

Oh. I was crying.

"Come," he said, taking my arm. I sucked in a jerking breath and let him lead me.

He stopped at the first carriage, where a big brown horse stood, bottomless eyes and velvety nose, breathing its warm breath on my hand, which was shaking. Jonathan took out his wallet, handed the guy some bills and muttered something.

Then he handed me up into the carriage and got in beside me. The driver clucked to the horse, and we started, turning into the park, the horse's massive hooves clack-clacking on the pavement.

"Ainsley, I'm sorry," Jonathan said. "I should never have asked you to do that."

I wiped my eyes. I needed to blow my nose, but this was his handkerchief, and it was kind of gross—oh, screw it. I blew my nose. "It's fine."

"No. It's not. I apologize."

The rhythm of the carriage was soothing, the pull and jerk of it. I swallowed and looked off to the left.

New York City is a good place to come to forget your misery. So many people, so many ages and races and stories. Virtually everyone had had, was currently nursing or would have a broken heart. There were a thousand stories worse than mine.

It was just that I always thought Eric and I were special. That our love wasn't tainted by selfishness or jealousy or pettiness. We were truly Plato's two halves of a whole, as I'd learned in my very first philosophy class.

I was wrong. For eleven years, I'd been wrong. I blotted my eyes again. "What's your horse's name?" I asked the driver.

"Truman," he said, turning back with a grin.

"Does he like his job?"

"Oh, yes, miss. Look at his ears, how they're pointed forward. He's having a wonderful time."

"And what's your name?"

"Benicio."

"I love that name. Tell your mom she chose well."

Another smile. "I will, miss. Thank you."

Truman clip-clopped around a turn. The dogwoods were in bloom, and a light breeze ruffled my hair and dried the last of my rage-tears.

Jonathan was staring at me. "Why do you do that?" he asked.

"Do what?"

"Try to make everyone like you. Your charm offensive. Here you are, crying over your idiot of a boyfriend, but you—"

"It's called being friendly, Jonathan. Not being rude. Noticing the world around you. Would you rather have me smiting myself with ashes and tearing my clothes? And I didn't try to be friendly. I just am. Right, Benicio?"

"*Sí, senorita.* Very friendly." He smiled back at me.

"So take a note, Mr. Kent. This is how humans act." I was tired of him, of me, of Eric, of feeling sad.

"Would you like to have dinner?" he asked.

My mouth opened, then closed. "Is that a trick question?"

"No. It's the least I can do after putting you through that. I feel very bad about your…distress."

Dinner would mean I'd have to talk to him for an hour or two. But going back home would just have me lying in bed, revisiting every stupid word between Eric and me. "Okay."

An hour later, after our lovely ride through Central Park and a fond farewell to Benicio and Truman, Jonathan and

I were seated in a typical East Side restaurant—quiet, posh, expensive. Jonathan had ordered a bottle of wine, and Carl, our waiter, poured me a generous glass. "Are you ready to order?" he asked.

"What's your favorite thing on the menu, Carl?" I asked.

"Well, everything's wonderful here," he said. "But I did have the lobster and asparagus risotto before my shift, and it was stellar."

"That's what I'll have, then."

"Any appetizers?"

"How about three Wellfleet oysters?"

He winked at me. "A wonderful choice. For you, sir?"

"I'll have the veal Oscar," Jonathan said. I winced. I had an issue with veal. "Not the veal," he amended. "The chicken. I assume it's free-range, organic, and led a happy and productive life?"

"Yes, sir."

"That and the tomato salad, then."

"Very good." Carl smiled and walked off.

"You made a joke," I observed.

"Did I?"

"I'm almost positive." I took a roll from the basket. "Oh, God, these are still warm." I was suddenly starving. Whole wheat, soft, hot with honey butter mixed with a pinch of truffle salt. "Oh, bread, I love you," I murmured, taking a bite and closing my eyes. "Jonathan, have a roll so I don't eat them all."

He obliged, breaking off a small piece of bread and buttering it with care. "So how did you meet Eric?" he asked.

"Junior year of college. One look and I thought *that's the guy I'm gonna marry.* He was my first boyfriend." Best not to think of happy times.

"Ainsley, why *don't* you reveal his exaggerations, as you

suggested earlier?" Jonathan asked, leaning forward. "You could show him as the fraud he is."

There was that British lord lingo again. I dropped my eyes to the table and sighed. "Yeah, I could," I said. "But when someone hurts you, is it right to hurt them back? I could, sure, but then I'd be stooping to his level. And while that would be very satisfying... I don't know. That's not who I want to be."

His eyes flickered. "Good answer."

I suddenly got the strong impression Jonathan knew exactly what I was talking about. "Let's change the subject. How did you meet your wife?"

He looked up, then back down at his roll. "We were childhood friends."

"Did you take her to the prom?"

"No," he said. I waited for more. *More* stayed put.

"Let's have a conversation, Jonathan. You did ask me to dinner, remember? You wanted to make up for that debacle, which I correctly predicted. Hate to say I told you so, but I did."

"True," he said. "I didn't quite imagine you trying to assault him, but I can't say he didn't deserve it, either."

"So let's pretend we're friends and talk."

"Sure." He took a sip of wine and said nothing.

Carl returned with our appetizers, and I slurped down an oyster, which tasted perfectly of the sea and had a nice, buttery after-flavor. "Oh, that was amazing." I sighed happily. Took a sip of wine. "Want one?" I offered my boss.

He hesitated.

"Have you ever had one before?"

"No, actually."

"Oh, fun! Give it a try! Smell it first. It should smell like the ocean. Then just slurp it in. You'll taste the brine, and then give it a few chews. Don't make it into paste, though. Just let it ride."

He did as instructed. "What do you think?" I asked.

"Very good." He smiled.

That smile was… It was kind of…adorable.

*That's the wine talking*, I told myself. I ate the last oyster. "So you and your ex…you were childhood friends and then what?"

"We got married and had two daughters."

"That's really crappy storytelling. How about you fill in some blanks?"

He straightened his cutlery. "Yes. Well, we ran into each other again after college and started dating and got married two years after that."

Still pretty crappy. "What's her name?"

"Laine."

"Were you happy together?"

"We were. For a time. I thought so, anyway." He sighed and looked at me. "Were you and Eric happy together?"

"You know what?" I said, leaning forward. Yep. Definitely a little buzzed. "We really were. We were so happy."

"Until…?"

"Until Nathan died. And then Eric snapped like a tooth-pick."

"What made you happy?" he asked. Once again, I had the impression that he was data-gathering so he could report back to his home planet.

But that was just his way, maybe. I thought for a moment. "I loved every day. I loved doing things together. I loved talking to him, and just…being part of a couple. Showing him I loved him."

"How did you do that?"

"Oh, the usual, I guess. I left him little notes in his brief-case and taped to his toothbrush. Cooked his favorite stuff.

Made sure I told him how nice he looked. Bought him little presents. I helped him at work a little, you know, giving him suggestions of how to deal with difficult bosses and stuff." I shrugged. "Nothing special."

He just looked at me for a beat. "It sounds very special."

I'd have to be careful with that voice. Just because he'd been blessed with a lovely baritone didn't mean anything. It was the same voice that irritably asked me not to ignore the toner light on the printer and noted how many minutes late I was.

But man, it was a good voice.

We looked at each other for a long second. Then Carl appeared and set down our plates in front of us, and my lobster risotto smelled the way I hoped heaven would when I crossed through the Pearly Gates. "Oh, thank you, Carl." I took a bite and groaned. "You were right. So good! Thank you, thank you, thank you!"

Carl beamed and put Jonathan's chicken in front of him. "Would miss or sir like anything else?"

"No, we're perfect," I said. "But I love how you call me miss."

Carl nodded and went off to his other (less charming) customers. I was sure he missed me.

"There you are, making friends again," Jonathan remarked, refilling my wineglass. "The carriage driver, the people in Divorce With Integrity."

"You need a new name, by the way. Whoever thought of DWI?" His mouth moved in what may or may not have been a smile. Score. "Yes, I guess I do. I like people."

"I can see that."

"Is that a plus or minus in my column?"

Another near miss with the smile. "I'm still deciding."

If I hadn't almost beaten my ex to a pulp tonight, if I hadn't had a glass of wine in me on top of a straight-up martini, I might have thought Jonathan Kent sort of…liked me.

Or pitied me. Shit, there was that, wasn't there? This was his apology dinner, after all.

"So what happened to you and Laine?" I asked, deciding I hated that name. Too snooty.

His eyes dropped to his meal. "My father had a massive stroke, and I took over running the magazine. I worked a lot. He needed a lot of help, ah, transitioning. The children were small, and it was difficult for her."

"That's it?" There seemed to be a good chunk missing from the story.

"Pretty much."

"She couldn't cut you a little slack? Your father was sick, you were trying to earn a living and she dumped you. That's pretty cold."

"I dumped her," he said, cutting his green beans.

I blinked. He always had a slightly martyred air; I just assumed he was the dumpee.

"Why?" I asked.

He didn't answer, just kept cutting those green beans into one-inch pieces, eating steadily.

Oh.

"I'm sorry," I said.

"About what?" Still no eye contact.

"She cheated on you."

He stopped chewing for a second, then swallowed. Took a sip of wine. "Yes."

"Would you like to talk about it?"

"No, thank you."

I put down my fork. And then, maybe because of the wine, maybe because he took me for a carriage ride like any good Prince Charming, I reached out and gave his hand a squeeze.

He looked at our joined hands—*human contact, how curious*—then up at me. "Would you like to tell me more about Eric?" he asked.

There it was, the little flash of gold in his left iris. "I would," I said taking my hand back, and I felt myself smiling. Why, I wasn't sure. Wine. Stress relief. Suddenly, our conversation in the Algonquin, all of us looking like Blue Man Group rejects, seemed funny. "He's become a grade-A dick, hasn't he? But honestly, Jon, he wasn't always like that. He used to...I don't know...need me."

I took a bite of risotto and thought. Jonathan waited.

"And I loved that. Then when he got sick and he was so scared, I just kind of...stepped it up. Took care of his appointments, his medications, went to the doctor's office with him—"

"Yes, I know," Jonathan said. "You still have minus fourteen days of vacation."

"Thanks for reminding me, boss." I pushed my excellent risotto away. A place like this would have boffo desserts, and I wanted to save room. "When Eric had cancer, I was completely...necessary."

"I would imagine you were completely necessary well before then."

As was so often true, his formal language kept a distance between the words and the sentiment. I *thought* it was a compliment.

I thought it was a very, very good compliment.

Jonathan looked steadily at me, not blinking, the impeccable suit, the muted tie. One hand was on his wineglass, his long fingers graceful on the stem.

Suddenly, I could feel my heart beating. My skin seemed to tighten at the same time my bones grew hot.

Jonathan Kent was smiling at me. Just a little. Just enough.

"Did you read the piece on the pumpkin farm?" I blurted. "That's pretty interesting, right? All those...pumpkins."

"Yes."

"Was it okay? The piece?"

"It was fine. Very good. I liked the bit about the dogs. That was your addition, wasn't it?"

I nodded.

"You're not as bad at your job as you pretend to be, Ainsley." He was still looking at me. His voice seemed to creep under my dress and caress my skin.

Clearly, two glasses of wine on top of a martini was way, way too much for me. He hadn't said a single thing that was even in the same neighborhood as flirty or dirty, and I...I was just overly emotional tonight.

"Would miss or sir like dessert?" Carl asked.

"No, thanks," I blurted. "I need to get home."

# Chapter Eighteen

*Kate*

On Friday, I went to my parents' house for a family dinner. Ainsley had to be in the city for work, which may or may not have been coincidental. My mother often held family dinners when Ainsley was out of town. Every summer, when Ainsley and Eric were off on vacation with the Fishers, Mom held a neighborhood picnic, too.

I wondered if Nathan and Madeleine had ever gone on vacation with his parents. I'd never asked.

I hadn't read those emails yet, either. I just couldn't, and now the thought of them sat in my mind like a tumor.

Being with my family would be a good distraction.

My parents' house had been redecorated since the last time I was over, before Nathan died. Everything was now white, save for the abused "pop of color" notion that embodied itself in orange throw pillows—three in a line on the couch, one on each white chair.

I went into the kitchen. "Hi, everyone."

"I'm so glad you're here," my mother said. "We all want to see how you're doing."

"I'm okay," I lied. There was no way in hell that I'd tell them about finding the emails.

"One month is usually a turning point," she said. "Especially since you really didn't know Nathan very long." She poured herself some wine and fluffed her stiff hair, ignoring the fact that her words had just stabbed me.

I remember going to one of her book signings, where people would break down, telling her how her wisdom and kindness had changed their lives. She'd take them in her arms and often wipe away her own tears. Genuine tears.

She'd always been better with strangers.

"Hello, my darling!" said Gram-Gram. "Oh, you look so pretty! Shall we have lunch together sometime?"

"That would be really nice, Gram-Gram."

"I have a wake to go to tomorrow. Would you like to come to that? We could get sushi afterward. Did you know sushi is raw fish? I just found that out!"

"Yes to the sushi, no to the wake," I said, forcing a smile.

"How's my princess?" Dad asked, coming inside from where he'd been avoiding the rest of us. He squeezed my shoulder.

"I'm fine, Dad. How are the Yankees?"

"Horrible this year. The Orioles, though—shockingly good so far."

"Nice call the other night. At second?"

He grinned, the eternal boy of summer. "Thanks, babe. It was a close one, but the replay proved me right."

"Hey, Kate," Sean said, giving me the requisite fraternal half hug. Even better, he gave me Sadie.

"Hi, sweet pea," I said, kissing her head and breathing in

her smell. "Hi, Esther, hi, Mattie." The other kids gave me dutiful hugs. "God, Matthias, you're getting tall."

"So good to see you," said Kiara, kissing me on both cheeks. "The kids have missed you!"

"Is this true?" I asked my nephew.

"Absolutely," he lied, the good-hearted boy.

Sadie wriggled to get down, then tugged on Esther's skirt. "Come play!" she demanded, the little tyrant. My arms felt lonely without her.

"Please stay off the white chairs and couch," Mom called.

"How have you been?" Kiara asked, her eyes kind. "Do you need anything from me?"

Drugs? She *was* a doctor. How about some nice anesthesia? For a second, I thought about asking her to come stay with Ainsley and me for a few days. We could make margaritas and binge-watch trashy reality TV shows.

But Kiara was a surgeon, and a mother of three. She didn't have time to babysit her middle-aged sister-in-law. "I'm doing okay, I think," I said. "Sleeping better." A total lie.

"Good, honey," she said. There was a crash from the living room.

"Kiara, those couches are brand-new." My mother sighed. Kiara lifted an elegant brow at me and went to check on the state of the white.

Still, this night was the Check On Kate Night, and in a way, it was nice. Sean, being the provider of the grandchildren and a surgeon, usually got the most attention, and Ainsley got a fair amount, too (though not always the best kind...the sort of sad, squinty type my mother was so good at). Then again, Ainsley was Dad's favorite, being Michelle's daughter.

Me, I was always a little invisible. Which was usually okay, being able to drift in and out without so much attention or criticism. Sean called me the family ninja. But now, with

Nathan gone, I felt too invisible, like I was disappearing bit by bit, parts of me dripping onto the sidewalk and evaporating. I wasn't Kate O'Leary as much as Nathan's Widow, left alone in his house, in his town, in his life.

And knowing that he'd kept a secret from me—a huge secret, it felt like—made me wonder if the validity of my widowhood was being taken from me. I was in mourning for this guy I'd known less than a year, but maybe he wasn't the man I thought. All those emails might tell a different story, one of infidelity or longing for his old life.

"It's so good to have all of us together," Mom said. I gave her a pointed look. "Well, except for Ainsley, of course. How is she? She's well rid of that Eric. Oh, there was something your father wanted to ask you." This was her line whenever she had something awkward to say.

Dad stayed mute, so Mom kept going. "He wanted to know, did Nathan have life insurance? That is to say, will you be all set financially?"

I sighed. "I can support myself, Mom. I have for a long time, in case you forgot."

"I haven't forgotten. Please stop taking offense at everything I say, though it's natural to lash out at those with whom you feel safe when you're grieving." She looked pleased with herself at the line, which basically excused her from any responsibility and made me look like an unstable ass. "Did he, though?"

I paused. "Yes."

"Is it enough?"

"It's fine. Yes. It was…generous."

"Oh, hooray!" Gram-Gram said. "You're a wealthy woman! Let's take a trip!"

I *was* wealthy. His insurance policy had been for more than a million dollars. The house was also in my name. There'd been some money for Atticus and Miles, too, but the bulk of everything was left for me, his wife of ninety-six days.

Now it reeked of guilt-money.

I would have to read those emails, damn it.

"Did you guys see Eric on TV?" Matthias asked. "I can't believe that guy! He's such a d-i-c-k." He smiled at Sadie. "That means stupid person."

"I not stupid!"

"Nope. You're supersmart."

We passed the platters of food around—salmon, spinach and Mom's special couscous with the pine nuts. All my favorites. Though she wasn't the cuddliest mother in the world, it was awfully nice that she'd made this dinner for me.

We fell silent for a few minutes, and I watched as my brother, parents, nephew and nieces shoveled in the food. Kiara shook her head and gave me a smile. Nathan once told me his mother insisted that he and Brooke take a bite, put the fork down, chew, swallow and pause before taking another bite. They'd have starved to death in our family.

I took a bite of the fish. It tasted like nothing. There was only texture, and therefore disgusting, too mushy. The spinach was no better, slimy and limp. I forced myself to swallow.

"This is so good, Ma," Sean said, already getting seconds.

"Good, honey. I made all your favorites."

I should've known.

My mother tapped her glass in that pretentious way she had when announcing a new book deal or tour. "Kids, there's no easy way to say this. Your father and I—grandfather and I, Matthias and Esther—are getting a divorce."

"And here we go again," Sean muttered.

Esther sighed. Kiara drank some wine.

"This time we're serious. Phil, tell them."

"Kids, we're getting a divorce."

"Kate, I thought I'd come live with you," Mom said. I flinched. "No."

"Why? I could take care of you!"

"I'm fine, thank you."

"Grandma," Esther said, "this is probably the fifth time you've told us this."

"Well, sweetheart, this time we mean it."

"So you were just playing with us all those other times?" I asked.

"Kate," Mom said in a low voice, "you know your father's a serial cheater."

"Grandma!" Esther dropped her fork with a clatter. "Gross. Grandpa, you're not, right?" He smiled and winked at her and didn't answer.

"He always did like the ladies," Gram-Gram said. There was a piece of spinach on her chest. "That's how Ainsley came into this world, after all."

"Can I be excused?" Matthias said.

"Actually, we'll all go," Sean said. Kiara didn't need to be nudged twice and leaped to her feet. "I have a surgery in the morning."

"Me, too," Kiara said. "Lives to save and all that."

"You pull that card out way too often, you two," I said.

"Sorry," said my brother. "You're on your own. Your widow card is no good here."

"Sean!" Kiara gave me an apologetic glance. "But we do both have surgeries tomorrow, and the kids have homework." She scooped up Sadie, who was smashing salmon into paste, and ten seconds later, they were all out, the lucky bastards.

"We feel it's time," Mom said. "A conscious uncoupling at long last." My father jerked as she no doubt kicked him under the table."

"We do. It's been a long time coming," he said, like a doll whose string had been pulled.

Gram-Gram took out her phone and started clicking. Ainsley had told me she was on Tinder.

I rubbed my forehead. "Well, get a divorce or don't. I'm leaving, too. Mom, just to be clear, you're not coming to live with me."

"I think it's exactly what you need."

"Nope. It's not."

"Phil," Mom snapped, "don't just sit there like a concrete block! You said we'd discuss this together."

"Right, right," Dad said, looking up from his phone, on which he was no doubt checking baseball scores. "Your mother and I haven't been intimate for months now."

"Did I ask? I did not." I could feel my neck muscles tightening. "Do you guys remember when I was a freshman in college, and you called to tell me you were getting a divorce? I came home expecting you to be packing and instead walked in on your sexy time!"

"I don't remember that," Mom said, frowning.

"Well, I do, and believe me, I wish I didn't. When Ainsley graduated from college, you did it again. That time, Mom, you were going to live with Aunt Patty in Michigan. But you stayed. And then again after Sadie was born, you were all set to buy an apartment in the city, yet here you are. Why do you bother?"

"We mean it this time." My mother raised a thin eyebrow, insulted that I'd questioned her sincerity.

"Good. Do it. I dare you. I *want* you to get divorced. I want you both to remarry so I can have stepparents. I'm leaving now, by the way. Bye, Gram-Gram."

"Bye, sweetheart! I love you."

My mother rolled her eyes. "Kate, you barely ate anything. Don't be such a drama queen."

I sputtered. I was *not* a drama queen! But you know what? I could turn into one, and fast.

"Has it occurred to you that I'm a widow?" I barked. "That I have real problems and issues going on? That I can't sleep and I can't stay awake, and I'm living this half-life like some kind of zombie? Maybe you can use your degree and help me out here, Mom! And, Dad...jeez! You were a widower, too. Don't you have anything for me?"

"Everything you're feeling is normal," Mom said.

My father shrugged helplessly. "It gets better? Not really, but sort of? For what it's worth, I don't think you're a zombie, honeybun."

"I love that show about zombies," Gram-Gram said. "Such handsome men! I like Glenn the best."

I patted her shoulder. "Well, I'm one of them, the walking dead, and the last thing I want to hear from you two is that, once again, you find each other lacking and you're pretending to get a divorce for the seventeenth time."

"It's hardly been seventeen times," Mom said.

"Whatever. Bye."

I slammed out of the house, got into my car and just headed south. I'd go to the diner and get a slab of cheesecake, or drive down to Tarrytown to look at the bridge, or...or...

Why was I so mad? This wasn't anything new.

Because being alone wasn't a choice for me. Because I didn't have the luxury of thinking about divorce. Because I'd thought that everyone was worried about me, and that dinner was for me, not stupid Sean, and I was oddly irked that everyone had bought my feeble declaration of *doing fine*.

I wanted someone to help me. To fix me. To tell me what to do.

Abruptly, I pulled into Bixby Park at the southern edge of Cambry-on-Hudson and got out of the car. It was a beautiful place, paths winding throughout, a view of the Hudson, a playground. The trees had leafed out fully this past week, and the sound of the breeze swishing through them was fresh and full.

I strode westward, my face hot, joints zinging painfully with the adrenaline rush.

There were benches placed along the path with plaques on them—*In celebration of the life of Howard Betelman. In loving memory of James Wellbright.*

Maybe I'd get one for Nathan. He'd like that. We'd come to this park last fall and made out on one of these benches. I wondered which one. It was under a tree, I remembered that.

*In honor of Marnie and Joel Koenig from their lucky children.* Nice. This might've been the bench we sat on that beautiful day. The tree's leaves had glowed with gold so intense the air seemed to shimmer, and it had been so incredibly romantic, like the stock photos I occasionally sold to Getty Images. Type in the search words, and you'd see just such a picture—*adults, love, romance, autumn.*

Maybe it wasn't this bench. Maybe it was the next one.

Did he bring Madeleine here, too?

The thought punched me in the stomach. It was too hard to think about. Better to be pissed off about Mom making salmon for Sean and not me.

I came upon the next bench and lurched to a stop.

*In honor of Nathan Vance Coburn III, a wonderful son, brother, uncle and friend.*

What? *What?*

He had a bench already? Who did this? Why didn't anyone tell me? I was his widow, for God's sake! *I* was going to buy him a bench, did I not just have that exact thought two minutes ago?

*And hold on one second*, my brain said. *There's a word missing, isn't there?*

*Why yes, there is.* Husband. *The missing word is* husband.

The Coburns had bought a bench for Nathan and not told me about it. Why? Eloise and I had had another lunch at the club last week, and she'd said *nothing*!

I yanked out my phone to call them and demand an answer, then shoved it right back in. I was too mad. Furious, in fact. I turned around, not wanting to see his name, not wanting to see that bench with its stupid bronze plaque, and stomped back to the bench for the couple with the lucky kids.

My heart was roaring, my face on fire.

This was turning into a really shitty night.

There was the playground. *Watch the little kiddies, Kate. They don't have a care in the world.*

Three little girls about Sadie's age chased each other around, laughing and shrieking. Their mother (or nanny) had long blond hair and a serene look on her face. A cute guy approached and handed her a cup of coffee (or booze) and touched her shoulder briefly.

On autopilot, and so I wouldn't have to think about that stupid bench, I fished my Canon out of my bag and aimed it at them.

They were still new, these two. He had smiley eyes and dimples not reflected in the little girls' faces. They were sisters, maybe even triplets, I guessed; the blonde woman was clearly their mother, but this guy wasn't the dad. And he was smitten.

There was a story there, I was sure.

That was what I loved about photography. It told me more about a person than I could ever discern in real life.

What would I see in those last pictures of Nathan? A man who'd made a mistake? Who wanted to be with his ex-wife? Who was biding his time until he could get free of his impulsive rebound marriage?

I put my camera down and squeezed the bridge of my nose.

There were more happy screams from the playground as a fresh batch of kids came streaming in, running, climbing, hurling themselves down the slide without any thought of danger.

*Oh, God, be careful,* I thought. *Don't bump your heads. Don't fall down. Don't have a tiny vascular defect. Don't die.*

My breath was scraping in and out, in-out, in-out, in-out. Gray spots splotched my vision, and I bent over, but no, that didn't help, was it supposed to help? I was here all alone, no one knew where I was. Ainsley would come, she'd help me, she was so good at this, but shit, she was doing something for work and I couldn't breathe, my lungs were stuck closed, I was about to die.

Sweat blossomed over me like a virus, and my hands started to shake.

I groped for my phone to call my dad, but it spilled out of my numb fingers. I reached for it, sliding off the bench, my knees stinging on the asphalt.

I was fainting. Or dying. The sound of my own breathing grew fainter.

"Kate?"

Someone had me by the shoulders.

Daniel the Hot Firefighter. Good. I wouldn't die alone. I clutched his arms. *"Hehn-hehn-hehn-hehn-hehn,"* I managed.

He smiled. "You're having a panic attack, aren't you? Okay, don't worry. They're not fatal." He pulled me back onto the bench and put his arm around me. "Jane!" he yelled. "Over here. I'll be a while."

*"Hehn-hehn-hehn-hehn."* If this Jane person answered, I didn't hear over the sound of my terror. What was that horse movie? Where the horse ran all day and all night across the desert? *Hidalgo*, that was it. I sounded like Hidalgo.

"So I'm here with my sister and her bratty kids," Daniel said, as if I was a normal person and not a dying horse. His fingers were on my wrist. "The ice-cream truck comes around, so I'm using that as a bribe. The little one? She's the devil, I swear to God. I told my sister to call the exorcist."

"Heart…attack," I managed.

"Probably not. Just take a deep breath and try to calm down."

"No!" I squeaked, my throat too tight to get out normal sound. "My husband died getting me—*hehn*—a glass of wine! I can't—*hehn*—calm down. Do something!" Because my heart was way, way too fast and pretty soon it would explode.

"Okay, okay," he said, sliding onto his knees in front of me. "Let's see if you can answer a few questions. Put your head down and try not to pant, that's a good girl." I did, feeling his hand on my shoulder. "That's it. Nice and slow. What color panties have you got on?"

My head snapped up. "What?"

He pushed my head back down. "Answer the question. Or I could check for you if that would be easier."

"Aren't you supposed to ask about—*hehn*—the President?"

"I don't care about the President's underwear. What color are yours? Throw me a bone and say a red thong."

"You're such—*hehn*—a pig," I said, staring at the grass. The gray splotches were getting smaller.

"I know, I know, red thong, such a cliché. But I'm a guy. We like visual stimulation. White lace panties, they'd be good, too, I guess. Or black. Or none, now that I think of it. Any chance you went commando this morning?"

"I can't believe they...let you do this...for a living." I sucked in a slow breath, held it, let it go. Did it again.

"Good point. But guess whose panic attack is dying down, huh?" He lifted my head with both his hands and smiled into my eyes. "Ta-da."

He was right. I was still sweaty, and my heart was thudding fast, but the panting had stopped, and I didn't see gray anymore.

"God, I'm good," he said with a grin, sitting back on the bench with me. "FDNY, baby. We live for this shit. Now, don't compliment me just yet. Just sit there and breathe. I'll stay with you."

An hour later, after I'd calmed down, met Jane, Daniel's sister whose "rat-faced shithead husband" walked out on her, as well as her two adorable sons and demonic daughter, after Daniel had handed his sister some money for the ice-cream truck, he informed me he was driving me home.

I didn't protest. For one, I felt weak and wobbly. For two, I didn't want to go back to that house alone. And for three, having a firefighter around made me feel safer. He made me take his arm on the way to the car, then fished my keys out of my purse and slid the driver's seat way back. "Tell me which way," he said, and I directed him through Cambry-on-Hudson.

"Holy shit," he said as we pulled into the driveway.

"Yeah. It's impressive."

I tapped the security code in, opened the door, then tried to turn on the front hall light. The den (or study) light went on instead. Good enough.

We went into the kitchen, and I heard Ollie's dog tags jingling as he came down the stairs, dragging his blanket, wagging his tail so hard his whole back swayed.

"Hi, Ollie!" I said, bending down to pet him. "Did you have fun napping today? You did? Did you miss me?" I looked up. "This is Ollie. Ollie, this is Daniel the Hot Firefighter."

Daniel was looking around, openmouthed. "Nice house," he said.

"Nathan was an architect."

"It could be in a magazine."

It had been in several, in fact. Nathan had copies framed in his work office. One of his coworkers had packed up his stuff and sent it over, but I hadn't managed to open the box yet.

I finished worshipping the dog and stood up, leaving Ollie to trot over to seduce Daniel's shoes. "Want something to drink?"

"I'm starving," he said. "You got any food?"

"I have a freezer full of sympathy meals," I said. "What would you like? I can thaw just about anything."

"Anything is fine." He looked a little uneasy, glancing around. It was an intimidating kitchen, I'd grant him that. He picked up Ollie, who began licking his chin. The dog loved everything with a heartbeat.

"Would you like some wine?" I asked.

"Got a beer?"

"Maybe." I dug around in the fridge. God, we had a lot of food! It looked like the fridge of a woman in a commercial, full of leafy dark greens and organic yogurt. All my sister's doing.

I found a beer in the back and took it out, then glanced at the label.

Hurricane Kitty IPA.

Nathan bought this. We'd spent a chilly Sunday afternoon in March at Keegan Ales microbrewery, sipping beers at the tasting bar after the tour, the lush smell of hops seeping into our clothes. Brought a twelve-pack home with us.

For a second, I could picture him so clearly it made me dizzy—Nathan reaching into the fridge, wearing his blue sweater with the four buttons at the neck.

"I'll have wine. Wine's good," someone said.

Right. Daniel the Hot Firefighter.

I put the beer back, grabbed some wine and pulled a Tupperware container of something from the freezer. "Chicken stew," I read from the label. "Sound good?"

"Sounds great. Hey, I don't have to stay, Kate. I'll call a cab and go to my sister's."

"No, no, that's fine. I mean, if you have to go back…"

"I don't have to. I just don't want you to feel like you have to entertain me." He folded his impressive arms. He didn't have a jacket on, though the night was cool, just a T-shirt. God forbid we should miss those biceps.

The thought brought a smile to my mind, if not my face. "Stay," I said. "And open this wine."

After the block of chicken stew had been pried from the Tupperware into a pot on the stove, the gas set on the tiniest flame, Daniel and I went into the living room, where I tried light switches until we could see each other, but not every pore.

I sat in one of the leather chairs; Daniel on the hard gray couch. He looked out of place here, too big for the sofa. Ollie leaped up next to him and put his chin on Daniel's thigh. Even dogs had a weakness for hot firefighters, apparently. Daniel petted Ollie's head with a big hand. "Hey, I started the porch swing, by the way."

"Great. The Coburns will love it, I'm sure." He'd sent me three designs, and I'd picked one and sent it back. Couldn't remember now what it looked like.

"How's your sister?" Daniel asked.

"She's good. She's staying with me for a while. How's Lizzie?"

"Oh, man, she's great. Those pictures were scary beautiful." He set his wine down on the coffee table. "I never thanked you for figuring out she had a problem with that little shit-stain boyfriend, by the way."

"Oh. You're welcome. A little magic trick of mine. Sometimes you can see things through the camera that you can't without it." It sounded stupid, saying it aloud. "So your other sister Jane…she's doing okay? She seems pretty together."

"She is. Her husband's an idiot. We never liked him. I didn't, anyway." He shrugged. "Then again, Jane hated Calista, so I guess we're even."

Rain began to fall, pinging in the copper gutters. This house was beautiful in the rain—the gutters had releases where the water would flow down in a controlled gush onto piles of white rocks before filtering into the irrigation system. Nothing was by accident with Nathan. Except his death, of course.

Which meant he'd kept those emails for a reason.

"You ever hear from her? From Calista?" I asked.

"No." He took a sip of wine, grimacing a little. I should've given him the beer. "Do you?"

I hesitated. "I get a card at Christmastime."

"She doesn't celebrate Christmas."

"Fine, fine. It's a winter solstice card." He gave a rueful smile. "So what happened with you two?" I asked. After all, he'd asked me about my panties today. I could pry a little, too.

"I don't know," he grumbled.

"Sure you do."

He sighed. "She loved me, then she didn't." He looked out the window, where the outside lights had magically gone on (still hadn't found those switches). "People change."

"She found yoga."

He snorted. "Yep. That was the beginning of the end for us. All of a sudden, she was talking about balance and mindfulness and inner quiet. I just nodded and smiled, and she got pissier and pissier because I was a dolt who just wanted to work and come home and get laid and have kids and be happy. I don't really know what being mindful really means."

"It means—"

"I also don't care." He smiled to soften the words. "So she left me not for another man or another woman, but for her *journey*. Which I wasn't allowed to be part of." He paused, shifting his gaze to the window. "If you ever want to make someone feel like they're nothing, that's the way to do it."

The words sat between us, heavy and sincere.

I took a sip of wine. "I always hated her name." I didn't; it was a beautiful name, but solidarity was called for. I smiled, and Daniel grinned crookedly, clearly relieved.

"Let's talk about something other than my ex-wife."

"Wait, wait, one more question," I said. "Why do you date all those teenagers?"

"Kate, cut me some slack. I've never dated a teenager, not even when I *was* a teenager. Let's make that very clear. They're all over twenty-one."

"Their IQs, too?"

"Good one." Ollie shifted his head so it was resting in Daniel's danger zone. Not that I noticed or anything. "I don't know. They want bragging rights so they can tell their friends they slept with a firefighter. I oblige, part of my civic duty."

"You're a prince."

"They're uncomplicated, at least."

"That does seem to be true."

"Besides," he added, "if Calista could gut me the way she

did, just imagine what someone like you could do, Kate." He winked, and I rolled my eyes.

"Oh, please. In your mind, I'm old enough to be your mother. All this flirting is just you on autopilot."

"It's a gift, I'll admit it." He looked at his wineglass. "So how are you these days?"

"Well, as you could see in the park, I'm doing great. Totally together."

"You lonely?"

The question jammed the spike through my throat. "Yes."

Daniel kindly looked outside, where the rainwater rushed down. "You know what I hated?" he asked, still not looking at me. "I mean, not that it's the same, divorce, but...well, I hated doing laundry after she left. When we were married, it was— God, I sound stupid."

"No, I know what you mean. It's like even your clothes are lonely."

He nodded. "Exactly."

"My husband had an ex-wife," I heard myself say. "And they stayed in touch right up until he died, but I didn't know about it. He saved all their emails, and I know I shouldn't read them, but I'm pretty sure I will."

"Don't."

"Easy for you to say."

"Kate. Don't."

"Why? Because then I'll see that I was his runner-up? Because then I might find out that he was going to come home one night and say, 'On second thought, Kate, I'm still in love with Madeleine. Can you move out this weekend?'" I took a hit of wine. "And no matter what they say or don't say, he's still dead. I'm still the widow, and I barely got to be a wife."

Daniel didn't say anything.

"Sorry," I muttered. "Verbal diarrhea. I better check the stew."

The stew was ready, bubbling and hot, and I found a loaf of gorgeous bread that smelled like rosemary and olive oil. I set out some cheese and got down the bowls, and we ate in the kitchen like two old friends.

Which I guessed we were.

"I better get back," Daniel said after his third bowl of stew and half a loaf of bread. "I have to work in the morning."

"Let me drive you."

"To Brooklyn? Nah."

"I meant to your sister's place, or the train station."

"I'm taking the train, but I'll walk. I like rain." He gave me a hug, and I registered the hard muscles and strong frame, the nice smell of him. "Don't read those emails. But if you do, call me if you want."

A kiss on the cheek, and he was gone, the smell of rain gusting into the kitchen, leaving me alone once more.

# Chapter Nineteen

*Ainsley*

Over the weekend, I fluttered around Kate's house, bought a few pots of flowers from the garden center for her patio, which looked so lonely, then made spaghetti and meatballs for dinner. We watched a movie in her home theater, and Kate fell asleep halfway through. It was a good thing, anyway. The husband in it died, and why hadn't I checked that first? Granted, it was billed as a suspense, filled with unexpected twists, but there should've been a widow-warning on it.

On Sunday, I went to Rachelle's, in case Kate wanted some time without me. Rachelle made margaritas, bless her heart, and we stalked men on the internet who had liked her Match.com profile. We *didn't* look up Eric.

At night, back home in the chic bedroom that still felt like a hotel, I held Pooh to my chest and surprised myself by crying. Honestly, while I didn't envy Kate losing Nathan, at least Nathan got to stay...pure. More than a decade of happiness with Eric was now tainted by the *now* of him. I'd never be able to think of him without remembering that smug look on his face at the Algonquin. I hoped he'd get eaten by a bear *and* an orca whale out in Alaska.

But still, tears trickled into my hair. Where was the boy who stayed in the bathroom with me when I had food poisoning that time, when I was so drenched in sweat that I kept sliding off the toilet? Forget roses and diamond rings, *that* was love. Where was the guy who held me every night because, by his own admission, he loved the smell of my hair and couldn't fall asleep unless I was snuggled against him? Had he found someone else with nice-smelling hair? Or did he now carry a lock of his own to sniff?

How did you just stop loving someone in the space of weeks? That guy in the blue light drinking a pink martini… that guy was a stranger.

I tossed and turned, filled with half dreams that we never broke up, or that he, and not Nathan, had died. That he'd written another column about me, and I didn't know what it said, but everyone was mad at me because of it, even my dad.

So no wonder I slept through my alarm, which I'd set ten minutes earlier than normal so I could get to work on time.

I did not get to work on time. I was four minutes late.

"Ainsley, can I see you in my office?" Jonathan said.

My face flushed.

I'd thought about him, too, this weekend. How unexpectedly kind he'd been. How his eyes were so special and hypnotic up close. How I was almost positive that twice, he'd said something nice to me.

I went into his office and closed the door behind me. "Hi. Did you have a nice weekend?"

"You were late again."

"Sorry about that."

"Is it really so hard to be on time, Ainsley?" His voice was irritable.

I blinked. Apparently, those two nice things were signs of my overactive imagination. "I'm sorry. I'll stay four minutes late tonight."

"It happens at least four times a week."

"I tried! I did set my alarm earlier this morning, but I slept through it. It's the wind chimes ringtone. I guess I need a foghorn or a siren alert, because I just dreamed that it was windy, and so I kept sleeping, and—"

"That's enough explanation. Thank you."

He stared at me. Today, his eyes didn't look like a beautiful mosaic of green and blue and gold—they just looked icy. It made me feel off balance. Here he'd taken me out to dinner on Friday *and* for a carriage ride. Now he was acting like he could barely tolerate me. Again.

"Was there anything else, Mr. Kent?"

"Yes. I need your pitches for the December issue by ten o'clock."

"Okay." I started to get up, then sat back down. "Jonathan, I won't be going to DWI anymore. That's your group, and I'm sorry if I made you uncomfortable."

His eyes flickered. "I appreciate that."

"I am having a makeover party with Carly and Marley and Henry tomorrow night, though. You're more than welcome to come."

His mouth pulled up just the slightest bit on one side, and I felt a strange tug in my stomach. "I'll pass, but thank you for the offer."

I reached into my bag and pulled out his handkerchief from Friday night, which I'd washed and ironed yesterday. "Nice and clean," I said, putting it on the desk.

"Thank you."

"Thank *you*." Okay, all this civility was getting awkward. I stood up and went back to my cubicle. For once, I was relieved to get working.

My cheeks still felt hot.

I opened my email and found a message from Gram-Gram, typed all in capital letters and 18-point font because it was getting hard for her to see.

DEAR AINSLEY, I HOPE YOU OR KATE CAN TAKE ME TO A WAKE TONIGHT. WEAR SOMETHING PRETTY BECAUSE THERE ARE ALWAYS SINGLE MEN IN CASE YOU ARE READY TO MEET SOMEONE NEW.

Ah, Gram-Gram. She always had my back.

I AM ON THE LOOKOUT, TOO. GOD KNOWS I'M NOT MEETING ANYONE HERE. EVERY SINGLE MAN IN THIS PLACE HAS A LINE OUT THE DOOR, AND TRYING TO SIT NEXT TO THEM AT DINNER IS A BLOOD SPORT. OR THEY ARE DYING! XOXOXOX GRAM-GRAM.

I emailed that I'd be happy to go to the wake with her, *not* to ask Kate and that I'd pick her up at 5:30.

Then I got to work on some ideas for Christmas stories that weren't too similar to all the Christmas stories *Hudson Lifestyle* had done in the past.

At 4:00, Rachelle buzzed me. "Your beautiful grandmother is here to see you!" she sang. Gram-Gram was universally adored.

I went out to the foyer. "Hey, Gram-Gram! What are you doing here?"

"For the *wake*, sweetheart. Oh, don't you look pretty!

You'll definitely find a nice boyfriend, I'm sure." She patted my cheek. "Such firm skin! I remember those days!"

"Thanks, but I was going to pick you up at 5:30," I said.

"You did?"

"I emailed you right back."

"I forgot to check. Oh, dear." She smiled happily. "Betty was coming downtown, so I asked her to drop me off."

"Well, I don't get off for an hour, Gram-Gram, and my boss is a little uptight about—"

"Hello."

I closed my eyes. More trouble with Jonathan. "Gram-Gram, do you remember Jonathan Kent, my boss?"

"Hello, dear," she said to him. "I love your hair!"

Jonathan gave me that look that told me he was suffering from sharp gastrointestinal pains caused by yours truly.

"My grandmother and I crossed signals, Jonathan," I said. "I was going to pick her up for a wake, and she thought she was supposed to meet me here."

"Calling hours started four minutes ago," Gram-Gram said. "I wanted to get there before Anita Duran. She's like a fox in the henhouse. Or a fox in the rooster house, as the case may be. She'll have that poor widower's pants around his knees before we even get in the door if we don't leave right now, Ainsley."

Rachelle clapped a hand over her mouth. Jonathan just kept staring at me.

"Then by all means, off you go," he said.

"Thank you, Jonathan," I muttered. "I'll make up the time."

"Yes. You will."

"Ticktock, honey," Gram-Gram said.

The deceased, Darleen Richmond, had quite a crowd. My grandmother pointed out an elderly woman with jet-black hair at the front of the line, holding the widower's hand and patting it.

"Oh, that Anita!" Gram-Gram hissed, "She's *such* a slut. I knew I should've picked you up at three."

"Well, we'll have our turn." The line shuffled along. "So how did you know her?"

"Who?"

"The lady. The deceased."

"Oh, I don't know her," Gram-Gram said blithely. "I'm just here to check out her husband. I read the obituary this morning."

The woman in front of us turned around and scowled.

"Do you see anyone for yourself?" Gram-Gram asked, oblivious. "There are some handsome men here. Maybe someone for Kate, too."

What the heck. I did a discreet check. "Anyone catch your fancy?" Gram-Gram asked.

I shook my head. Smiled awkwardly at one of the actual mourners.

"The night is young. Don't give up!"

"Do you mind?" snapped the woman in front of us.

"No, dear, not at all," Gram-Gram said. "Go ahead, it's your turn. Don't take too long, all right?" The mourner went up, and Gram-Gram turned to me. "Oh, goody! The widower is quite handsome, don't you think?"

"Uh...sure."

"By the way, someone asked me if I wanted to have *sex* on that little phone game of yours!"

"Inside voice, Gram-Gram."

"I thought it was a little soon, so I suggested we have dinner, and guess what? He never wrote to me again! Oh, it's our turn! Come on, honey!" She dragged me to the casket, barely paused and trotted over to the grieving widow. She hugged him tightly for a long, long minute.

"She was a wonderful woman," Gram-Gram said, holding his face in her hands.

"Thank you, uh…"

"Lettie. Lettie Carson."

"And how did you know my wife?"

"Oh, gosh, we went way back. High school."

"So you're from Ohio, too?"

"Not exactly! So how are you, uh…Edmond?"

"Edward."

"Yes, yes. How are you, poor man? Can I offer you some advice, since I've been a widow for thirty-four years? Don't become a hermit. In fact, why don't you come to movie night with me this week at Overlook Farms Retirement Community? That's the official name, but I call it Village of the Damned. They're showing *The Ten Commandments*." She dug into her purse and handed him a piece of paper. "My name and all the details are here. I'll see you Thursday!" She hugged him again, winked at me, then released him. "And this is my beautiful granddaughter Ainsley. Also single, in case you have any grandsons under forty. Her boyfriend strung her along for eleven years! Eleven years, can you believe—"

"And we're leaving," I said, taking my grandmother by the arm. "So sorry for your loss, Mr.… Uh. Yes."

I steered her out of the funeral home, not missing the triumphant look she gave Anita. "Did you have fun?" I asked as we drove back to her apartment.

"Oh, yes, honey!" she said. "Your mother would lecture me, but where else am I supposed to meet someone?"

I was never really sure how much of Gram-Gram's dottiness was her personality or dementia. But Candy *was* pretty hard on her, and Kate was a little too dignified to do things like pick up men at wakes or turn a blind eye when Gram-Gram crammed her purse full of jam packets and creamers at Denny's. Me, I didn't mind.

"Maybe we can do an event at the Village of the Damned," I suggested, turning into the giant residence. "Speed dating or something."

"Honey, the women outnumber the men five to one. Why do you think I'm reduced to scoping out widowers while they're burying their wives?"

"Or we can start a local senior citizen matchmaking service. I met a widower recently. George. He's very sweet."

"Probably gay," Gram-Gram said. "But sure, honey. Give it your best shot."

"I could do a story for the magazine. Dating After 70—The Challenges and the Fun. What do you think?"

"I think I have to go to the bathroom, honey," Gram-Gram said, opening the car door. I slammed on the brake, since we weren't quite stopped yet. "Hurry up if you're walking me in!"

We speed-walked to her apartment, and I managed a kiss on the back of her head before she bolted inside. "Love you!" I called, then headed back down the long hallway.

A senior dating story would be great. We could tie in some key advertisers, too—gerontologists and hearing aid places, a yoga studio that might offer special classes for seniors. We could do a contest on the website... *Win a romantic date for two, limo included, home before 9:00 p.m.*

My phone buzzed with a text. It was from Eric.

Ains, I'm working on my cancer memoir and I can't remember the name of the chemo drug that made me so sick. Do you? Also, packing for AK! Super excited.

I had to read it three times before answering.

It was the yellow fin tuna that made you sick. You waltzed through chemo, Baron Munchausen.

It took only a few seconds for him to respond.

I understand you're still bitter and hope you find a more fulfilling path.

I took a cleansing breath. Took another. Turned off my phone.

As I walked through the beautiful foyer, I heard a commotion down the hall. Two little girls, one significantly taller than the other, stood outside a room. From within, a man was yelling. A nurse or aide came running down the hall, and the girls looked wretched.

I hesitated.

Then Jonathan came out into the hall and knelt in front of the girls. He looked back in the room, where the man was still shouting, and ran a hand through his hair, ruining the perfect combed-back sleekness and allowing a few subdued curls to spring into life.

He was frazzled. Not something I'd seen before. Ever.

"Hi," I said, walking toward them. "Can I do anything?"

"This is not my house!" yelled the man inside the room. "I want to go home! Right now!"

The smaller girl's bottom lip trembled, and the older one—whose eyes were the same hypnotic blue as her father's—had the same set to her jaw as Jonathan had when he was irritated with me.

There was a crash from inside the room. "Please stay calm, Mr. Kent," the nurse said.

"I will not!" the poor old guy yelled.

"Maybe I can take the girls outside," I suggested.

"That would be very helpful," Jonathan said. "Emily, Lydia, this is my, uh, my friend Ainsley. She works at the magazine. She'll watch you until I get Grandpa settled. I won't be long. Is that all right?"

"I hate it here," said the younger one. Lydia, if I remembered correctly. She was six, and Emily was eight.

"It's no fun when grown-ups get upset, is it?" I asked. "Come on, let's go outside. It's beautiful tonight."

Jonathan gave me a terse nod, then went back in the room.

The sun was still high over the Hudson. The Village of the Damned had beautiful grounds with wide, smooth paths and lovely landscaping, but no playground. They should think about that…a playground would give the grands and great-grands something to do when they visited.

"Let's make fairy houses," I said.

"What are fairy houses?" the little one asked.

"You make a house for a fairy, and sometimes they leave you a little treat," I said.

"Fairies aren't real," said Emily. Her father's girl, clearly.

"I don't know about that," I said. "I've heard they're getting braver, since so many people believe in them these days. Come on, let's make them a house and maybe they'll visit. I'll show you."

We went to the edge of the grounds, in sight of the front door so Jonathan could see us when he came out. "The first thing you have to do is find a place that's a little bit hidden, because they're shy."

"How about here?" the little one said, pointing under a rhododendron bush.

"Perfect," I said. "We need to find some sticks and maybe some moss and a few leaves."

"And pebbles?"

"And pebbles. Great idea."

"What's your name again?" asked Emily.

"Ainsley. And you're Emily, and you're Lydia, and I know this because your daddy has a picture of you in his office."

"I hate visiting Grandpa," Lydia said. "He smells funny."

"He yells at Daddy, and I hate him," Emily added. Her eyes filled with tears.

My heart tugged, and I slid my arm around her. "Sometimes when people get old, they're confused and scared."

She dashed the tears away. "That's what Daddy says, but I don't care."

"Daddy says it's nice for us to come see him," Lydia said, "but mostly he doesn't know who we are." She held up a stick for my inspection. "Will this work?"

"Let's see." I sat down on the grass and started making a little structure, digging the sticks into the soft ground, making a lean-to. "How about that moss for a roof?" I suggested. "And maybe some flower blossoms to make it pretty." Emily carefully placed the moss on top, and Lydia got some flowers.

"It's pretty," Emily said. "Even if fairies won't come."

Aha. Progress. A few minutes ago, she didn't believe in them at all; now they were a possibility. I smiled at her, earning a small, shy smile back.

The girls got into it, making a little path of stones to the structure, chatting away about what the fairies would like, asking me if I ever got any presents. I'd have to make sure to come back here and leave a little something (just in case the fairies didn't come through).

The girls were getting pleasingly grubby, the knees on their tights stained with dirt. Sign of a happy childhood, I always thought. Candy always liked us clean; childhood baths from her were scrub downs, rather than the bubble baths I started taking the second I had a place of my own.

Well. A place with Eric.

But I did love baths, more than ever now that I was living with Kate.

Not once had she suggested I look for my own place. Not once had she given the vibe that she found me irritating or too chatty. She didn't complain about Ollie, even when he'd barfed up some grass on the rug.

I felt a rush of love for my sister. Pulled out my phone and took a picture of the fairy house, then texted it to her. Playing with two little girls and thinking of you. Glad you're my sissy. xoxox.

I hoped she wouldn't think it was dumb.

A second later, my phone buzzed. You're so sweet, Ains. Thank you. Same here!

It was bittersweet that grief had made us closer.

Jonathan was taking longer than I expected. It occurred to me I didn't know where he lived. A sterile condo would be my guess. "Are you staying at Daddy's place tonight?" I asked.

"No. Mommy's and Uncle Matt's. We live half with them and half with Daddy," Emily said.

"Yes, he told me." How icky, making the girls call him uncle!

"Daddy hates Uncle Matt," Lydia said innocently.

"Lydia! Don't talk about it," said Emily, shooting me a worried glance.

"Why?" she said. "Annie's nice." She ripped up some grass from the perfect lawn to scatter around the fairy house.

"Ainsley," I corrected. "I think you're nice, too, both of you. But don't worry, Emily. I won't say anything." I ripped up some grass, too. Nothing but the best for the fairies.

"What have you got there?" came Jonathan's voice, and I

jumped a little. I hadn't heard him coming. He stood behind us, hands in his pockets, tie off, jacket missing, his shirt un-buttoned at the neck.

"Ashley taught us to make fairy houses and the fairies might come back and give us presents!" Lydia said, yanking his hand. "Look, Daddy, look!"

Jonathan hunkered down and studied our work. "I like the little path," he said. "And the roof will keep them nice and dry if it rains."

I felt an odd pressure in my chest. An odd, lovely pressure.

"Daddy," Emily asked, "there aren't really any fairies, are there?" The look on her face practically begged him to con-tradict her.

He put his arm around her and looked into her serious face, the expression so similar to his own. "I don't know," he said in that low, beautiful voice. "I haven't seen one since I was a little boy."

"You saw one?" Lydia asked. "When, Daddy, when?"

Jonathan stood up. "Oh, I was about seven," he said, art-fully picking the age just between his daughters. "At first I thought it was a dragonfly, but it hovered in the air in front of me, and it had a face almost like a person, but a little strange, a little different."

"Was she very beautiful?" Lydia asked.

"Did she have hair?" Emily added.

"She was beautiful, and yes, she had silvery hair. She seemed very curious about me. Then, just like that, she zipped away."

"*I* want to see a fairy!" Lydia said, hopping up and down.

"Is that a true story?" Emily asked.

"It is." He smiled at them, that small, slight lift to his lips, and that feeling came again.

Who knew that Jonathan Kent had a whimsical streak?

"Why don't you make another down there?" Jonathan suggested. "In case there's more than one fairy who needs a house. Maybe over there, where that big tree is."

The girls bolted down the lawn, Emily reaching out to hold Lydia's hand.

The sun was setting over the Hudson, high cumulus clouds piling up in a creamy glow. We could see the lights of Cambry-on-Hudson wink on down below, and in the distance, the shining bridge. The Village of the Damned had the best view in town.

"How's your dad?" I asked, not getting up from the grass. To my surprise, Jonathan sat down next to me.

"He's calmer now." There was a pause as he weighed what to tell me. "The stroke took away a lot." His face was hard to read.

"I'm sorry," I said.

He inclined his head. "Thank you. I bring the girls here because...well, because he's their grandfather. He loved them a great deal before."

There was a lot unsaid in that sentence. A lump formed in my throat. "And your mom?" I asked.

"She died eleven years ago. Cancer."

"I'm sorry."

"Thank you." He kept staring straight ahead. "My daughters mentioned their uncle, I take it?"

"Matt?"

"Yes."

"They did." I paused. "They said you hate him."

"Yes. It's somewhat hard to forgive your brother when he sleeps with your wife."

My mouth fell open. Holy guacamole! So *uncle* wasn't an honorary title.

"Oh," I managed.

He kept staring ahead. "They had an affair shortly after my father's stroke. They're still together."

"Jonathan, I'm so sorry."

Another incline of the head. "Partly my fault, I'm sure."

"No, I don't think it is."

He did look at me then, a flicker of amusement in his strange eyes.

"Your wife and your brother?" I went on. "Nope. Definitely not your fault. That's just shitty luck in relatives. And spouse. Low morals. Cheatin' hearts. Slimeballs. Did they take your dog, too?"

He laughed unexpectedly. "As a matter of fact, yes."

I leaned so my shoulder touched his just for a moment. "At least you have the makings of a good country song."

He slid a look at me, and something turned over in my stomach. "I suppose that's true."

The sky had turned an intense red at the horizon, and for a moment, we didn't say anything, just watched the girls as they busied themselves at the edge of the lawn. Two swallows dipped and whirled as they made their way home, and the Hudson shimmered silver and pink.

"Have you seen Eric lately?" Jonathan asked.

"Only on *Jimmy Kimmel*."

"You seem to have taken it well."

"Don't be fooled. I'd stab him in the eye if it wouldn't get me arrested." I shifted slightly, the grass feeling a little damp against my legs. "Do you ever get over it?" I asked. "That feeling that you didn't know the person you were sleeping with at all?"

Maybe I'd gone too far, because he didn't answer right away. "Sorry," I said.

"No," he said. "You don't. But it does stop hurting quite so much."

"You still go to the support group."

"I'm not sure how to extricate myself from that, actually. Also, they're nice people. My friends."

It struck me as odd that Jonathan had friends. I always pictured him alone. Not very fair of me. Until very recently, I'd pictured him only as a work-obsessed robot. Captain Flatline.

Who told his daughters that he'd seen a fairy, and faithfully visited his sick father.

"Daddy! Come see our fairy house! You, too, Abby!" The girls charged back at us, dirt-stained and happy.

"It's Miss O'Leary to you, sweetheart," he said.

"Or Ainsley," I said.

He stood up and offered me his hand, which I took, and he pulled me up. For a second, we were almost pressed together, and I smelled him, his laundry detergent, his soap.

I took a step back. "I should go," I said, my voice a little off. "It was so nice to meet you, girls. Check the fairy houses in a week or so and see if they left you a prize, okay?"

"We will!" Lydia announced.

"It was nice meeting you," Emily said, a little shy.

Jonathan smiled at me, a slightly crooked smile, as if he didn't quite know how to do it, and there it was again, that pressure, this time deep in my stomach.

"Oh, um, Jonathan, I thought we could maybe do a story on senior citizen dating," I babbled. "My grandmother? Who came to work today? Anyway, she's— Well, we can discuss it at work."

"All right," he said. "Good night, Ainsley."

"Bye," I said and walked off, acutely aware that my boss may or may not have been watching me go.

I hoped my ass looked good in this skirt.

"Cool it," I muttered to myself.

But the flustered feeling stayed with me all the way home.

# Chapter Twenty

*Kate*

On the first Friday in June, two months into the all-fun, all-the-time journey that was widowhood, I came home from shooting a wedding and decided to read Nathan's emails to and from Madeleine.

I don't know why then. Maybe because the bride and groom had seemed genuinely happy, their faces showing me nothing through the lens except simple joy. It made me wonder if my marriage had been as happy as I'd thought.

Maybe it was because I'd been to the widows and widowers group again. LuAnn, the orangey woman who'd lost her police officer husband, had told us about cleaning out his closet and finding a Christmas present for her, already wrapped, or possibly forgotten from last year, unsure of whether or not she should open it.

Maybe it was because the house was quiet; Ainsley was out with friends. One of these days, I'd have to call Jenny and Kim and let them know I was up for a night out. Jenny had mentioned her sister, too, newly divorced, a mother of three. All I had to do was reach out, which had always been a little hard for me.

Maybe I decided to read those emails tonight because I got an invitation from the Re-Enter Center—a fund-raiser next week, one of many they had throughout the year—and it reminded me of Daniel. The last time I'd seen him, we'd talked about those emails, and I still hadn't pulled the trigger.

Whatever the reason, I poured myself a big-ass glass of wine, chugged half of it and went into the den (or study). Hector, who'd clearly felt ousted as number one pet since Ollie had come to live with us, was delighted to see me, wriggling vigorously in his bowl. "Hi, buddy," I said, waving at him. "You got my back here? Yeah? Good. Let's do this."

I sat in Nathan's chair and turned on Nathan's computer. Swallowed some more of Nathan's wine and dived right in. There was the MRT folder.

I clicked on the earliest email and started, taking care to read every sentence slowly, every reply from my dead husband.

Madeline Rose Trentham was a good writer, I'd give her that.

The nutshell version: she'd asked him to dump me and give her another chance, and she wanted his babies now, and theirs was a love too great to be denied, even if it would be hurtful to "her." (Me, of course. Madeleine referred to me only in pronouns. Didn't type my name once, the bitch.)

He said no.

But he didn't say *No, I love Kate more than I ever loved you. She's the moon of my life, my sun and stars.* (Yes, yes, I'd been watching *Game of Thrones* again.)

He didn't say *She's everything to me and I love my life with her.*

He didn't say *Piss off, Madeleine, and stay out of my life.*

Instead, he said it was too late. Things with me had gone too far. He'd gotten used to life without her. He and I were a good match.

I know. It sets the heart afire, right?

He said he loved me in a different way, and if it wasn't as *tempestuous* as the way he'd loved Madeleine, he felt he and I would be—wait for it—*content.*

The *bastard.* If I could've ripped the spike out of my throat and shoved it into his, I would have.

Content, my ass. I rocked his world. Didn't I? We had sex against the wall, thank you very much! Of course I rocked it! The ingrate!

And yet, reading his words made my whole body ache, because I could hear Nathan's voice, even if he wasn't talking to me.

The gentleness, the kindness.

The love.

Because he did still love her.

There was anger, too. That was one emotion I'd never heard from my husband. We'd bickered here and there, and he'd been irritable and sulky once or twice (it was once), but he'd never been *mad* at me.

Suddenly, that seemed like a big problem.

So he was settling for me. *She* was the love of his life— passion, anger, fire, love—and I was contentment.

Yay, me.

Their emails started back when Nathan and I were getting serious. When I was starting to let myself think that maybe I had actually found *the one*, Nathan was debating with his ex-wife.

Him: I can't do that to her just because you're afraid of being alone.

Her: You know how I feel. You've always known.

Him: It's not the same as it was with you.

What did that mean, huh? Was that a compliment or an insult?

The emails were mostly from before we got married, when Madeleine clearly thought she had a chance to change his mind. However, on January 6, five days after our wedding, she'd sent him this: I can't believe you went through with it. Oh, Nathan, what have you done?

He didn't answer that one.

Another one, telling him about a dream she'd had where they were together and had a baby, and they were so happy, and it was so right. Gack.

On Valentine's Day, which was apparently their anniversary, she'd sent another one:

My whole soul is shredded by thoughts of you. Our tenth anniversary—ten years today! How can my life be going on without you? I ruined everything. I'm sobbing right now, alone and broken, and I know I shouldn't be writing to you, but I'm so very, truly sorry for everything, Nathan. I miss you more than I can say, I love you so much, and I know I have no right to tell you that, but it's true.

She sounded drunk to me. Speaking of, my wine was gone.

Nathan had brought me a beautiful bouquet of orchids for Valentine's Day, a glorious riot of white veined with red. I made him dinner, rare for me, and went all out—oysters, Cornish game hen stuffed with cranberries and corn bread, early asparagus and scalloped potatoes. For dessert, I'd made tiny red velvet cakes in the shape of hearts; I'd bought the cake pans at Williams-Sonoma a month before. I gave him a framed photo of the two of us, that selfie I'd taken in September, me standing behind him, kissing his cheek, him smiling right into the camera.

He'd been preoccupied. A sticky issue with a zoning ordinance, he said.

Ordinance, my ass. He sure as hell didn't mention that today would've been his anniversary to his first wife.

He did answer that tragic Heathcliff Loves Cathy Valentine's email. Not the way I wished he had, oh, no. What I wanted to read was *Kate completes me. She baked me tiny red velvet cakes, and they were fantastic! By the way, I can't even remember your face.* I wanted him to threaten a restraining order.

But the truth was now in front of me, because he answered:

I miss you, too. But Kate is my wife now.

Daniel had been right. I shouldn't have read these.

On December 12 of last year, it had been snowing heavily, and Nathan and I had gone for a walk. Most of Cambry-on-Hudson was closed in the way that the 'burbs shut down in the snow, no one trusting their Range Rovers and Mercedes SUVs to actually handle five inches of the white stuff.

It had been almost completely quiet, the only sound the slight hiss of snow falling and the squeak of our boots. We walked and walked, our cheeks pink, hands cold, but it was so magical, the tree branches bending with the heavy weight of white. We walked through the nature preserve that his great-grandfather donated to the town until we stood at the top of a ridge that overlooked the Hudson River, our breaths fogging the air, laughing as we slipped a little, holding hands, steadying each other.

Then Nathan dropped to one knee. "Will you marry me, Kate?" he asked, and I remembered how sweetly shy he looked, those blond eyelashes, his eyes so blue, the snow falling on his hair.

Of course I said yes.

Now, staring at my fish in his fancy bowl, the roots of the plant waving gently in the water, I had another answer.

"On second thought, no," I said, my voice too loud. Hector seemed to flinch.

Because if I'd known Nathan still missed his ex-wife—if I'd known that he'd categorize our relationship as *contentment*—I wouldn't be his widow now.

On Saturday, I went to see my in-laws.

"Kate, deah," Eloise said. "Do come in. Shall I get you some coffee? Perhaps some iced tea? Please, come sit on the patio."

Their house was a brick Georgian, gracious and old. Nathan had grown up here, played hide-and-seek with his sister. Once, he fell asleep in the cupboard under the window seat, legend had it, and it had taken hours to find him.

Probably, he and Madeleine had made out here a few times. Possibly more. Nathan and *I* had never done more than hold hands in the presence of his parents.

"Hello, Kate," Mr. Coburn said, rising to kiss my cheek.

"Hello," I said, never able to call him by his first name. "It's good to see you."

He seemed sober, but my God, how he'd aged in these past two months! The skin on his face was loose, and his eyes seemed to have faded in color.

We sat awkwardly on their slate patio, where Nathan had envisioned the new bedroom/bathroom/sunroom addition. I accepted some iced tea, though I hated it. The lemon always made my teeth feel stripped like old wood.

"How are Miles and Atticus?" I asked.

"They're very well," Eloise answered. "Miles will start at camp next week, and Atticus is enrolled in an art class. He's quite a gifted painter, Brooke says."

My heart hurt. As ever, I wondered how Eloise could do it—make pleasant small talk, allow that gleam of pride in her eyes as she smiled over her grandsons. Mr. Coburn stared into the middle distance.

"I was in the park the other day," I began. "Bixby Park?"

"A lovely time of year to visit," Eloise said.

"Yes. I, um...I saw the bench."

She raised an eyebrow. "Which bench is that?" she asked.

"The bench for Nathan."

They glanced at each other, and I immediately knew they didn't have any clue what I was talking about.

"I'm sorry," I said. "There's a bench dedicated to Nathan. I thought it was from you."

"Did Brooke do it?" Mr. Coburn asked.

"No, I don't think so," Eloise murmured. She looked at me, her brow furrowed with concern.

I looked into my iced tea. "Maybe Madeleine, then."

She put down her teacup. "I'm sure her heart is in the right place. But I'm so sorry if this makes you uncomfortable. I'll call her."

"No, that's fine," I said. "Listen, I know it's... I brought my camera for your portrait. We never got around to it, and I thought something more spontaneous might be better."

"Our portrait?" Mr. Coburn asked.

"For our anniversary," Eloise said. "The party."

"We're still having that?"

"I told you, deah. Remember? Because of the scholarship fund?"

"Right, right."

"I'll make it as painless as possible," I said, faking a smile.

And so I told them where to sit, adjusted Mr. Coburn's collar under his crewneck sweater and saw something I'd never seen so clearly—Nathan's parents loved each other. They'd never recover from their son's death, but they had each other. They'd love, honor and cherish each other for the rest of their lives, and the magnitude of their loss had brought them closer together.

"You're a beautiful couple," I said, and my voice was husky.

"We've been blessed," Mrs. Coburn said, her voice trembling a little. "We've been very blessed."

Mr. Coburn covered her hand with his and smiled at her, his eyes full of tears. She smiled back and touched his cheek.

Sometimes, a smile was the bravest act of all.

# Chapter Twenty-One

*Ainsley*

On Sunday, I left the fairy presents in the little houses Jonathan's daughters and I had made—two flower beads, and two tiny glass figurines of a snail and a cricket. I spent far too much time agonizing over what the fairies should leave, but I loved picturing the girls finding the gifts.

And imagining their dad smiling when they showed him.

I was visiting my grandmother that day, and it just so happened that Gram-Gram's apartment had a nice view of the side lawn, and yes, I found myself lingering there, glancing out the window.

Gram-Gram was trying to remember her computer password. Ollie sat on her lap, helping by putting his little paws on the keyboard occasionally. Chances were strong he'd figure it out before she did.

"Do you want a sandwich, honey? I made a ham this week."

"I love ham!" I said, always happy to eat.

"Sniff it first, in case it's just about to go bad."

"Roger that." I went into the kitchen and sniffed; there was probably enough salt in that sucker to kill any salmonella or E. coli anyway. "Smells good enough to me!" I took a knife and started hacking away.

"Thanks, sweetheart. Your mother is so fussy about these things." She gave me a squeeze. "Don't use that knife, honey, it's sharp. I'll do it for you."

Dear Gram-Gram. She did love having someone to fuss over. Candy treated her like she had a foot in the grave, raising her voice so Gram-Gram could hear her, even though hearing loss wasn't one of her problems.

"How is your mother?" Gram-Gram asked, reading my mind.

"Oh, fine," I said. I went to the computer and started entering random passwords. *LettieCarson. lettiecarson. lettiecarson1. Gram-Gram.*

A few days ago, Candy had been on the local television lifestyle show, where she was a regular for parenting issues. The host asked her how many children she had and she'd said, "Two children and one stepdaughter." The truth, but still.

I tried Gram-Gram's birthday, her anniversary to her late husband, the date of his death.

Nothing. "Did you have a pet when you were little?" I asked.

"I did," she said. "Blacky the cat. Oh, he was wonderful!" *Blacky. BlackytheCat. blackythecat.*

"I'm going to throw that thing out the window!" Gram-Gram said. "I hate technology! What happened to the good old days when people could just talk to each other? Here you go!" Gram-Gram said. She handed me a sandwich, which had at least half a pound of ham on it, and beamed.

I typed in *SeanKateAinsley*.

And I was in.

"Aw, Gram-Gram," I said. "Your password is us. You're so sweet! Here, I'll write it down, okay?"

"What if the terrorists find it and hack me?" she asked.

"That's a chance I'll take."

"Well, you're a genius. Thank you so much, honey! Now eat your sandwich before it spoils."

Mmm.

"Do you remember my mother, Gram-Gram?" I asked, taking a bite. Oh. Okay, maybe the ham wasn't so fresh. I discreetly spit it into a napkin and fake-chewed.

"Candy? Of course, honey! I'm her mother!"

"I meant Michelle."

Gram-Gram frowned. "The one who died? No, honey, I never met her. I don't think I did, anyway. I'm sorry."

"It's okay. I just wondered. Now, let's check your dating profile." I'd finally found SunsetYearsDating.com. I set my sandwich aside and pulled up the site. "Oh, look! You have five men interested, you hussy!"

"I do?" She clapped, delighted.

"Here's StillGotIt25. I wonder if that's his birth year."

"Then he's only in his nineties! Is he handsome?"

I clicked, then flinched. "Okay, it's best not to go with a guy whose profile picture is of him in tighty-whities."

"Not so fast," she said, putting on one of her many pairs of glasses and peering at the screen. "Oh, dear, no. That's some serious droopage. Looks like a turkey wattle in there. Next." She picked up my sandwich and took a bite.

"Oh, Gram-Gram, that's my sandwich. And you know what? I'm pretty hungry." I'd also have to figure out how to get the ham out of there so she wouldn't get food poisoning.

We clicked on the next picture. It showed a collage of

pictures—an elderly man, nice-looking, smiling. Another of him holding a toddler. And the most recent one, lying in a hospital bed, eyes closed. Good God. His interests were listed as *custard night*. Yes. He looked like a soft diet kind of guy. I glanced at my gram.

"Is that Bill Parsons?" she said, blinking at the picture. "I think it is. He died a few weeks ago. Next."

The next profile had no photos. It just said I'm looking for someone to take care of me. Must not be squeamish about bowel rinses. Also, my daughters do not approve of this, so you would have to leave or hide when they visit.

"Charming," I murmured.

An announcement came over the intercom, which was in everyone's apartment. "Good afternoon, residents! A reminder that our salsa dance class starts in ten minutes."

"Shall we go to that, Gram-Gram?" I said. "A lot of times, meeting someone in person is best."

"Only women go to salsa dancing."

"Maybe you should become a lesbian, then. It would solve that pesky life expectancy problem."

"Oh, you're such a hoot!" She laughed. "Sure, let's go. This is getting us nowhere." She paused. "I'm just lonely, honey. Your grandfather's been gone so long I can't even remember what a hug from a man feels like, let alone sex. I hope you don't mind helping me."

I wrapped my arms around her little shoulders and gave a gentle squeeze. "I love helping you," I said.

I'd never met my grandfather—well, Candy's father—who died before I was born. Pictures always showed a smiling, bald man with Malcolm X–style glasses. I remember how jealous I used to feel, seeing the old home movies of him carrying Sean on his shoulders, holding Kate as an infant.

Dad had been raised in an orphanage, back in the days

when they had orphanages here in the United States. My mother's parents had never met me, according to Candy. They'd sent birthday cards until I was about ten. Otherwise, Gram-Gram was it.

At least she was fantastic. I waited while she doused herself with rose-scented perfume that made my sinuses itch, combed her hair, fussed with her earrings, put on a scarf, took it off and finally was ready to go. "Shall we bring Ollie?" I asked.

"Oh, yes! He'll help me stand out in that crowd of shriveled hags. Men love dogs."

"Good point. Come on, Ollie, let's go." I scooped up my dog, who was looking extra cute today, and kissed him on the head.

The Village of the Damned did a nice job of offering different things. Cooking classes, tai chi, dancing, crafts, holiday parties, outings… It was just that not many people seemed to want to do them. Or weren't able to do them.

As Gram-Gram predicted, there were roughly thirty women in the gym and three men. Each man had at least four dance partners vying for his attention.

Wait. There were five men.

Jonathan Kent stood in the doorway, his hands on the back of his father's wheelchair.

My face grew hot, same as the time I'd hidden in the boys locker room in eleventh grade to see Juan Cabrera without his shirt. Would Jonathan think I was stalking him? *Was* I stalking him? I'd been at that window a long time.

He looked over, saw me and gave a cool nod.

Right. Captain Flatline.

His father looked distressed, however, and I knew how to fix that. "Do you know that gentleman over there in the wheelchair?" I asked Gram-Gram. "Mr. Kent?"

"I don't think so," she said. "He's rather handsome. Is he senile?"

"I'm not a hundred percent sure. He's my boss's father."

"Well, if he's nice, who cares about a little senility? Let's go say hello." She marched over to them, using her sharp little elbows to negotiate the crowd. I followed, Ollie trying to lick everyone we passed.

"Hello, hello, hello, boys!" Gram-Gram said, neatly cutting off an incoming female, who glared at her.

"Hi," I said to Jonathan. "Fancy meeting you here."

"Hello." He looked tense. Normal, in other words.

"You remember my grandmother?"

"Of course. Mrs. Carson, lovely to see you again."

"Oh! Don't you have the nicest manners, young man! This is your father?"

"Yes. Malcolm Kent. I'm afraid he's not—"

Malcolm Kent caught sight of Ollie in my arms. "Good dog," he said.

"Would you like to hold him?" I asked. "He's very friendly."

Gram-Gram took Ollie from me and put him gently on Mr. Kent's lap. The old man lifted a gnarled hand and petted him, then smiled at my grandmother.

"Shall we get out there?" Gram-Gram asked. "Come on! It's fun." She hip-checked Jonathan out of the way and grabbed the wheelchair handles.

"Is that all right, Dad?" Jonathan asked, but they were already out there, Gram-Gram's head bouncing to Michael Jackson's "Billie Jean." Not what I'd consider salsa music, but hey.

Jonathan's eyes were on his father. "He'll be okay," I said, hoping it was true.

"He likes dogs," he said.

"And Ollie likes people. We actually volunteer here, Ollie and me. Well. Mostly Ollie. But I tag along."

He dragged his eyes off his father and looked at me for the first time.

Damn. Those eyes did not play fair. The gold chip in his left eye just invited staring. I dragged my gaze off him, my stomach hot and tight. "Are the girls here?" I asked.

"No."

I watched the seniors for a minute. "Does any white person really know how to salsa?" I asked. "Where does a person even learn salsa dancing?"

"You should know," Jonathan said, "since you wrote a story about it for the magazine last fall."

"Did I? Right. I did, didn't I? I forgot."

"Clearly."

"I never took a class, though."

"I did."

I snorted. Jonathan, dancing. It was probably against his religion. "Oh, yeah? Can you *paso doble*, too?"

"No. I can jitterbug, though."

"Get outta town! So when did you become lord of the dance? Was it to meet women?"

"No. It was when my wife and I were engaged."

I winced. "Sorry."

"Why would you be sorry?" He gazed at me with that expression—*human apologizes for no apparent reason.*

Out on the dance floor, my grandmother was shimmying in front of Mr. Kent, who didn't seem to notice, as he and Ollie were staring deeply into each other's eyes.

"Would you like to dance, Ainsley?"

I actually jumped. "What?"

"Would you like to dance?"

"Um…no. I mean, I'm not very good. I inherited my grandmother's gift, in other words."

His mouth twitched. "Well, then, at least you're enthusiastic."

"If uncoordinated."

"Don't be a coward." He took my hand, and a jolt ran up my arm. He pulled me out to where his father was, put his hand on my waist and, much to my shock, seemed to know what he was doing.

I stepped on his foot and found myself against his chest.

"It's sort of a rocking thing," he said. "Eight counts. Step forward, step in place, step back, pause. Or in your case, back, in place, forward, pause."

Whatever. He was holding my hand. I tried to follow him and tripped.

This time, he did smile, and my legs threatened to splay.

"One, two, three, back, five six seven pause."

I stepped on his foot again.

He laughed, the sound low and sooty, and everything inside me seemed to swell and squeeze.

"Okay, let's freestyle it, what do you say?" he asked and stepped a little away from me (self-preservation, no doubt). But he kept holding my hand and twirled me.

"Good girl, Ainsley!" Gram-Gram crowed. "You look like a professional!"

Jonathan twirled me again, and this time, I found myself with my back pressed against his chest. "Thank you for the fairy presents you left," he murmured, and my bones practically dissolved. "I went to leave something and saw that you beat me to it. And your gifts were better." He moved me so we were facing each other again.

Then I accidentally smacked one of the female residents in the cheek, got a glare, apologized, then looked at Jonathan.

He was definitely smiling. It was an odd smile, and he looked dorktastically adorable and so, *so* appealing that I didn't quite know what to do.

Captain Flatline, smiling. At me.

"Son," Mr. Kent said, and Jonathan's smile dropped.

He knelt next to his father. "Yes, Dad."

"I want to go home. Will you take me home?"

"Of course." He straightened up, then gently picked up Ollie and handed him to me.

Our eyes held for a second.

"Thank you," he said.

Then he turned to my grandmother, took her hand and kissed it. "Mrs. Carson, always a pleasure."

"Oh! So courtly!" she cooed.

He looked at me once more. "Try not to be late tomorrow," he said.

Then he left, pushing his father's wheelchair. He didn't look back.

Damn.

Gram-Gram put her hands on her hips and looked around. "Well, I don't have a chance in hell at getting close to a man. Let's just dance, sweetheart."

And so we did. As Jonathan said, what we lacked in skill, we made up for in enthusiasm. We might as well have been blood relatives after all.

# Chapter Twenty-Two

❦

*Kate*

On Thursday when I got home from a day of photo editing, my eyes bleary from the computer, Ainsley was waiting, full of her usual energy. "We're going out tonight," she announced. "Margaritas! The cure for everything! I know just the place."

"It's a nice thought, but I'm supposed to go to a fund-raiser in Brooklyn. The Re-Enter Center. It's a wine and cheese thing." I didn't want to go. I wanted to nap until next year.

"Oh, the ex-cons! Right. Well, I'll come with you, maybe flirt with some of your students. Those tattoos can be very attractive. I love the little teardrops."

"That means they've killed someone."

"It does? Are you sure?" I nodded. "Well, there goes my plan to find a new boyfriend. Come on, it'll be fun."

I didn't answer. "Kate," she said, "I know you're tired, but you need to get out. You need to wash your hair and moisturize. And shave those legs. It's a forest down there. Come on! Up and at 'em!"

I closed my eyes for a second, then went off to do her bidding.

When I was clean (and smooth), Ainsley brought in her enormous tray of makeup and went to town on me. "You used to do this when you were little," I said, trying not to move my lips as she applied lipstick.

"I remember," she said with a smile. "You should wear makeup once in a while. You're gorgeous without it, but come on. A little cat's-eye here, some blush here, and it's really not fair how beautiful you are."

Nathan used to tell me I was beautiful, too.

Ainsley took out a giant brush and began sweeping my cheeks. "So what's new these days?"

"Nathan's ex-wife bought him a memorial bench in Bixby Park," I said.

Her mouth dropped open. "Are you serious? How dare she! *So* not her place."

"Thanks. I agree." I thought about telling her about the emails, then decided not to. It was too much. Besides, she had loved Nathan.

But maybe, if I saw Daniel tonight, I'd tell him.

"Okay, take a look," my sister said. "Ta-da!"

I looked.

For the first time since Nathan had died, I didn't look exhausted or stunned. Ainsley had done my eyes with dark gray eye shadow, and her mascara was obviously better than mine, because my lashes looked long and feathery. My lips were red, and my skin looked perfect.

"Gorgeous," she said. "Those ex-cons won't know what hit them."

★ ★ ★

The Re-Enter Center looked weird to me; I hadn't been here since February, when Nathan and I had come for the spaghetti dinner. It smelled the same, though, like all schools—disinfectant and books, boredom and potential.

Ainsley got us some wine and cheese. I waved to Greta, the director, who flashed me a huge smile. She was talking to someone but held up a finger to indicate I was to wait.

Other than Greta, I didn't know a lot of people here, and the familiar awkwardness fell over me. I smiled at a woman who taught computer basics. We'd both taught here for years, but I couldn't remember her name, and the window for asking had closed.

"Okay," Ainsley said, "I see four guys with teardrops. Are you *sure* it means what you said?"

"Very sure."

"Kate! Oh, my God, it's so good to see you! I was so sorry to hear about your husband."

It was Pierre, one of my less egregious parolees (no teardrop, in other words). We hugged, and I introduced him to Ainsley.

"So what did you do?" Ainsley said. "I know, I know, I'm not supposed to ask, but tell me anyway."

Pierre smiled. "I stole a hundred and seventeen cars. Chop-shopped them. Nice profit margin, I gotta say."

Then I heard Daniel's voice, and an unexpected rush of happiness filled me. Yay for Ainsley for making me look hot and wear heels and a dress that wasn't black. Daniel and I could talk and pal around, and I wouldn't feel so strange.

Oh. He was here with a False Alarm.

Right.

I'd forgotten about them. And like all of them, she was

young (it pained me to think half my age, but we were getting there). A redhead, in a skirt so short I had no idea how she'd sit.

Well, that was Daniel for you. This was what (and who) he did.

"Kate?" I turned. It was Paige. "What are you doing here?" she asked.

God, she was rude. Had it always been like that? "I'm supporting the Re-Enter Center with both my money and my presence," I said. "And you?"

"I teach here now. A class on appeals. Daniel talked me into it."

Did he? I found that a little hard to believe. Then again, she was a lawyer, and most of our clients could probably use some legal advice.

She turned to Ainsley. "Hi, I'm Paige Barnett."

"I'm Ainsley, Kate's sister. We've met at least ten times, and you never remember me." Love for my sister and gratitude for her forthright ways flooded through me.

"Have we? Well." Paige turned back to me. "You look... good."

I didn't respond with a similar compliment, just took a sip of crappy wine and stared at her.

She huffed. "Whatever, Kate." With that, she left, sauntered over to Daniel and squeezed his arm. Tilted her head against his shoulder and fake-laughed, her eyes on me.

"I always hated her," Ainsley said.

"You know what?" I said suddenly. "I'm starving. Are you starving?"

"I am indeed."

"Let's go somewhere." I waved to Greta, pointed at my watch as if I had somewhere else to be, and a second later, Ainsley and I were out on the street, walking down Flatbush Avenue toward where we'd parked. I glanced over my shoulder. Daniel was not following us. Not that he even knew we were there.

We got into the car, and Ainsley didn't ask questions, didn't grill me, didn't judge me.

"You're such a good sister," I said, looking out my window, a little embarrassed at my statement. A second later, I felt her hand in mine.

"So are you," she said. The spike pierced my throat.

"Not really."

"Oh, yes, you are."

"I wish I could do it over," I said, swallowing. "I was so jealous of you—Dad's favorite, the cute one, the boyfriend who adored you."

"Oh, my God, I'm so jealous of *you*! The smart one, the cool one, the one who had a real career." She glanced at me. "Seriously. I was jealous of Nathan, even. You got the best guy in the world."

There was the spike again. "I should've been nicer to you."

"I was the other woman's kid," she said. "You were allowed to have mixed feelings." She was quiet for a minute, negotiating the streets with ease. "You know, you never told me to bug off," she said. "It must've been irritating, having a little kid always knocking on your door. But you always let me in. You brushed my hair, you did my nails, you let me tag along with you, you came to see me at college, you invited me over. And I'm living with you! You're a great sister."

"I loved your mother," I said unexpectedly, and again, the tears that were locked in my chest gave a mighty kick, wanting to get out.

"Really?" Ainsley smiled at me, delighted. "What do you remember? Oh, shit, the guy almost hit me. Watch it, idiot! Where are we going, anyway?"

I directed her to a rooftop bar in SoHo where I'd photographed an engagement party. The views of the city were breathtaking, and we managed to get a table by some miracle. The crowd was too sophisticated to be overly rowdy, so we could really talk.

"Should we call our worthless brother and see if he wants to come?" Ainsley suggested.

"Nah. Let's just have it be us sisters." I paused. "Do you think he's worthless?"

She shrugged. "Not really. Not to you."

It dawned on me that Sean was pretty worthless where Ainsley was concerned. I started to apologize for him, then stopped, as always torn between loyalty to my family of origin and sympathy for Ainsley, the outsider.

"Ooh! A lavender martini! I'm definitely getting that."

For a very long time, I'd seen Ainsley's übercheer as a character flaw, hiding some shallowness. Now, suddenly, I saw how thick her skin was, how much energy and strength it took to be so forgiving, and so happy, and so...nice all the time.

"This is so great," I said. "Thanks for making me shower."

We ordered a martini apiece and some appetizers. Tomorrow, I was photographing a newborn baby and his parents in one of those *let's all get naked and remind this child how he got started and then hide the portrait once he turns six* shoots. I could use a drink.

The waiter brought our food, and we devoured it in true O'Leary fashion. One of the things about grief—my appetite sucked, and I was looking a little skeletal these days. But tonight, I was hungry, and the food tasted like food.

"It's so pretty here," Ainsley said, looking over SoHo, the pretty cornices on the building across the way, One World Trade Center looking a bit like a narwhal, its antenna piercing the low-hanging clouds. "We should do this more."

"We should," I said, and unlike a thousand times in the

past when I'd said just that, it felt real this time. Like we'd really do it.

"So. Tell me about my mom," she said, folding her hands.

I took a sip of my drink. "Well, she was really pretty, which you already know. And so nice. She never bossed Sean and me around when we went over, and she always made something fun for dinner." Was this the first time I'd ever told her this? Shame on me.

"Like what?"

"Oh, macaroni and cheese, but the homemade kind, with these crazy curly noodles. And she bought special place mats for us. Sean's had the solar system on it, and mine had these cute chickens on it."

"Did she like you? I mean, she was pretty young to be a stepmom."

"She was great. She was like this cool aunt. Not like Aunt Patty, who tells you about her irritable bowel syndrome the second she sees you."

"Yeah, I know way too much about her colon."

"Michelle really loved you," I said, remembering. "She'd hold you for no reason, even if you were asleep. And she shared you. She let me play with you and hold you, and she always took pictures of the two of us, and the three of us, and the next week, there they'd be, in a frame."

"What happened to them?" Ainsley asked.

I frowned. "I don't know. I thought you had them."

"No. I don't think I've ever seen them."

We both sat in silence, thinking the same thing. Of course our father didn't know. He couldn't find the butter without help. That left my mother, and it was totally in her character to toss the photos from her husband's other wife, other life.

Ainsley looked away. "I guess if Candy threw them out, I... I don't know. She'd have her reasons."

"No, she wouldn't. She'd find some way to justify it, but she'd only do it because she was so jealous. Your mother was lovely, and it drove my mom crazy."

Ainsley's eyes widened. That's right. I'd done it; jumped the breach and said what was true. Because Ainsley had been so wonderful these past horrible weeks. She didn't just say words; she came through, damn it. I took another sip of my drink, enjoying the buzz and the honesty it seemed to bring out. "I don't blame Dad for leaving."

"Don't say that," Ainsley said. "He cheated on Candy. That wasn't right. And she took him back—and took me in. That was superhuman."

"She could've done better by you, Ainsley."

"She did well enough. I mean, she doesn't hate me. And I don't hate her." She paused. "I kind of love her."

"I loved your mom, too. And I love you, too. Even if you are Dad's favorite."

We looked at each other for a second, then laughed. "No more booze for you," Ainsley said. "Look at you, getting all sappy." She gave my hand a squeeze. "I love you, too."

"Believe me, I can tell." I was a little buzzed, but I meant it. Why were we just doing this now? Why hadn't we always been close?

*Because you couldn't be bothered, that's why. Because you and Sean liked to act superior with Ainsley. Because you were always jealous of her.*

I'd do better now.

"Hey, did you hear?" I asked. "Mom and Dad are getting a divorce."

"Not this again."

"She wants to come live with us."

"God, no. I mean, not that I get a say, but…"

"Don't worry. I already turned her down." My drink was gone. "Have you heard from Eric?"

She closed her eyes. "He keeps emailing me to fact-check his cancer journey. And his parents are starting to turn. Judy said she was proud of him the last time we talked."

"She once told me he was regarded as the Christ child when he was born."

"That sounds about right." Her smile was a little sad.

"You know what we should do? Let's go to his house. *Your* house. He's in Alaska now, right?"

"Um…I think so. He started another blog, but I've been superstrong and haven't read it."

"Come on," I said, pulling out my wallet to pay for dinner. "Let's spy. It'll be fun."

Forty-five minutes later, there we were, sitting two houses down from her place. The house was dark.

"Let's go inside," I said. "We can take a few things that are rightfully yours."

She shook her head, smiling. "Look at you. Little Miss Perfect, committing a crime."

"You still have a key, don't you?"

"Hell's yes, I do."

It was awfully dark (which was good, since we were breaking and entering). I followed her up the walk. She peeked in the garage. "No car," she reported.

A second later, we were inside. "Don't turn on any lights," Ainsley said. "I don't want anyone to know we're here."

"Won't the car parked on the street tip them off?"

"Oh, shit, yes," she said, giggling. "Then again, who doesn't drive a white Prius? It's like Wonder Woman's jet. Practically invisible." She turned on the flashlight on her phone and shone it around. "I guess he hasn't left yet." There were piles in the living room—backpacks and hiking boots and climbing gear. "Look at all this crap. And from a guy who was never allowed to climb a tree in case he broke a bone."

"Think he's home? Maybe he sold the car. Maybe he's asleep upstairs, right now," I whispered. This made us laugh uncontrollably for some reason.

"Let's put his hand in a bowl of water and see if he wets the bed," Ainsley suggested, and I laughed so hard I had to go to the bathroom. Went into the little powder room and peed. Opted not to flush. Let him wonder.

When I came out, Ainsley was standing there. "He's not home," she said. "I checked. Come on, let's get some of my stuff." She looked around, the light from the bathroom illuminating the rooms. "I loved this house," she said, her voice a little forlorn.

"It always felt so happy here," I said, meaning it.

"When he kicked me out, I never thought he meant it." Her mouth wobbled.

This was the first time she'd really talked about her breakup, and I didn't know what to tell her. I was hardly a relationship expert, was I?

"Take that pillow," I said, pointing to the couch. The pillow said *love you* in pink letters, such an Ainsley kind of thing. "And this little flower vase. It's very pretty."

"I don't want them. But here. For you," she said, grabbing them. "He can't prove I didn't buy them. At least, I don't think he can. I handled all the finances when we were together. He probably has his mommy doing it now."

We went upstairs, Ainsley grabbing a little statue of a dachshund off a table. "He hasn't even been to see Ollie," she said. "The bastard."

"The sign of a sociopath," I said. "Can I have this?" I asked, pointing to an antique clock.

"No, that was his grandmother's. Sorry. Here. Take this instead." She gave me a wooden giraffe.

We went into the master bedroom. The covers were askew, a pillow on the floor. Ainsley paused, then went into the master bathroom, turned on the light and began scooping up moisturizer, mascara, lipsticks out of a drawer, and shoving them in her purse.

"This is in addition to the stuff you have at my house?" I asked.

"I know, I know, I'm an addict. But it costs a fortune. I'm not leaving it here."

Eric's toothbrush and razor were on the counter, which had blotches of toothpaste and stubble staining the sink. "Men are disgusting," I said.

"No kidding. We're better off without them. Oh, shit, sorry. I'm better off without mine. You, of course, are much worse."

I snorted. "Thank you. I appreciate that."

I put down my loot, took Eric's toothbrush, pulled up my shirt and leisurely rubbed the brush in my armpit. Ainsley shrieked, then laughed so hard she bent over.

My reflection showed a happy, flushed person. Nice to see a smile on my face. For once, the thought didn't make me immediately revert to sadness. "Shall I spit on his pillow?" I offered, and Ainsley went off again into gales of silent laughter.

Then we heard the door open downstairs. We froze.

The door closed. There were footsteps.

"Oh, God! He's back," Ainsley hissed. "Hide!"

I grabbed my stuff and obeyed, trying not to snort with laughter. We tiptoed down the hall, and Ainsley opened the door to the guest bedroom, dragged me to the far side of the bed and pulled me down onto the floor with her. She was laughing, too, her eyes streaming with tears.

Then we heard his voice…and a woman's voice answering. Our laughter died a quick death.

"I love your place," the woman said. They seemed to be right under us, in what I thought was the living room, and the insulation must've sucked in this house, because we could hear them clear as day.

"Thanks. It's a little soulless, but I'll deal with that when I get back. Probably, I'll sell the place and donate the money to my charity."

*His* charity. Because there weren't enough charities for cancer research. The putz had to have one with his name on it, of course.

Ainsley had grown very still next to me. I slid my arm around her. "He's a prick," I whispered. "You deserve better."

"So how is a guy like you still single?" the woman asked, her voice playful.

"Oh, I was with someone for a long time," he answered. "I don't think she could handle my illness. She said the right things, but she never honored my journey, you know what I mean?"

Ainsley sucked in a breath, her eyes narrowing dangerously.

"You're kidding!" the woman said. "That's horrible!"

"Well, it happens. Not everyone is open to tackling the hardships of life. Enough about her. Come here, you."

There was quiet then.

"They're kissing," Ainsley whispered. "That's his come-on line. 'Come here, you.' Worked every time."

"It's a *really* stupid line," I whispered back.

"They're gonna do it. Here. In my house. In our *bed*."

"No, they're not," I whispered.

"Yes, they are. In two minutes, he's going to bring her upstairs, take a shower, because that's his idea of foreplay, and then he's going to have sex with her in our bed." She was shaking.

"Give me your bag," I whispered. I clicked on my phone light and grabbed some mascara. Rubbed it under my eyes.

"What are you doing?" she whispered.

"Just be ready to get out of here when I distract them. We don't want you to be seen." *For legal purposes*, I didn't add. Hey. I was a grieving widow. Time to get a little mileage out of that.

I took out her lipstick—super red—and put it on, making sure to smear it with a heavy hand. "How do I look?"

"Insane."

"Good."

We sat there in the dark, holding hands. "Make sure you bring my loot," I said, and we started to laugh again, silent, wheezing, unable to look at each other. She grabbed a pillow off the guest bed, took off the pillowcase and loaded it up with my goodies. Added the cute bedside clock, too, which made us laugh even more.

Sure enough, Eric and his friend came upstairs. We could hear little bursts of laughter and murmuring.

"I'll just take a quick shower," he said. "Make yourself comfortable."

"Why don't I join you?" she said in a sultry tone.

"Excellent idea."

I thought so, too. We heard the shower start. More laughter from the frisky couple. "Time for you to go, Ains," I whispered, standing up.

"Oh, I wouldn't miss this for the world."

We tiptoed down the hall toward Eric's room. Ainsley stationed herself outside the doorway like a cop expecting gunfire.

I went in.

Screwing another woman in the bed he'd shared with my sister? Not on my watch.

The bathroom door was closed. Since they'd left the lights on, I could see myself in the bureau mirror. Yep. I looked crazy. I messed up my hair for that added asylum look, took a deep breath and threw open the bathroom door.

"Eric!" I bellowed.

He screamed. She screamed. She also flailed, her elbow jerking back and catching Eric in the face. He screamed again, the wuss, one hand going to his nose, the other to cover his junk.

I jammed my hands on my hips. "Where's my sister, Eric? What did you *do* to her?"

"What are you talking about? How did you get in? God! I'm naked here!"

Naked, and no longer *homo erectus*, either, I was pleased to note. Also, his nose was bleeding. "Where is she, Eric?"

"Who *is* that?" the woman shrieked, trying to cower behind Eric, who was trying to cower behind her.

"Where is she?" I demanded. "What have you *done* with her? Did you kill her?"

"Of course not! I don't know where she is!"

"Oh, my God," the woman whimpered. She scrambled out of the shower and started pulling on her clothes.

"If Ainsley doesn't turn up," I said, "I'm calling the police on you. And I'll be watching you, Eric." I turned to the naked woman. "My husband is dead, and it's Eric's fault," I told her. "Or maybe that's the grief talking, but you should be very careful around this one." I gave her a mournful look, then looked back at Eric. "Shame on you, by the way."

"Kate, are you... Is this a..." He straightened up. "You'd better leave, or I'm calling the police."

"Or maybe *I'll* call the police, Eric, and tell them my sister is missing. Gotta run. Things to do. Have a great night!"

I bolted. Ainsley was waiting at the top of the stairs, and we ran out, across the front lawn to her car, the bag of loot glowing in the darkness. Got in, and Ainsley floored it, laughing so hard she had to wipe her eyes. We fled silently thanks to the Prius's electric motor. A few streets away, Ainsley pulled over, both of us laughing so hard we were holding our stomachs.

Then Ainsley's ringtone went off, a series of little chimes. She looked at the phone. "Why, it's Eric," she said, tapping it. "Hello?" Her voice was very calm. "Oh, hey, Eric. You sound stuffed up." She hit Mute so he couldn't hear us laughing, then returned to the call. "Kate? She's out with a friend. Fund-raiser or something. Really? Huh. Are you sure it was my sister? No, I'm here with Ollie, reading. Listen, you sound ungrounded. Take some cleansing breaths and commune with the grizzly bears."

I wheezed, tears streaming down my face. God, this felt good.

There was a pause as he spoke. "Oh, so you're *not* in Alaska. Huh. Guess you haven't quite cut free from the corpse of your old life. Easy to blog about it, harder to do it, isn't it? Oh, and don't you dare write about my sister. First, you have no proof. Second, she's Nathan's widow and still grieving. And third, I'll make sure she sues you for libel if you do. *Namaste,* asshole."

She hit End, and we both sat there for a few minutes, occasionally snorting, until the laughter ran out, and we were both quiet.

A few raindrops hit the roof, then more, then a steady hiss, the beads running down the windshield, our view blurring. Thunder rumbled in the west, and a flash of lightning lit up the belly of the clouds.

"I guess it's really over," Ainsley said, her voice quiet. "The Eric I knew is gone. I'm sitting here, jealous of you, because at least Nathan gets to stay Nathan in your memory, whereas I have to deal with the new and unimproved Eric."

"I'm sorry, Ains."

She nodded. Wiped her eyes.

"You know, Nathan's given me a few surprises since he died," I added.

She glanced at me. "Really?"

"He stayed in touch with his ex-wife. I found emails."

"Are you kidding me?"

"Afraid not. It seems like they weren't really...done."

"An affair?"

"No. But I think he still...loved her."

Said out loud in the intimacy of the car, the words seemed to lurk there in front of us.

"You have to wonder if you ever know anyone at all," Ainsley said.

"Ain't it the truth?"

The rain kicked up, drumming on the car roof, and still we sat there, closer now than we'd ever been in our lives.

"You know what?" I said. "There's a Pepperidge Farm coconut cake at home."

"Say no more," Ainsley said, and home we went.

# Chapter Twenty-Three

*Ainsley*

Though I showed up on time eight days in a row, I failed to dazzle Jonathan.

Not that I was trying.

Fine, I was *totally* trying. Why, though, I didn't know, because A) I was still furious with Eric, who finally did go to Alaska, according to Judy's Facebook post, and B) dazzling Captain Flatline was impossible.

Not only did I get into work on time, I also refrained from shopping online. I realized my bar wasn't terribly high, but I'd been hoping it would make a difference to Jonathan. If it did, he hid it well.

On another front, I unfriended and unfollowed Eric on all his social media platforms. When he texted me a question about his bad reaction to latex (he had no bad reaction to latex, for the record; he'd had a mosquito bite), I blocked his phone number.

Eric had broken up with me. He'd brought another woman back to our house. He was in Alaska now.

We were done.

His mother and I hadn't talked in two weeks. Of course, the Fishers had to side with their son. I understood that. I'd never spend Hanukkah with them again, or go see *Phantom* with Judy, or watch a Sunday afternoon football game on the couch with Aaron, cheering vaguely when he did as Eric smiled and read.

Those days seemed like a dream now.

On Friday afternoon at 4:45, my email chimed.

Please be ready to leave for the tool museum in ten minutes. Thank you.
Jonathan Kent, Publisher
*Hudson Lifestyle*

Tool museum? Was that a metaphor? I checked my calendar. *AITM*. A quick Google search reminded me what the initials stood for. Antique Ice Tool Museum.

Super exciting.

I texted Kate to let her know I had a work thing. She was making dinner for some of the people from her grief group, which was nice. I'd been planning to lay low anyway and read. I asked her to feed Ollie, since I might be late; previous work excursions had shown that Jonathan was the type of person who read every plaque in every museum. And since the museum would be taking out a full-page ad to coincide with the story, we'd have to schmooze the director, which was something *I* could do in half an hour, and something that Jonathan could do only by memorizing every fact about the place.

Antique ice tool museum. Who thought of these things?

"We can take my car," Jonathan said as we went to the parking lot.

"Sure." I got in; his car was ridiculously clean and neat. Two booster seats were in the back. "How are your daughters?" I asked.

"They're fine."

"And your dad?"

"Also fine."

That was it. Was this the guy who'd forced me to dance with him? "I am also fine, Jonathan."

"Yes."

I rolled my eyes and looked out the window. The rest of the ride passed in silence.

The Antique Ice Tool Museum was about an hour north of Cambry-on-Hudson, and surprisingly charming—an old stone barn overlooking the river, filled with fearsome-looking saws and old photos and ads. As predicted, Jonathan studied every word of every bit of print in every place while I chatted up the director, a sixtyish man (my specialty) whose name was Chip.

"Do people call you Ice Chip?" I asked, and he laughed, making Jonathan startle a little. "Chip off the old ice block?"

"They will now," he said, proud of his new nickname.

"Correct me if I'm wrong," I said, "but I'd think the Hudson wouldn't freeze this far downstream with the tidal patterns being what they are."

"Most people think that!" Chip exclaimed, delighted with my mistake. "But back in the 1800s, you could skate right into New York Harbor!"

"Really!" I said. His enthusiasm was infectious.

"It's all about the salinity of the water," he continued, his eyes glazing over with love of his subject.

By the time we left, the sky was growing dark with a summer thunderstorm, black clouds piling up across the river, the wind fluttering my dress. Chip and I hugged goodbye, as we were now close personal friends, and I promised to come back in the winter to see the ice-carving demonstration.

"Thank you so much for your time," Jonathan said, shaking Chip's hand.

"That's a great girl you've got there," Chip said. Same thing Eric's bosses used to say.

"Yes," Jonathan said. "Have an enjoyable weekend."

Captain Flatline struck again, I thought as he got into the car. I texted Kate to see how dinner was going as he backed out of the parking lot.

Really well. Thx for checking! Be careful, okay? The weather map shows red.

"Bad weather's coming," I said to my driver. "Big boomers."

"Excuse me?"

"Thunderstorms, Jonathan."

He turned on the radio, and sure enough, the meteorologists were practically peeing themselves with joy. "Wind gusts up to fifty miles per hour, heavy rains, some local flooding. Stay inside, folks!"

Jonathan sighed.

"Do you have to pick up your girls?" I asked.

"No, not till tomorrow." He drove with both hands on the wheel, looking straight ahead. "You did well with the director," he said.

"Thank you."

"You're good with people."

"I like people."

His mouth curled up in a flash smile, then returned to its normal straight line.

A gust of wind rocked the car, and rain abruptly slapped the windshield. Jonathan switched the wipers to high.

The farther south we drove, the worse the weather. The lightning was getting intense, and twigs littered the road. Thunder rolled overhead, sometimes so loud that the car vibrated with it.

Then there was a crash, a flash and a huge branch came down about twenty feet in front of us.

"I'm going to bring you to my place," Jonathan said. "It's closer. You can wait out the storm there. Is that all right?"

I glanced at my watch. It was 7:30 anyway. And it wasn't like I had plans. "Sure. Thank you."

The power seemed to have gone out; the houses we passed were dark. We saw more downed branches, and sure enough, a Con Edison truck passed us, lights flashing.

Jonathan turned onto a road that wound through the woods. The rain was so loud now, the wipers slapping frantically. Outside, the trees waved and bent, and clumps of leaves hit the car. I hoped nothing bigger would fall on us. It was getting a little nerve-racking.

Jonathan turned again, onto an even narrower road, this one dirt, that brought us out into some farmland. No trees to fall on us here, but the road was like a river, water gushing along the side of it. The headlights showed only rain and mud. The clouds were so thick and black that it seemed like midnight.

We turned again, and when the lightning flashed, I saw a big white farmhouse and red barn. Jonathan's headlights illuminated a stone wall. "Wait for me," he said, turning the key. He got out and, a second later, opened my door, holding his suit jacket over my head. "Let's make a run for it."

There were leaves all over the slate walkway, and the sharp smell of rain and summer thick in the air. Jonathan unlocked the door, and in we went. It was pitch-black. He took my hand and led me farther inside, my footsteps short and uncertain. "Stay right here," he said. "I have a generator. I'll just be a second."

Then he was gone, the thunder swallowing all other sound.

I waited, my clothes sopping wet despite Jonathan's effort to cover me. It smelled nice in here, like wood and maybe a little bit of cinnamon. A cluster of lightning flashes showed me that I was in an entryway with a bench and a door leading into the house.

A woman stood in front of me.

I screamed, my hands going up in front of me.

"Ainsley?" Jon's voice was sharp.

"Who's here?" I shrieked. "Someone's here!"

Then the lights came on, and I looked up and saw my reflection.

I was standing in front of a mirror.

"Never mind," I called. "I— It was me. Sorry." And speaking of me, my hair looked ridiculous. I fluffed it up, ran my fingers under my eyes and fluffed out my soaking wet dress, sending raindrops pattering to the floor.

"Are you all right?" Jonathan stood before me, also soaked, though his hair looked quite...well, Darcy-esque; there was really no other word for it. Colin Firth and Jane Austen had ruined us chicks for other men, let's face it.

"I saw my reflection. But I didn't know it was me. Sorry for the screaming."

He looked me up and down. "Would you like some dry clothes?"

"Um...sure. Thank you."

He led me through his house, which was not at all what I expected. I'd pictured him...well, in many places. Hell, for one. A casket, for another, like Dracula needing to sleep on Transylvanian soil. That sterile condo.

But this house was big and rambling and filled with comfortable furniture and the occasional antique. Not the fussy kind that you don't want to touch—rough, battered, *we're here because we've earned it* kind of pieces. A grandfather clock, a big brown sofa with a patch of pink fabric on one arm. We went upstairs, and Jonathan went into his room, which featured a sleigh bed and fireplace. Old chest of drawers, pictures of his girls, a view of the fields from his windows.

"I don't have any women's clothes," he said.

"Really?" I asked. "You're not a drag queen?"

He ignored that. "And you won't fit into my daughters' things."

"Of course I won't, Jonathan! I'm a grown woman. Just give me some sweats, okay?"

He complied. "You can change across the hall. There's a bathroom, as well."

"Thank you, Mr. Kent." I took the clothes he handed me, went across the hall and fell instantly in love.

It was the girls' room, clearly; bunk beds, two desks filled with cheerful clutter and construction paper, a giant box-turned-playhouse with windows cut in it, flowers drawn in Magic Markers at the base. Bookcases surrounded a huge window seat, the shelves filled with piles of books and photos and little treasures—a music box, a porcelain cat. A hammock was strung across one corner, filled with stuffed animals. There was an enormous soft chair on one side of the bed, perfect for reading and cuddling.

I took off my dress, laid it across the desk chair and pulled on Jonathan's sweatpants (which fit far too well; I'd have to go on a diet very soon). He'd given me a flannel shirt, too. Huh. I didn't picture him owning one. An ascot, yes. Flannel…not so much.

The photos on the bookshelves called to me.

Damn.

There he was, holding a little white burrito of a baby, smiling into the camera with all the happiness a man could have. Emily, I decided. He looked so young in the picture. And there was another, Jonathan holding toddler Emily in one arm, infant Lydia in the other, smiling at Emily as she touched her baby sister on the nose with one shy finger.

Another of him with the girls on Halloween. One of him coming out of the water with Lydia. Nice abs, I noted. His, not Lydia's. Another shot of him holding Emily, pointing at something in the sky.

He was a good father. If I didn't believe it already, I'd have known from these pictures.

"Are you hungry?"

I jumped, flushing with guilt. Jonathan's voice was right outside. "Yeah. Sure! Thank you." Opening the door, I smiled. "This is a lovely room," I said. "The whole house is beautiful."

"Thank you. It's been in my family for five generations. This way, please."

Ah, yes. I was a servant in the family wing.

He led the way back to the large kitchen, which had wooded plank floors and tile counters, a fridge covered in children's artwork and photos. "I need to call my daughters," he said. "Please have a seat."

I wriggled onto a stool at the counter. To my surprise, Jonathan poured me a glass of red wine without asking if I wanted one, then one for himself. Took out his phone. "Hello, Laine," he said. "Are you safe?"

His jaw clenched, and yet his first question was for her safety.

"I'm home now. Yes. Do you have power? Good. Don't go out. There are branches down all over town. Are the girls available? Thank you."

Very civilized. I took a sip of my wine.

"Hello, honey bear," he said, and my heart melted a little. His face gentled, and his voiced deepened even more. "Oh, it's not so bad. No, nothing's broken. It's just windy. Don't forget, the house has been here a long time." His smile flashed and was gone. "Sure. I'll pick you up at ten. I love you, too, bear. Put Lydia on, okay?" He glanced at me, and I dropped my gaze, suddenly fascinated by the floorboards.

"Hello, Lyddie. How was your day, pumpkin? What did you have for lunch? You did? Three pieces? How's your tummy?" Another lightning smile. "The fairies?" He glanced at me, his eyebrow rising. "I imagine they have places to go. Sure. A hollow tree, maybe. A bee's nest? I'll ask. Okay, sweetheart. I love you. See you in the morning. Bye-bye."

My heart felt achy and sore.

A man who loved his children that much should not have had to leave them. I hated his wife. Hated her.

"Lydia was concerned about the fairies," he said. "But she thinks they must be friendly with bees and wanted me to check with you."

A warm prickle crept across my chest. "Yes, she's right, of course. Bees and fairies are very good friends. They also use mushrooms as umbrellas."

His eyes crinkled with a smile. "I'll let her know." He looked at me. "Well. Let me make you dinner." He opened the fridge. "Are you a meat-eater?"

"Yes. I love meat."

"Good."

I was suddenly nervous. Drank a little more wine. "Can I help?"

"You can make a salad."

He set out some lettuce and tomatoes, dug around in the fridge and found a pepper, as well. I got to work, rinsing the lettuce and patting it dry, slicing the tomatoes. Opened the fridge and found some carrots and avocado, too. "Can I use these?" I asked.

"Of course."

There were herbs growing in little pots on the windowsill. "How about these?"

"Make yourself at home," he said.

It was so strange to be here, the rain still pounding the roof and gurgling in the gutters. Jonathan turned on the gas stove and set a cast-iron frying pan on it and began slicing up the beef.

Making dinner with Captain Flatline. Very strange.

"So this house is quite something," I said when it became apparent he wasn't going to initiate conversation.

"Thank you. My great-great-grandfather built it in 1872. Part of it burned down in the 1950s, so this kitchen and the family room are new. Newer, that is."

He moved quickly around the kitchen, cooking efficiently. Occasionally, we'd get in each other's way, doing that awkward left-right-left thing. The smell of beef filled the air. He sliced some potatoes and seasoned them with salt and pepper, then drizzled olive oil on them. Took some rosemary from the windowsill and added that.

Gotta love a man who knew his way around a kitchen.

He wore jeans and a henley shirt, the sleeves pushed up over his forearms. Beautiful forearms, muscled and smooth.

Had he always been this tall, or was it just because I was barefoot?

I finished making the salad, sat back down at the counter and watched as he nudged the meat and potatoes. Drank the very good wine.

Felt some feelings.

A thunderclap shook the house, and if possible, the rain fell harder. "It should clear up soon," Jonathan said. "These storms don't usually last very long."

"I know."

I poured myself a little more wine, then topped off his glass, as well. He nodded his thanks.

I was getting used to that formality. It occurred to me that he might be a little shy.

"Dinner is served," he said, not quite meeting my eyes.

He *was* shy.

I couldn't believe I'd never noticed it before.

We ate at the table, not talking, just letting the storm blow and rumble around us. The food was fantastic, simple and flavorful, and I was suddenly starving.

Jonathan ate carefully and precisely, holding his fork in his left hand, like a European. Probably learned that at boarding school. I pictured the bleak place in the James Joyce novel, the little boy crossing off the days till he could go home at Christmas.

Yes. Jonathan fit that picture.

"Did you go to boarding school?" I asked.

He looked up. "Yes."

"I can tell."

He smiled. I smiled. The cat smiled.

He had a cat!

"You have a cat!" I said. Maybe shouldn't have had that second glass of wine. Too late now.

"Ainsley, this is Luciano. Luciano, meet Ainsley. Miss O'Leary to you."

"Call me Ainsley, Luciano. Is he named after Pavarotti?"

Jonathan looked surprised. "Yes. How did you know?"

"I only know one guy named Luciano."

"Ah. Well. This Luciano also likes to sing." The cat obliged with a squeaky meow, then regarded me with a delightful lack of interest.

"I have a question for you, Jonathan," I said.

"Deeply personal, no doubt."

"Yes." I put my fork down and leaned back in my chair, the intimacy of the weather and the cozy kitchen making me relax. "Why are you running *Hudson Lifestyle*?"

He chewed carefully, his strong jaw flexing hypnotically, then swallowed, which forced me to look at his throat. "It's the family business."

What were we talking about? Oh, right, the magazine. "Do you like it?"

"I do."

I shifted in my chair. "Why? All those kiss-ass articles about plastic surgery and day spas, all those phony, gushing restaurant and gallery reviews...you could be doing a lot more. You're so smart."

He didn't answer.

Shit. That had been a really rude question. "I'm sorry," I said.

"Yes. Well, the kiss-ass articles and gushing reviews do make our advertisers happy, and our advertisers pay your salary. And the salaries of the rest of us."

"That's true."

He looked at me for a few beats. His eyes looked green now, but there was the little piece of gold. "I love this area," he said. "The river that seems to go unnoticed, the farms that are fighting to survive. The little towns and ice tool museums. The whole history of our country is embodied here. If kiss-ass articles and gushing reviews get people to at least get a glimpse of a place like the ice tool museum, then maybe they'll stop for a minute and learn something. Appreciate where we are and all that we have here."

He turned his attention back to his plate.

"That was a good answer," I murmured.

"Let me ask you something," he said.

"Go for it." I took another sip of wine.

"Why do you work at a job you hate?"

I sputtered, spraying a little wine. "Uh, I don't hate my job!" I said, dabbing my lips with a napkin. "I... It's fun. Today was fun. Chip, that is. That part was fun."

He folded his hands in front of him, looked me straight in the eye and sighed.

"I don't hate it *that* much," I said. "I'll probably like it much more after what you just said so poetically."

"When you're paying attention, you're not a bad editor. That being said, I think I can count on one hand how many days you've paid attention. And most of those days have been this week."

"Yes, well, we live in a distractible society."

He stared at me. Unfortunately, he was not distractible.

"Why haven't you fired me?" I asked.

He took his time answering. "I like your mother," he finally said.

I laughed. "Good for you. It's not easy. Also, she's my stepmother."

He resumed his tidy eating. "How old were you when your parents divorced?"

"They didn't. My mom died when I was three. Candy was my father's first wife. And also his third." I stood up and cleared our plates. "Thank you for dinner. It was very good."

"I'm sorry about your mother."

"Thank you."

"Also, you make a good salad."

I smiled at his awkward attempt at conversation. "Everyone has special gifts, Jonathan. Mine is salad."

He glanced at me uncertainly, then finished clearing the table, and we loaded the dishwasher in silence.

"I'll check the forecast," he said, going into the other room.

Right. So he could get me home.

I followed him into the family room, where there were more framed photos of the girls on the mantel. Stone fireplace. I'd always been a sucker for those.

I sat on the couch, which was soft and comfortable. There was a yellow crayon stuck between the cushions, which made me happy for some reason.

The TV showed another red blob headed our way.

"Do you mind waiting till that passes?" he asked.

"Not if you don't."

"I don't."

He went back to the kitchen and returned with the wine bottle. Poured me a little more. "I don't have anything to offer you for dessert. I'm sorry."

"Life without dessert is sad, boss."

Another robust crash of thunder. Jonathan turned off the TV and sat next to me on the couch. I curled into the corner and stared at him. He didn't return the look. Then again, this allowed me to study his profile. The gods of bone structure had had a lot of fun with him—razor-sharp cheekbones, hard, well-defined jaw.

Funny that I used to think he was unattractive.

"How are you doing with your ex-wife and that, um, situation?" I asked.

The eyebrow I could see lifted. "It's...difficult."

"You were very polite on the phone."

"Yes. Laine is the mother of my children. It wouldn't help them to have us be at each other's throats."

I couldn't imagine Jonathan at anyone's throat.

I could, however, imagine him heartbroken.

"Do you ever talk to your brother?"

"No."

"That's a tough one."

"Yes." He swirled the wine in his glass. "My father and brother and I were very close, and when my father had the stroke, it was devastating. I worked at the magazine at the time and took over my father's job there, as well." He paused. "You may have noticed that I'm not the best at…" The hand that wasn't holding his wineglass flailed a little as he searched for the words.

"Expressing human emotion?" I offered.

"That. Yes." The cat jumped up on his lap, and he began petting him, eliciting a silky purr. The cat narrowed his eyes at me. I narrowed mine back. "So. The magazine was struggling, and I was working long hours so we wouldn't have to lay anyone off. My brother was grieving, my wife was lonely, I was *emotionally unavailable*, according to Laine. So they found comfort with each other. For the sake of the girls, I'm trying to be civilized."

"It's still shitty, Jon. You're allowed to be mad."

"Oh, I was. Believe me, I was." There was that deep voice again, low and dangerous and kind of…hot. "No one calls me Jon, by the way."

"Do you hate it?"

"No. But no one calls me that."

"Except me."

The lips quirked again. "Yes."

Luciano jumped down and began licking his privates,

which were publics if you were a cat. Jonathan nudged him away, and the cat left with an impressive yowl.

"How's that woman you mentioned?" I asked. "Remember? In divorce group? You said there was someone you liked."

"I'm quite sure I never said that."

"Well, Carly said you said it. In a prior session."

"So much for the group's confidentiality clause."

"You were on a date the night Eric dumped me. Was that the woman?"

"No. That was my cousin."

"Oh. Well, according to rumor, there was a woman, and you liked her." I pulled a throw pillow against my stomach. "Come on. It's raining, we have wine, I'm Dr. Lovely's stepdaughter. You can tell me. How is she?" I felt oddly jealous. But of course he'd be dating someone. Though a little clenched, I'd discovered that Jonathan was...well, a kind man. A good father. He had those eyes and that voice. "There *was* a woman, right?"

He glanced at me. "Yes."

"And? How's it going with her? What's she like?"

"It's...complicated."

"Why?"

"She doesn't know what she wants."

"Oh, one of those." So she was stringing him along, then, huh? Sounded like she needed a hearty slap.

"Have you made your move?" I asked.

"No."

"Why?"

"I repeat—it's complicated."

"Why is it complicated? God, this is like pulling teeth! Can you put two sentences together, please?"

He turned his head to look straight ahead once more. *These humans and their interactions. So maddening.* "She just got out of a long-term relationship."

"So? Maybe she needs a good bang to get over him. A little boom-boom-pow."

Jonathan didn't answer. Thunder rolled across the fields outside, but it was fainter now.

Then he turned those beautiful eyes to me. "Also, she works for me."

I sat bolt upright. "Really? Who— Oh."

*Oh.*

I felt hot. My whole body felt flushed and tight and tingly.

"I'm not quite sure she even likes me." He shifted so he was facing me. "Though recently, she seems to like me a little more."

My heart jerked in my chest. "Just to be clear," I said, my voice husky, "we are talking about me, right?"

He closed his eyes for a second—*why do I get the idiots?*—then opened them. "Yes," he said, his voice so deep it was just a rumble. He didn't look away, and there it was, that glimmer of gold in his strange, beautiful eyes.

"I do like you," I murmured. "But only when you smile."

Very slowly, he obliged, one side of his mouth leading the way, a crooked, small smile, and God, he was just ridiculously appealing. My heart jackrabbitted in my chest, furiously pounding, and I was pretty sure I couldn't feel my legs.

"Are you going to kiss me, or are you just going to sit there staring?" I asked.

He leaned forward, set his wineglass on the coffee table, took mine from my fingers and set it down next to his. His movements were slow and precise. He looked at me a beat or two (or seventeen, it seemed), then cupped my face, his long fingers sliding into my hair, and then he did kiss me.

His mouth was gentle but sure, his lips perfect against mine.

He was warm and solid and my hand went to the side of his neck, feeling the strong thud of his pulse there, his smooth skin. Then his mouth moved, and good God, Jonathan Kent could kiss like there was no tomorrow. His tongue touched mine, and that was it, I was abruptly lost and found at the same time. My whole body throbbed, and it was a wonder I didn't just dissolve into a big puddle of *yes*.

I grabbed his head and kissed him back, crawled onto his lap, still kissing him, pushing him back against the cushions, straddling him. I groped for the buttons on my shirt, and God, his mouth, I loved his mouth so much, and who *knew*? Who even knew Jonathan Kent could kiss like this, long, luxurious, hot kissing that rendered me blind with lust, and who *cared*? I had two fistfuls of shirt in my hands and was pulling and tugging, and he was doing the same, and now his hands were on my skin, burning me in the most wonderful, intense way, and all I could do was feel.

There was just one thought left. It didn't make sense, but it felt true all the same.

I'd been waiting for this kiss all my life.


"I'm sorry, but you need to leave now."

Not really the words a woman wants to hear upon awakening the morning after she was banged silly.

But Jonathan was holding a cup of coffee, and his expression was…well, it wasn't clenched, angry or disappointed.

It wasn't quite happy, either. I accepted the coffee and sat up, covering my naked self with the sheet, unsure of how to feel. On the one hand, I felt amazing. I'd been shagged to within an inch of my life. Three times, mind you.

On the other hand, Jonathan was kicking me out.

"I have to get my daughters in half an hour."

"Right. Okay. Well." I took a sip of the coffee and looked up at him.

He sat on the edge of the bed. "Thank you."

"Oh, sure. Salads and sex. My specialty."

His hair was mussed, curling over his forehead, and my hand wanted to smooth it back. But my hand wasn't quite brave enough to do that, because you know that old saying about the cold light of day. Also, his resting bitch face was on.

Or maybe it was the shyness again.

"I'll call you tomorrow," he said.

"Okay. Great. I'll just…get out of bed, then."

"Good."

Back to Captain Flatline. Still, a man without a heartbeat couldn't do the things he'd done to me last night. Nuh-uh.

He seemed to read my thoughts, because he leaned forward and kissed my bare shoulder, the faint scrape of razor stubble in contrast to his soft, warm lips, and my hand worked up the courage to stroke that hair.

"You need to go," he murmured.

So much for my dreamy state. "And you need to work on your pillow talk," I said. He gave a nod of acknowledgment, and I couldn't help a smile.

I got out of bed, grabbed my dress, which he'd thoughtfully brought in, and got dressed in the bathroom. The mirror showed a serious case of bedhead, smeared mascara under my eyes and a glow to my complexion. I couldn't wait to tell Kate about this; I'd sent her a quick text last night between rounds one and two, letting her know I wouldn't be home.

Jonathan was waiting downstairs, standing by the door. "Okay. Uh…talk to you tomorrow," I said.

"Yes." He started to say something else, then opted against it, leaned forward and kissed me gently.

Everything in me softened. Brain, heart, bones. I felt a

blush creep into my cheeks. "Bye," I whispered, then fumbled with the door handle. Left, right, push, pull, nothing worked.

He reached around me and opened the door. "Bye," he said, his voice so deep it was just a vibration in my chest.

I glanced back at him as I walked down the path.

He was smiling.

I tripped, staggered, managed not to fall. "I'm fine," I said. "Bye. Have fun with your daughters."

"Ainsley?" he called.

"Yes?"

"Your car is at the office."

Right. There was that. "So do I have to walk back?"

"You do not." He came down the walk, keys in hand.

As usual, the ride was mostly in silence. This time, however, it felt different. Silence, I was coming to realize, could mean quite a lot.

When we got to the parking lot of *Hudson Lifestyle*, I leaned over, kissed my boss on the cheek, earning a flash of a smile. "I'll call you tomorrow," he said.

"Roger dodger," I replied, not even minding the fact that I sounded idiotic.

I almost hit a tree on the way home, thinking about that mouth, and those hands, and his eyes. And his voice. And his smile.

He'd call me tomorrow. And that would be lovely.

# Chapter Twenty-Four

❧

*Kate*

On Sunday afternoon, as I was leaving the studio after reviewing approximately a million and twelve photos Max had tweaked in Photoshop, I saw a woman walking down the street. She held a bouquet of yellow flowers in her arm and was beautifully dressed in a red pencil skirt and white top with capped short sleeves. Strappy black shoes with heels so high and sharp they could be used as a murder weapon.

I myself was sweaty and stale, since the air-conditioning wasn't working in the studio. I wore skinny jeans and a T-shirt that said I ♥ Mac & Cheese, the heart made of macaroni noodles. Beat-up sandals. In Brooklyn, I'd look normal. In Cambry-on-Hudson, I looked homeless. I'd have to go shopping soon. I was a wealthy woman now, and I lived in a wealthy town. If I wanted to, I could dress like that woman, every day, even.

I studied her for a minute more, hoping to impress her fashion sense into my brain, then realized who it was.

Madeleine.

"Hey!" I called sharply. "Madeleine!" I ran down the street. "Madeleine!"

She stopped in front of Bliss, turned and saw me. Her face froze.

"Hi," I said, coming to a stop in front of her, already winded from the half-block run. Must make use of Nathan's elliptical more often. And how was this for irony? The ex-wife and the widow in front of a wedding dress store.

·Her lipstick was perfect. And that haircut, damn. Eons better than my sloppy ponytail.

Her eyes wandered over me, full of judgment, and I felt a biting, acidic anger churn in my stomach.

"What?" she said. No niceties, then.

Just then, Jenny opened Bliss's front door. "Hey, Kate, I thought that was you!" she said, giving me a hug. "Great to see you. Gorgeous day, isn't it?" She looked at Madeleine. "Hi. I'm Jenny, a friend of Kate's."

Madeleine didn't answer.

"This is Nathan's ex-wife," I said flatly.

Still Madeleine didn't stop looking at me.

Jenny looked back at me. "Well. I have a dress to make. Uh…see you later!" She gave me a smile and went back inside, leaving me alone on the sidewalk with *her*.

"You do remember me, right?" I asked sharply. "Kate O'Leary. Nathan's wife."

"Of course I remember," she said.

"I've been meaning to talk to you. Would you like to get a drink?"

She glanced at her watch, her perfectly groomed eyebrow rising a bit in disapproval. "It's only two o'clock."

"You can have water," I said. "Maybe somewhere more private. How about that bar in Tarrytown? Where all those new condos are?"

She made me wait.

The bar was new but was trying to look old, with distressed wood and reproduction light fixtures. It was fairly empty, as we were between the lunch and dinner crowds. Outside, though, it was crowded; a band played over by the marina, and there was a bounce house. Kids of all ages rode their bikes, and well-dressed couples walked along the riverfront path. Very cheerful, very Americana, very different from the bitter black hate that tarred my insides.

Finally, she came in. "Sorry about the delay. I went to the cemetery."

The first shot across the bow.

"What can I get you ladies today?" our server asked.

"Grey Goose, straight up," I said.

"Perrier for me with a slice of lemon, please," Madeleine said.

We waited in silence, eyeing each other. A staring match, almost. Finally, the girl came back. "Anything to eat today?" she asked.

"Just the drinks," Madeleine said. "We'll need some privacy, too." She smiled up at the girl, who nodded and scurried off. Then she looked at me, her smile dropping. "Well?"

I took a glug of my vodka, welcoming the icy burn. "Guess what I found? Your emails to my husband, telling him you never stopped loving him."

"I never did stop," she said, raising an eyebrow.

"Or you didn't want to see him happily married to someone else and got a bug up your ass to make him miserable."

"I'm sure he *was* miserable, since he was with the wrong woman."

Wow. I had to admire her nerve.

"If you were so right, you should've stayed married. You could've had four more years with him." *You could've been his widow, not me.*

"Believe me, I'm well aware of that."

I slurped down the rest of my vodka. One didn't confront one's dead husband's ex-wife without fortification, no, sir. "So why did you let him go? And for the love of God, why did you torture him with those emails after we got married?"

She took a sip of her drink and smoothed her red hair behind one ear. "He didn't tell you about me, did he?" she asked, her voice low and smug. Yeah, smug.

"He told me quite a bit, actually." That was a lie.

"Mmm-hmm. Did he tell you I was a foster child? That I was moved fourteen times in eighteen years? That I was abused and neglected?"

Ah, shit. Now I was going to feel sorry for her. No, no, I wasn't. I imagined Ainsley giving me an elbow to the ribs.

"I guess you didn't know that," she continued. "But I didn't let that define me. I went to college on a full scholarship. Graduate school, too. That's where we met. And we loved each other in a way you can't possibly imagine."

My mouth fell open. "Wow...your ego is *really* healthy."

"I'm just stating a fact. We were so happy together, so in love. Our life was perfect."

"Except for the part where you got a divorce. Tiny detail, but one worth mentioning."

"That was a rash decision. We were always so passionate. The fights we'd have..." She smiled fondly. "The makeup sex. Did he tell you we didn't stop seeing each other after the divorce?"

He had not.

But the Nathan I'd known wouldn't have cheated on me. Would he?

"Oh, yes. We saw each other regularly." She took a sip of her water. "Right up until he met you. But I knew he still loved *me*."

I unlocked my jaw. "Not quite enough, though, right? Since he married me and all."

She gave me a pitying smile. "He was going to leave you."

"I'm not so sure about that. We were trying to have a baby."

"Yes, he did want children. And you're right. I didn't realize he'd marry someone for the sole purpose of breeding." She gave me another once-over. "He probably should've chosen someone a little younger."

"Jesus! You're breathtakingly rude."

"You're the one who wanted to have a drink. Would you like another? Maybe some macaroni and cheese to soak up some of the alcohol?"

"I'd love some. Miss?" I waved to the server. "Can I have an order of macaroni and cheese? And another round?"

"Of course," she said. "Would you like bacon or lobster with that?"

"How about both?" I beamed at her—at least the server would like me better, if not my husband. "Anything for you, Madeleine? A blade of grass to chew on?" *That's right, bitch. He told me you were a vegan. We ate meat together. Deal with it.*

She rolled her eyes. The happy sounds from outside grated against my brain like a dentist's drill.

"Do you get visits from him?" she asked, leaning forward with mock compassion. "I do. Little signs, things only he would know. Sometimes I hear him say my name."

"Usually after a few drinks, am I right?"

"I don't seem to be the one with the drinking problem."

Shit. Good retort.

The girl returned with my food and refill.

I didn't want to eat, but now it seemed like a moral imperative. Spooning up some of the gooey dish, I took a bite. It wasn't hot enough and it didn't taste very good, either.

"How is it?" Madeleine asked with a condescending smile.

"Delicious. Want some?"

"I don't eat things that once had a heartbeat."

"That's what he said," I mumbled around the food.

Madeleine narrowed her eyes. "Look, Kate," she said, making my name sound like a curse. "I don't know what I can tell you. I loved him. He loved me. Because of my difficult childhood, I didn't think I wanted children. When I saw how desperate he was to be a father—desperate enough to date *you*, a stranger—I changed my mind about children. And from then on, it was just a matter of time before we got back together."

"Riddle me this, then, Batman," I said, the vodka loosening my tongue. "He met me. We dated. We had a blast. We had so much fun and happiness that we got married. And it was great! So yeah, he answered your pathetic emails. Politely, because he was a kind person. But he *didn't* leave me. He loved me."

"Tell yourself what you need to. I know in my heart what was true. We were..." She shook her head, the image of her and Nathan's love too big for mere words. "He felt obligated to you. I think he felt sorry for you, honestly. So yes, he stayed. For a little while." She gave an elegant shrug. "And then you needed another glass of wine, I heard. And now he's dead."

I let that sit a moment.

Then I took my bowl of mac and cheese, stood up and dumped it on her head.

She gasped and lurched back from the table. "Lunch is on me," I said. "Well, figuratively, of course. Literally speaking, lunch is on you."

My hands were still shaking ten minutes later.

I was too angry to drive (not to mention the two vodkas), so I walked around out to the park, sloppily dodging dogs, joggers and kids on tricycles. It was wide-open here and flat, not like Bixby Park with its woods and paths. Not like Prospect, which was practically a forest.

I got to the lookout and stared at the new bridge. Sailboats dotted the blue of the water and speedboats motored past, coming in and out of the marina. Somewhere behind me, a band played Van Morrison's old hit "Brown Eyed Girl."

*I* had brown eyes. Had Nathan and I ever heard this song together? Had he ever called me his brown-eyed girl? We'd never danced to it; we'd danced only a couple of times, at one of his parents' benefits, and it was more of the Benny Goodman type of event.

Well, meeting Madeleine had been a *huge* mistake. Hopefully, she wouldn't sue me.

I pulled my phone out of my backpack and called Eloise. "Hi, it's Kate," I said.

"Kate, deah, how are you?"

"I'm… Listen, I'd like to get rid of that bench in Bixby Park, okay? It's upsetting me."

"Of course. Let me make the call, deah. No need for you to do it. I agree. It was very inappropriate of her."

We made plans for lunch, and this time, it didn't feel so awful. It felt, in fact, like I had an ally.

Speaking of allies, I called Ainsley. The call went to voice mail. Shit. Wasn't it always the way? Just when I wanted to talk, she wasn't around. "Hey, I'm down at the river walk in

Tarrytown," I said. "I'll be later than I thought." *Because I got a little drunk with Nathan's ex-wife and dumped food on her head.*

I wandered over to a tree and sat down, leaning against the trunk. Took my camera out of my bag and shot the bridge, the boats, some kids, a dog. None of the shots were any good. Everything looked fake and staged.

Also, the tree trunk was grinding into my spine. So I lay down instead. The grass prickled my arms. The sky was so fiercely blue I had to close my eyes.

*Are you up there, Nathan? Are you okay? Did you really love me, or was she right?*

I didn't get an answer. Instead, I fell asleep.

I woke up sometime later with one of those sharp snore-snorts, then blinked. The sky wasn't quite as blue as before.

Daniel the Hot Firefighter was sitting next to me. "Hi," I said.

"Hi. Hope you don't mind, but we just had sex."

I snorted again—laughter this time. "Did we emotionally scar any children?"

He gave me a steamy look, sleepy eyes and raised eyebrow. "You *were* pretty dirty."

"What are you doing here? Other than molesting sleeping widows?"

"I was helping Jane with her horrible kids. Thought I'd get a beer and called your landline. Had it mixed up with your cell phone, and your sister told me you were down here."

"Yeah. Just taking it all in."

"I thought I saw you at the Re-Enter Center a couple weeks ago. At the fund-raiser?"

"I made an appearance."

"You left pretty early." He started picking blades of grass.

"I did. My sister and I had plans."

My cheeks felt hot, whether from the drinks, the sun,

the nap or the fact that D the HF was sitting next to me, I wasn't sure.

It was also a little embarrassing to admit that I'd left a party because he'd shown up with a date.

"So how are things?" he asked.

"Good."

"You read those emails."

I nodded.

"And they made you feel like shit?"

"Yep."

"You should've listened to Uncle Dan." He stretched out next to me, all male beauty and muscle. "What did they say?"

I watched as a little girl ran after her older brother, which reminded me—Sean hadn't called in a while. Too busy living his perfect life.

I cleared my throat. "His ex still loved him and wanted him to leave me, but he was very *content* with me and didn't want to hurt me." My words were careful.

"That's it?"

"I thought it was pretty earthshaking."

"Doesn't sound that bad to me." I cut him a look. "But then again, I'm a guy, so I'm thick." We were quiet for a minute. "No, it's not so bad," he said. "Content is pretty great. You want what you have and have what you want. Nothing wrong with content."

"She said he was going to leave me. He just felt guilty."

"So? What does she know? He *didn't* leave you. Let it go, Kate."

I sighed. "It's just that if I had known any of this was going on, I would never have married him."

"Why?"

"Because he was...torn."

"Was he? He married you. That seems pretty decisive."

"And then he *died*, Daniel. I'm a widow. If I'd known he'd been uncertain or conflicted or whatever, I would've said no, let's wait. And then…maybe he'd even be alive today."

He gave a huge sigh. "But he's not. It happened. You want some ice cream? I hear the truck."

"That's all you've got?"

"You need more than ice cream?" He stood up in one quick, athletic move. "Come on." He offered his hand, and I took it.

He didn't let go, either. For maybe twelve or thirteen paces, he kept holding my hand, and it was only when a soccer ball rolled our way did he let go, run up to the ball and kick it back to a kid.

I ordered a Good Humor vanilla nut cone and let him pay.

"Did you ask Paige to teach at the Re-Enter Center?" I asked as I wolfed the thing down (my lunch having gone on Madeleine's head).

"No," he said, licking the side of his hand where ice cream was melting. "Somebody did, though. Why?"

"I was just surprised to see her there. I asked her to teach a dozen times back in the day."

"Well, she's there now. Being quite a pain in the ass, from what I hear, trying to run the place. You should come back. Everyone misses you." He nudged my shoulder with his. "Especially me."

"Aw, thanks, you big lug."

He smiled around his cone. He was just pointlessly beautiful, Daniel was.

Even better, he was nice.

"Walk you back to your car?" he asked.

"Sure."

There was no hand-holding on the way back to the car. I was irritated that I even thought about it.

"Thanks for the ice cream, mister," I said when we got to my car.

"You're welcome." He gave me a hug, practically crushing me in his big brawny arms, then messed up my hair. "Let's have dinner sometime, okay?"

"Okay."

With that, I got in the car and drove home, feeling a lot better than I had before.

Daniel Breton was a very nice man. A good friend.

Who would've guessed?

# Chapter Twenty-Five

*Ainsley*

Stupid-Head didn't call on Sunday. I checked my phone maniacally all the livelong day. Stayed home, even, in case he wanted to swing by.

He didn't.

So on Monday morning, feeling very pissy indeed, I stomped into work at 8:29.

He was on the phone in his office. I glared in his general direction.

"How was your weekend?" Rachelle asked.

"It was great!" I said—it was half-true. A quarter true, at least. I dropped the glare and smiled at her. "How about you?"

"So good. I met someone! He seemed straight, didn't have a doll collection or long toenails and lives in a cute apartment, but his grandmother is the landlord, so there's a red flag."

"Well, it could be legit," I said. "She's not living with him, is she?"

"I didn't see her," Rachelle said. "I thought I smelled old lady powder, but I didn't find hard evidence."

"Ainsley, can I see you for a moment?" Jonathan said.

"Sure, Jonathan!" I said, my voice hard. I whirled around and swept into his office.

He closed the door behind me, then sat at his desk.

"Thanks for the call yesterday." I folded my arms and resumed glaring.

"I didn't call you."

"I know."

He blinked. *I don't understand this sarcasm you employ, human.*

"What do you want, Jonathan? Are you firing me? Finally?"

"No. I need you to sign this."

He passed a sheaf of papers across the desk, then folded his hands. I glanced down.

Consensual Romance in the Workplace Agreement
We, the undersigned...voluntary and consensual...not
have a negative impact...public displays of affection...

I tossed the papers back on his desk. "This your form of snuggling?"

"Excuse me?"

"*This* is the conversation we're going to have after—" I lowered my voice "—sleeping together? Don't you want to say anything to me first?"

"Absolutely not. I need you to read that. If you wanted to sue me right now, you'd be well within your rights."

"Why? Because we *did* it?"

He flinched. Less than flattering. "Please keep your voice down, and yes."

"You are the least romantic person I've ever met."

"I'm simply trying to protect—"

"I know. I'm not stupid. Give me your pen." I grabbed it, scrawled my signature on every page, initialed in four spots and tossed the pen back at him. It bounced off the desk and hit him in the chest.

"This is necessary, Ainsley. Please make sure you read the paragraph on public—"

"Jonathan, enough. Okay?"

He stood up. "I'm sorry if this has insulted you somehow."

I threw up my hands. "It would've been nice if you called me. I was feeling a little unsure on Saturday, since your first words to me upon waking were 'Get out.'"

"Actually, I believe I said—"

"I didn't even know you *liked* me on Friday, and the next thing I know, we're doing the wild thing, and then you didn't call, even though you said you would, which is breaking a commandment in the dating world, and now you greet me with a form from your lawyer."

He took a slow breath. "Lydia was under the weather yesterday, so the girls stayed over last night instead of going back to their mother's."

"Which you could've let me know."

"I don't want my daughters to overhear me talking to someone I'm...potentially involved with. Their mother has confused them enough."

"Text, Jonathan. Email. We live in a wondrous modern world."

He tilted his head, not quite looking at me. "I wasn't sure what to say."

Right. I was dealing with Captain Flatline.

"How about 'Hi, Ainsley, I trust you had a pleasant weekend. I know I did, especially Friday night. Unfortunately, my daughter is sick, so I can't talk, but I'll see you tomorrow.'"

His mouth curled up the tiniest bit. "I did have a pleasant weekend. Especially Friday night."

Though they were my words, his deep dark voice made them seem...delicious. "How's Lydia feeling now?"

"All better."

"Would you like to say anything personal to me, Jonathan?"

"No. We're at work." But the smile grew.

I smiled back at him, feeling gooey and melty and happily stupid.

"Don't you have articles to edit?" he asked.

"Right," I said. But my smile stayed put, even as I went off to read articles on how more and more family physicians in our area were offering their patients Botox.

A few hours later, as I was reading Candy's latest warm and touching response to a daughter whose mother was cold and unloving, my father walked in.

"Dad!" I said, fear shooting through my limbs. He'd never come to see me at work before. "Who's dead?"

"Is someone dead?"

"I don't know. You tell me!"

"Is it Gram-Gram?" He looked startled.

"I don't *know*! Is it?" We stared at each other a second. "Dad, are you here to deliver bad news?"

"No," he said. "I thought we could go out to lunch." He paused. "Should I call your grandmother?"

"I'll do it." We were both superstitious, Dad and me. Him, because he worked in baseball, and those men fell apart if they didn't wear their special pants or cross themselves three times before batting or turn in a circle three times at first base.

Me, because I'd grown up in a world where moms went for a bike ride and got hit by trucks.

"Hi, Gram-Gram!" I chirped when she answered, giving Dad the thumbs-up. "Just wanted to say hi. How are you?"

"Oh, honey, you're so sweet! You are! I'm fine. Well, I'm lonely. I'm a lonely old woman waiting to die."

"Don't say that," I said. "I'd miss you too much."

"Well, it's true. I have nothing to look forward to."

"What about that date you went on?" I'd fixed her up with George from Kate's grief group, and they had lunch the other day.

"All he talked about was soup."

"You like soup."

"That's true. Bisque. I really like bisque."

"See? It's a start."

"You're wonderful. Do you know that? You're my best friend. I love you, honey!"

"I love you, too, Gram-Gram." I hung up, feeling relieved, adoring, adored and rather pimpish.

Jonathan was staring at me from his office. Not only did I have a family member at my desk, I was making a personal call at work. "I'd like to schedule that employee review, Ainsley," he called.

Apparently, sleeping with the boss wasn't going to win me any points. There was no hint of a smile in his dead-eyed stare. "It was an emergency," I said. "We thought Gram-Gram might be dead. She's not. I'm going to lunch. You remember my dad, right? Bye!"

My father drove me in his little convertible, and it was like old times, doing errands/visiting his girlfriends when I was a kid. We talked about baseball, how much we both missed Derek Jeter, where Dad's next game would be, the pulled pork sandwich he'd had in Kansas City.

"Shall we eat here?" Dad asked, pulling up in front of Hudson's. "I've never been." He and Candy didn't go out together a lot (or ever), and the place was relatively new.

"Sure. I came here for drinks with the girls a few weeks ago. It's really cute."

A few minutes later, we had a nice table overlooking the river and had placed our orders—fettuccine Alfredo for both of us, rich and delicious and unhealthy, the kind of food Candy never made. "So, Dad. This is nice. And strange. I don't think we've had lunch together in ten years."

"I know, Ainsburger. That's my fault. Too much travel!" But he smiled; he really did love his job. "I wanted to see how you were doing about Eric."

Dad, worried about me? That was new.

It dawned on me that I hadn't thought too much about Eric in the past couple of days. I mean, sure, he'd crossed my mind; Jonathan was only the second guy I'd ever slept with, so there was some comparison. I was happy to say that Jonathan won. "Well," I said, "I'm getting over it, I guess. He's making it easy by turning into a total idiot."

"I always thought he'd take good care of you. That's why I liked him. Nice parents, too."

They *were* nice. But the last time I'd called Judy, she hadn't called back. The thought made my throat swell, but I smiled at my dad anyway.

"How are you doing for money?" he asked.

I sighed. "I have a little saved up. But I have to find a place of my own. Kate won't want me with her forever."

"It's awfully nice, you staying with her."

"It's awfully nice of her, putting me up."

"She never could ask for help. I'm glad you're there." Our lunches arrived, and we dug in. It was heaven, this food. Heaven.

"The reason I asked about money, Ainsburger, is I have some for you."

"That's okay, Dad. I'll be fine."

"It's from your mother."

I blinked. "It is?"

He nodded, not looking at me. "She had life insurance. Not a lot, but it's been earning interest all these years. Close to a hundred thousand now."

I sputtered in shock. "A hundred thousand *dollars*?"

"Yes. I figured I'd give it to you when you got married, but…well, it's yours."

I sat back in my chair. "Why didn't you ever mention it before?"

"The truth is, I kind of forgot about it. It was supposed to be yours when you turned twenty-five."

Leave it to my father to forget a *huge* sum of cash. I closed my mouth.

My mom had been twenty-five when she died, almost twenty years younger than my father. Did most young mothers take out life insurance? "When did she do that?" I asked.

"The week before you were born. She had this… Well, it doesn't matter, does it?"

"It does, Dad. You never talk about her. Please tell me." The truth was, I'd learned more about my mother from Kate a few weeks ago than I had from Dad in three decades.

He sighed. Looked out the window. "She had a dream that she was dying," he said very, very quietly. "That she was giving birth to you, but she knew she wouldn't make it, and all she wanted was to last long enough to see you. She woke up so upset. Cried and cried." He rubbed a hand across his forehead. "I used to tease her about it after you came. Tell her at least she got to hold you, see you walk, see your first tooth. I never thought…" His voice broke.

"Oh, Daddy," I said, reaching for his hand with both of mine. "I'm so sorry."

"I was ruined when she died. I felt like I died, too." He

wiped his eyes in the way men do, pinching away the tears with his free hand. "You're so much like her, Ainsley. In all the good ways."

I kissed his hand, my own eyes filling with tears.

He squeezed my fingers, then pulled free. Wiped his eyes with his napkin, shook his head, smiled at me and resumed eating. I watched as he retreated back behind his amiable mask. Somewhat fitting that he wore one for work.

Not everyone could cope with a broken heart. Some people never recovered. My dad seemed to be one of them.

Kate *would* recover. I'd make sure of it.

Our heart-to-heart was over. I told him about the ice tool museum and suggested we visit it in the fall when baseball was over, and he told me that he'd gone to see a movie in Seattle at a theater where the seats reclined, and he'd fallen asleep and woken in the middle of the next movie.

I never realized how lonely my father was. All those girl-friends, all that cheating, all those years with Candy, who couldn't get over him the same way he couldn't get over my mother.

"Are you and Candy really getting a divorce?" I asked.

"What? Oh, that," he said. "No. She just likes to go through the motions once in a while to get my attention."

A man dressed in chef whites came over to our table. "How was everything today? I'm Matthew, the chef and owner."

"Fantastic," Dad said, shaking his hand. "Best pasta I've had in years."

"And Dad eats out a lot," I said. "All over the country. He's an umpire for Major League Baseball."

"Oh, man! What an awesome job! You ever meet Derek Jeter?"

"Sure have. He's a great guy."

The men talked baseball for a few minutes, then the chef shook both our hands, thanked us for coming in.

"Hey," I said, suddenly remembering my job. "I'm the features editor at *Hudson Lifestyle*. I don't think we've covered you." That in itself was weird; we did a story on a bead store opening last year. There was nothing too inconsequential for us, so long as it was in the area. We *always* covered new restaurants.

"Yeah," he said. "Um…"

Dad's phone chimed, and he looked down at his phone. "Oh! Clancy canceled for tonight's game. I have to get to Camden Yards. Can you get back to the office on your own, Burger-baby?"

"Sure, Dad. I'll walk. It's beautiful out."

He kissed me on the cheek, shook the chef's hand again and left, once again buoyed by our national pastime.

"Do you know our magazine?" I asked Matthew. "We do lots of restaurant features, and this is a lovely spot."

He sat down in Dad's vacated seat. "I do know the magazine. I'm Matthew Kent."

My mouth fell open, and a rush of heat rose up my chest.

Jonathan's brother. Jonathan's brother, who slept with his *wife*.

"Oh," I managed. "You."

"Yeah."

Now I could see a resemblance. Matt's hair was lighter, and his eyes lacked the odd beauty of Jonathan's, but he had high cheekbones and beautiful hands.

"Have you worked there a long time?" he asked.

"Two years."

"So you know my brother well?"

*I know him biblically.* "Mmm-hmm."

"And based on the hate shining from your eyes, I guess you know about me."

"Yep."

He sighed. "Yeah." His fingers drummed on the table. "Well, I'm not proud of the way it happened, but I do care about my brother."

"Funny way of showing it."

"There's no excuse, I realize that," he said, staring down at the table. "For what it's worth, I really do love Laine and the girls."

"Of course you do. They're your *nieces*."

His gaze snapped up to me. "Look. I was in love with her years before Jonathan even noticed her, okay? And when our father had the stroke, Jonathan just closed up. There was no room for me, no shared grieving or whatever, and Laine was alone all day long with two little toddlers. All he did was work."

"So you thought you'd help by *shtupping* his wife."

He looked away. "As I said, I'm not proud of it. And I didn't just *shtup* her. Long before it got to that point, I was buying the groceries, cooking dinner, playing with the girls, fixing the furnace."

"Wow. You should get a sticker."

"I know what a shitty thing I did, Miss…"

"O'Leary."

"Miss O'Leary. But if you work for my brother, you probably know he's not the easiest person in the world. I'd like to make things right with him, or at least try." He looked out the window again. "I miss him."

"Sounds like someone needs to buy a well-worded card," I said, standing up. My hand hit my father's water glass, which tumbled into Matthew's lap. "Whoops."

With that, I left, my head buzzing with the feels.

Quite a lunch. In an hour, I understood my father better than I ever had. I learned that my mother had somehow known she wouldn't always be there for me and tried to provide for me before I was even born.

And I'd met the man who'd ruined Jonathan's life.

# Chapter Twenty-Six

*Kate*

"Booty tooch!" the mother yelled. "Come on, Brittannee! Make it high fashion!"

"High fashion?" Max muttered. "Or porn?"

It was Thursday afternoon, a beautiful July afternoon, and we were doing a high school senior shoot for a very nice girl whose mother clearly wanted her to model, rather than go to Vanderbilt on a basketball scholarship, as she was planning.

"She's wasting her looks!" the mother said, throwing up her hands.

"Ma," Brittannee said. "I want to be a doctor. I don't need looks."

"Well, you have them. You should take advantage. Can't you just work with me? I know I could get you in at *Elle*."

We were at Bixby Park, and while the eighteen-year-old seemed content with the *look at the camera and smile* approach that usually worked best, the mother had a different concept.

She stomped over in front of the cinder block wall of the public restrooms, which she had deemed "editorial."

"Like this," she said, thrusting out her rump so hard I heard a joint pop. "Booty tooch. Bing, bang, boom. Tick, tick, tick. And now, swivel your arms forward. Gucci tooch!"

"Are you speaking in tongues?" Brit asked. She rolled her eyes at me, and I gave her a sympathetic smile.

"This picture is for *me*," the mom said. "It's how I want to remember you when you're gone."

"Okay, first of all, I'm not dying. I'm going to college. And second, you want to remember me with my ass out? Can't I just smile like a normal person?"

Speaking of modeling, Daniel's youngest sister, Lizzie, had texted me. She'd signed with Ford Models, and I was thrilled for her. I told her to let me know if she needed anything, since I knew a few people in the fashion world. Lizzie had talent. I thought so, anyway. And she *wanted* to be a model.

Brittannee of the difficult spelling did not.

I focused on the mother, who had that gaunt, stringy look of a body-obsessed middle-aged woman.

"Lori," I said to her. "You have fabulous cheekbones. Do you mind if I take a few shots of just you?"

"Me? Well, if you *want* to," she said, immediately pursing her lips at me. She tootched and gooched and did whatever else it was Tyra Banks said on TV. *Thank you*, mouthed Brittannee, then smiled at her mom.

"Fantastic, Lori. Love that! Hold that pose, long neck!" Hey, I didn't live in a cave.

A half hour later, when Lori was done dangling from a tree branch and squinting at me, I focused on the child. "Brit, why don't you take a seat on the grass there and make yourself comfortable?"

And so it was that I got at least ten beautiful shots of Brittannee looking like what she seemed to be—a lovely, athletic girl with a pretty smile. And her mom got to pretend to be a model for a little while. They left holding hands, which made my throat ache.

I would've loved a daughter.

Maybe I'd adopt after all, in a year or so. The grief group members all told me not to make big decisions in the first year.

And it had been only three months, one week and six days.

Nathan's bench had been removed. I'd have to call Eloise and thank her.

For the past four days, I'd been in the city, looking after Esther, Matthias and Sadie while Sean and Kiara went to a surgeons' conference in Napa, sponsored by a manufacturer of surgical equipment, where they spent fifteen minutes looking at technology and three days getting mud masks and massages.

It had been fantastic, playing Scrabble with Matthias and Esther at night, binge-watching *The Walking Dead* with them, taking Sadie to Central Park during the day, pushing her in the baby jogger along the West Side Highway, letting people assume she was mine. I made Sean and Kiara promise to go away more.

But today, I'd have to go back to Cambry-on-Hudson.

"How you doing?" Max asked as we packed up.

"Not bad, I guess." I looked at him, my old pal. "Sometimes it feels like I was never married. It's—" I cleared my throat. "It's tough."

Max nodded. "Don't be so hard on yourself," he said, his whispery voice always sounding a little scary. "Don't overanalyze everything. Let yourself have a little fun."

"You know me well."

"I should."

"Give the family my love."

He nodded and walked off to his car.

★ ★ ★

I was thawing dinner, the last of the bereavement food, some sort of bisque, when Ainsley came home that night. "Hi!" she said. "I missed you! How were the kids?"

"They're great," I said. "Esther's gonna put them through their paces, though. She's starting the terrible teens."

"Good," Ainsley said. "Sean's always had it too easy." She beamed at me, clearly about to explode with news.

"So how was your week?" I asked.

"You'll never believe it!" she said. "I wanted to tell you immediately, but I knew it would be better in person, and I forgot you were going to Sean's. You ready?"

I nodded.

"I slept with *Jonathan*! And I have reason to believe we're in an actual relationship, because he made me sign papers."

"Holy crap," I said, smiling. I didn't need to ask about it, because she buzzed around the kitchen like a happy bumble-bee, scooping up Ollie, smooching his face, putting him on one hip while she grabbed the wine from the fridge.

"I got stuck at his house on Friday night in the storm, and he made dinner, and we had some wine, and then he told me he *liked* me! I had no bleepin' idea! But I've actually been having these feelings about him here and there, because aside from being sort of an alien-robot, he's got this Mr. Darcy thing going on, a little bit, anyway. And it was so *cute*, how he told me! And then we kissed, and next thing I knew, we were doing our best to break his headboard."

I laughed. She poured me a glass of wine and set the dog down, then took a seat at the counter. Ollie dragged his blanket over to my feet and curled up there.

"So what do you think? Too soon after Eric?" she asked.

"Oh, I don't know. What do *you* think?"

"Come on. Give me some big-sister advice. I have a date

with him in forty-five minutes. Out of town, of course. He's freaked out someone from work is going to find out."

"He's divorced, right?"

"Yes, and you wouldn't believe that story! His wife cheated on him with his *brother*."

"Are you kidding? Yikes!" Oh, the fun of juicy gossip! It reminded me of happier times with Paige. "Well, all the more reason to be careful with him. I imagine he has trust issues."

"See? Excellent big-sister advice." She finished her wine. "All right. I have to change and find some slutty shoes. And, uh, I might stay over at his place."

My heart sank a little. I'd missed her, too. "Okay. Have fun."

She must've picked up on something, because she said, "You want to do something tomorrow night? Just you and me, or maybe you and me and some friends?"

Hell, yes. I was tired of my own company. "Sure. I'd love to. I'll invite a couple people from the grief group, okay? LuAnn is hilarious, and she could use a night away from her kids."

"Super! We can have a party! Put this house to good use." She gave me a hug, then clattered upstairs.

So. Just me and the dog tonight. That was fine. I could edit the pictures I'd taken today. Or read a book. Or clean the bathroom.

Or start to clear out Nathan's clothes.

It had to be done sometime.

Ainsley left, and I ate my lonely soup at the counter, feeling a bit like a Dickensian orphan. "Please, sir, I want some more," I said aloud. Ollie barked and wagged, so what the heck? I scooped him onto my lap and let him lick out the bowl.

There was still some soup in the pot, enough for another bowl, at least.

I dumped it down the drain.

No more bereavement food. I was sick of it.

It's funny how time is measured after you've lost someone. Everything relates back to that second your life swerved. The calendar isn't measured by the names of the months or seasons anymore, but by those significant dates. The day we met. The first time we kissed. The first dinner with his family. The anniversary of his death. The date of his funeral.

And every day takes you further from the time he was alive, slicing you with the razor-sharp realization that those days would never be celebrated again. Nathan's birthday would come and go, year after year, but he'd never grow older. All the anniversaries we'd never have. *It would've been our first, our third, our twenty-fifth.* All those dates that held no meaning for anyone on the outside but were slashed into the hearts of those of us who'd been left behind.

In our group the other night, LuAnn talked about that first year, how she'd steeled herself for every first. "The three hundred and sixty-sixth day, though…things inside me, they just kinda relaxed, you know? Like I proved I could survive it, even when I never believed I could."

Janette, whose husband had died of cancer on their anniversary, said it was the opposite for her. "Every month seems harder. All the things he's missing. And here I am, pathetically getting older, wandering through life without him."

"For me," Leo said, "it was like a car was parked on my chest, crushing me, and even breathing hurt. Now it's been almost three years. The car's still there, but it's moved off and made some room."

"For Jenny," I said.

"Yes." He smiled. "For Jenny. And other people, too. My students. You guys."

I still had such a long way to go, the newest in the group.

I refilled my wineglass and wandered into the study (or den). Maybe I'd look at those last photos of Nathan, still sitting in the Nikon on the shelf.

But what if I saw that he didn't really love me? What would I do then?

And then...no matter what I saw in his face...I'd never have anything new of him again. As long as those photos were unseen, it felt like there was something left of Nathan still in the world.

"Not tonight, Hector," I said. My fish swam amiably in his bowl. Still alive, still bucking the fishy odds of life expectancy.

I clicked on my computer. I had to erase pimples from a dozen high school seniors' faces and put together a slide show for two sets of newlyweds. Ollie came in, dragging his ratty old blanket, made a nest on the floor and fell asleep, his soft little doggy snores keeping me company.

I adjusted light and smoothed skin and cropped relatives. It was easy work. Ah, here was a gorgeous shot—the bride was African American, in profile as she said her vows, a tear glistening on her cheek, echoing the diamond earring she wore, the contrast in her skin tone and dress stunning. I'd submit that one to a photography magazine. "Nice work, don't you think, Hector?" I asked. I'd really been on my game last weekend. Good for me.

A knock slammed at the front door, and I nearly jumped out of my skin. *Boomboomboomboom!* Ollie leaped up, grabbed his blanket and went racing to the door, his barks muffled by fleece. I followed.

It was Daniel. And it was past nine.

"Is everything okay?" I asked.

"I'm an uncle again!" he said, giving me a big hug. "Congratulate me! I was in the delivery room, which, believe me, was not on my bucket list, seeing my sister spread from east to west. I need some acid to wash out my eyes." He let me go, grinning like an idiot. "Oh. Shouldn't have hugged you. I have all sorts of fluids on me. I came right from the hospital."

His happiness was contagious. "Oh, hell, it's okay. Boy or girl?"

"Girl, and please God, she won't be the little demon her sister is. Maisy Danielle—I totally earned that middle name, by the way, hauling my sister's leg back so she could push, telling her she was amazing while trying not to look at her parts. Nine pounds, two ounces, head like a frickin' moon. My sister won't be able to walk for weeks." He folded his brawny arms across his chest, still smiling. "Nice name, right?"

"Very nice. Congratulations, Uncle Dan. Come on. I might even have champagne somewhere."

"I'll take a beer. Actually, I'm kind of gross. A brother tends to sweat from every pore when his sister's water breaks. In my truck, no less. Any chance I could take a shower first?"

He was clearly buzzed with adrenaline. "Sure, come on in. There are seven bathrooms in this house."

"See this stain?" he said, pointing to his shirt. "It's blood. How gross is that? And I don't even want to think what *this* is." He continued to talk as I led him upstairs. "She was a champ, though, my sis. Hardly yelled at all. Then my mom got there, and she was all irritated that she missed the drama, but it was Jane's fourth, you know? The kid slid out like a greased otter. We barely made it to the hospital. I think she pushed five times."

I led him down the hall to one of the unused bedrooms. Couldn't remember the last time I'd been in here, but it was clean, vacuum marks still on the rug, a splotchy painting on the wall.

Strange, that there were rooms in my house I didn't go in.

Daniel opened the door to the bathroom. "Wow. This is bigger than my apartment."

Yeah, it was a little on the obscene side. Tasteful, sure, but enormous. Nathan had deemed white and glass bathrooms very "last decade," and so this one was made out of dark wood and soapstone. One side of the room had a counter with double sinks, elaborate lighting above, below and alongside the counter, as well as four live orchids. Someone was keeping them alive, Ainsley or the cleaning service. There was the toilet room (with bidet, which, being American, I found creepy). A giant tub with water jets, and, in the far corner, the shower, hidden by a wall of smoked gray glass.

"Towels are everywhere," I said, indicating the row of a dozen symmetrically rolled white towels. "Take your time. Enjoy."

"I will. Thanks. Hey, got a clean T-shirt I can borrow?" he said, pulling off the one he was wearing.

Good God. Muscles everywhere, and skin, glorious skin.

"Sure. I'll be right back. Keep your pants on, mister. No flashing me."

He winked, and I found myself smiling as I went down the hall to my room. I had a giant Yankees T-shirt my father had brought me that I slept in sometimes. I wasn't about to give him something of Nathan's. That... No.

I grabbed the shirt and came back to the bathroom. Daniel was now barefoot, fiddling with the controls in the shower. His work boots and socks were by the door, his mighty torso rippling like Thor's. I said a brief prayer of thanksgiving to FDNY, their training program and gyms. I was a widow—I wasn't dead. He had an eight-pack, and just above the waistband of his jeans were those wonderful V-lines. A happy trail.

"How do you turn the light on?" he asked, and I jumped and cleared my throat. Hot in here.

"Oh. Um…I'm not sure. Wave your hands. Some of the switches are motion sensors."

The bathroom was big enough that the shower required its own lights. It was gloomy-dark in there. Daniel waved an arm, the motion causing his shoulder to bunch and flex hypnotically. Nothing happened (light-wise, though my ovaries were sighing happily). I tried a few light switches—under the sink, next to the sink, in the toilet room, the tub's underwater lights.

I went over to the shower. It had three showerheads—north, south and above—one of those rainshower things, as well as a detachable sprayer. On the shelf, there was a line of products—lemongrass soap, shampoo, conditioner and moisturizer. A razor. A loofah. There was a control panel (don't judge me…this was all Nathan's idea) where you could adjust the temperature of the water and which showerheads to use.

I waved a hand. Nothing. Jazz hands failed to get us light. I moved closer to the control panel, thinking there must be a switch there. Temperature, steam feature, tile heating. Nothing that said *light*.

I waved again. This time, for some reason, the lights went on.

So did the water, from every possible source. And it was *freezing*. I scrambled back with a yelp and collided with Daniel.

He was laughing. "Yay for you," he said, holding on to my elbows. "You found it."

The water from the rainshower had soaked me through. Daniel, too. It got warm almost immediately, running down my face, my back, soaking my jeans.

Streamed in fascinating rivulets down Daniel, pooling in the indentation above his collarbone, down his beautiful, thick chest and arms, into the waistband of his jeans.

"Well," I said, my voice husky, "have fun."

"I will." But he didn't let go of my arms, just looked at me with that slight smile.

Then he kissed me.

For a second, I didn't move.

Then I did. My mouth did, anyway, and all the loneliness and emptiness I'd been feeling seemed to leap out of me. Daniel's hands slid into my wet hair, and my arms went around his neck, feeling the power of his muscles, and he felt so good, so beautiful, that I almost cried.

I missed being touched. I missed touching another person who wasn't my sister or niece. I missed someone wanting me.

And hot damn, he knew what he was doing—he was Daniel the Hot Firefighter, after all, and I was finally seeing what all the fuss was about. He kissed me like he was planning to do just that for hours, slow, intense, wet kisses, his mouth moving and testing. His big hands wandered down my back, then he bent and picked me up and pressed me against the shower wall, his mouth never leaving mine.

He felt *so* good. I mean, he was basically a god, physically speaking, and he felt so strong and big, his skin slippery and wet and warm, his muscles rolling, holding me up without apparent effort, his arms rock hard under my hands.

And he was smiling against my mouth. For some reason, that did more than everything else.

I missed this. I missed sex. I missed the feeling of a man, the scrape of his razor stubble, the amassed strength. After all these months of me fading away, someone knew I was here.

"I don't have anything with me," he murmured against my ear, "but I think I can make you happy just the same." Then his mouth moved to my throat, and lower, and my hands fisted in his hair, tugging his mouth back to mine.

"I have something. Just…just… I'll be back in a second." On legs that barely worked, I staggered out of the shower, down the hall to my bedroom, leaving a trail of water the whole way. I didn't even care.

There were condoms in the night table drawer on Nathan's side of the bed, back from before we were trying to get pregnant. From before we were married.

I wouldn't think about Nathan now. He was gone, he'd still had feelings for Madeleine and I was so, so tired of being sad. I'd been disappearing for months now.

Daniel *saw* me, and not just because I was standing in front of him. He'd come here, to me, to tell me about his new niece. That day in the park, when I'd fallen asleep, he'd been sitting next to me when I woke up.

*Don't overthink this*, I told myself. I heard Max telling me to be nice to myself. Ainsley saying I deserved some fun.

I ran back down the hall, the half-empty box in my hand. He was getting out of the shower.

He really was beautiful. There was no other word for it. But his expression was somber. "I'm sorry about that," he said, not looking at me. "Obviously, we don't have to do anything, and I get the feeling I really, uh, overstepped there."

"You didn't."

He looked at me a long minute. "You took your time."

"I wanted to make sure this was a good idea."

"Is it?"

"It is."

His mouth pulled up in an abrupt smile. "Thank God. I thought you were trying to figure out how to get rid of me." Then he crossed the room and kissed me again, a hard, whole-body kiss, and, being that he was six foot three and a wall of perfection, just scooped me right up and kept going till we hit the bed. Bounced me down on it and said, "Let's get you out of those wet clothes, then," and proceeded to get me naked. Fast.

It was fun. It was fun and horny and hot, and he was beautiful and smiley, chiseled and rippling, heavy and delicious on top of me, and for a while, I felt like my old self again.

Happy.

# Chapter Twenty-Seven

*Ainsley*

Jonathan's house seemed more beautiful each time I saw it—the old farmhouse high on a hill, no neighbors in sight, a view of fields and woods, and in the distance, the silvery wink of the Hudson.

But it was now Friday morning, and he was kicking me out so we could both get to work, so I had to go. The birds were singing full-on, and the mist was rising off the river, and the world was beautiful and new.

Last night, we'd had an honest-to-goodness date. A glass of wine while sitting out on the slate patio, under a big maple tree that shushed with the breeze, watching the sun lower in the clear summer sky. Then we drove across the river to a beautiful restaurant in a former mill building, our table overlooking a waterfall.

At first, I did my usual *isn't she wonderful?* repertoire, gently flirting with both Jonathan and the waiter, making sure

Jonathan remembered he did indeed like me. Sleeping with the boss was harder than it looked; this whole week, there'd been absolutely no affection or lovey-dovey stuff between us at work. So it was normal, in a sense, but every time he walked by, I felt my cheeks warm. I was so used to being in trouble at work, I couldn't tell if it was lust or guilt. And he seemed completely unaffected that he'd seen me naked. It was a little bruising on the old ego.

So I tried to bring it on our date, in case he was thinking that I was a terrible mistake. I told what I thought was a pretty funny story involving my old job at NBC. It was a classic cocktail party story in my repertoire, in which a goat had gotten loose from a set and ended up falling asleep under Matt Lauer's desk, making Matt scream when he sat down and the goat bolted past him.

"Nothing to say?" I asked when he just nodded at the end of the story.

He shook his head.

"Well, that sucks, because that was one of my best stories."

"You don't have to impress me, you know."

"Well, I'd like to. It beats unimpressing you."

"You're fine the way you are."

I almost sighed before realizing it was—possibly—a compliment. He looked at me from across the table, still in his suit from work, though he'd taken off his tie.

"If it makes you happy to talk, then talk," he said. "But I like just being with you, too."

Which he proved later, in bed. Twice.

It was funny, I thought as I drove home. My role in the relationship with Eric had always been to be charming and funny and bright and animated with him, with his parents, with his friends and coworkers.

Just being… I wasn't a hundred percent sure how to do that.

But one thing was for sure. I was not about to turn myself inside out for Jonathan, or any guy. I'd based my life around Eric and our relationship. That wasn't going to happen again. At least, that was what I told myself. Jonathan was my boss and boyfriend now, and it could be said quite truthfully that a huge part of my life was indeed based around him.

I pulled into Kate's driveway, once again doing the walk of shame (though damn proud of it), went into the kitchen and screamed.

A very large man was there.

"Hey," he said. "How's it going?"

"Who are you, and why are you wearing my sister's shirt?" I yelped.

"How do you know it's your sister's?" he asked calmly.

"Because Derek Jeter's signature is on the back, and our dad got us those for Christmas a few years ago."

He smiled. "I'm Daniel Breton."

"Daniel the Hot Firefighter?"

He smiled. "One and the same."

"And you're here because…" My eyes widened. "Did you sleep with Kate?"

His smile grew.

"Holy guacamole! I'm gone for one night, and this place turns into a sex palace! Pour me some coffee and tell me what happened."

He got another cup and poured. "Keep your voice down. She's still sleeping."

I melted a little. He cared about my sister's sleep. I loved him already. Plus, he was freakin' beautiful. In all the years I'd visited Kate in Brooklyn, I had only heard the legend of Daniel the Hot Firefighter.

The stories hadn't done him justice.

"Say I was trapped in a burning building," I said. "You

burst in, you carry me out, I'm not breathing. Describe the mouth-to-mouth I'm about to get."

He laughed. "Well, in reality, we'd use a ventilator mask—"

"Oh, come on! No reality. Please continue."

"What are you wearing?" he asked, lifting an eyebrow.

"A very flimsy something, and my hair looks amazing."

He grinned. Oh, *mommy*! That was a killer smile.

Just then, the kitchen door opened, and Brooke walked in. At the sight of Daniel, she stopped abruptly, horror flooding her face.

Oh, shit.

"Hey, Brooke!" I said, jumping up to hug her. "It's so good to see you!" She looked blank. "How are the boys? They're in camp, right? Kate said something about camp? Anyway, uh, do you know my, uh, friend? My friend Daniel? He's my friend."

It really sucked to be a terrible liar.

"Oh, he's *your* friend," Brooke said, her entire being sagging with relief. Clearly, she'd assumed the exact truth of the situation.

"Daniel," I said, "this is Kate's sister-in-law. Nathan's sister."

"You came to the wake," she said, her eyes narrowing.

"Yes," he answered. "I'm so sorry about your brother."

"Daniel's a good friend of the family," I said. He gave me an odd look—I'd just met him, obviously—but mercifully didn't contradict me.

"I need to talk to Kate about my parents' anniversary party," Brooke said.

"Right! That'll be very...uh...yeah."

Just then, Kate came into the kitchen looking exactly as if she'd been up all night making sexy time with a hot firefighter. Her long hair was tangled, her eyes were still heavy with sleep and she had a certain glow about her. (Go, Daniel!)

She was barefoot and wore the silky short kimono I'd given her a few years ago.

She saw Brooke and lurched to a stop. Her eyes swiveled to Daniel.

If I was bad at lying, my sister was incapable of it.

"Hey, Kate!" I barked. "I ran into Daniel and asked him if he'd like to have coffee with me. Us. Here. Anyway, he came over. Sorry it's so early! And Brooke's here to talk about the anniversary party!"

Sure, I sounded like a chattering monkey, but my sister unfroze. "Right. Hi. Hi, Brooke."

"You okay?" Brooke said.

"Um, yeah. Yep."

"I can reschedule, if you're not feeling well."

Kate closed her eyes briefly. "No, no. I just overslept. Sorry."

"Of course you're not sleeping well," Brooke said. Her face wobbled. "I should've called or texted first. I'm so sorry."

Kate had that stake-through-the-heart look.

"Daniel, let's go out for breakfast, why don't we?" I said, grabbing his beautiful arm and pulling him toward the door.

"Actually, I can't," he said. "Uh…thanks for the coffee. Good to see you, Kate."

*Don't look at her*, I thought, because I could feel the air vibrating between them.

Out he went, raising a hand as he strode down the walk.

"Nice guy," Brooke said. "Are you dating him, Ainsley?"

"No! Nope. I mean, I *would*, but, uh… Well! I should… I'm going to, uh, grab some stuff, and then I'll be gone, too," I said.

Twenty minutes later, which was a land-speed record for me, I'd showered and dressed and even put on makeup. I slipped out the back door without saying goodbye, unwilling to lie anymore.

But seriously. Nathan's family couldn't know she'd just gotten it on with the poster boy for FDNY.

Cambry-on-Hudson's business district was hosting a Sidewalk Festival on Saturday, and *Hudson Lifestyle* was doing a web feature on it, written by yours truly. This meant I got to spend this morning wandering through the shops to get the latest info to update our website. It was the kind of work I really enjoyed.

My first stop was Bliss, the wedding dress shop I'd ogled from the outside many a time when I was with Eric. I'd always thought it would be bad luck to go in before I had a ring on my finger (pause for ironic and slightly bitter laughter). But now I had a good reason to go.

It was paradise inside. I mean, what woman didn't love wedding dresses? And these were ethereally beautiful—a blush tulle dress with tiny rosebuds along the bodice; a velvet lace gown that would make the bride look like a winter princess. Each one was more beautiful than the last.

"Hi, I'm Jenny," said a pretty woman dressed in black as I fondled a sleeve. "You're Kate O'Leary's sister, right? She took my picture a while ago. I still owe her dinner out."

We played the Cambry-on-Hudson two degrees of separation game; I told her I'd met Leo at Kate's grief group, and it turned out Eric and I had lived down the street from Jenny's sister.

"So Rachel Carver is your sister! Wow!" I said. "We used to chat when I walked Ollie. How's she doing?" She'd gotten a divorce, I knew that. I always thought her husband was a little too smug.

"She's doing really well," Jenny said. "She'll be here on Saturday. Her daughters are going to model flower girl dresses for me."

"Oh! So cute!" I said. "They're such beautiful girls. I miss seeing them. I, uh… My boyfriend and I broke up, and I'm staying with Kate now."

"That's so nice of you," she said. "She told me that. My sister and I are super close, too."

Did Kate say we were super close? God, that made me happy!

I asked Jenny a few more questions for the article and left reluctantly, thanking her for her time. Next stop: Cottage Confections. Kim, God bless her, felt it was necessary to feed me a red velvet cupcake as I sat there asking questions, then send me off with four more.

Too bad more of my workdays weren't like this. Speaking of, I had to take a good hard look at my life. I had options. I always had, but now I had funding because of my mother's insurance policy. What would she want me to do? Travel? Live in Paris for a year, drive across America?

But I loved this town.

And there was Jonathan. Too early for him to be a real factor in any decisions I had to make…except I was kind of falling for him.

Well. I had two clothing boutiques and three jewelry stores to check next. Not quite as fun as wedding dresses and cupcakes, but not bad, either.

As I was crossing the street an hour later, someone called my name.

It was Matthew Kent.

He came down the steps of Hudson's (which was *not* on my list). "Hey, Ainsley."

I had to give him points for remembering my name. Most people didn't on the first try.

"Uh, listen. I…I tried calling Jonathan this morning, but I'm pretty sure he's blocked my number."

"I wonder why," I said.

"Would you do me a favor?"

"Nope."

He gave an exasperated sigh, and I caught a glimpse of the resemblance between them. "Would you tell him I'd like to see him? Tell him we can't go on like this forever, and... Shit. I don't know. It's not good for the girls."

"Probably their uncle sleeping with their mother was also not good for the girls." I cocked my head and stared him down.

"It was more than two years ago," he said, "and they were little, and look. I know what I did was wrong. But it's done. It can't be undone."

"Sounds like you need to go to confession," I said. "I'm working. Bye."

"Tell him I miss him."

"Not gonna," I called, walking away.

When I got back to the office, it was nearly quitting time. "How's it going with the new boyfriend?" I asked Rachelle.

She let her head flop back against her chair and sighed.

"That bad?"

"He's a sex offender."

"Oh, man! Again?"

"Flashes senior citizens at nursing homes."

I nodded. "Oh, okay. Yep. My grandmother mentioned him. She said it livened up bingo, for what it's worth."

"I'm giving up," she said. "Want to go get a drink or something?"

I glanced at Jonathan's office. He was on the phone. "I need to check in with the boss," I said.

"Poor you."

"Ah, he's not that bad."

She snorted, then grabbed her purse. "See you tomorrow, Ains."

I scrolled through my emails, waiting until Deshawn had left, too. Jonathan was still on the phone. I needed to talk to him. No matter how grouchy it might make him, he should know that his brother had talked to me. Twice.

And I wanted to kiss him. Office hours were over, baby.

Finally, he hung up, only to have his cell phone ring immediately. I sank back into my seat to wait some more.

Almost everyone I knew seemed to be estranged from someone. Candy no longer spoke to her sister, because Aunt Patty never visited Gram-Gram. Rachelle didn't speak to her uncle—for good reason, though; he enjoyed walking around family events in his boxer shorts, testicles dangling past the hem. Kate had that bitchy Paige, who'd dumped her.

And here I was, estranged from the Fishers and the man I once loved without question.

Against my better instincts, I went to his blog, which was no longer called *The Cancer Chronicles*. No. It was now called *New Life Horizons*, which sounded to me like a cult or a weight-loss center.

There he was, looking bundled up and healthy on a snowfield. No grizzly bear in sight, unfortunately. He looked… good. Happy. Sunglasses against the glare, a few days of downy scruff.

I glanced through the blog. He used the word *pure* a lot. Pure sky, pure air, pure snow, pure rush. If I still edited his pieces, I'd have fixed that.

Ah. Here was a mention of me. *While I know Sunshine has yet to get over me, I can't help thanking my guardian angel, Nathan, for setting all this in motion.*

I almost punched the computer. For the love of God! Yes, by all means, Nathan, well done! I'm sure this was exactly what he intended.

The comments held a surprise—there were only four. The blog had been posted six days ago.

From one of his fraternity mates: Nice pictures, dude!

From his parents (Judy, of course; Aaron wouldn't know how to comment on a blog): Make sure you're eating right! You could also call sometime! xox Mom & Dad.

From Anonymous: Cool.

From Jeannie8393: I've struggled all my life to lose weight and finally found a supplement that REALLY WORKS!!!

Seemed like Eric's fifteen minutes of fame had expired.

I clicked off the site and checked the magazine's Twitter and Facebook pages. Jonathan was still on his cell. He opened his door, glanced at me, did a double take, then went back in, leaving the door open this time.

I could hear him talking now.

"What did Mommy say? Everyone else was invited? Everyone? Ah. Well...sometimes people can be thoughtless. I know she's your friend, sweetheart. But if she didn't invite you... No, no, you're wonderful! It doesn't make you any less nice. Just her. I know it's her birthday, but... Oh, Lyddie, don't cry."

Ah, shit. That sweet little girl was getting stiffed by a friend.

"It does sound like a fun party. But maybe you and I can do something fun on Saturday, too. We could go horseback riding, maybe. No? Okay, well, we could go to the painting place, how about that? Oh. Okay, something else, then."

I whipped out my phone and texted Jenny Tate. Any chance you could use another flower girl model? Six years old. A little friend is having a bad day.

She responded right away. Sure thing! Can she come about 10?

Yay for Jenny! I scrawled a note on a piece of paper and ran to Jonathan's office, where he was still trying to find something to assuage her. "Well, what about a movie? No, you're right, they're very loud."

I held up the paper. *Bliss Bridal Shop needs flower girl models for Saturday at 10.*

He scowled at me. "No, Lydia, I can't get you a puppy."

I shook the paper and pointed to the phone. Realization dawned on my boss's face.

"Hold on, Lyddie. Do you remember Ainsley? The fairy house lady? She wants to talk to you."

I grabbed the phone. "Hi, Lydia! How are you, honey?"

"I'm fine, thanks," she said, her sweet voice so small.

"Listen, I was wondering if you could do me a favor on Saturday. Do you know what a model is? A lady who puts on fancy clothes and gets her picture taken?"

"Like the ladies on *Project Runway*?"

I was glad to hear Jonathan's daughters weren't being raised only on Dickens. "Exactly. Anyway, there's a store that needs little girl models, and I thought you would be perfect. You'd have to wear a couple of very fancy dresses and be with a few other girls and look cute and smile."

"What kind of dresses?"

"The extremely beautiful kind. Like flower girls wear. Or princesses." Jonathan smiled at that, and my ovaries swelled.

"Really?" asked Lydia.

"Really. Will you do it? Pretty please?"

"Okay! Yes! That sounds like so much fun!"

"Great! I'll see you Saturday, then. I'll be at the store."

"Say thank you, Lydia," Jonathan said, raising his voice.

"Thank you, Amy!" the little girl sang. "Mommy, guess wh—"

I smiled at my boss. "She hung up," I said, handing the phone back to him.

"I'll call her later."

"Mean-girl troubles, huh?"

"Yes." He leaned back in his chair, looking at me directly for the first time. "Thank you."

"You're welcome, Mr. Kent." I closed the door behind me. Reached up and undid a button on my blouse.

"You planning on seducing me in my office?" he asked, his voice low, eyes on my fingers.

"Yes, Mr. Kent," I said.

"I see lawsuit all over this."

"Deal with it."

I went behind his desk and straddled his lap, held his face in my hands and kissed him.

"Ainsley," he said.

"Check the thing I signed," I said. "It specifically allows workplace nooky if no one else is here." I paused. "You haven't dated at all since your divorce, have you?" I asked.

"Are we dating?"

"Yes, Jonathan," I said, rolling my eyes. "You take me out to dinner, we talk, we sleep together. That's dating."

He took my hands in both of his and studied them a few seconds. "And you're not dating anyone else?" He looked up at me, and there it was, that little speck of gold in his clear eyes.

"No," I said. "And neither are you."

His smile started in his eyes, and another good bit of my heart was his.

Then I kissed him, and he surprised me by standing up and laying me on his desk. Papers went everywhere, and the phone fell on the floor.

He didn't seem to mind.

No, he was a little too busy taking off my panties.

Jonathan followed me to Kate's house afterward. She wasn't home, but Ollie seemed quite happy to see my guest. He put his paws on Jonathan's knee and used his beautiful brown eyes to good effect until Jonathan picked him up.

I started cooking—chicken piccata, because Kate loved it. I texted her that Jonathan was here and we hoped she'd make it home for dinner. She said she probably wouldn't be back in time. She was in Brooklyn, seeing Daniel the Hot Firefighter, I surmised.

"She's out with friends," I told Jonathan, getting out the flour and bread crumbs. "Have a seat. Would you like some wine?" It was nice, having him here, my goofy little dog sitting on his lap. Ollie was already fast asleep, snoring slightly. He missed male company.

I busied myself with dinner prep—sliced the lemons, gently pounded the chicken breasts.

"This is very different from your place," Jonathan commented.

"Yeah, well, Nathan was an architect."

"Will Kate stay here, or will she sell the place?"

I lay the chicken in the frying pan. "I don't know. She hasn't mentioned moving."

"It must be hard, being in Nathan's house. His family lives just up the road, don't they?"

"Yeah. Hey, speaking of family, I met someone recently." I covered the frying pan, adjusted the heat to low, washed my hands, then came over to sit with Jonathan. "Your brother."

He barely blinked. "Where was that?"

"My dad and I had lunch at Hudson's. I didn't know it was his place."

"Yes."

"He came out to press the flesh, and lunch had been very good, so I suggested that we review it. Then he told me who he was." Jonathan's face was tight, but unreadable. "He asked me to tell you something," I added.

"And what is that?"

"He'd like to see you."

He bent down to put Ollie on his blanket, then sat up straight again. "I'd prefer not to have this discussion with you," he said. "I— Yes. I'd prefer not to."

"Okay. I felt like I should mention it." I bit my thumbnail. "Um, I saw him again today."

"Really."

"Yes. When I was getting stuff for the Saturday stroll, he came over to me, he must've seen me through the window, and—"

"Did you tell him we're dating?"

"No."

"I don't want my children to know about you. And he would tell them."

"I didn't say anything."

"Are you sure?"

"Yes." I thought so, anyway. No, I was sure.

Jonathan stared out the window. His jaw looked like I could hit it with a crowbar and end up with a broken piece of metal in my hands.

The mood was broken, that was for sure.

He turned to look at me. "Maybe we should talk a little bit. About…us."

"Sure. Go ahead."

He took a deep breath. "I'm not going to bring my children into this. They don't need to know I'm seeing someone until…quite a long time from now."

"Well, they do know me."

"They've met you. They don't know you. You work for me, that's all they know." He opened his mouth, closed it, then tried again. "You're fresh out of a relationship. It could very well be that I'm just a rebound for you."

"I can think of easier men for a rebound."

"I don't want my daughters to get attached to you if things don't work out. They've been through a lot of change in the past two years. I won't do what their mother did and shove a new relationship into their lives."

Couldn't fault him for that. Still, his verbiage could've been a little nicer. "I understand."

"Good."

I waited for him to say something nice to take the edge off. He didn't.

"Okay. I'll check the chicken."

I got up and went to the stove, shoved the chicken around a little, turned it. Didn't really feel like cooking for him anymore. In fact, I felt like being alone.

Then his arms were around my waist, his mouth at my ear. "I'm sorry," he said, sending a shiver down my spine. "It's complicated."

"I know." My voice was just a whisper.

Then I put down the spatula and turned around to face him. "Jonathan, sometimes I feel like you don't really like me a whole lot."

One second. Two. Three. Four.

"You're wrong."

"I know you like sleeping with me, but that can't—"

"I like you, Ainsley."

Oh, that voice, so deep and rumbly. That wasn't fair.

He reached behind me and turned off the stove, then cupped my head, his fingers firm on the back of my scalp. My bones started to tingle. "I like that you always seem happy. I like how you talk to strangers. I like your silly dresses. I like that you're completely different from me. I like the way you smell. I like your hair and your eyelashes and your smile."

The faintest smile was on his face, and he didn't look away.

"Okay, you pass," I whispered.

He smiled full-on then, and my knees buckled. "Go sit down," he said. "I'll finish dinner."

No doubt about it. I was falling in love.

# Chapter Twenty-Eight

*Kate*

I had to talk to Daniel.

All the *give yourself a break, have some fun* rationale had turned to dust the second I'd seen Brooke standing in my kitchen.

Thank God for Ainsley, making it seem like Daniel was hers.

Sitting there in Nathan's living room, talking to Nathan's sister about Nathan's parents' party the night after I'd slept with someone who was not Nathan...

Brooke looked like hell. Her hair was falling out, she told me. She kept dreaming that Nathan was alive. She told me Miles was sucking his thumb again. That she was afraid her father's drinking was getting out of hand. That her mother was too quiet. That she couldn't bear the thought of never seeing her brother again. That she wanted to talk to a medium.

I felt each statement like a punch to the heart, and that

spike through my throat twisted. "Oh, Brooke," I said, holding her as she sobbed, my own eyes dry and hard and wrong. "I'm so sorry."

"You loved him so much, didn't you?" she asked. I nodded helplessly, even more guilt sloshing over me.

But I *had* loved Nathan. Even if he'd never fallen all the way out of love with Madeleine. It occurred to me that I could ask Brooke about that.

But of course, I couldn't. In the face of Brooke's grief, it seemed petty, asking about his ex-wife, trying to see just how much Nathan loved her. He was gone, and if I was an insecure widow, I should probably keep that to myself. Especially after sleeping with Daniel.

"We'll get through this," she said, blowing her nose. "And God, I'm so sorry, coming over here, crying on your couch when you're the one who's really suffering."

I smiled weakly. Images of Daniel and me last night, in the shower… I was going to hell.

When Brooke finally left, I took a punishing shower, scrubbing every inch of myself as hard as I could. Pulled my hair into a ponytail, put on one of my Cambry-on-Hudson dresses, a pink-and-green Lily Pulitzer dress with strappy sandals that aged me ten years. Drove to Brooklyn, the VW's air conditioner not up for the task of truly cooling the sticky summer air. There was traffic, of course. There always was.

Daniel was working. It hadn't occurred to me to check first, idiot that I was. Come on over, he said after I texted him from the sidewalk in front of his apartment building. Meet the guys.

Super. I went to Rescue 2, home of the most elite firefighters in the world, and got out of the car. My back was wet with sweat, and my face felt tight and red. I kept my sunglasses on.

The humble, two-story brick building had a logo painted

on the red door. Like all FDNY departments, they'd suffered a lot of tragedy, and I wished abruptly, after three hours in stifling traffic, that I'd thought this through.

Two firefighters were sitting outside the firehouse. One winked at me. "Hi," I said. "Is Daniel around?"

"Breton!" yelled the other. "Your woman is here!"

Oh, shit. I was not his woman. I hoped to God he hadn't told them I was.

The door opened and Daniel came out, a big smile on his face. "Hey," he said, coming over. He bent down for a kiss, and I turned my face so it landed on my cheek.

"Hi," I said.

The smile slid off his face. But he turned to the other two. "Bruce, Jay, this is Kate, an old friend of mine."

"Nice to meetcha," they said in unison.

"Same here. Thanks for being so badass and brave and everything."

"You got it, pretty lady," said the winker.

"We live to serve," the other one said.

"Come on," Daniel said. "There are benches over here."

Given the heat of the day, no one was out. The firehouse was near a school, and there were tennis courts and tracks behind chain-link fences. A row of benches sat in the shade.

"What brings you to Brooklyn?" he asked. "And what the hell are you wearing?"

"Goofy, isn't it?" I wiped my palms on my dress. I had no reason to feel bad about this, I told myself. We were friends. There had been benefits. Those benefits were now suspended. That was all. "We need to talk."

He folded his arms. "Funny, that's usually my line."

"I'm so sorry about this morning. That was Nathan's sister who came in."

"Yeah, I got that." He sighed. "So you made a terrible mistake and it should never happen again."

"It's like you're psychic."

He didn't smile.

"Daniel, you've been a really good friend these past few months. I...I appreciate last night more than I can say. But I can't do anything more. Or again. You know what I mean? I'm a new widow. I... If you thought—"

"No, I didn't think anything," he said, his voice hard. "You know me. Just out for a good time."

"Yeah. Okay."

"I should get back to work."

"Right."

He stood up, offered his hand and then let mine go the second I was upright. "You didn't have to drive all the way here just to tell me I was a one-night stand," he said.

"We're friends. I just... I didn't want... I *did* need to. I'm sorry if I hurt your feelings."

"You didn't. I'll see you around, okay?" With that, he went back into the firehouse.

Feeling like shit, I decided to visit the Re-Enter Center. I got back into my stifling car and drove there. The door was unlocked, and my footsteps echoed down the hall. Greta, the director, was in.

"Kate!" she exclaimed. "So good to see you!" She stood up from her desk and gave me a hug. "Hot out there, isn't it? How are things?"

"Things are okay," I lied. "Better." No one really wanted to hear the truth. It was a much-discussed topic in the grief group.

We chatted about easy things, some of the students, where they were, if they'd gotten any jobs.

"We're having a show in a few weeks. Ex-con art is all the rage, apparently. Did Paige tell you about it?" Greta asked.

"No. We're not as close as we used to be."

She nodded. "Well, you should come! There'll be paintings, sculptures, some furniture and, of course, photos. In fact, why don't you judge that category? Say yes! I won't lie, I want you back here, and I know it's a bit farther for you now, but please do this for us! Who better than our Kate?"

"Sure, I'll do it," I said. "You bet. But I better head back home. It was great seeing you."

Rather than get back in my car, I walked through my old neighborhood, avoiding my street, which held too many memories. I didn't see anyone I knew, not even Ronny, the homeless guy I used to buy breakfast for.

The feeling of disappearing slammed into me. Maybe I really was becoming invisible. What if I had a heart attack? Who would save me? Would anyone even notice? Would someone call 911?

In for three, hold for three, out for three, hold for three. I wouldn't faint. I wouldn't die (not yet, anyway). But my heart felt like a hard, dead thing inside my chest, heavy and useless.

*I could really use some help here, Nathan*, I thought. But from my dead husband, there was nothing.

# Chapter Twenty-Nine

*Ainsley*

The summer plodded through the dog days of August, when half of Cambry-on-Hudson left for Martha's Vineyard or the coast of Maine. Despite the muggy weather, I rode my bike to work every day, through the park and cemetery. For some reason, I managed to show up on time every day, something I hadn't managed with a car.

Jonathan and I were a couple. A real couple, and it was at turns wonderful and maddening. Sometimes I wanted to kick him, sometimes I wanted to crawl over him and lick every inch of his skin. At work, he was more anal-retentive than before, if such a thing was possible. But I tried to give him fewer reasons to get irritated with me. I did my work, stopped the online shopping...except for when Zappos had a huge one-day sale, and please, every woman in America was online that day, the website crashed (but not before I'd ordered three adorable pairs of shoes).

As I rode home through the park one soft evening, the sun turning the western sky purple and the most amazing shade of nectarine, I saw someone sitting in the cemetery.

It was Kate.

If she visited Nathan's grave regularly, she never mentioned it. Since I'd taken to riding my bike, I stopped by, making sure the plantings were watered. Sometimes, there'd be a drawing from one of his nephews, which I tried not to look at, because they weren't for me. Nonetheless, they made me cry—the sweet, childlike printing, the swirls of Crayola.

"Hey," I called, getting off my bike and leaning it against a tree. "Want company?"

"Sure," she said.

*Nathan Vance Coburn III, loving husband, son and brother, a wonderful man, always smiling.* There was a bouquet of fresh white roses there, from Kate, I assumed.

I sat next to my sister and put my arm around her, and she leaned her head against my shoulder, her hair tickling my cheek.

A year ago, this kind of interaction would've been out of the question. It just wouldn't have been us.

It was us now.

"Today's the one-year anniversary of the day we met," she said.

"Oh, honey." I squeezed her a little closer.

"It was this awful wedding, and he asked me out, and I thought he must be a serial killer or something."

"But he wasn't. Or he was really secretive about it."

She gave a little snort.

"How's Daniel?" I asked.

"We're not... I haven't seen him recently. That night was a mistake."

I smoothed her hair out of my eye. "You sure?"

"Yeah. I can't have a fling, Ainsley. I'm a widow."

"So no sex forevermore?"

"Probably."

"Well, I think you should cut yourself some slack. Let's face it. Maybe it was the grief that drove you into his magnificent arms—" Another snort. "Or maybe it's just that he likes you and you needed a little fun."

"I feel like I cheated on Nathan."

"You didn't." I paused. "Kate, you knew Nathan less than a year. You're allowed to get over him, you know."

Her head snapped up. "I *loved* him."

"I know, honey. I do. But don't do things because you feel like there's a handbook you should follow. If Daniel makes you happy, let him. You don't have to marry him next week."

She sighed. "It all sounds very wise until you walk into the kitchen, all postcoital, and your dead husband's sister is there with her hair falling out."

"Yeah, that was bad. But you're allowed to be alive, Kate. If you find something that makes you smile, don't worry about it. Have fun. Nathan would want that. He was crazy about you."

"Yeah. Me and his ex-wife."

I had no answer for that. "Well, we hate her, so who cares? He loved you, Kate. You have to know that."

She swallowed hard. "I do."

I smoothed her hair back and gave her another squeeze. A red-winged blackbird sang from the top of a pine tree, and a train whistle sounded in the distance.

"Oh, there you girls are!"

We both jumped and turned. Candy, in the flesh, strode up through the graves, dressed in a red suit and black Manolos that made me start to drool with envy.

"How did you find us?" I asked.

"I have a GPS app on your phone, Ainsley."

My mouth fell open. "You do?"

"Of course I do."

"Why?"

"So I know where you are." She gave me a puzzled look and sat down on Kate's other side. "Is today a significant day?"

Kate sighed. "Nathan and I met a year ago today."

"It's important to acknowledge these milestones in your healing journey." As always when talking about anything emotional, she sounded smug.

"Roger that." Kate was a master at not being offended by our mother. Her mother. Whatever.

"So! I left your father, girls," she said, lying back and folding her hands under her unnatural hair. "Don't worry, I'm not moving in. You made it clear I'm not wanted."

"You're wanted," Kate said. "Just not as a roomie."

"I signed the papers on a little place of my own today. You know those condos right on the Hudson in Tarrytown? I bought one. I also signed another book contract. *The Toxic Marriage: Why We Stay.*"

"Wow," I said, lying back, as well. The grass pricked the back of my neck, but the view of the sky was amazing. Also, this was big news, and lying down seemed appropriate. "Wow."

Kate lay back, as well. "Why now, Mom?"

Candy sighed. "Oh, I had a client come in, and she reminded me of myself. Stuck in a stupid marriage, perpetually unhappy, and I heard myself telling her she had choices, and inaction was a choice, too, and I thought, Hello? Candace? You've been doing the same damn thing for thirty years."

"I thought you loved Dad," I said.

She didn't answer for a minute. "I do," she finally said, and her voice was smaller. "But let's face it. He never got over your mother. Don't be like that, Kate. Get over Nathan and live again."

"Thanks for the advice."

"I'm tired of being bitter," Candy said. "I'd like to try something else."

"Does Dad know?" I asked.

"I just called him. Left a voice mail. He's working a Cardinals game."

We were all quiet for a minute. A crow flew over us, cawing, the last of the sunlight turning its feathers iridescent.

"Why did you take him back, Mom?" Kate asked. "You were so angry when he divorced you. Sean and I thought you hated him."

"I did."

"So?" Kate continued. "It must've been clear he was just using you. And if you had said no, he would've married someone else within the month. Dad couldn't make himself a sandwich with a gun pointed at his heart, let alone raise Ainsley alone."

"I know," Candy said. "But I couldn't leave that poor innocent child out in the cold, could I?"

"So all these decades of unhappiness are on me?" I said. "Sorry for being born."

"No, Ainsley." Her voice was overly patient, that *I'm sorry you're so dense* voice I knew so well. "Part of me hoped he'd… well, you know, girls. I hoped he'd fall in love with me again. But he didn't. There were times when I thought he was close, but I was always wrong." She glanced at me. "You were the best part. The sweetest little girl in the world."

My eyes widened, and I had to sit up a little to make sure Candy had just said what I thought I heard.

Kate was smiling. "You win, Ainsley. Mom loves you best."

Candy smiled and looked back at the sky. "Every child is a mother's favorite."

"I thought I was the recalcitrant stepchild," I said.

"That book isn't based on you, Ainsley. Please."

"Sean is your true favorite," Kate said.

"Sean," Candy snorted. "He's useless, that boy. But he did give me grandchildren. Who wants dinner? I'm starving. Or are you too busy for your poor soon-to-be single mother?"

I was pretty sure she was talking to both of us, and the word *step* had not been used.

"*I'm* not too busy for my poor single mother," I said, jumping up. "Kate, are you too busy for your poor single mother?"

"I don't seem to be," she said. I offered her my hand and pulled her up, then did the same to Candy. For a second, I thought we might hug, but then the moment was gone.

We were still us, after all.

Us, but a little better.

On Sunday, I decided to look at some classes at the local colleges. I took my laptop out onto the patio—the heat had relented, and it was about as perfect a summer day as could be. Plus, who knew how much longer I'd be living here? I had to enjoy the koi pond while I had one.

I scanned the class selection. I'd fallen into my job at NBC. I didn't mind working at *Hudson Lifestyle*, now that I was actually making an effort (and shagging the boss). But I didn't love it (the work, that was). It was a job, not a career.

For Jonathan, it was different. In the past month, I'd learned that his grandmother had started the magazine in 1931 at a time when no one thought a woman had the business savvy to run a business. *Hudson Lifestyle* had never laid off a single employee. When a freelancer's kid had gotten leukemia, the magazine (i.e. Jonathan) had paid all her bills, and the girl was now at Columbia, getting her law degree.

So it was all very noble and lovely. It just wasn't me.

I wasn't a hundred percent sure what was. Unlike Kate and Sean, I never had a calling. I liked people. I liked being useful. That was about all I knew.

Maybe it was time for me to travel. Or live alone. Or get a degree that might serve me better than philosophy.

My phone rang from somewhere in the depths of the sofa where Ollie had hidden it. I dug around, pulled it out.

*Judy.*

"Hello?" I said.

"Sweetheart? It's me."

My eyes welled unexpectedly at the sound of her voice. "Hi," I said. "How are you?"

"We're fine. We miss you."

A longing for their kitchen, for Judy's pancakes, for Aaron's bear hugs, for family game night, swamped me. "I miss you guys, too."

"How are your parents?"

"Uh…they're fine." Dad had taken Candy's news with grace (I hoped he noticed Candy had moved out), then gone off to Anaheim for a few days. But I wasn't going to tell the Fishers about my parents. A few months ago, Judy would've been the first person I called. That had obviously changed.

"Would you come over, honey? We have a little something for you."

I looked at the time. Two o'clock. "Okay. I'll be there in about an hour."

I showered and dressed carefully in a white dress with pink poppies printed on it and pink canvas shoes. Put on a little makeup. "Come on, Ollie," I said. "We're going for a ride." The Fishers loved Ollie.

On the drive over, I wondered what they had for me. Maybe something from our house? Maybe my Hanukkah presents, since Judy shopped all year round to find the perfect gifts?

I pulled into their driveway, and the lump came back to my throat. I couldn't count the number of times I'd been here. Hundreds. I was in at least five framed photos that hung in the house—more than at my own parents' house.

I opened the door, which was never locked. "Hello?" I called, setting Ollie on the floor. My little dog tore off into the kitchen, barking madly. "It's Ainsley."

"Come on in, honey!" Judy called. I walked into the kitchen, the smell of baked goods in the air.

And jerked to a stop.

Eric was here, holding Ollie in his arms as the overjoyed and traitorous dog licked his face, whining with happiness.

"Sweetheart!" Aaron said, hugging me. My arms stayed at my sides.

My never-fiancé smiled at me. "Hey," he said. *Hey.* After all this, hey? Please.

He looked confident and gorgeous. He was wearing contacts, which was unusual, and had a beard, like in the picture. His hair was longer than I'd ever seen it, scooped back into the dreaded man-bun, and his face was ruddy from sun exposure, his nose a little burned.

His rugged man appeal hit me straight in the gut. "Eric," I said flatly. "You're back."

"I did what I needed to do," he said.

"Well, surprise!" Judy said. "We'll leave you kids alone to talk. There's cake! And cookies. And some ice cream in the freezer. And if you're hungry, Ainsley, there's a roast chicken in the fridge."

"We're good, Mom. Thank you," Eric said, setting down the dog.

"We'll just go outside, then. Ollie, do you want a ball? Can you catch the ball?" Ollie flew out with them, and Judy tossed a tennis ball, but if I knew her, she'd be at the window eavesdropping in ten seconds.

"Have a seat," Eric said, pulling a chair back. "You look fantastic."

"I won't be here long, Eric."

"Well, hear what I have to say, okay? I mean, we have ten years together."

"Eleven."

"Even more reason to stay." He smiled and poured me some coffee, stirring in sugar and cream. Irritating, that he remembered how I took it.

He sat down next to me. "Want cake?"

"Just get to it. I have things to do. That man-bun looks ridiculous, by the way."

He laughed, not bothered in the least. "Yeah, I need to get a haircut." He looked at his own coffee. "Thank you for seeing me."

"I was tricked into it."

"Well, thanks anyway." Another smile. "Okay, I'll cut to the chase. I can't say I made a mistake in going to Alaska, but I sure made a mistake leaving you." He looked at me steadily.

"Fascinating," I said. "Are you done?"

"Ains, I don't know what happened. To say I freaked out would be a gross understatement."

"Agreed."

"I think you know better than anyone—better than I do, even—what was going on. It's just like you said. I was scared of dying, then Nathan's accident... I just lost it." He squeezed the bridge of his nose. "I lost *you*. I threw you away, and it was the stupidest thing I've ever done in my life. For the past month, I've been meditating on it and I'm so, so sorry, Ainsley. You're the best thing—"

"Why don't we stop here?" I interrupted. "Apology not accepted. Was that all?"

He put his hand over mine, and it was still there. The tingle. The connection. The familiarity that I used to love with all my heart. My Eric, our life.

Which he'd shat upon.

I pulled my hand back.

He leaned forward, his face earnest and serious, none of that glazed-over zealousness he'd had all through his cancer months.

"You have every right to be mad and hurt," he said. "Of course you do. And, babe, if I could have a do-over on the past four months, I'd take it in a heartbeat. If you gave me another chance, I'd spend the rest of my life making sure you didn't regret it. I love you. I've always loved you."

"That's not what you said in the restaurant that night. And that's not what you blogged about."

"I think I was having a psychotic break."

"Oh, please."

He nodded. "Okay. A midlife crisis, then, a decade or so early?" He smiled, then grew serious again. "Ainsley, for eleven years, we were so perfect together. We've had a hundred and thirty-seven months together. I did the math," he added with a wink. He knew I couldn't multiply in my head. "Four of those months were me being a complete and total ass. Does that wipe out everything else? Because I *did* want to marry you. I still do. I want you to be the mother of my—"

"Stop," I said. "I don't want to hear this." But my voice was trembling with an emotion I couldn't pin down. Anticipation? Happiness? Hate?

He reached into his pocket and pulled out the ring. "Let me make it up to you, Ainsley. Marry me. Let's have that life we were meant to have. I'll never let you down again." He gave a crooked smile, his lovely brown eyes warm.

And there was my ring, the first time I'd seen it since the night Nathan died. The beautiful, hypnotic ring.

I suddenly knew what the trembling was. Fury.

"Are you out of your mind?" I said. "You smug, spoiled, entitled little *shit*. You broke my heart, humiliated me every chance you got, called me a corpse dragging you down, and you think I'm going to *marry* you?"

"But I'm sorry," he said, his eyebrows coming together. "I didn't know what I was doing. I was wrong, and now I want to do what's right. Let me fix this. I didn't mean what I said or did."

"I disagree. You did and said *exactly* what you wanted to. And now that you've communed with the Inuit and listened to the wolves and your fifteen minutes of fame is over, you think you can just pick up where we left off? No."

"But...but... Ainsley, listen. Honey. Listen." He sat back in his chair and put both hands on the table. "I talked to Ryan Roberts. He'll interview us on his show."

Fresh shock slapped the hell out of my face. "You gotta be kidding me."

"No! I can undo everything I did! I was an ass on television, and now I can go back on the air and eat humble pie and tell the world how much I love you." He paused. "And you love me. I know you do."

I stood up and pushed my chair back into the table. "No, Eric, I don't. I did, but you smashed that, and it doesn't get glued back together."

"Well, I know there's not someone else, because you're

not the type to sleep around for revenge." He stood up, too. "Are you?"

"My personal life is no longer your business. Good luck with everything." I opened the slider. Aaron and Judy froze, Ollie leaping around their feet.

They knew. Their faces fell.

"Bye, you two," I said, and then my eyes did fill with tears. These people had been the family I always wanted. But they weren't mine anymore. "Thank you for everything."

"We'll always love you, sweetheart," Aaron said, and I choked on a sob. Then I scooped up my dog and left.

Cried all the way home, Ollie whining from the backseat.

When I was in the center of Cambry-on-Hudson, I decided to call Jonathan. "Are the girls there?" I asked.

"No, I just dropped them off with their mother." There was a pause. "Are you all right?"

"Can I come over?"

"Of course."

When I parked at his house, I wiped my eyes and blew my nose. My chest and neck were blotchy, and Ollie licked my face, then whimpered to get out.

I went inside, Ollie nearly killing me by tangling in my feet so he could beat me.

"Hello, Oliver," Jonathan said, bending down to pet him, though his eyes were on me. "Has something made your mommy sad?"

"Eric's back in town."

He stood up and folded his arms. Adjusted his gaze so it was over my shoulder. "I see."

"He wants to get back together. I didn't even know he was back, but his parents called me, and—"

"Oh, no, by all means, get back together," he said, his voice almost a growl. "You have eleven years with him, right? So what if he humiliated you in front of eight million people and left you so he could find his spirit animal in Alaska? Absolutely, you should get married and have little Erics and—"

"I said no, idiot."

That stopped him. "Oh."

"And it wasn't because of you, either, so don't think that."

He blinked. "Why was it, then?"

"Because! Because he's a self-centered, narcissistic ass-pain who didn't appreciate all the love I gave him and thought there was something better out there and now he's found out that there's not, but you know what? Too little, too late."

"I see."

"Yes, you should see! Did you really think I'd get back together with him?"

"I probably shouldn't have—"

I jammed my hands on my hips. "Well, why wouldn't you? You have no idea who I am, do you? You made me sign that paper so I wouldn't sue you, as if I would. And you make us date in secret. And you won't let your kids see me, which I actually respect. Still, it hasn't escaped my attention that you're probably 60 percent in love with me and 40 percent positive I'm a terrible idea. So don't worry, Jonathan. I'm not counting on you for anything. I didn't tear Eric a new orifice because I have a secret boyfriend. I did it for me. He doesn't deserve me."

"Got it."

"By the way, I quit."

The grandfather clock ticked from the living room. Ollie dragged a throw pillow off the couch and curled up on it.

"Yeah," I said more quietly. "I quit. It's time, don't you think?"

"I...I don't know."

"I do." He was standing very, very still, and it occurred to me that he hadn't contradicted me once. "I would still like to date you, by the way," I said. "Even if we're only dating 60 percent."

"Good."

That one word made my heart swell almost painfully. "I'm leaving now," I said.

"Very well."

"I'll give you two weeks' notice so you can find someone else."

The almost-smile struck again. "I appreciate that."

"Okay, I'm really leaving. I want to ride this wave of moral indignation."

He grinned then, and I couldn't help it, I smiled back. Then I got my dog and left, feeling more proud of myself than I had in a long, long time.

That night, Candy came over, and she and Kate and I made dinner and then Skyped with Sean and Kiara and the kids, which was ridiculous because he lived forty-five minutes away and could, one imagined, get in his damn car once in a while and visit his family.

Still, it was worth it to see Sadie blowing us kisses and showing us her stuffed animals, and to get a glimpse of Esther and Matthias, who graced us with hellos.

Then there was a knock on the door. "I'll get it," I said, though I was already in my Yertle the Turtle pajamas.

It was Jonathan.

"Oh, Jonathan! Hello!" Candy said.

"Hello, Dr. O'Leary," he said. "Kate."

"Hi, Jonathan," she said, a smile in her voice.

"What can I do for you, boss?" I asked.

He took my face in his hands and kissed me. A deep, thorough, fantastic kiss that made my heart turn into hot caramel goo.

"Well, this is surprising," I dimly heard my mother say.

He pulled back and looked at me with those beautiful, changing eyes. "Sixty-five," he said.

"Excuse me?" My voice was husky.

"Sixty-five percent, at least. Possibly sixty-seven." Then he looked over my shoulder. "Good night, ladies," he said and then left, glancing back at me with a smile.

Sixty-seven, huh?

I'd take it.

# Chapter Thirty

*Kate*

August was a long month. Maybe there was something to what my mother had said about milestones, because I found myself looking forward to the fall, to the end of this year, the year Nathan died. To next spring, when it would be a year, when my head would be clearer and I'd know what to do. Because these days, my brain was fuzzy and the heat pressed down on me, and all I wanted to do was nap.

"Perfectly normal," LuAnn said in grief group. "You leave the house with the wrong clothes sometimes, am I right?"

"Grief is wearying," Lileth, the social worker, said in her singsong voice.

"Fucking exhausting if you ask me," LuAnn said.

Leo wasn't there this week. His presence had been sporadic lately, which we knew was a good sign. George, too, had been absent; he'd had lunch a few times with Gram-Gram, in fact. Ainsley's doing, of course.

My sister had left her job, started work at the Blessed Bean and was taking two classes at the community college. She wanted to be a nurse, she thought, and in my opinion, she'd be perfect—so energetic and sweet, so eager to take care of people.

I heard all about Eric, and I loved her so much for her ferocity. A year ago, I never thought I'd say it, but I admired my little sister more than just about anyone else. She had the biggest heart of anyone I knew. She had convictions, and she put her money where her mouth was.

And it was awfully nice to see her and Jonathan together. He watched her closely; I wasn't sure if she noticed, but he barely took his eyes off her. She blushed a lot around him. I liked that, too.

The Coburns' anniversary benefit was a few weeks away, and I had to get the porch swing from Daniel. If he'd finished it. If not, I still had the plans for their house expansion finished; Phoebe had done the job for me (and cried when she came here to drop the plans off).

That party would be an incredibly difficult event.

I missed Daniel. Our little friendship hadn't felt little at all.

Last week, I turned forty and asked Ainsley and my parents not to do anything for it. Ainsley had left a little gift— an antique heart locket—and a Carvel ice cream cake in the freezer and said nothing.

Sean had needed no prompting to forget my birthday; he never remembered. I got a card from Kiara signed with all five of their names and the message *Happier times ahead, my darling sister-in-law.* She was awfully wonderful. Sean didn't deserve her.

I slept and I ate and I waited, though for what, I wasn't really sure. The Nikon stayed on the shelf. Every day that passed made it harder to bear the thought of looking at the

last pictures ever taken of Nathan, my gentle, sweet husband
of ninety-six days.

I didn't see Madeleine again. I hoped that would remain
true for the rest of my life. Honestly, I felt sorry for her. She
really had loved Nathan, and she'd lost him, just like I had.
The fact that she'd been a royal bitch, well…people told themselves what they needed to. If Nathan had kept a secret from
me, what could I do about it? I was just too tired to carry it
anymore.

"I forgive you, Nathan," I said to the empty air one night
when Ainsley was at Jonathan's. "If you loved Madeleine,
it's okay."

I listened for an answer. Nothing, as usual.

With a sigh, I got up to make myself a milk shake, because I was a widowed adult and who cared if I gained thirty
pounds, and also the *I can't eat* phase of grief had passed. So
yeah, a milk shake would be just the ticket.

The windows and doors were all open, and the crickets
made a deafening chorus along with the katydids, always the
sound of summer's end.

A year ago today, Nathan and I had been on four dates.

I scooped out the ice cream into the milk shake maker—
Nathan had been in love with kitchen gadgetry, so of course
we had one. Added milk and some vanilla, and pushed Start.
I waited till it was done, then took the cold metal glass and
sipped the drink. Perfect. Nice and cold.

And then I smelled his cologne, smelled *him*, and my whole
body tingled in a warm, strange wave. I froze, then inhaled
again slowly.

Yes. That was his smell. That was *Nathan's* smell. And oh,
God, I missed it.

"Honey?" I whispered. Not that I expected an answer. The
tingle was still rolling over me.

*I love you*, I thought with all my heart.

Then it—he—faded away, and it was just me and the ka-tydids again. I closed my eyes, inhaled again, but now there was just the smell of vanilla.

"Thank you," I said, my voice squeaking a little.

Madeleine had said that he visited her. Maybe he did. If Nathan was as wonderful as I thought he was, then yeah, he'd visit everyone.

I hoped he visited Brooke. And Atticus and Miles. And God, I hoped he visited his parents.

*Be happy, Nathan. Don't worry about me too much. I'm fine.*

The afternoon of the Re-Enter Center's art show, I was at the studio just after a shoot, and my phone buzzed with a text.

Hey, Kate. Just wanted to say I hope I see you tonight. I'm almost done with the swing for your in-laws and I should have it in time for the party, no problem. We've known each other for a long time. Let's not be dicks about sleeping to-gether, okay?
Daniel
the hot firefighter

I laughed. Kind of loved that he signed his name that way. I wrote back:

Okay, hot firefighter. See you later. And thank you for not being a dick.

I went home to get ready. Ainsley was coming, too, which was really nice. Paige would be there, too, but the thought didn't bother me.

I took a shower with my special lemon soap, which smelled

extra nice today. Felt a little…happy. Maybe it was the notion that I'd felt Nathan's presence the other night. Maybe I'd just turned a corner. I had loved Nathan, but I didn't have years of memories together, which was both crushing and…well… easier.

And knowing that Daniel wasn't sulking in a corner made me feel better, too.

I looked into Nathan's closet. Maybe this weekend, I'd start cleaning things out. Before I could turn maudlin, I shut the door and lay down on the bed and surprised myself by falling asleep.

A few hours later, Ainsley and I walked into the Center. Greta came over, hugged me, shook hands with Ainsley, who was unabashedly looking for teardrop ex-cons, then led us through the crowd to the photography exhibit.

Pierre was there. "Ah, Kate, my love, my love! So good to see you! This one is mine, just sayin'. In case you like it best."

"Pierre, shoo," Greta said with a laugh.

"I would've guessed this was yours, though," I added. It was a picture of a naked woman.

"Ten bucks if you pick it as the winner," he said, then melted back into the crowd.

"So just mark down your top three," Greta said, "and we'll announce it, and then the auction will start, okay? I better go press some flesh. Take your time. Just not too much time." She flashed a smile and went back to schmoozing.

Ainsley and I walked slowly down the line, and I told her what I was looking for. There were the usual marks of the amateur—poor composition, negative space used the wrong way, not enough color saturation, bad lighting.

But what I loved was the subject material. All of the fifteen or so pictures were taken outside, even Pierre's naked woman. All of them showed heart, whether it was the picture of the homeless man and his dog, or the little kid drinking from a water fountain. These men had suffered while in prison, as many of them richly deserved. Hopefully, they'd learned some things, too. The value of freedom, the beauty of an ordinary day.

"This is the winner," I told Ainsley, stopping at the second-to-last photo. It was of a little girl with big brown eyes, laughing as a pigeon fluttered up toward her. "See how much life and movement there is? The bird's wings, the girl's braids flying up, her hands, the way he caught her in midjump."

"It makes me happy to look at it," Ainsley said.

"Exactly. A lot of emotion here."

"You're so cool, Kate. You should start teaching here again."

"I think I will," I said. Even if it was a bit of a haul, it was worth it. I marked down my choices for first, second and third (Pierre's) and sealed the envelope.

"Making a celebrity appearance?" came a voice. Paige.

"Hello," I said. As always, she looked fantastic.

She scrunched up her face in an approximation of a smile. "So nice of you to grace us with your presence."

"You're welcome. You remember my sister, of course."

Paige didn't spare her a glance. "I met someone," she said. "It's pretty serious. I'd love for you to meet him."

No *How have you been*, no *I'm sorry I've been such a bitch*. I glanced at my sister, who just rolled her eyes. "Yeah…no. We're not friends anymore, Paige."

She exhaled in disbelief. "Why? Because I'm finally happy? You only liked me when I was a loser?"

"What about when I was happy?" I asked. "I seem to remember you telling me to fuck off when I got engaged. I seem to remember that you didn't email or call me even once after my husband died. Now I'm supposed to throw confetti because you finally found someone to put up with you? No, thanks."

Her mouth hung open.

"Hear, hear," said my sister. "For the record, I always thought you were a bitch, too."

She whirled and stomped off, and I had to admit, it felt pretty great. Ainsley and I grinned at each other for a second.

Then Daniel was there. "Hey, gorgeous," he said, hugging me. He smelled very clean, very Ivory soapish. "Hi, Ainsley," he added, letting me go to kiss her cheek. He looked back at me. "Did you finally tell her off?" he asked, nodding in the direction Paige had gone.

"I did," I said. "And it felt great."

"I love her shoes," Ainsley said. "I hate her, but those are some killer shoes. I bet you two have some talking to do, so I'll just slip discreetly away," Ainsley murmured.

"No, no, that's not necessary," I said. "How are you, Daniel? How's the family?"

"They're good," he said. "Want to see pictures?" He pulled out his phone and started sliding his finger across the screen. "Here's Lizzie. You know she booked a runway show? My mom is freaking out, but the money, holy shit. College is not going to be a problem, let's put it that way." He slid to the next one. "And here's the baby, Maisy. She smiled the other day. Cutest thing in the world. Here's the demon child. She's my favorite, of course." He looked up from the phone and grinned.

We were normal again. The knowledge made my chest loosen with relief.

"Hey, come on down the hall and see the porch swing," he said. "You, too, Ains. It's really nice. The students have been helping. It's sort of a class project. We still have to put on some more varnish, but it'll be ready. When's the party again?"

"Two weeks from tonight," I said.

We left the gym and went down the hall to the wood shop. Ainsley pressed a glass of wine into my hand. "Thanks," I said, taking a sip.

Oh, God, it was horribly off. I forced myself to swallow it. "There's something wrong with this," I said. "Don't drink it."

"There is?" she asked. She took my glass and sniffed. Frowned at me and took a sip. "Seems fine to me."

"It's really bad."

"It's not Chateau Lafite, but it's not horrible," she said.

Daniel took a sip, too. "No, it's fine." They looked at me, puzzled. "Anyway, here we go, ladies. After you."

He opened the door of the shop, and the sharp smell of polyurethane hit me hard. There was the swing, dangling from two chains. It was made of narrow strips of a honey-colored wood and curved beautifully, the shape modern but classic.

Nathan would have approved.

"Go ahead, sit on it, girls," he said. Ainsley and I scootched up, and it glided gently, back and forth, back and forth.

Then I bolted. Ran to the sink in the corner and puked. God! What the heck? I retched again, my whole body convulsing.

"Kate, are you okay?" Ainsley asked, handing me some paper towels. Daniel stood there, too, rubbing my back.

"I'm so sorry," I said. "I hardly ever throw up." I rinsed my mouth, my stomach still quivering, and took the paper towels. Straightened up.

Ainsley was looking at me with her mouth half-open.

The fatigue. The sleepiness. The bloodhound sense of smell. And now puking.

"Oh. Oh, no. Nope," I stammered. "No. It's not… Nope."

Daniel covered his mouth with a big hand.

"No," I whispered.

"Oops," Daniel said.

"No!" I barked. "No, it's…it's— I can't… Oh, God."

"Okay, okay," Ainsley said, holding out her hands in a conciliatory gesture. "Let's get out of here. Daniel, do you live nearby?"

"Yeah," he said. "Oh, shit. Holy crap. My God. But we used… Oh, God."

"Enough," she said. "Move it, you two."

We got out of there faster than bank robbers, into Ainsley's Prius, Daniel barely fitting in the back. There was a Duane Reade a few blocks down. "Stay here," Ainsley said, hopping out of the car. Daniel and I didn't speak.

It couldn't be true. Please. Not now.

Six minutes later, she was back with a plastic bag. I looked inside.

Two boxes, four pregnancy tests all told.

No one said anything as we drove to Daniel's. He unlocked the door, and we clomped up the stairs. "I'll come in with you," Ainsley ordered. "Daniel, wait here."

"Okay," he answered faintly.

I knew the drill. Somewhere, I could swear I heard the Fates laughing.

My hands were shaking as I held the test.

*One line*, I thought. *One line. One line.*

I set the test on the wrapper and tidied up. Ainsley and I didn't look at each other.

"You guys okay?" Daniel's voice was a little on the strangled side.

"We'll be with you in a second," Ainsley said.

*One line. One line.* All the times I'd prayed for two came

back to me. *Please*, I told my body. *Please be consistent. Do that for me. Let there be just one line.*

When I got to a hundred and eighty, I looked.

There were two lines.

# Chapter Thirty-One

❧

*Ainsley*

Because they had a *lot* to talk about, I left Kate at Daniel's and drove back to Cambry-on-Hudson by myself.

Oh, my poor sister. I'd spent half an hour sitting with her on the couch, looking at her white face. Daniel, God bless him, didn't say much after I opened the door and said, "Congratulations."

Instead, he made her a sandwich. "It'll be okay," he said, whether to himself or Kate or me or all three of us, I wasn't sure. "It'll be okay."

There wasn't much else to say.

As I drove up the FDR Drive, Jonathan called. "Are you free?" he asked.

I glanced at the time. Wow. It was only seven o'clock. It felt like a lifetime had passed since we'd left for Brooklyn late this afternoon. "Um...yes."

"Are you hungry?"

"I am."

"Would you like to come here for dinner?"

"I would. I'll be there in about an hour, okay?"

"Very good." There was a pause. "Drive safely, sweetheart."

My grip loosened on the steering wheel. "I will," I said.

Sweetheart. He called me sweetheart. The endearment nestled in my heart, a warm little jewel on this complicated night.

An hour later, I pulled into the driveway. "I'm on the patio," he called, and I went down the slate path, past the tree where the girls had a swing, past the front door.

The sun had set, but remnants of orange and red held on. Jonathan had lit a fire in the copper fire pit and a bottle of wine rested in an ice bucket. Two lounge chairs sat side by side.

"It's lovely to see you," he said, kissing me, and my heart swelled.

"You, too." I rested my head against his shoulder. "How was your day?"

"Very good, thank you. Your replacement lacks your, ah, unique energy, but he's doing a competent job so far."

"Glad to hear it."

He poured me some wine. He'd changed into jeans (I was surprised he owned a pair, but he did, and he was rocking them) and a maroon crewneck sweater, and he looked very much like what he was—a son of the Hudson River Valley, established, sure of himself, confident, wealthy.

Happy.

Then he sat down next to me, glanced down at the ground and did a double take. I followed his gaze.

Oh. My purse was open, and there was the backup pregnancy kit. Kate had opted to believe the first two tests. He raised his eyes to mine and didn't so much as blink.

"About that," I began.

"Yes. Is there something you want to tell me?"

"It's not mine. The kit, I mean." I took a sip of wine.

"So you just carry around pregnancy tests?"

"I repeat," I said. "It's not mine."

He continued looking at me, the flickering light of the fire making it hard for me to read his expression. "I see." He sat back, tension radiating off him. I would've loved to tell him it was for Kate, but I hadn't asked if that would be okay.

The sky was now almost black with a thin deep red line on the horizon.

I sighed and took another sip of wine. The bugs chirred and sang, and a mosquito whined by my ear.

"If you *were* pregnant," Jonathan said, not quite looking at me, "for one, you shouldn't be drinking—"

"I'm not pregnant."

"—and for two…that would be… We'd figure it out."

"Jonathan. Listen to me. Read my lips. I am not pregnant, I'm on the Pill, as I'm sure I've told you ten or fifteen times."

"I know. I just… But if you were pregnant, it…it wouldn't be horrible."

I rolled my eyes. "That's very touching. Why don't you stop now? We don't need to have this conversation."

He dipped his head in exasperation. "What I mean is, I…I like children. I'm sure I'd like your children quite a lot." He paused. "Our children."

And there it was again, that stealth missile of sentiment that hit me right in the heart. Captain Flatline was trying to say something lovely.

"Well, I already like your children quite a lot," I said, my voice a little husky. "I bet our children would be very nice, too."

The almost-smile rose, changing his face from unreadable to frickin' adorable.

"Maybe in a year or two, we should have this conversation again," he said.

A year or two. He was thinking toward the future, and with me in it.

And that was fine with me. I didn't need more than that right now. No engagement ring, no plans, just *maybe someday*, and that was enough.

Then he reached over and took my hand, and we sat side by side as the red faded, and the dark blue sky felt like a blessing.

"I think you may be at 70 percent," I said, and he laughed and kissed my hand and then pulled me onto his chair and kissed me properly, long and deep and wet, his hands under my hem, unzipping my dress, until the mosquitoes drove us inside to bed.

Hooray for mosquitoes.

# Chapter Thirty-Two

*Kate*

Sitting in Daniel's living room, two pregnancy tests telling me that, yep, I was knocked up, it dawned on me that God had a helluva sense of humor.

How many times in our marriage had Nathan and I done it? Seriously, how many? I'd taken my temperature, counted days, pressed on my abdomen to see if I felt the pinch of ovulation. In ninety-six days, I'd bet we'd had sex at least a hundred times, even taking into consideration his trip to Seattle and the days my period was too gross. We'd been newlyweds. Not young newlyweds, but enthusiastic newlyweds just the same.

How many times had Daniel and I had sex? Twice in the same night. Both times with a condom. Trojan was going to get a very strongly worded letter, yessiree.

"I'm so sorry about this," I said for the twentieth time.

"It's fine. Eat your sandwich. I don't want you to faint."

There was, I supposed, a microscopic chance that I was

pregnant with Nathan's baby, not Daniel's. No matter what those fourteen pregnancy tests and two periods had told me.

But logic and all the signs told me what I was sure science would confirm. I'd been so tired lately. Peeing more than was normal. The smell sensitivity.

Oh, boy.

Daniel sat down next to me. "What do you want to do?" he asked.

"I have no idea."

He put his arm around my shoulders and pulled me against him. I sat there stiffly, my heart still thudding. My boobs hurt. Why hadn't I noticed this before? Should I be cuddling here on the couch? Then again, cuddling was a little bit like closing the barn door after the horse had bolted, wasn't it?

Daniel took a deep breath. "Look. I always wanted kids. I love kids. We've known each other a long time, you and me. I like you. This is not the worst thing in the world." He looked down at me. "We can get married if you want."

"Daniel, my husband died four months ago."

"Yeah, the timing isn't great." He paused. "Kate, do you want to have the baby?"

"I don't know. I mean, I don't think I could…terminate." I bit my lip. No, that was not something I could face. "I'll have to go to the doctor. And I'm forty. God knows, a million things could go wrong. Miscarriage. This might even be a blighted ovum or something. An ectopic pregnancy."

"Right."

"So maybe I should go to the doctor tomorrow and we'll talk again. Okay?"

"That sounds good. I'll come with you."

"No, no. Not this time."

He sighed again. "Okay. Whatever happens, though, I'm here. I'm with you. I know I'm not your type and I'm a big dumb firefighter, but I'm here. Now, you're staying over tonight. You can sleep in the bed, I'll take the couch, but I'm not driving you home tonight. If we're gonna be parents, we should spend more time together."

"Bossy, aren't you?" The words were automatic, my lips numb.

"I have four sisters. Of course I'm bossy. Oh, man, they're gonna go crazy about this."

"Let's not get ahead of ourselves."

"Right." He looked me up and down. "Since you're already pregnant, you wanna—"

"No, Daniel. Jesus."

He laughed and messed up my hair. Ah. A joke. Then he went into his room to put clean sheets on the bed.

The doctor in Tarrytown—recommended by Daniel, because his sister used the same one—confirmed everything.

The condoms in Nathan's night table drawer were two months past their expiration date. Yes, the doctor said with a wry chuckle, those dates *did* matter. Hahaha. She asked some embarrassing questions about what Daniel and I had done and when. If Daniel had, er, lingered a little, that could've done the trick.

I was pregnant.

Four weeks along, based on my blood work. The ultrasound showed a gestational sac; the baby was too small to be seen.

It was a high-risk pregnancy, given that I was forty. Certain tests would be recommended later on. Chances of miscarriage were higher. I had to take folic acid and prenatal vitamins and stop drinking coffee and alcohol. She told me the receptionist would schedule monthly visits for me.

I was *pregnant*.

I called Daniel with the confirmation. He offered to come

over, but I told him I wanted to be alone. Called Ainsley, who was working at the Blessed Bean, and told her, too.

Then I went home, numb, and sat in the den (or study), watching Hector swim around his beautiful bowl, Ollie curled up on my lap, moaning with love from time to time.

What would the Coburns say? What would Brooke say? She'd hate me. They'd all hate me. I didn't blame them.

"Nathan?" I whispered. "Hey." I started to say the words, then stopped. Even his ghost didn't deserve to hear my news.

My breath began to shake, and my hands tingled so hard it hurt, and the familiar dread rose up like a cold tide.

But I couldn't have a panic attack. I couldn't. I was pregnant. What if hyperventilation was bad for the baby? Huh? What then?

*In for three, hold for three, out for three, hold for three.*

Ollie's tail wagged.

What was I going to do? I kept breathing as best I could, Ollie's cold little nose burrowed in the crook of my elbow, grounding me. I should get a dog, probably. Or just steal Ollie.

I'd have to move, for one. I couldn't stay here, in Nathan's house, percolating another man's baby. So yeah. I'd clean out his closet, finally. Get at least something in motion. Then, if I didn't lose the baby—already, even though it was about as big as a pen dot, I was thinking of it as a baby—I'd...I'd go. I'd tell the Coburns. There was no point in saying anything until after the twelve-week mark. Why break their hearts sooner than I had to?

I closed my eyes and wished so, *so* much that I'd never asked for that second glass of wine.

"I'm sorry, Nathan," I whispered. "I'm so sorry."

Of course, it was Ainsley who looked on the bright side. Ainsley, and Daniel. They double-teamed me the next night,

Ainsley making grilled fish and spinach and rice pilaf for dinner, Daniel refilling my water glass so often I had to pee every fifteen minutes.

"She always wanted to be a mommy," Ainsley told Daniel, who was helping himself to thirds of dinner. "And you know, call me a little ray of sunshine, but I kind of think Nathan had a hand in this."

I flinched. "No, no. Don't go there. Please."

"Seriously, Daniel," Ainsley said. "He *died* on her. He totally screwed up her life and didn't even get her pregnant. Um, may he rest in peace and all that. But is it too much to believe that he felt bad about all this and maybe used his influence to make sure you knocked her up? I don't think that's such a stretch."

"What church do you go to?" Daniel asked. "Because I'm Catholic, and from where I sit, I'm going to hell, impregnating the poor widow here."

"I'm still in the room," I reminded them. "Can you not talk about me like this?"

"Fine, fine," Ainsley said. "But it's a *baby*, Kate! I'm pretty excited."

"Me, too," Daniel said, grinning.

I rubbed my eyes.

"Aren't you? Even a little?" he asked, putting his hand over mine.

"It hasn't really sunk in yet," I said. "I'm a little preoccupied with the shit storm part of this." I took my hand back. "So here's what I am thinking. I'll tell the Coburns I can't live here anymore. Because I can't. It was hard enough before."

"You can move in with me," he said.

"Or me," Ainsley said. "I was thinking of getting a two-family house with the money my mom left me. You can live downstairs, I'll live upstairs, I can watch the baby when you have to work."

"Or I can. Because I'm the *father*," Daniel said.

"Yeah, but you have a lot of girlfriends," Ainsley said. "Bad moral influence. So I win. I get the baby."

"First of all, the baby is half mine. And second, I haven't slept with anyone since your sister."

"Okay. I need a nap," I said. They both stood up, ready to tuck me in. "Stay here! I need some breathing space."

I went upstairs into my bedroom. Sat on the edge of the bed.

There was Nathan's closet. I hadn't been in there since he died.

I guess it was now or never.

It would be awfully nice—and very convenient—to buy into what Ainsley had said. That Nathan had magically pulled some strings and brought about this conception. But until my husband died, I'd had only a vague sense of the afterlife. It didn't seem fair to suddenly chalk this all up to divine intervention, to a husband who was beaming down at me, giving me a wholehearted blessing.

I went into the closet and closed the door.

The closet held a little bit of Nathan's smell, not as powerful as the milk shake night, but there just the same. Still, it was enough to make me sink to the floor. All Nathan's shirts. All his clothes. His shoes. His beautiful cashmere sweaters.

Tears burned behind my eyes. I couldn't cry here. Not now. It wouldn't be right. But I *missed* him. I missed hearing his voice. I missed his whistling as he shaved. I missed what we never got a glimpse of—familiarity. The truth was, I was more comfortable around Daniel than I'd ever been around Nathan.

If I had to pick a baby daddy, Daniel was probably a good

choice. I wondered if it was true; that he'd left behind the False Alarms.

And if he had, what that meant.

I was pregnant. Right now, that little cluster of cells was growing like crazy. According to the best information I could find on the internet, that little cell clump had a 66:1 chance of being a healthy, normal baby.

I'd take those odds.

And suddenly, the guilt and shock were swept away as I sat in the dark, and a wave of love rolled over me like nothing I'd ever felt.

I was going to be someone's *mother*. And no matter what, no matter if I miscarried or the baby had problems, I was going to love her with all my heart, without reservation, and I was not going to pollute my love for this little speck with anything negative. I could judge myself and deal with my actions.

But my baby—my baby!—would feel only love.

# Chapter Thirty-Three

*Ainsley*

So I was going to be an auntie again. I thought it was pretty great.

Sure, the timing sucked. But Kate had been so solitary for so long. For years and years. Then Nathan had come into the picture and made her into something else—a wife, half of a couple, something she'd never been before. His death was all the more cruel because of it; she'd been happy before she knew him, then reduced to a ghost.

But now she had a new purpose in life.

The three of us—Kate, Daniel and I—were going to keep this a secret until she passed the first trimester and felt safer about the baby's odds. But she'd already set some things in motion.

Last week, a few days after she found out, she'd talked to Brooke and told her she wanted Miles and Atticus to own Nathan's house someday, and would set up a trust to cover taxes and upkeep until they were old enough. "It's his most beautiful work," she said, "and the boys should have it." Brooke had cried and cried, the poor thing, hugging Kate and thanking her.

Kate was thinking she'd move back to Brooklyn. Let's face it; she'd never really loved Cambry-on-Hudson, and she still did have that great old apartment. There was a reason she'd never sold it.

And she'd be close to Daniel. "He's the father, after all," she said. "He deserves as much time with the baby as he wants."

"He really likes you," I said. "Do you like him?"

"Sure," she said.

"Do you love him?"

She gave me an amused glance. "Not yet."

"Give him a chance, okay? He's gonna be a great dad."

She shook her head, smiling, no doubt thinking her dopey little sister was a hopeless romantic. She was right.

My own love life was boffo, thank you very much. Not working for Jonathan had made him much more attractive. The feeling was probably mutual. We talked almost every night, and I saw him a few times a week.

Also, I was crazy in love with him.

But I'd done that total immersion relationship. And so had Jonathan, for that matter. I wanted to layer my life a little better than I had eleven years ago. I wanted to get my nursing degree. In a few weeks, I'd finish a class and become a certified nursing assistant. The Village of the Damned was hiring, and I could work there while I kept plugging away at a registered nursing degree.

In the meantime, I worked at Blessed Bean, serving up coffee to Cambry-on-Hudson's stay-at-home mommies and teenagers. My boss, Rig (short for nothing), was twenty, tattooed and pierced with those hideous spacer earrings. He was also quite a sweetheart and viewed me as the authority on all things romantic. And hey, I was Dr. Lovely's daughter, after all.

Speaking of, Candy had expressed the expected dismay at my change of career when I visited her at her beautiful new condo. "Nursing? Oh, honey. All you'll do is change old people's diapers."

"Well, just think. I can change yours when you decide to let loose."

"You'll have to change your father's sooner than mine. That man can barely dress himself as it is. We had dinner the other night, and he forgot his wallet, for the love of God."

"Are you guys staying friends?" I asked.

"Of course," she said in the voice that meant *that's a good one.* I felt for her, though. Somehow, I'd never known how much it had hurt her, being on the wrong side of unrequited love.

"I have something for you," she said. "I found it when I was packing."

She got up from the table and came back with a shoe box.

Inside were a couple dozen photos.

My mother, so young, younger than I was now, and so *beautiful.* Kate, holding me, smiling a gap-toothed grin. Sean, looking up from a book, his glasses smeared, a plate of cookies next to him.

My mother and father and me at about two. I'd never seen a picture of the three of us together.

"These were in the attic," Candy said sharply.

"Thank you," I breathed, leafing through them slowly. My parents on a date night, dressed up and smiling. Me, asleep in a lawn chair, Pooh beside me.

"Do you remember anything?" Candy asked.

I wanted to. Maybe I would someday, maybe the pictures

would trigger something. But for now, there was nothing. "No," I said, looking up at her. "I'm afraid I don't."

But I remembered Candy, holding my hair back when I had the pukes. Showing me how to do long division. Sitting with me during a thunderstorm, not exactly happy that I was terrified, but there nonetheless.

I got up and hugged her and kissed her brittle blond hair. "Thank you," I said again, and my voice was husky.

She patted my hand, then pulled back. "Your father's dating someone about Sean's age," she said, changing the subject.

"Yick," I said. "Wish I could say I was surprised. How about you, Mom? You know I found Gram-Gram a nice widower to date. I could do the same for you."

She snorted. Didn't mention my little slip with the M-word. It wasn't really a slip, after all.

One afternoon in September when I was grinding a freshly roasted batch of Arabica at Blessed Bean, the bell over the door jangled, and I looked up.

Matthew Kent saw me and did a double take.

He had his nieces with him. Jonathan's daughters.

"Hello," he said, approaching the counter.

Lydia was jumping up and down next to him. "I want a cookie! No, cake! No, I want a latte, Uncle Matt!"

"Hello, girls," I said, unsure if they remembered me.

"Hello," said Emily shyly.

"I want a scone!" Lydia said. "Oh, hi, Angie! Hi! Hi! Can I have a scone?"

"It's Ainsley," I said, smiling at her. She had her father's eyes.

"So you're not working at the magazine anymore?" he asked.

"What can I get for you today?" I kept my voice pleasant for the girls' sake.

"Did you ever mention those things I asked you to?"

"We have a fresh batch of Arabica. And some hot chocolate if you girls are interested."

His jaw hardened, just like Jon's did.

"Lyddie, Em," he said, squatting down to their eye level, "wouldn't it be fun to have Mommy and Daddy and me and you all get together? Wouldn't that be great?"

"Yes, yes!" Lydia said, jumping up and down. Emily, who was wiser, just looked at me.

"Rig!" I called. "I'm going on break." I turned back to the girls. "It was really nice to see you both. I hope you like your goodies!"

Then I went into the back room where we washed coffee urns and took a few deep breaths.

What a *shitty* man to use the girls to get what he wanted. Then again, this was the guy who'd slept with his brother's wife. I shouldn't be surprised.

I stayed there until Matthew left and then got back to work, cheerfully serving coffee and cappuccinos, scones and slices of pumpkin cake. The second my shift was over, I bolted. It was a little chilly outside, and I hugged my denim jacket closer. A cold front had moved through the other day, and all of a sudden, the leaves were bursting into color.

Blessed Bean was two doors down from Matthew Kent's restaurant. There was a bench across the street from both, excellent for spying. Was Matthew working now? Should I go in and say something? I wondered if Jonathan's ex-wife knew her boyfriend was campaigning for a family reunion.

"Hey, Ainsley!" It was Jenny Tate from the wedding dress place, and the lovely Leo, holding hands.

"Hi, cutest couple," I said.

"We're going to Hudson's for a drink," Leo said. "Want to join us?"

"Oh, that's sweet. But no. You guys are good?"

"Jenny's a very lucky woman," Leo said, getting a punch on the arm from his beloved. "How's Kate?"

"She's doing okay, I think." I'd let Kate tell them the details of her life.

"Anytime she wants to call me, she can," Leo said. He had such a sweet smile.

"I'll remind her," I said. "Have a nice night, you two."

This was what I loved about Cambry-on-Hudson. This beautiful little downtown, the hills rising from the noble river, the people who walked around at night, holding hands. Regardless of my history with Eric, and no matter what happened with Jonathan, too, I wanted to stay here. This was my home.

I pulled my phone out of my purse and called Jonathan. "Jonathan Kent," he said, caller ID or no caller ID.

"Yes, I know," I said. "Listen. Can you come meet me? I'm on the park bench across from the Bean."

"Are you all right?" he asked, and I loved that he always checked that first.

"I'm fine," I said, my voice softer. "Come on down."

Ten minutes later, he was walking down the street toward me, wearing a navy blue wool coat and a scarf that made him look very British. He kissed my cheek and sat down. "What is it?" he asked.

"Your brother came into the Bean today," I said. "With the girls."

He was silent as I told him what happened, but his jaw grew harder and harder until I feared for his teeth.

I took his hand, needing to uncurl his fingers in order to hold it. "Look," I said gently. "The thing is, he has a point. The girls are caught in the middle. What if he and your ex get married? Then he's their uncle *and* their stepfather. He'll show up at school concerts and birthday parties. You're going to have to talk to him someday."

"And say what, exactly?" There was that dragonesque growl that indicated high emotion, I knew by now. He stared straight ahead, and I reached up and turned his face to me.

"Say that you forgive him."

"I don't."

My heart ached. "You can. You will."

"Really. How do you know this?" His eyes were ice-cold, as we were apparently at the *kill the messenger* part of the conversation.

"Because you're the better man, and you always put your children first."

He looked down, then away. The wind blew, and some red maple leaves drifted down around us.

"You're right," he said. Then he was pulling me across the street, his coat flapping, right past the Blessed Bean and up the stairs of Hudson's.

"Are we, uh— Right now?" I asked.

"Yes." His grip on my hand was nearly painful. We burst into the place. "I'd like to see Matthew Kent, please," he told the maître d', who came into the Bean every afternoon. Eva.

"Oh, hi, Ainsley!" she said. "Um, Matt is in the kitchen. I'm afraid he's really busy. You know, it's Friday night and everything."

"Get him right now, please," Jonathan said in that *you're in trouble, young lady* voice I knew so well.

"Tell him his brother is here," I added.

Her eyes widened. "Oh. Oh, wow. Okay. Hang on." She rushed off.

The restaurant was filled with patrons, even at six o'clock. We were hardly Europeans around here. There were Jenny and Leo at the bar. Jenny gave a little wave. I tried to smile back.

Jonathan squeezed my hand harder. "Deep breaths," I murmured. He didn't answer.

A second later, Matthew came through the restaurant. A few people tried to get his attention, but to his credit, he came right to Jonathan, who dropped my hand and took a step forward, stopping Matthew in his tracks.

"Hey," he said. "Thank you so much for—"

"Don't you *ever* use my daughters to further your own agenda," Jonathan growled.

"I... Yeah. I'm really sorry about that. It was a bad move." Matt wiped his hands on his chef's jacket. "I regret that. But I was a little desp—"

"I understand you want to say something to me."

The restaurant was growing quiet.

"Um, yeah. Jonathan." Matthew straightened up. "I...I miss you, buddy. I know I fucked up, and there's no excuse, but you're my brother, and I love you. And Laine really cares about you, too, and of course the girls think you walk on water."

"And?"

"I just hoped that maybe we could... I don't know. Put the past behind us. For the girls' sake. And mine. You were a good brother. You didn't deserve what I did."

Jonathan looked at him with that ice-cold stare I knew so well, the one that used to be leveled at me.

"I accept your apology," he said.

"Really?"

"Yes."

Then Jonathan drew back and punched his brother in the mouth. Hard. Matthew fell to the floor, and there was an intake of breath and a few exclamations of *Oh, my God!* and *Holy crap!*

Matthew lay there, looking up at his brother, then smiled, a little blood staining his teeth. "Thank you," he said.

"You're welcome." Jonathan turned to me, and only then did some expression seep back into his eyes.

"Well done," I said, and he kissed me, right in front of everyone. Took my hand, and led me out.

"How are your knuckles?" I asked as we walked in the near-dark, the lights of the green making a pinkish glow.

"Sore," he said, then looked at me and smiled. "Thank you, by the way."

"You're welcome," I said. "I also accept gifts."

"You're very good with people, Miss O'Leary. Especially me."

"Well, I love you, so…"

He stopped. "Do you?"

"Afraid so."

He looked at my mouth, then back to my eyes. "Good," he said. "Good." Then he kissed me again, and since it was Jonathan, I think we could tell this was his way of saying *I love you, too.*

# Chapter Thirty-Four

*Kate*

On the night of the Coburns' anniversary party, I was seven weeks pregnant. The baby was about as big as a bean, or a blueberry, according to the internet. Disturbing that they always compared it to food. She—or he, the sex was already decided, though I wasn't sure I wanted to find out—was ten thousand times bigger than when she began. In five weeks, my chances of miscarriage would plummet, and I was counting the hours. Just eight hundred and thirty-three to go.

My breasts were sore, and I was still tired a lot. In fact, I fell asleep at my desk the other day and woke up in a puddle of drool, another fun pregnancy symptom.

I loved the baby so much it was like living in another dimension. My little traveler had replaced Ollie as the creature I talked to the most.

My plan was to get through tonight, which was going to be horrifically difficult on its own. Later this week, I'd tell the Coburns I was moving back to Brooklyn and get out of Cambry-on-Hudson before I started showing. The urge to disappear into Brooklyn and simply never contact them again was strong, if wrong.

This pregnancy would hurt them so much.

In two months, my tenants' lease would be up, and I could move back to my apartment and start the next phase of my unexpectedly complicated, sad, wonderful life. Daniel was campaigning for me to live with him until then; he had a second bedroom. I was thinking about it.

He'd been great these past few weeks. He called every night and came over at least once a week. One day, I found the fridge full of fresh vegetables and a roasted chicken. He left me little presents, like a huge vat of Tums—I had wicked heartburn—and a nice almond-scented shower gel. A gift certificate for a pedicure. You could tell the guy had four sisters.

This would be my last regular night in the house. Tomorrow, Ainsley and I were going to start packing my things. Not that there were too many—mostly clothes and a few photos.

I'd miss it here, the house that never felt like mine. It had always been like winning a vacation in a fabulous place you could never afford. But the few short months of my marriage had happened here. Every day of our marriage, Nathan and I came back here. Slept here. Made love here.

The spike shoved through my throat once again.

It was time to get dressed. I had a navy blue gown to wear, a simple V-neck.

The dress looked a lot different compared to the last time I'd worn it (also to the Cambry-on-Hudson Lawn Club, to another fund-raiser), courtesy of my pregnancy boobs, but it was too late to try to find something else. I put on a necklace Nathan had given me—a single dark gray, iridescent pearl on a silver chain. My wedding band and engagement ring.

I'd have to stop wearing those. The spike turned again.

I had the architectural plans finished, rolled up and tied up with a gold ribbon. The Coburns had asked me to come early so we could all drink a toast to Nathan first.

I picked up the picture of the two of us from last fall, the selfie I'd taken, me over his shoulder, kissing his cheek. For the first time since he'd died, I really studied it. It had been September, a year ago.

He looked happy. A little unsure, maybe? It was hard to tell, knowing what Madeleine had said, reading those emails.

"Time to go," I whispered to my bean-sized embryo.

The Coburns, Brooke and Chase, and I were ushered into a private room at the Club. We all kissed each other on both cheeks—it took a while.

"Kate, deah," Eloise said. "Thank you so much for coming. I know how hard this is for you."

"Oh, I…I wouldn't miss it," I said.

"You look beautiful," Chase said kindly. He was a nice man. "And, Kate, about the house…thank you. It will mean so much to the boys. It means so much to Brooke."

"Well," I said. "It felt like the right thing." I forced a smile, inwardly cringing. I'd also donated Nathan's life insurance to the Coburns' scholarship fund. Anonymously.

A waiter handed out glasses of champagne, then left, and we all stood around, not making eye contact.

"It's hard to celebrate this year," Mr. Coburn began, and Chase put his arm around Brooke, who immediately began to cry. "But I'm grateful to you, my love." He turned to Eloise, tears in his eyes. "Thank you for fifty years. Thank you for our daughter. Thank you for our son." He raised his glass, his hand shaking. "To Eloise," he said, the tears tracing down his wrinkled cheeks.

"To Eloise," we echoed.

She looked so dignified and beautiful...and tragic. Her whole life was written on her face, the smiles, the love for her children and grandchildren, the pain of her unfathomable loss.

"To our son," she said, and then they were in each other's arms, sobbing quietly.

I bent my head. *Oh, Nathan, please help them*, I prayed.

"He loved you all so much," I said. "He was so proud to be your son and brother." Eloise glanced at me gratefully, and Brooke squeezed my hand.

Then, from my purse, I heard the buzz of a text. Shit! Daniel was supposed to drop the swing off here. But I'd forgotten to text him earlier so he could get here before the Coburns. Just plain forgot, one of the many fun symptoms of pregnancy. I checked my phone discreetly. Yep.

When do you want me to drop off the swing? I'm in the parking lot. Are you here yet?

"Mama," Brooke said, her voice ragged, "I have something for you." She went to the table and picked up a gift-wrapped package. "Open it."

It was a family portrait, taken at our engagement party. The eight of us—Nathan and me, Mr. and Mrs. Coburn, Brooke and Chase and the boys, standing stiffly, a rather terrible shot, slightly blurry. Brooke's eyes were closed, and Atticus was out of focus, and I looked uncomfortable (because I had been). Nathan's arm was around me.

It was the only picture I'd seen of all of us.

"Oh, darling, it's perfect," Eloise said, and they hugged, too, Brooke's shoulders shaking.

This was agony.

"Kate?" Chase asked. "You have something, too, right?" He nodded at the scroll I'd left on the table.

"Yes, yes," I said, breaking out of my inertia. "Here." I handed them the plans. "One of Nathan's coworkers put the finishing touches on, but this is from… This is from Nathan. He wanted you to modify the house a little."

"Nathan did this?" Mr. Coburn asked as Chase and I unrolled the blueprints.

"You remember, darling," Eloise said. "He wanted us to have a bedroom downstairs for when we're older. I didn't realize he…he'd started." Her chest started to hitch, but she pressed her hand against her heart. "Kate, this is so thoughtful. Thank you, darling. Oh, look. A porch! He knew I always wanted a covered porch." She reached out and grabbed my hand. "Kate, thank you. Thank you, deah."

"You're welcome," I whispered.

"I had a dream he came to the house for lunch," she said, her voice faraway. "It was so wonderful to see him…"

"Mr. and Mrs. Coburn," said one of the club staffers from the doorway. "Your guests have begun to arrive."

"We should get out there," Eloise said. "Is everyone ready? As ready as we'll ever be, I suppose." She gave a smile that wobbled at first, then grew stronger, and I admired her more than I could ever possibly say.

It was a relief to get out of that room of pain and loss. Older people in tuxes and gowns streamed in, and I hugged the edge of the foyer, trying to make it outside without having to talk to anyone. The smell of perfume was thick, and a wave of nausea rolled over me. Outside, one of the staff was directing people inside, welcoming them to the party.

"Is there a man in a pickup truck around here?" I asked.

"Around the corner of the building," the kid said. He smelled horribly of Axe body spray, and another heavy wave of nausea rolled up my legs, into my gut. Oh, God, I was going to throw up. Walking as fast as I could, I saw Daniel's truck at the kitchen entrance. He was leaning against the tailgate.

"Hey," he said. "You look amazing."

I puked on his work boots.

His arm went around me, guiding me to the passenger side of the truck so I'd have a little privacy, anyway. Not that I could think much, as my insides tried to surge up my throat.

Good thing I'd worn my hair up, I thought distantly. Daniel pulled the hem of my dress out of the way as I retched until I was clean. Then he sat me down on the passenger seat, opened the glove box and handed me a Dunkin' Donuts napkin so I could wipe my mouth.

"Here," he said, handing me a bottle of water. "Rinse and spit."

I obeyed. Realized I was gripping his hand.

"Rough night?" He knelt down in front of me and smiled, his eyes kind.

"You're a good guy," I whispered.

"That's what they tell me."

For a second, I just looked at him.

"It's gonna be all right," he said, and I believed him. "I know it's complicated, Kate, but we're in this together. I'll be a good dad, you'll be a great mom and…and this is gonna be fine. Okay?"

"Okay." I took a deep breath and looked at the Club's front door, where people were still streaming in. "You know what? Maybe it's best if you just drop off the swing at the Coburns' house. I sort of missed the moment. Is that okay?"

"You bet." He stayed where he was a moment longer. "Feeling better?"

"Yes."

He smiled, and I loved him a little then.

Daniel helped me out of the truck, held me by the shoulders for a minute to make sure I was steady.

"Their house is on the same street as mine," I said. "Half mile down. It's a big brick place with a white front door."

"Got it. I'll call you later."

I could feel his eyes on me as I walked back to the main entrance. Up the four stairs, holding my gown up so I wouldn't trip. Then I looked up and saw Madeleine.

"You nasty whore," she said. "You're pregnant with that man's baby."

Why she'd been invited, I didn't know. Maybe she hadn't been. It hardly mattered now.

We went into the room where I'd just been with the Coburns.

She'd seen me from the window, leaving when everyone else was coming in, she said, and suspected something was off. It was one of the many things Nathan had loved about her, she said—her uncanny intuition. And so she'd spied.

"I guess we know what kind of a person you really are," she said, her lips white.

"Madeleine, I…I would appreciate you not telling the Coburns."

"Oh, believe me, they're going to know."

"Not tonight, please. This day is hard enough."

"They should know what kind of pretender their son married."

I closed my eyes. "I'll tell them tomorrow." My hands were shaking, and I felt dizzy and starving and wretched. "I'm moving soon. Back to Brooklyn."

"Good. I hope they never see you again. You never deserved their son."

"Why are you here, Madeleine?" I asked.

"Because I support their foundation," she said. "Because I love them."

Because she would never recover from having drawn that line in the sand with Nathan—children or her. She'd never get over the fact that he didn't desert me. She thought they'd have more time.

Just as I did.

"I'm sorry for your loss," I whispered. "I know you loved him so much."

Her eyes narrowed into slits. "I don't need your pity," she snarled. "Just make sure you tell the Coburns. I'll call Eloise tomorrow night to make sure."

"Kate!" Brooke stood in the doorway. "There you are." She looked from me to Madeleine. "Is everything okay?"

"We're fine," Madeleine said. "Excuse me." She left the room with her head held high, her gown swishing.

"I'm sorry if she upset you," Brooke said, putting her arm around me. "You're white as a ghost. She wasn't invited. I think she's a little...psycho." She gave me a smile. "Come on. Mom and Dad are worried about you."

And so I spent the rest of the night with Nathan's family, Eloise occasionally holding my hand, Mr. Coburn making sure I had enough to eat, Brooke sitting next to me at dinner, Miles climbing onto my lap.

For the last time, I was one of them, and it hurt more than I could have ever imagined.

The next day, dressed in jeans that were feeling a little tight, I went over to my in-laws' house.

"Kate! That swing! Oh, darling, it's beautiful," Eloise said. "And last night...it was special, wasn't it? I think it was the right thing to do. I think Nathan would've approved. We raised so much for the scholarship fund! Someone donated more than a million dollars, can you imagine?"

"That's wonderful," I said. "Um, Eloise… I need to talk to you and Mr. Coburn."

"Hi, Kate!" Brooke was here. "How are you?"

So they'd all hear at once. Maybe it was better this way.

"Are you all right?" Brooke asked, her face changing from a smile into concern.

"I need to tell you something. All of you."

"Come, come, let's all sit. Nathan, where are you, darling? Oh, there you are."

We sat in the living room, a vast, chilly place. On the mantel was the photo Brooke had given them last night.

"We've already called a contractor," Eloise said. "We're just so excited to start Nathan's plan for the house. It's like having a little bit of him back, in a way."

"Good. That's…that's what I hoped. Um, listen." My heart started clacking against my ribs. "I have some news."

"What is it, dear?" Mr. Coburn asked, leaning forward.

Shit. The words I'd practiced last night evaporated. The thing I wanted most to avoid was the idea that this baby was Nathan's. I couldn't let them think that, even for a second, then take it away.

"Well, I… There's a friend of mine. Brooke, you met him. Daniel Breton?"

"Oh, yes. Your sister's boyfriend."

"No, he's not. Um…no, he's an old friend from Brooklyn. He actually made the swing for you."

"And we love it," Eloise said. "It's simply stunning. Please give me his address so I can write him a note."

They'd probably want to burn the swing in a few seconds. "Uh, well…" I licked my dry lips. "The thing is, Daniel and

I, we…we've been friends for a while now. Ten years. And um…this past July, we, um…we slept together. Once."

Eloise's smile slowly sagged. Mr. Coburn's bushy eyebrows drew together. I couldn't look at Brooke.

"And now I seem to be pregnant," I whispered.

Their silence was absolute. My hands were clenched so hard they were white.

"Wait," Brooke said. "You slept with someone three months after my brother died? Are you *kidding*? Is this a joke? Because it is *not* funny."

I bit my lip so hard I tasted blood. Didn't say anything.

"So my brother was barely cold and you fu—"

"Brooke, that's enough," Eloise said. She was looking at the coffee table. "Kate, I'm sorry. We'd like you to leave."

"Okay," I whispered. "I just want you to know that it wasn't planned and… I loved Nathan so much, and all I wanted was—"

"Get out," Mr. Coburn said, his voice shaking with rage. "Get out right now."

I did. My head screamed with all the months of unshed tears, and the spike made swallowing impossible. I walked to my car like I was walking to the gas chamber, got in and drove the half mile back to my husband's house.

It was time to go.

# Chapter Thirty-Five

*Ainsley*

I was supposed to go to the Coburns' anniversary party, but I had to go to the hospital instead.

My father got injured when a rookie first baseman slid into him at home plate. Dad still made the call (out by a mile and a half) but had to go to the ER with a broken tibia and a dislocated kneecap. Luckily, it was at Yankee Stadium, so I met him in the Bronx and drove him home. Texted Kate that I'd be staying with him tonight and maybe for a few days. I also called Candy.

"Well, he's on his own," she said merrily. "We're separated. Besides, he's *your* father."

"And Kate's and Sean's. And Sean is a doctor," I reminded her.

"Right," she snorted. "Try getting that lunkhead to actually do something for his parents. No, it'll be you, sweetheart. You can practice your nursing skills. Good luck!"

"Mom doesn't care," I told my father, who grunted. It was fine.

And once I'd gotten him into his recliner, gave him a pain-killer and made him some soup, I went out to my car and brought in the pictures of my mother that I'd been carrying around. Captive audience and all that.

"What?" he asked. "I want to watch SportsCenter."

I turned off the TV and tossed the remote control on the couch, out of reach. "Sorry, gimpy. No time like the present."

"Fine," he grumbled. "What do you want?"

I handed him the first photo, and he melted a little.

"You sure were a cute little bugger," he said. He looked at the pictures slowly. "And your mother...she was terrific."

"Can you tell me anything else about her?" I asked.

"You're a lot like her."

"In what ways?"

"I don't know, Ainsburger," he said, shifting in the chair. "In the good ways. She was... She was fantastic."

Men.

But his eyes lingered on every photo, and once in a while, he'd touch one. "Happy times," he said gruffly. "We were happy."

I wedged myself into the chair next to him and hugged him tight. "I'm sorry, Daddy."

When he spoke, his voice was thick with tears. "I never thought I'd last this long without her. I'm an old man being taken care of by his spinster daughter, but Michelle will always be young."

"I'm not a spinster," I said. "And she did give you me."

"Yes," he said, hugging me. "Yes, she did." There was a pause. "What do you mean, you're not a spinster? You and Eric back together?"

"No, Dad. But I'm dating my boss. My former boss, I mean. Jonathan Kent, from the magazine."

"What magazine?"

"You should pay more attention."

He nodded, his chin scraping against my hair. "It's always been easier not to."

"I love you anyway."

Another squeeze. "Right back at you, sweetie."

The next afternoon, I got a call from Kate. "Hey, I'm… I'm moving out. Sorry it's so sudden."

"What happened?" I asked.

"They know. The Coburns."

"Oh, shit."

"Yeah."

"Want help?"

"No, but you'll have to move out, too. Not immediately. But soon." Her voice was tight.

"Sure, sure. I was planning to anyway. Um, Dad broke his leg, did you get that message?"

"Yeah, sorry. Is he okay?"

"He's fine. I'm gonna stay with him a few days, I think." I paused. "You sure you don't want help?"

"Yeah, I'm good."

I went over anyway, leaving Dad on the couch with a tube of Oreos and the remote control. His broken leg was all over ESPN, and he wanted to enjoy it. Gram-Gram was on her way over to babysit him.

Kate had three suitcases on her bed when I found her, and was tossing things in a little wildly. "Oh, hey."

"Sit down," I said, taking a pair of boots from her. "Have you had anything to eat or drink today?" Really, I was going to make an excellent nurse.

"I did. See?" She picked up a glass of water and took a long drink, then told me what happened.

I sighed. "Well, it was gonna happen sooner or later. Sort of ripped the Band-Aid off. You won't have to skulk around for the next few months, afraid that they'll find out."

"They're really upset."

"Of course they are." I sat on the edge of her bed and looked at her. "But, Kate, you loved Nathan. This baby doesn't change that fact. You took a little comfort with Daniel and now you're going to have a baby, and you always wanted that."

"True," she said. She was quiet for a minute. "I'll miss you. I loved living with you."

My heart swelled. "I loved it, too. And I'll come to Brooklyn and stay with you, I promise. And you can come up here when I get a place of my own."

"I will," she said. "I don't want us to stop being close." Then she stood up and hugged me, long and hard, petting my hair the way she used to when I was little.

"I don't know how I could've gotten through this without you. And don't think you're off the hook now."

I squeezed her tight. Nothing she could've said would have made me any happier.

# Chapter Thirty-Six

*Kate*

It was funny how quickly my presence was erased from Nathan's house. Ainsley had taken Ollie with her when she left, and I was alone.

My suitcases were by the door. My toiletries were cleaned up from the bathroom. Max was coming to pick me up after rush hour. Daniel had offered, but I put him off. It carried too much weight, him coming to take me away from Nathan's.

Brooke had sent me an email, telling me not to touch any of Nathan's things. She would take care of that. It's very hard for us to believe you loved Nathan if you found it so easy to fall in with another man. I think it would be better if we didn't hear from you for a while, the email said.

But I did take one thing. A navy blue cashmere sweater, tucked at the bottom of my suitcase. He had so many, and I wanted something that had touched him.

I went into the cellar and brought up the Apple boxes. Into

the den (or study) to pack up my equipment, the Apple, the cords and accessories, tucked back into their nesting foam.

Otherwise, there were a few books on photography—Ansel Adams and Margaret Bourke-White. The photo of Nathan and me. And Hector, of course.

Otherwise, there still wasn't much of me in this room. There never had been.

Nothing of mine had ever made it from storage.

Did some part of me know I wouldn't be married for long? Did I believe Nathan and I would last? Was the feeling of strangeness that permeated our marriage trying to tell me something?

There was my Nikon.

I guessed it was now or never.

Slowly, I reached for the camera. The last time I'd held this was the last day of my husband's life, and yet it fit into my hands the same as always, comfortable, a solid, reliable workhorse of a camera.

If I was going to do this, I'd do it right. I dug through my bag of cords and found the one that would download the photos onto Nathan's computer. Tapped the space bar of his computer. It took a minute to wake up, since it hadn't been used since I looked at his emails from Madeleine.

And there they were, his neat folders.

I plugged the cord in and waited. Looked at Hector as the photos loaded, my heart thumping.

Then I looked at the screen. *Import seven pictures?* the computer asked me. I clicked Yes.

Oh, God. There he was, that last morning, his face so dear, so plain and rugged and...and...*loved* that my knees crumpled, and I slid into his chair.

*Nathan. Oh, Nathan. How can you be gone forever?*

I drank in the details; the shape of his mouth, the freckle

under his eye, the blond eyelashes, the sweetness in his almost shy expression.

Thank *God* I'd gotten up early to see him that day. Thank God I had this picture.

The next one was from Eric's party—my sister, lit up with happiness. Eric, that smug bastard.

Jonathan Kent, looking intently at Ainsley as she talked to someone else. Another little revelation caught by the camera.

The next one was of the back of Nathan's head. He'd turned at the last second, and there was his head, hiding that vascular malformation. His soft ginger hair.

Ainsley with Eric's mother, both of them teary-eyed.

It would be just a few minutes later that Nathan died.

One picture left.

I clicked, then sucked in a breath.

It was *us*. Nathan and me. That's right, some girl from Ainsley's work had asked to see my camera and clicked a shot.

It was a little off-center. But it didn't matter, because there it was, the answer.

We were in love. I looked strangely sweet, my cheeks flushed, my arm around Nathan's waist, my eyes shining. And Nathan...

I heard a noise just then. It was me. I was crying. Finally, I was crying. Gushing, really, and sobbing, the sound so strange and so wonderful, too.

Tears made the picture go out of focus, but I dashed them out of my eyes.

Nathan looked so happy. So...*content*. And God, there was nothing wrong with that. He had the look of marrow-deep satisfaction, and a little hint of pride, and love, yes, absolutely, love. The moment in time, stopped and caught forever.

We had been so happy.

I bent my head and cried. Cried and cried with happiness

and loss and gratitude and grief. I had loved my husband, and he died far, far too young, and if he had lived, we'd still be together, pregnant or not, taking care of each other, the way people do when they love each other.

"I love you," I whispered. "Nathan, I loved you so much."

And there it was again. The wave of warmth, the smell of my husband, and such a sweet, strong pressure in my chest that I knew he was here.

Here to say goodbye.

# Epilogue

— • —

*Kate*

On May 7, one year, one month and one day after I was widowed, I became a mother.

The time had passed slowly, and also with breathtaking speed. My body flew ahead with pregnancy, but it seemed like the longest fall on record.

I moved back to Brooklyn, staying with Daniel for two months until my apartment was once again mine. I slept in his spare bedroom and acted like a guest, keeping my room tidy, paying for half of the utilities, working as much as I could to save up for when I had the baby. Daniel didn't push things, but he jumped at the chance to do anything for me, whether it was pick up some food or rub my feet.

We kept things platonic.

During those eight weeks, I'd often go to Cambry-on-Hudson to stay with my dad and sister. In December, Ainsley put a down payment on a sweet little bungalow with three bedrooms, and I stayed there most weekends. She and Jonathan were in no hurry to take things a step further, she said; if she was going to be his children's stepmother, she wanted to do it right. Slow and steady seemed to be the plan.

On one weekend in COH, I saw Brooke leaving the cemetery. She didn't see me.

Yes, I still visited Nathan's grave. Those pictures had shown me that despite being unsure and unsettled, I had also been happy in a way I'd never been until then.

And I was happy now. Still in mourning, but moving forward. The two feelings didn't cancel each other out.

Moving back into my apartment was odd; once, it had been so important to me. Now it was just a place. A lovely place, but I had learned that home had a lot more to do with the people than the floorboards and closets. Nathan's house had never been home. He, on the other hand, had been.

My mother surprised me by sneaking a little closer. After she left Dad, the weight of bitterness had slipped off her shoulders. She called me every few days and had stopped reciting from her books, content just to talk. Dad remained his usual self, always one step removed.

Sean and Kiara and their kids stayed where they were, on the fringes of our family, always around just enough, never so much that familial responsibility actually interfered with their perfect lives. It was okay. Now my family was my little bean. Ainsley and Jonathan.

And Daniel, too.

After I moved back into my old place, Daniel started coming over at night. We'd talk and eat and watch TV. He told me about the downside of being a firefighter—the bureaucracy's needless interventions, the bad calls, the lazy coworker, the hidden dangers, the uncomfortable hero worship. Seemed like the hot firefighter routine had been as much armor as a way to attract women.

Sometimes he fell asleep on the couch, tired from his shift, and I'd look at his ridiculously handsome face and feel a rush of tenderness. He was a simple guy, was Daniel the Hot Firefighter, but in all the good ways. He loved his job, protected his woman, as he called me, and talked to our baby through my stomach.

There was a lot to love there.

Eventually, the nights on the couch morphed into him sleeping in the guest room a few times a week, then every other day, then most days.

Then one night, when I was in bed, tossing and turning and occasionally chomping down a Tums, he came into my room in his boxer shorts. "Move over," he said and got in next to me, holding me in his big arms, one hand on my stomach, where our baby slid and flipped inside.

When I was thirty-nine weeks pregnant, with swollen ankles and acne on my chin and a backache in its fifth week, he took my feet in his lap. "I love you, you know," he said, not looking at me.

A beat passed. "Thank you," I said.

He cut me a sideways look. "That's all you got?"

"I love you, too." I smiled as I said it, because it was true. It was different from Nathan, but different didn't mean less.

Then Daniel pulled me, bulk and all, over onto his lap, and we made out, our baby kicking him as well as me, making us laugh.

Two days later, she was born.

Our daughter weighed seven pounds, three ounces, had a tubular head from twenty hours of labor, a red, squishy face, and was the most beautiful thing I'd ever seen.

*We'd* ever seen.

Daniel cried unabashedly when the midwife said, "It's a girl!" So did my sister, who was with us for eighteen of the twenty hours, never flagging in good cheer and words of encouragement.

When the baby had been weighed and wrapped and handed to me, Daniel put his arm around me, and we just stared at her face.

"She's so perfect," Daniel said. "Look at her. She looks just like you." He smiled and gave me a quick kiss.

"Do you have a name picked out?" the nurse asked.

"We do," I said, looking up at my sister, who had my Nikon and was snapping pictures. "Ainsley Noel."

"Are you kidding me?" my sister said, bursting into tears. "Oh, guys! Thank you! Hi, little Ainsley! I love you, honey!"

The next day, my parents came to visit, as well as Daniel's mother and four sisters and several of their kids, in addition to Sean and Kiara and Sadie, who was thrilled to have a baby cousin. Jonathan came to pick up Ainsley the Elder and brought a beautiful soft elephant stuffed animal.

I was surrounded by love. By family. Tears filled my eyes, and suddenly, I yawned.

"All right, everyone, get out," Daniel said, and I smiled at him gratefully. "I'll walk them out and come right back. You need anything, honey?"

"Ice cream?" I suggested.

"You got it. Ben & Jerry's Pistachio coming up."

Our families were herded out of the room, and I snuggled little Ainsley closer, smelling her head, a smell I already recognized. I'd cheerfully kill for her, happily lay down my life for her without a second's hesitation and with a smile on my face. My beautiful baby. My gift.

"Hey." Daniel stood in the doorway.

"You forget something?"

"You're gonna marry me," he said, and his voice was rough. "Whenever you want, but you are. I love you, Kate. Okay? You'll marry me?"

My heart, which was already so full, threatened to overflow. "Yes, I'll marry you. Someday."

"Don't make me wait too long." He came to my side, bent down and kissed me, then kissed Ainsley's head. "Back in ten with the ice cream, my beautiful girls."

I lifted Ainsley into the clear plastic bassinet next to me. She gave a tiny snort—so cute!—and grunted. I touched her cheek. "Mommy's right here," I said, then closed my eyes.

I'd be happy with Daniel. I already was. The fact that the universe had given me two lovely men and a baby in the space of a year...well, the universe was full of tricks and mystery.

I opened my eyes to make sure my baby wasn't a dream. She was still there, pink and beautiful, eyebrows like her daddy, long, beautiful fingers. I smiled and closed my eyes again.

It seemed like ten seconds later that a soft knock came on the door. I jolted awake.

It was Eloise Coburn.

My God.

I scrambled to sit up, wincing at the pull of stiches.

"I'm so sorry if I woke you," she said.

"No, no. Please come in. How are you?" I adjusted my johnny coat and swallowed.

"I'm doing well, thank you." She stood in the doorway. "Your sister called me."

"Oh," I said. "Um...have a seat."

As always, she was beautifully dressed, her hair whiter now than the last time I'd seen her. "How's the family?" I asked.

"Everyone is doing well," she said. "The boys are growing so fast, and we finished the house expansion."

"Great, great," I said. "Um…this is Ainsley. My daughter."

Eloise looked, a soft expression coming over her face. "You named her for your sister. How lovely." There was a pause. A page for Dr. Somebody came over the PA. "May I hold her?" Eloise asked.

Would she hurt my baby to get revenge? Would she bolt out of here with Ainsley in her arms?

She wouldn't. Eloise Coburn had never done a cruel thing in her life.

"Of course," I said.

With great care, Eloise lifted the baby out of the bassinet and settled her in her arms. She looked down at her, and when the baby reached out a flailing arm, Eloise offered a finger for my baby to grip.

"Aren't you beautiful," she murmured.

This might have been her granddaughter, this child of her son's wife. Tears slid down my cheeks; crying had not been an issue since the day I left Nathan's.

Eloise touched Ainsley's cheek and smiled just a little, and I saw Nathan in her face.

"Well. Here you go," Eloise said, handing her to me. "She's just lovely. I brought her something."

She reached into her purse and pulled out a little package. "Let me unwrap it for you," she said, doing just that, her movements brisk and efficient. It was a small box. She lifted off the top and showed me.

It was a silver baby brush, the bristles as soft as rabbit fur. And it was inscribed: NVC III.

"It was Nathan's," she said softly. "More of a showpiece than a practical gift, but...well. I wanted you to have it. I know he loved you very much."

My breath shook out of me. "Oh, Eloise. I loved him, too." The words were barely audible.

"Yes," she said. "I believe you." She looked away then, at the room. "I should leave you. You need to rest."

"Eloise? Would you like to...to stay in touch?"

Her face didn't move. Then it crumpled for just a second, before she regained her composure. "Yes," she said. "I'd like that very much."

Because we were two women who'd loved her son, and that was a bond that wouldn't be broken. Brooke would never forgive me, but Eloise... Eloise already had.

"Hello." Daniel stood in the doorway, a pint of Ben & Jerry's in his hand. "I'm Daniel Breton."

"This is Nathan's mother," I said, wiping my eyes with the edge of Ainsley's blanket.

"Yes, we've met," Eloise said. "You came to Nathan's wake." Daniel nodded. "Congratulations on your beautiful daughter. Kate..." She turned to me. "It was good to see you, deah."

Then she was gone, the strongest, most generous person I'd ever met.

"You okay, sweetheart?" Daniel asked. He put the ice cream on the bedside table and sat on the edge of the bed, his eyes worried.

I looked at him, then down at our little baby. "Never better," I said. "Look what she brought the baby."

He picked up the brush, tiny in his big hands, and glided it over Ainsley's thatch of hair. "That was very nice of her."

I swallowed. "Yes."

"The nurse says we can go home tonight if you want." He put the brush down and then placed one hand on our baby's head, looked at me and smiled. Daniel the Hot Firefighter was gone, and in his place was Daniel the Daddy.

He put his other hand against my cheek, and I turned my head and kissed it. "Yes," I said. "Let's go home."

\* \* \* \* \*

# Acknowledgments

———●———

Thanks to my editor, Susan Swinwood, who never fails to make my books better and is so much fun to work with. The entire team at Harlequin gets a huge shout-out for their encouragement, support, enthusiasm and talent, not just for this book, but for all my books.

My agent, Maria Carvainis, gets a thousand thanks for so ably guiding my career, and thanks as well to Elizabeth Copps, Martha Guzman and Samantha Brody at Maria Carvainis Agency, Inc.

To Kim Castillo, Sarah Burningham and Mel Jolly, thank you for helping me in the thousand ways that we authors need to be helped or we would otherwise wander around in the hallways, bumping into things.

To Marie Curtis, an amazing photographer and, even better, an old friend, who advised me on Kate's profession, and who also has taken pictures of my family and me for the past few decades. Thank you, Marie!

To Jennifer Iszkiewicz, Huntley Fitzpatrick, Karen Pinco and Shaunee Cole for the friendship, laughter and all-around fabulosity that makes the very air shimmer when we're together. I love you guys so much.

To my mom, the funny, wonderful, generous woman who puts up with her middle child.

To my kids, who are simply everything, always—first in my heart and last on my mind.

To the love of my life, Terence Keenan, who makes life fun, reassures me when I'm worried and brings me coffee every morning.

And to you, readers. Thank you for picking up this book. It's an honor and a privilege, and I am so very, very grateful that you chose to spend some time with this book.

# Questions for Discussion

1. Kate and Ainsley have a somewhat odd relationship thanks to their father's two marriages. Do you have firsthand experience with a blended family? What do you think makes them difficult, and what makes them work? Do you think Kate and Ainsley's relationship is typical of sisters, regardless of the circumstances?

2. Why do you think Ainsley loves Eric so fiercely? What in her childhood makes it logical for her to think he's the perfect man for her? Why doesn't she question their dynamic more? Do you think her father's personality makes her accept less than she deserves in a relationship?

3. On the other hand, Kate is surprised by falling in love at the age of 39. She's almost suspicious of Nathan for being as wonderful as he is. What's your take on that? Do you think it's true that after a certain age, all the "good ones" are taken?

4. Candy—Kate's mother and Ainsley's stepmother—is a family therapist. What did you think of her role? Could you blame her for being resentful? Do your feelings about her change throughout the book?

5. Daniel the Hot Firefighter is more than a pretty face. (The author's husband is a firefighter, too.) Kate never senses his attraction to her, but Daniel hints at it later on. Do you think Kate kept him stereotyped for a reason, or do you think

Daniel did that to himself? Was there a moment in the book when you saw Kate's view of Daniel change, or was it more gradual?

6. Jonathan and Ainsley are clearly a case of opposites attract. Ainsley has a history with lying men—her dad, her former boss at NBC and now Eric—while Jonathan is unable to be anything except forthright and blunt. Do you know anyone like him? Do you like that person, or did it take a while to warm up to him or her?

7. Becoming a wife and then a widow strips away Kate's outer shell as a person who's in complete control of her life. As a newlywed, she's a little awkward. As a widow, she's completely lost. Have you ever been rocked by a life event and felt adrift in the same way? What helped you recover your equilibrium?

8. One of the most important relationships in the book is between Kate and Eloise. What did you think of Mrs. Coburn?

9. One theme in this book is being there for someone else. Kate and Ainsley, who've never been particularly close, find that they're truer sisters than either thought. Talk about a time when someone surprised you by coming through for you at a difficult time.